## DATE DUE

# THE UNRAVELING

## OF MERCY

## LOUIS

# THE UNRAVELING

## OF MERCY

## LOUIS

*A Novel*

## KEIJA

## PARSSINEN

**HARPER**

*An Imprint of* HarperCollins*Publishers*

This book is a work of fiction. The characters, incidents, and dialogue are drawn from the author's imagination and are not to be construed as real. Any resemblance to actual events or persons, living or dead, is entirely coincidental.

FIRST EDITION

*Designed by Fritz Metsch*

Library of Congress Cataloging-in-Publication Data has been applied for.

ISBN: 978-0-06-231909-8

16 17 18 19   ov/rrd   10 9 8 7 6 5 4 3 2

For Malcolm Lee Robertson,

*for teaching me courage;*

and for Malcolm Fionn Robertson,

*for teaching me a new kind of love.*

# The Unraveling

## of Mercy

## Louis

ARLY FRIDAY MORNING in Port Sabine sees a ragged
crew gather at the Market Basket on LeBlanc Avenue. After
clocking out at the refinery, the night shift guys load up on NyQuil
where, eight hours before, they'd bought black coffee and NoDoz.
Because the store is close to the highway, drifters hitching to Galveston or farther south, to Corpus or Mexico, loiter around the bathrooms. They strip off their undershirts and soak their hair beneath
the faucet, sponge-bathing their gritty chests with soiled handker-
chiefs before standing in the hot blast of air from the hand dryer.
The cashier has orders from the manager to kick them out if they
keep the dryer going too long, so he keeps the TV above the register
on mute and listens for the machine's high whine through the wall.

On weekends, Fenceline kids drift over from Park Terrace looking to score weed from the cashier, whose bloodshot eyes and slack
jaw are the calling card of his trade. Today, though, even the stoners
are asleep, crashed out in the Gulf Breeze apartments if they're the
kids of refinery grunts, or on the hill if they're kin to the managers
and office workers, still poor but at least off the Fenceline, where
every kid seems to have asthma or a rap sheet.

Today is the last day of school, and kids are eager to prove that the rules no longer apply to them, if they ever did. One day is a slim buffer between six hundred teenagers and summer. Pity the teachers, who themselves have been counting down the days since spring break.

Before the high school kids show up to buy their breakfast of champions, Slurpees the color of glass cleaner and day-old sausage biscuits and Krispy Kremes, the cashier bundles the trash. It's the last task before his shift ends. *Garbage bags cost money,* the manager told him. *Don't go wasting them or I'll dock your pay.*

Outside, the cashier hobbles to the dumpster hauling the two bags, each one feeling as heavy as a dead man. He throws back the plastic lid, which reverberates loudly when it hits the metal siding, silencing for a second the birdsong from the scrub forest behind the store. With effort, he heaves first one bag over the edge of the dumpster and then the next. Breathing hard, he shakes out his arms, already anticipating the first jay of the day. This is his morning ritual—dump the trash, then take a few puffs while waiting for the clock to strike seven a.m. He likes the sound of the mourning doves, which in his mind is spelled *morning dove* because that makes more sense. He likes the dense smell of honeysuckle underscored by the brininess of the Gulf, whose gray waves shove and suck just beyond the seawall, out of sight but always there, constant as the refinery lights. While he tokes up, he enjoys looking across the street at the high school, knowing he never has to go back, even if it looks kind of pretty, its orange bricks turned golden in the rising sun, its flag snapping in the breeze off the Gulf.

He reaches into his pocket for the joint and lighter but realizes he has neither. What the hell? He always keeps them close. He darts back into the store, examines the ground by the garbage cans, the counter around the register. Then he remembers just moments before, how he leaned deep into the trash can to compress the garbage.

*Shit.* He *needs* that joint. He stays clean on the clock, eight whole hours, but by seven a.m., he's jonesing hard. From behind the register, he takes another pair of the disposable plastic gloves, then jogs back outside.

Gripping the edge of the dumpster, he hoists himself up. Nothing too nasty down there, as far as he can see, mostly big black trash bags like the two he just tossed. He lowers himself down, again holding his breath, cursing his wimpy lung capacity. He's about to tear into one of the bags when something catches his eye. A cardboard Lone Star case, streaked in red like it's been painted. Almost immediately he understands it's not paint. It's the distinctive dark red of dried blood. Tentatively, he reaches for the box and parts the flaps. There, lying on a bed of balled-up toilet paper, is the tiniest baby he's ever seen, about the size of a banana, matchstick arms and legs pulled tight to its tummy. And just as he knew the red was blood, he knows the baby is dead.

Gently, he closes the flaps. He balances the box on the edge of the dumpster before climbing out. From a distant corner of his memory, the Lord's Prayer drifts to mind, *forgive us our trespasses*. He carries the tiny coffin inside with the dignity and reserve of a pallbearer and then calls the police.

# Part I

Be sober-minded; be watchful.
Your adversary the Devil prowls around like
a roaring lion, seeking someone to devour.

— 1 PETER 5:8

# MERCY

—————  ——

SOMETHING WILL BE lit on fire today. Noses and windows
will get busted. Girls will cry. It's the last day of school, and
endings are always extreme. Like the Great Tribulation before the
Rapture, the sun and air dark with smoke, armies of locusts with faces
like men, tails like scorpions, two hundred million of them riding to
cleanse the earth of those who lack the seal of God on their forehead.

Already, summer breathes through the hurricane shutters outside my room, wet and close. Along the ceiling, a green anole lizard
moves in fits and starts, pausing to puff its orange throat. Maybe if
I stay right here in my room in the stilt house, the final school bell
won't ring, dismissing us into the anarchy of summer.

The whole world falls apart in summer. Murder rates rise with
the heat, hurricanes brood off the coast, waiting to batter us. On the
streets, girls go practically naked, a carnival of flesh so that when we
pass by, Maw Maw sings under her breath, *Bless them, give them purity at the gates.* By the time school starts in August, some of them are
vanished—they drop out, move across the state line into Louisiana,
gone to join all the other lost girls, my mother included, in that city
called *easy.*

I throw the sheet back and grudgingly slide out of bed. Only because I know that after summer comes basketball season, and I have to get through one to get to the other. Out on the balcony, I feel the wood warm beneath my feet, listen to Chocolate Bayou humming with insects and bullfrogs. After Hurricane Alicia, we put the house on stilts. No concrete foundation anymore, just beams and floorboards, like a tree house. I like being up high, eye to eye with the birds. When I look toward the bayou, I can imagine myself a mermaid on the prow of a ship that has made a wrong turn and gotten stuck here.

When Alicia was still a green swirl over the Gulf, Maw Maw prophesied the flood and warned Mayor Sanchez. But the weatherman told him the storm would miss us, and since the mayor didn't want to shut down the refinery, he didn't order an evacuation. By the time the water peaked, four people had drowned. After the storm passed, the watermark on the walls of our house went clear up to the ceiling. Maw Maw used the insurance money to prop it up on these chopsticks, making the house a spindly four-legged creature whose lamplight eyes glow yellow by night. She never told Mayor Sanchez *I told you so.* It's not Christian to gloat, especially when death comes calling.

Padding to the kitchen, I pull a string cheese from the fridge. As I sit peeling it, a moan issues down the hallway. It's the kind of sound women make on TV when they're laboring with a baby, before the screaming starts—a growl that vibrates with pain. I quiet my breathing. She's prophesying again, and even the groan of a floorboard can interrupt the vision. Vivid and gut-socking, they come on every few weeks now, leaving her pale. *Like turkey vultures aswarm around the dying,* she says of the visions. *This world is in its death throes,* ma petite.

Maw Maw says it's only a matter of months before the Tribulation begins. Everything is a sign of the times, like what happened with the president and that intern, when even the special prosecutor's name, Starr, was a portent. Like the government shooting up that man and all his wives in Waco, and those people who tried to get to heaven on the back of a comet. The thread of Maw Maw's visions start in her fingertips. When she touches something, it tells her a story. Some nights she sits for hours on the dock where Paw Paw Gaspard died, running her hands along the cedar planks, trying to summon his spirit. She's been ready for heaven since the day he left us seventeen years ago.

At the sink, I fill a water glass and take a drink. A bright blast of sunshine spills over the counter, but otherwise, the room is dark, the wood paneling on the walls soaking up light. Other than being hoisted on stilts, the house hasn't changed a shred. When I move the living room furniture to vacuum, I run my hand over the deep grooves left behind in the carpet. Paw Paw's navy wool blanket stays folded over the back of his easy chair, as if at any moment he'll return for a snooze. He was fishing at the end of the dock out back of the house when the stroke buzzed through his brain and toppled him into the bayou. By the time Maw Maw got to him, he had drowned, the canvas pants and jacket he wore turned heavy as stone with water. He was fifty-six years old. Though Maw Maw told people that the Lord don't make mistakes when He takes someone home, she wore widow's weeds for over a year, like she hoped God would see her huge sadness and restore Paw Paw to her.

Another moan, long and low. I fight my instinct to check on her. What's it like having the world as it doesn't exist yet reveal itself to you? At church she's begun laying hands, running her fingers along the brows of upturned faces, touching temples where she can feel the pulse of brains through the scalp. She's so tender when she does it that the women go soft, the men yearn toward her palms. Before bed, I wish for her to touch me like that, but she stays in the doorway and says the same thing each night: *Live to meet the end without dread, Tee Mercy. Be better than good.*

Even though I've been taught my whole life that the Rapture will happen *in the twinkling of an eye,* I never expected it to come so soon. I should be glad to go to heaven, but all I can think about is that December 31 falls in the middle of basketball season. If the world ends that night, we won't make it to State. I won't ever feel the weight of that gold medal in my hand. Perhaps in heaven, I'll grow wings and finally know what it's like to soar above the rim. But I wonder if even that would be enough to replace the pleasure of winning, that *zing* of happiness when the buzzer goes and you're exhausted, but best, the feel of a sweat-soaked uniform when you've left a part of yourself behind in it. Maybe it's better that Maw Maw doesn't touch my forehead before bed; these thoughts would burn her like fever.

From her room comes a series of thuds, and the moaning stops. I hurry down the hall and peek past her door, where she's slumped on the ground, eyes closed, nightgown spread around her. I rush in and kneel beside her, then lean in close to see if she's breathing. *Thank God.* Her shallow breath is feathery against my cheek. Before pulling back, I kiss her papery skin. It's a gesture she wouldn't tolerate while awake, but I can't help myself, I'm so relieved she's not dead. When the last day arrives, I know we'll rise together, neither one of us will get left. There's comfort in that.

Surrounded by the nightgown, Maw Maw looks so small, like Thumbelina inside a rain lily. I take her hand, massage it, breathe warmth over it. "Maw Maw, can you hear me?" Angling her chin toward me, I see her eyelids flutter like she's in the middle of a dream. "Maw Maw?"

She opens her eyes and blinks several times, squeezing out a few fat tears. The visions come on fast and physical. In the last year, they've leached her hair white as a gull's breast. Afterward, she seems pummeled, disoriented. This is the first time she's fainted, though. "You're all right," I say, squeezing her hand. "Everything's okay." I almost say *I love you* but stop myself. Last time I slipped, she told me to save my love for the Lord.

She pulls her hand away, and for a second it's like she doesn't recognize me, her eyes small with suspicion. Where has she traveled to in her vision that I don't exist anymore?

"It's me," I say. "Mercy."

At the sound of my name, she relaxes a little. "I don't understand it," she says in a faraway voice, pushing herself to a seated position. "Been the same for weeks now, but I don't understand."

"What, Maw Maw?"

"Girls spread out on the floor, not dead but moving, dancing, maybe . . ."

"What girls?"

A pause, then: "Don't worry over it now," she says, her voice returned to its usual forcefulness. "He'll give me the knowledge when it suits Him. Help me up." I nod and scramble to a squat. With one hand she grips my arm and, with the other, scoops up the Bible from where it has landed on the floor. I brace myself and together we stand. She hobbles beside me until we reach the kitchen, where I pull out a chair for her and put the kettle on. Slumped into the seat, she rests one hand in her lap, the other on the Bible. Her fingers are elegant, like she ought to play piano. From the fridge, I take out the carton of eggs and a foil-wrapped hunk of corn bread. I light two burners, one for the skillet, one for the kettle, then set out two mugs for tea. "Can I fry you some eggs? Get up your strength?" I ask.

Staring out the window, she shakes her head. "Ain't hungry, but thanks all the same."

When the kettle shrills, I pour the water, then hand her a steaming mug. "Here," I say. She takes it with a nod of thanks.

I worry for her. Skinny as a rake and snow-headed, she looks a sight older than her sixty-seven years. Being privy to so much truth has aged her. Mothers used to bring their engaged daughters to her so she could caress their necks, skim their collarbones with her fingers to pause over beating hearts in order to discern whether the love was true, or the man worthy. Of course the girls had gone through father-guided courtship, the boys already put through their paces and groomed for guardianship, but that didn't stop these mamas wanting to be *absolutely certain* before marrying their girls off. Those visits stopped after several girls left in tears, stomping across the gallery, shouting that it was all superstitious nonsense, their marriages would sure as sugar last, and that Ray or Tommy or Bobby would love them much as they loved football and fishing and oyster po'boys.

Maw Maw doesn't mind upsetting people when it comes to delivering truth. She says Jesus was crowned with thorns for *His* troubles. Some people have a hard time accepting that the world keeps secrets from them, or that God shares those secrets with a chosen few. But accepting the world's mysteries is the root of faith, Maw Maw says. Most people just don't know when to listen or to whom.

I crack an egg into the skillet and watch as the white turns opaque around the bright yellow yolk. When it's done frying, I slide it onto a piece of toast and poke the yolk with the tines of a fork. Seated at the table, I watch it seep slowly over the bread, waiting for it to soak in; I like it soggy.

"Church tonight," she says, fingering the tag of the tea bag. Her hands shake with a gentle tremor.

"I remember."

"The year is over and done now, so no more of your moping. Don't forget, that game was part of His plan for you, Mercy girl. He don't make mistakes."

"Yes ma'am." I stab at my egg.

"Fruitless are our earthly desires."

"Yes ma'am," I say again.

The eggs are rubbery on my tongue. Around town, people ask me what went wrong in the state semifinal game, as if just because my body is my own, I understand what makes it fail. Even during the season, when we were winning, they asked me questions I couldn't answer, *How do you do it?* And *What does it feel like to play the way you do?* God gave me the gift of a sure shot and quick feet, a body too tall for a girl, bossy shoulders. Coach says that more than my physical gifts, my hunger to win makes me great. I want to win so bad, the wanting fills me until there's not a lick of room for anything else.

"Kids'll be wild tonight," Maw Maw says. "Good time to visit with the Lord. Ready yourself by seven o'clock."

"Yes ma'am."

Maw Maw believes that purity of spirit is all a person needs to be full up, that you can find peace only when you stop wanting, because desire is the trick the devil plays on human hearts. I long to look at the world as Maw Maw does, with a cool eye toward heaven; there's simplicity in stripping your heart like that. But I'm weak for the things I can touch—a basketball, a trophy, my best friend Annie's hand in mine.

Maw Maw rises and walks to the pantry, fumbling among the boxes of tea and dehydrated potatoes and onion straws until she finds what she's looking for—her tobacco. She chews after the visions to calm her nerves. I watch as she tucks a tiny wad of chaw in her cheek before going to the sink to wash her hands. She thinks I haven't noticed, and maybe I wouldn't have but for the yellow streaks of spit in the bathroom sink.

From behind, Maw Maw might be mistaken for frail; her spine curves slightly, her head tilts forward like the loop of a letter *P* tilted off its leg. But if you see her face, you know she's not to be crossed. That toughness is how she's survived so much—the stillborn baby; Paw Paw's death; my mother, Charmaine, leaving us;

and raising a child long after she ought. It's what makes her strong in faith, too.

"I better get going," I say, chair scraping the linoleum as I stand.

She dries her hands on a dishrag. "Mind yourself today, stay clear of the beach road. Don't let trouble find you, Tee Mercy."

"No ma'am," I say.

Outside, the grass sweats dewy beads, the sun bakes the mud banks of the bayou to cracking. From the backseat of the car, an old junker Maw Maw bought cheap off the scrap lot, I grab a towel and spread it on the torn pleather of the driver's seat so I won't burn my thighs. The steering wheel is squishy with heat; I touch it gingerly as I reverse out of the gravel drive. Summer is here—the long, empty days without the team, the egg-cooking heat. By the water's edge, cypress trees weep through their branches. Tangles of velvety morning glories grow inky blue and secretive in the thicket at the roadside, bursts of Mexican hat cascading into the drainage ditch like spilled paint. On the air, the smell of ripening things. Or maybe it's decay, like Maw Maw says. The world gone rotten.

At Annie's, I punch in the security code and the gate comes alive, opening on silent hinges. I drive up the driveway, hugging the concrete curve of the fountain, where a bronze fish rises from the center, spitting water in a sparkling arc. Annie hates the fountain, says it's nouveau riche. Last Halloween, she vandalized it, filling it with laundry detergent and red dye. Her father blamed it on one of the many disgruntled boys she had dated and dumped. Annie laughed mirthlessly when she told me. *Dated,* she said. *So quaint.*

I honk for her and wait, but she doesn't appear. I watch a Mexican man on a riding mower ride back and forth over the gentle slope of the hill that surrounds the house. Beau had the entire hill built special because he didn't want to live at sea level like the rest of us.

After a few minutes, I get out of the car. Passing the fountain,

I run my fingers through its cool water. A few pennies wink from beneath the water, and I wonder who in the Putnam house has been making wishes. Maybe Lourdes, the maid, hoping for a job in a happier home. At the door I ring the bell and she answers, wearing the same forlorn expression as always. I can never tell if she's actually unhappy or if her face is just made that way. Perhaps she can't help her haunted eyes, the mouth freighted with worry. I say a quick hello, then bound up the stairs to Annie's room.

"Annie?" I call.

"In here," comes the reply from the walk-in closet.

"For someone who says she doesn't give a crap what people think, you take an age to get ready," I yell through the open door.

"Just another sec, promise!"

Annie's bedroom reminds me of hotels I see in magazine ads, walls painted in earth tones, a huge neatly made bed covered with a shimmering duvet that calls out for a body, bland landscape art hanging over the headboard. Lourdes cleans the bathroom every day. In the dish to the right of the sink, she leaves soaps with French names on the wrappers. The bedroom is sterile, no overflowing bookcase or desk cluttered with ticket stubs and out-of-focus snapshots, no postcards sent by friends on summer vacation, *Wish you were here*. Only the shelf of basketball trophies reveals that someone lives here. I guess it makes sense that Annie inhabits her room like a guest; she swears she's moving out the day she turns eighteen, going to college on the West Coast, where the air smells like orange blossoms and not swamp rot and refinery gas.

I'm jealous that Annie gets to display her trophies; I have to keep my hardware stashed in a box in the closet where Maw Maw won't find it. She doesn't believe in keeping mementos, no sense in getting attached to this world when it's fixing to end. I wander to the shelf, finger the golden statuettes, the miniature plaques on the pale marble bases. Not a thing from State this year, though, not even a ribbon. *Fourth place is like kissing your brother,* Coach told us. *Don't forget how you feel right now. Because I want you to come back angry, I want you to come back for blood.* I didn't dare tell Coach that I wasn't angry, just scared. Twenty scouts in the crowd, but I left without the scholarship offer I'd thought was my destiny. When I passed the pack of them on my way to the locker room, they avoided my eyes. *Please,* I wanted to beg. *Give me another chance.* Maw Maw said the loss was a humbling. *Now the town'll remember that Mercy Louis puts her pants on one leg at a time, just like everyone else.*

At last Annie emerges, wearing a thin black tee stretched tight over her chest. In the morning sun coming through the window, I see the outline of her bra, a hint of nipple. Her wardrobe makes me blush, and I have to remember that it's not me wearing the sheer shirt, not my nipples like pencil erasers against the fabric. We are so close that I often forget her body is separate from mine. Since we were twelve, we've played every single league basketball game together. Last year we added them up: 155 games. 4,440 minutes. That's over three days of nonstop ball, not to mention all the practice hours. On the court, I know where she's going before she gets there. That's a kind of connection you can't deny.

"Morning, sunshine," she says with false cheer. She's a night owl, would probably do well as a vampire. "Let's go or we'll be late."

"Because tardiness is such a big concern for you," I say. She slaps my butt playfully.

As we tear down the stairs, we nearly crash into Beau, a column of a man, former lineman for A&M.

"Mercy Louis, you're looking well," he says. His eyes linger on Annie and I notice his mouth tug down in disapproval.

"Thank you, sir," I answer, out of breath, feeling like I should salute him. Standing there freshly shaved in his white ten-gallon Stetson and navy sport jacket, he looks like a man who runs things. Annie must have got her lizard blood from him. Never have seen the man sweat, not even during the investigation after the explosion or when he announced his resignation as refinery manager. They showed clips of the announcement on the evening news; halfway through, he held up his hand like he was choking up for the dead, but Annie swears his heart is so parched, the man can't cry. He's a showman, is what.

"Plans for the off-season?" he asks.

"Yes sir," I answer. "Going to train every day. Strength, speed, and agility stuff, mostly. Anaerobic and aerobic, too. At least a couple hundred made shots a day."

Annie rolls her eyes, hitches her thumb toward the door, then slips out. Though they live in the same house, she hasn't spoken to her father in years, not since the explosion three years ago. Sure, she says *yes* and *no* and sometimes *hello* and *goodbye,* but they don't converse. She blames him for what happened to those people. No criminal charges were ever brought, but Annie tried and hanged him in her head.

"Better work on your head game," he says. "Never thought of you as the choking type."

My face burns from his words. I hear Maw Maw's voice: *Nobody likes an angry woman.* But what can I do with this rage if not wear it? I manage to give a curt nod and follow Annie out. *Meek and mild, be meek and mild.*

"Kiss-ass," Annie says over the car's roof before sliding into the passenger seat. I duck down behind the wheel. She gives me a sour look. "Bet he wishes *you* were his daughter."

No AC in the car, and I can feel sweat trickling down my neck. "Can you not sit on those?" I ask, trying to clear old team meal plans off the seat beneath her.

"God, why do you hang on to this crap?" she says.

"In case I need them in the summer."

"The summer's *our* time, Mercy." She flips down the sunshade, checks her makeup in the mirror. "Girl, obedience is only attractive in dogs and small children." She pauses. "Sometimes I worry about you."

"That's new," I shoot back.

She shrugs. "Just saying you don't always have to be perfect."

"And you don't always have to be such a B." I ease into gear and we coast back down the driveway. Guilty at being sharp with her, I ask after her mom. If Annie has a soft spot beneath her spikes, it's for her mother.

"She's not doing good," she says. "She's in pain whenever she's awake."

"What does Dr. Morris say?"

"He says there's nothing they can do at this point. There are no meds to help with fibromyalgia. And get this: as he's leaving, he tells Mom she only has to *want* to be pain-free to start to see some real changes." She snorts. "What a dickwad."

When Beau made his first million in the late eighties, he threw a retirement party for Mrs. Putnam in celebration. There was this beautiful cake in the shape of a rainbow and pot of gold; the baker had sunk shiny plastic doubloons into the thick pink frosting. Mrs. Putnam was thirty-six years old and working as a nurse at County Hospital. When I went to the bathroom to wash my hands, sticky from cake, I found her sitting on the toilet, her face streaked with mascara, her red lipstick smeared clownishly from where she'd been holding a fistful of tissues against her mouth. Scared by the spidery black streaks, I tiptoed down the hallway to the other bathroom, hoping she hadn't seen me. *A man knows he's really made it when he can give his wife the gift of leisure,* Beau said, toasting Mrs. Putnam later that night. *Here's to no more late nights and long shifts at the hospital, sugar.*

Now she rattles around the top floor of the house and never comes down, taking all her meals on trays delivered by Lourdes, the only reminder of her existence the occasional thumping you hear through the thick carpeting as she paces overhead. I imagine her swathed in silk robes, eating off silver-rimmed china, reclining on her feather bed with a cool washcloth pressed to her forehead. When she hears the car doors slam in the morning, does she look out her window, watch us drive away? Does she envy us our movement? Can she even remember what it's like on the outside?

At the Market Basket on the corner of Main and LeBlanc, two police cars are pulled nose to nose in the parking lot.

"Someone got an early start on things," Annie says as we glide past. "My money's on Luke Fogarty. Or maybe they finally busted Half-baked."

Half-baked is the kids' nickname for the pothead cashier; he's standing by the dumpster, arms folded across his chest. The officers are crouched down, examining something on the ground. Inside the store, a line of students has formed. Kids driving into the student lot are rubbernecking, cars backed up all the way to the traffic light behind us. Ahead, someone's laying on the horn.

"That's helpful," I say to nobody, annoyed with the heat, with Beau and Annie, with the holdup and the end of another year. I should have a verbal agreement by now, a T-shirt to wear loud and proud on the last day of school: *Lady Longhorns* or *Lady Techsters* or *Lady Tigers* or *Lady Bears*. A promise for the future, four more years of ball.

"Wonder what's up," Annie says, hanging her elbow out the window and resting her chin watchfully on the back of her hand. She is drawn to trouble, magnetized by it. Because of this, Beau keeps her on a short leash. People are surprised when I tell them Maw Maw doesn't put a lot of rules on me; I don't even have a curfew. *The Bible is your rulebook, Tee Mercy,* she says. *The Lord gave us free will, every day man chooses between damnation and grace, but it's always a choice.*

There's Lucille Cloud sitting in front of the shuttered Mr. Good

Deals, watching the scene. Her large dog, a German shepherd mix, is flopped out on the pavement beside her, and Lucille's wearing the same oversize men's jacket and army pants as always, her long dark hair limp with grease. A blanket crowded with wares spans the sidewalk in front of her. Every day she sits in the same spot, promising students cures for all manner of ailment—potions for allergies, oils for asthma, necklaces to help you get a boyfriend, that kind of nonsense. Some days one or another of the women from church parks herself nearby, holding a cardboard sign with a verse from John: *Dear friends, do not believe every spirit, but test the spirits to see whether they are from God, because many false prophets have gone into the world.* Once in a while, the woman holding the sign is Maw Maw. For years, she has petitioned the city to get Lucille booted off the street where she sells her wares. Officially, the petition cites loitering, but that's only because there's no box to check for practicing black magic or devil worshipping, both of which Maw Maw believes Lucille does with her velvet boxes filled with semiprecious stones and crystals, her tinctures of oils and herbs.

From across the lot, Lucille's eyes meet mine. I look away, embarrassed to be caught staring. They say last year she broke up Gum Hibbard's marriage, that she prostitutes herself, luring boys and men to her lean-to in the woods under power of her spells to steal their cash. People claim to see lights dancing near her lean-to in the forest at night, flames of the fires Lucille builds for her rituals. At lock-ins and youth group socials, kids dare each other to sneak to her cabin to try and find the baby-bone pile she is rumored to keep buried nearby.

On the radio, a jumpy pop song comes on, and Annie sings along in her husky alto. When we finally pull into the lot, I notice someone has festooned the live oaks near the flagpole with toilet paper.

"And so it begins," Annie says, peering up into the trees. "My favorite season."

I think of three months without Coach, no meal plans, the semi-final looping in my mind. As I pull into a spot, I try to breathe, but the car's too hot, my chest won't expand. I park, then stick my head out the window like a dog, opening my mouth to feel air on my tongue.

"Mercy? You okay?"

"It's so hot," I say.

"Ding ding ding, the prize in observational arts goes to Mercy Louis!" Annie says, as she puts on another coat of lipgloss.

Gradually panic rolls off my chest and I can breathe again. Then Annie says my name in a more subdued voice: "Mercy?"

"Yeah?"

"I've got another one. I'll explode if I don't tell you."

"Okay," I say. "What?"

I wait for her to speak. Around us, kids hover in the lot, giddy from summer's promise, glancing at the action across the street. Girls in tank tops the color of sherbet sashay by, their calves slender in espadrilles and wedge sandals, their skin already burned from trips to the river and the Red Dump and Crystal Beach and Galveston Island. Boys hang out of idling trucks, cup the bills of baseball caps that bear the white salt lines of their sweat.

"I made Lennox hit me," Annie says after a while, looking down at her folded hands. "He didn't want to. See?" She lifts up the left side of her T-shirt. Underneath, the skin is striped with bruises. "Afterward, he was really upset. I think he might have been crying, but it was dark, so I couldn't tell."

I can't help it: I imagine Mama Charmaine doing what Maw Maw says she does—in a soiled bed grunting like an animal with a man who doesn't know her name. Annie, agitated, shifts back and forth in her seat, scratching her nails against her jeans.

"I'm such a fucking bitch," she says, her voice low and ferocious. "God, Mercy. I'm so fucking *hard*. Everything breaks against me."

Pitching forward, she rests elbows on knees and stares at the floor. From the school building, the first bell sounds. I vacuum up her words from where they hang unclaimed in the air; I perch them in the shadowed space where I keep her other confessions, a line of grackles on a bare branch by my heart. She looks at me with lost eyes. I think, *Put on the full armor of God so that you can take your stand against the devil's schemes.* Then, because she doesn't want Scripture, I pet her hair, say what I always say: "I love you, Annie."

But what if Maw Maw's right and we only have a few months before Christ Raptures the believers? Annie will need so much more than my love to be saved. I kiss her temple, say a silent prayer for her soul. She nods as if resigned to her fate, purses her lips, and then gets out of the car. As we stride across the lot, I take her hand. Together, we walk up the stairs to the main entrance, into the last day of our junior year.

In class before the second-period bell goes, kids are buzzing about the cop cars at the Market Basket: *I heard Half-baked found a finger in the dumpster, did you see that box of bloody tissue on the floor behind the register? Nah, dude, you got it wrong, they finally busted his ass for slinging dope. I'm telling you, something was bleeding hard-core by that dumpster.* I think of the vision troubling Maw Maw, girls sprawled on the ground, not dead but not well, either. The police should hire her, let her hold whatever shreds of evidence they find. How many cases could she solve with her gift?

The bell sounds, but kids keep chattering like they didn't hear. This Market Basket thing has put them near to a frenzy. Mr. Ball tries to shush them, but it's not until Krista Blythe walks in that everyone hushes up. She's a student aide for the front office, which means she's the one who delivers summonses to the principal. When she strides to my desk, someone whispers, "Oh, snap."

Holding out a letter, Krista says: "Ms. Custer found this in a pile of faculty mail when she was cleaning out the lounge." She inspects a fingernail, presses her lips together so the pink gloss glistens. "It's probably real late, but she only just now found it."

When I thank her and take the letter, I notice my hand is shaking. It can't be a recruitment letter, those usually go to Coach, and anyway, I haven't gotten one since the semifinal. Embarrassed by my hopeful heart, I set it down like it doesn't interest me. With a shrug, Krista turns and walks out. Mr. Ball uses the break in talk to try to steer us to order, but it's impossible. "Fine," he says after a minute, throwing up his hands. "As you were."

He goes to his desk and leans back in the chair, props his feet up. Everyone cheers and talk resumes. When I'm sure no one's watching, I slide my pinkie beneath the flap of the envelope and jigger it open. From the fold of the letter a photograph falls onto my desk. It's a perfectly ordinary photo—something that might appear on an ID card or driver's license—but I draw breath loud enough that a few students turn and look at me, eyes glazed with boredom or maybe booze.

Maw Maw keeps no photos of her stashed in cupboards behind the flour or buried under socks in a drawer. On low days, I've looked, ransacked every possible hiding place in search of something of her I can hold on to. So how can I be certain of the identity of the woman in the photo? To start: her skin is pale like mine, hair bluish-black and unruly, eyes large and dark-lashed, blue like mine; not a happy shade, like the sky or sea on a sunny day, but the lonesome blue of deep night hours when no one but the devil and the drunks are awake. They seize on me with their sadness.

*Good,* I think, glad that this woman who has caused Maw Maw such heartache knows something of pain. I want to stand, walk to the trash can, ball up the letter, and toss it away like it's as insignificant to me as an unwanted love note. I owe it to Maw Maw, the woman who raised me, not to care a fig what Charmaine has to say. But already I've glimpsed the looping script peeking from inside the creased page, and I'm struck hard by the fact that I've never seen my mother's handwriting—Sheryl Swoopes's autograph on the Tech poster hanging in my bedroom is more familiar to me.

I read the letter for the simple, pathetic reason that I want to know how Charmaine signs her name.

*March 5, 1999*

*Dear Mercy,*

*I have no right to contact you but I want you to know that I think about you every day. When people ask if I have any kids I say no because I haven't been a mother to you and that's the honest truth. I read in the paper that you are coming to Austin for the state basketball tournament. First of all congratulations but second would you let me buy you a Coke or something.*

*When I saw your photo in the paper I thought what a beautiful young woman you have become but it made me sad because you are seventeen years old and I found myself wondering what were you like before you were seventeen. What were you like when you were ten and seven and three. I remember you as a baby, you were a very sweet baby, you cried like a kitten, so quiet I could barely hear you.*

*When you were a baby I held you up to my ear like one of those seashells, I swear I heard whispering through your breath, you were from another world, someplace old and beyond me. I can't believe there was anything I loved more than you at that moment you were so sweet-smelling and soft but that is addiction, a bad romance that eats you up.*

*I will say sorry because that's what I am but the word looks a skinny thing written out here. Maybe I will come to your game just to see who you have grown into. You don't need to talk to me if you don't want.*

*I hope you will write me back: PO Box 1984, Austin, Texas.*

Love true,

*Charmaine Boudreaux*

She signs off sloppily, just a capital C and B followed by nonsense scriggles. Blinking back disbelief at the sight of her name, I look up at my classmates, who carry on with their gum-chewing and eye-rolling and gossiping, as if this is just another blah-blah day and not the first time in my life that I've had word from my mother. The letter is dated March 5, a few days before the state tournament. I remember how I felt in those days leading up to the semifinal game—like I was invincible, already thinking about which finger to wear my championship ring on. Imagine! Seeing the date written out makes me ache to go back and fix my head.

Was she there? I wonder. It makes me shiver to consider being so close to *Charmaine Boudreaux* without knowing it. Whenever Maw Maw speaks about her, she doesn't give her a surname, as if the minute Charmaine left us and Port Sabine, she gave up her right to family. If this letter landed in our mailbox at the stilt house, Maw Maw would have put it down the garbage disposal or let it sink beneath the rain lilies clogging the mouth of the bayou before it ever reached me.

For years, Charmaine has roamed through our house, a fleshless presence anchoring the tales that Maw Maw spins as often as her Bible stories and Cajun yarns. *The demon drugs bewitched your mama until she forgot herself, forgot God, forgot everything but pleasure. The devil knows how easily he captured her in spite of the godly household I kept. Beware, Mercy child, he knows your weak blood.* Hearing from Charmaine now is like receiving a letter from the Loup Garou or the old woman who lived in a shoe. Like Jesus and the devil, Charmaine is most alive to me in Maw Maw's stories.

As for my father, I've seen him only once in the flesh. He came by the stilt house when I was a girl of maybe seven. At the door, this scarecrow of a man scooped me up in his tan arms thin as straw. I screamed, which brought Maw Maw running from the kitchen. She snatched me back quick and sent me scooting to my room. On the way, I heard Witness say, *Cain't a man hug his girl when he comes round?* And she said, *Only if he put a cent toward the child's lookin' after and didn't flee the state to avoid the law on account of his being good-for-nothing.* He told her she still owed him money and he was come to collect it, and she said how dare he, and that was a lie. She called him a grifter and a fraud and sent him on his way. When I asked her later if that man was my father, she had said, *After a fashion,* and then returned to her needlepoint.

I reread the letter, then wish I hadn't, because this time, the words get me by the gills. Because I've never seen Charmaine, never touched her, can barely imagine her and only then with the help of stories, my mother's absence has seemed all right these seventeen years. But this featherlight letter makes me feel and want things I shouldn't, not after all this time. For instance, a mother to give a rose to on Parents' Night at the last home game of the season. And the story of how I came into this world. Annie has a pink baby book where her mother wrote out all the details of her birth: the nineteen hours of labor and how Annie broke her collarbone coming through her mama's bony pelvis, and how she was a colicky baby who didn't stop crying for the first three months of her life. Which surprises exactly no one familiar with Annie Putnam. All I know is I was born in the stilt house, and Maw Maw delivered me herself. She's not a trained midwife, but she helped her mother deliver four babies in

Calcasieu Parish before she met Paw Paw Gaspard and crossed into Texas so he could work the refinery.

When my birthday comes around, we don't celebrate with cake and presents. Maw Maw says I should use the day for prayer, for reflection and repentance for the sins of my mother, even though I'm not the one who got pregnant, loaded, and gone.

I look back down at the letter. *Maybe I will come to your game just to see who you have grown into.* It would be just like Charmaine to show up and ruin everything. Maybe Maw Maw's right—that the sins of your parents belong to you no matter how right you try to live. That game a reminder of where I came from. *A humbling.*

When the bell rings to dismiss us to third period, I steal another look at the photo while students jostle past.

She looks better than I imagined an addict could. Her cheeks are creamy and touched with pink, like she's embarrassed to have her picture taken. I'll admit, she's pretty; beautiful, even. I fold the letter around the photograph, tuck them back into the envelope, intending to toss it all into the trash.

But as I pass through the door and into the hallway, I slip the bundle into my backpack, stepping lightly as a burglar into the thrum of students. I half expect someone to appear and snatch the letter away before phoning Maw Maw with news of my deception. Part of me begs to be found out, but nothing happens.

I decide not to tell Maw Maw about the letter. The one time I told her I missed my mother, she got so angry with me I haven't ever forgotten it. I had just started kindergarten and realized that all the other kids had pretty young mothers to pick them up after school. I was ashamed of Maw Maw, with her creased face and brittle hair. That first day home, I cried and told her I wanted my mother instead. She told me my mama wasn't coming back, that she'd seen Charmaine on the streets of New Orleans, lips scar-bubbled from the crack pipe, hair scraggled, stockings torn, wearing the kind of towering shoes a woman puts on to spend her days flat-backed on a bed beneath a man. *Asking for your mother is like asking for a green-eyed demon to come take you away, that what you want?* For weeks I couldn't sleep, imagining every scratch to be the demon's toenails.

Walking to my next class, I carry my backpack gingerly, the letter snarling at me from inside.

# ILLA

NSIDE THE GYM, the basketball girls are scattered around the six hoops completing their warm-ups. There's Mercy, treating the ball like an outgrowth of her hand as she does ball-handling drills in the far corner, figure eights and spiders and over-and-throughs. Nothing more natural in the world than that girl on a court. Illa takes comfort in Mercy's gift. Since the explosion put Mama in the chair, watching Mercy play has been the only thing that makes Illa feel hopeful. She understands why the town blocks off Tuesday and Friday nights to come to the games. When those forty-seven people died in the refinery blast three years ago, Jesus and God and the Holy Ghost, as well as the other trinity of small-town life—drink and smoke and talk—left people comfortless, so Mercy became the town's beacon. The weekend of the state tournament, hundreds of people caravanned to Austin to see the Black Angel because they knew she would give them an hour when their lives would seem better.

Illa remembers the sense of deflation that pervaded the arena after the Lady Rays lost. An entire town sighing in defeat. That night and over the weeks that followed the loss, there had been an edge to people's voices when they talked about Mercy's shoddy play, words sharpened on a steel of betrayal. Illa worried that someone would stick a for-sale sign in Mercy's yard, so she cruised past the house from time to time, ready to uproot the sign before Mercy saw it. The yard stayed clear, though, likely because people feared Evelia. There was talk she could send a man to hell just by praying on it.

The track and softball and volleyball girls are draped over the gym bleachers. One girl, Callie Loggins, is already applying baby oil to her arms and legs, preparing for an after-school sunbath. Illa can hear them twittering about who's going to hook up over the summer, making plans to go to Crystal Beach and the bayou. On the last day of school, only the basketball team is still required to dress out. Coach Martin keeps them running drills until the very end. Technically they're bending the rules by doing so, but no one confronts Coach with this fact.

From outside, she hears the occasional lament of sirens from the Market Basket lot. The sound always gives Illa gooseflesh because it means that somewhere, the underside of life is revealing itself, a reminder that black luck and bad faith exist. She associates the sound with the refinery explosion and with her father's death, even though the police didn't have their lights on as they pulled into the driveway with the news. When her dad wrecked his car on the beach road, he was blind drunk. Illa was three years old, too young to understand death but old enough to register the absence of her gruff, bearded papa, and to know the noises coming from Mama's bedroom meant *sad*. Mama never spoke about Papa. Her mother took a job at the refinery soon after his death.

Illa blinks against the harsh fluorescence of the gym lights, which creates a checkered pattern behind her eyes. In her knees she feels the rhythm of the pounding basketballs. She loves everything about these practices, even drill sergeant Jodi, even the singular gym musk, heavy on cleaning solvent and stale sweat, with a tinge of concession-stand hot dog. Freshman year, Illa signed up to be manager because she needed a PE credit and it seemed like an easy way to knock it out. But after a few days with the team, practice became the highlight of her day. Not just because her duties allowed her to feel a part of something; she also appreciated the way the girls flew down the court, uninhibited, like when they put on that uniform, they forgot they were mortal girls living in a nothing town.

Illa understands she's just the manager, but she takes pride in her work. She knows that for ordinary people like her, value lies in what she can do for others, so she tries to make herself as useful as possible. She gave Chole Gomez the socks off her feet before a game when Chole forgot hers; when Corinne Wolcott's parents divorced, Illa let Corinne blubber to her in the locker room, leaving shimmering snail-trails of mucus on Illa's black T-shirt. How many hundreds of ankles has Illa wrapped, how many knee braces has she cinched, how many black eyes iced and shin splints stretched? Between looking after Mama and mother-henning the team, Illa has become expert at taking care of other people's needs. If only Mercy needed her the way the other girls did, surely they could become friends. But Mercy is not other girls; she is exceptional, always.

"Stark." In Coach Martin's mouth, Illa's name is onomatopoetic.

"Yes ma'am?"

"Get the equipment set up. Just because it's the last day of school don't mean we won't go hard."

"Yes ma'am."

Coach stares at Illa, caterpillar eyebrows raised. After a beat, she looks away to indicate they've finished their exchange, and Illa scrambles for the equipment room. Three years in and *yes ma'am* represents the sum total of her communication with Coach Martin, who wields her reticence so pointedly that even a mime could walk away from her feeling that he'd said too much. For years, Illa has watched the effect of Coach's broadsword of silence on the fawnlike freshmen girls who stumble onto her court. It usually takes less than a minute for the giggling and side conversations to cease, hacked to bits by Coach's aggressive muteness. Only Mercy has the power to make Coach lighten up, teasing out smiles from a mouth Illa had thought incapable of that expression. Coach and Mercy share a closeness born of respect and mutual need, like a jockey and a champion racehorse.

From the equipment room, Illa snags the camera bag, which she keeps wedged behind the ball cage for safekeeping. Even though the next game isn't till October, Coach wants to run the camera. Punching the button to release the bleachers, Illa clambers into position on the topmost bench, where she scans the lens back and forth over the court, trying to capture every bricked shot, every turnover and botched pass. During the season, the five girls with the fewest errors get to start the next game. Now it's just a little muscle-flexing by Coach before the girls disperse for the summer.

The scoreboard clock runs down, filling the gym with the mechanical grunt of the buzzer; warm-ups are over. Illa clicks the camera on, watching as the ten girls take position for the first drill, a full-court layup series in which each missed shot means running horses at drill's end. Illa rarely follows the ball. Instead, she finds herself drifting into photographer mode, attuning herself to the details of the scene: the ropy muscles in the girls' calves contracting with each explosive step, the decisive flick of a wrist in follow-through as a shot rolls off fingertips. The girls balance so perfectly between control and chaos.

As the video camera records, Illa takes the lens off her Canon and snaps a few quick frames, the rapid click of the shutter satisfying beneath her finger. After school, before the janitor kicks them out of the building, she'll develop the photos in the journalism room and show them to Lennox. He's not a photographer, but as editor of the student newspaper, he has strong opinions on just about everything. Which is okay, because she likes watching his mouth move. When Illa had learned that he and Annie were hanging out, she was surprised and disappointed; she'd always thought he had more imagination than that.

On the sidelines, Coach Thibodeaux paces with a clipboard. While they wait to go on, Jasmine Carter and Melissa Rivera do wall touches to keep loose. In between turns on the court, Annie and Mercy hip-check each other. Mercy drains a three just wide of the elbow, but Coach isn't satisfied.

"Want that shot from the baseline," she says as the girls reset themselves to try the play again. "Move farther down after Gomez sets the pick."

On the whistle, the play goes live, and Chole bodies up against Keisha Freeman, the backup point guard who shadows Mercy on defense. Then Mercy does exactly as she's instructed, taking an extra dribble down before pulling up for another three. She floats for a blink before releasing the ball, holding her wrist elegantly in follow-through like a woman waving goodbye to a lover at a train station.

Mercy calls the next play; she knows Coach too well to wait for praise. Mercy's delicate features, pale skin, and ice-pool eyes are more haunting than usual today. *Beauty* is too common a word for what she possesses. *Sublimity. Radiance.* Annie isn't lovely the way Mercy is, but she has the kind of obvious, shellacked prettiness that can carry you far in high school if you're the right amount of bitch.

Annie misses an easy bank shot, and the whistle shrills between Coach Martin's lips; play grinds to a halt.

"Now the time for sloppiness? That what you decide?" Coach, hand on hip, levels her falconine glare at Annie.

Illa holds her breath, waits for Annie's riposte. What Coach Martin does with silence, Annie does with words, carving up students and teachers with slicing quips. With practiced nonchalance, Annie shrugs. To Illa, it seems worse than a verbal response. She feels her body tense. Coach looks to her right, then her left, as if searching for someone to corroborate the sass she's just witnessed. "That what this game means to you, Putnam?" Coach shrugs in snide imitation, exaggerating the movement. This time Annie does nothing, her face statuesque in its cool neutrality.

"Don't have time for this kind of slack attitude," Coach says, talking through her teeth. It's what she does when she's especially pissed, and Illa finds it more unnerving than a good bellow. "Back to it," Coach says, turning away from the court in disgust. She shakes her head at Coach Thibodeaux, who's busy scribbling away on the clipboard.

Normally, Coach Martin wouldn't stop play to nag Annie for such a small infraction—if she did, they'd never make it through practice. But everyone's on edge over the Market Basket incident. From the gym you can see the convenience store parking lot, the police cars coming and going, the small crowd of gawkers that has gathered. Everyone is waiting to hear the bad news, whatever it is, and Illa can sense the tension moving outward from Coach Martin's telephone-pole frame, emanating from her stiff dome of brown curls.

Practice ends and Coach Martin calls the girls into a huddle. Illa jumps down from the bleachers and moves toward the tightening circle. This is her favorite part of practice. She presses in behind Mercy's right shoulder. From there, Illa can feel the warmth of the girls' perspiring bodies as they listen to Coach and try to catch their breath. Afterward, there will be the tumult of the locker room, the jokes and noise Illa can imagine belong to her. At the last minute, though, Annie shoves her way between Illa and Mercy so that Illa's hand is no longer connected to the huddle.

"God, would you quit *staring* at her?" Annie says under her breath, not bothering to look at Illa. "Freak."

Illa draws back, blood flooding her cheeks. Clumsily, she shifts a few bodies over. Coach starts talking, but Illa feels light-headed from embarrassment, the flush spreading, making her ears ring. Annie has it in for Illa, and Illa suspects it has something to do with what happened at a school assembly a few days after the explosion. Back then, Mercy had hugged Illa close and then forced Annie to apologize to her. *For what?* Annie protested. *Dad's the asshole, not me.* But Mercy insisted, saying that *someone* ought to say sorry to *somebody*. When Annie finally acquiesced, there was a bitter light in her eye. Annie didn't apologize to many people, and that temporary humiliation soured her permanently on Illa. But Mercy's kindness that day was worth Annie's anger. Though Mercy had enchanted Illa hundreds of times over the years—every single basketball game, for instance—it was the hug that stayed with Illa, cementing her belief that Mercy was not only a star but a saint, too.

As Illa's embarrassment fades, Coach's words begin to drift back to her: " . . . by this point, your bodies are machines we've tuned up over thousands of hours. Don't let things fall apart over the next few months. Summer is when championships are won or lost. Y'all gonna keep working hard?"

"Yes ma'am," the girls say.

"Are you?"

"Yes ma'am!"

"Bring it in."

Illa wedges her shoulder in so she can again place her hand in the stack among the others. She feels the press of the bodies against hers, the rough skin of someone's dry palm and the softer skin of a wrist.

"Lady Rays on three. One, two, three . . ."

"LADY RAYS!"

And just like that, the girls disperse, blown spores from a dandelion, away from Illa and into the locker room.

"Stark."

"Yes ma'am?"

"Don't forget to wash the warm-ups. The navy ones. Need 'em washed and packed up for the summer."

"Yes ma'am."

So she won't have the locker room one last day. That's okay. She's afraid of what Annie might say, anyway. Better to keep a low profile. In the laundry room, she loads the warm-up shirts and pants into the industrial-size washing machine. When she finally makes it back to the locker room, the girls have already showered and gone to class, so she hears none of the familiar ruckus: lockers banging shut, girls belting out Shania or Britney or hollering at each other, deodorant spray cans discharging. Illa passes the cement shower bank, which gives off a dank chill, and pushes open the door to the varsity locker room. There, in the subterranean space, the silence is total except for the muffled drips from the stripped showerheads next door.

She walks along the row of lockers, empty little cages now that they've been stripped of their owners' identities. She found it endearing the way each locker reflected the owner's personality: Corinne Wolcott's neat as a pin with a miniature Bible tucked in a corner (her daddy is a Baptist preacher); Keisha Freeman's stuffed with half a dozen drugstore perfumes, which she likes to spritz on her jersey just before game time; Chole's plastered with torn-out magazine photos of Selena. Chole, a tall, thick-calved girl with fierce black eyes set too close together, lives with her tia and tio on the east side of town, her parents back in Juárez. In the locker room, she likes to brag about all the stuff she can get away with, since her aunt and uncle spent all their time focused on their daughter Veronica, *their little angel*. Chole regularly steals Cokes and lotto tickets from the Market Basket, drives into Louisiana with Marcus Drab and a posse of other male jocks to gamble at the casino.

Illa looks inside Mercy's locker to see if she accidentally left anything behind. The cross she made out of a discarded wire hanger is still up, and below it, a forgotten Post-it note. Illa removes both items to toss in the trash, but the dense handwriting on the Post-it catches her attention. When she examines it more closely, she sees that it's a list, in Mercy's meticulous handwriting:

1. Be NOT proud.
2. Stick to the meal plan *every day*.
3. *Be twice as good as other girls.*
4. You *get out* what you *put in*.
5. No boy gets the privilege of *your flesh* until marriage.
6. Get *full D-I scholarship*.
7. Live to meet the end without dread.

Reading the list, Illa feels a mix of embarrassment and pity. It's like pulling back the curtain on the great and powerful Oz to find that he's just a man moving levers. Of course Mercy has goals— anyone with her drive and talent does—but these are not just reminders of physical benchmarks; they're instructions on how to *be*. *Live to meet the end without dread.* Y2K freaks, Lennox included, thought the computers were going to melt down at the end of the year, but did Mercy believe the *world* was ending that day?

Illa knows Mercy is religious—she always leads the team prayers, and she and her grandmother belong to some Holy Roller church out in the backwoods—but since Mercy wears regular clothes (no floor-length skirts or bonnets or whatever it was fundamentalists wear) and plays basketball and goes to school with the rest of them, Illa thought that maybe to Mercy, religion was a benign set of guidelines, kind of like a diet you cheated on.

Plunking down on the bench in front of the lockers, Illa realizes the list makes her feel protective of Mercy. There's something tragic and unnerving about the severe dictums Mercy had written out for herself. And yet the idea of *Illa* protecting *Mercy* from anything is laughable.

She folds the Post-it and sticks it in her pocket, feeling suddenly depressed. She stares for a while at the poster hanging on the wall: Michael Jordan tomahawking in for a massive dunk. Taken aerially, it casts Jordan against a bright blue floor, five fingers taut, arm popping with muscle. To the left, his shadow imitates the movement, a ghost player crashing in from the other side of the hoop. The picture has been hanging in the same spot for the three years that Illa has managed the varsity team; it's the image that first made her want to pick up a camera. That the photographer saw the game the way she did, as art and not just sport, and that he tried to capture it as such, had seemed important. So she had joined the newspaper staff because she heard they gave you access to decent cameras.

She also bought a print of the poster and tacked it to her ceiling. *Blue Dunk* was such a striking, elegant image that she wanted it to be the first thing she saw each morning and the last thing each night, a small reminder that the human body was a machine built for movement, capable of extraordinary things, and could be breathtakingly gorgeous. Living with her mother, it was easy to forget that.

And then one afternoon a few months ago, she was flipping through an old *Sports Illustrated,* the only magazine on the table, when she learned about a student sports-photography contest. Though she'd had months to try, she wasn't able to get the money shot. The theme, "Euphoric Sport," kept tripping her up. Whenever she thought she'd nailed it, she rushed to the darkroom to develop the roll only to discover that the shot was flat or blurry or pedestrian. Maybe the problem was her subject. The Lady Rays basketball team is many things—five-time state champs, run-and-gun, disciplined as marines—but *euphoric?* The word was probably long ago struck from Coach Martin's vocabulary, along with *fun, lose, can't.*

Illa doesn't expect to win the contest, but the act of putting one of her photos in an envelope and mailing it to New York City would be victory enough. Someone working at 4 Times Square (Times Square!) would look at her photograph and read her name. On the off chance that she *did* win, she'd earn a photo internship at *SI* next summer, working out of the Times Square office. It's probably better that she doesn't try, because then there would be the issue of what to do about Mama. Always there's the issue of Mama.

In the next room, a shower splashes on. On her way out, Illa peers in and sees that it's Mercy, her clothes piled messily on the floor by the entrance. The team's last meal plan, which Illa typed up the day before, puckers with moisture by Mercy's clothing. The plan's familiar headline, CHAMPIONSHIP BODIES START AT THE CELLULAR LEVEL, has begun to smear.

Mercy is usually so modest about her body that, in three years with the team, Illa has never seen her undressed. While the other girls paraded their nakedness, pinching their lean thighs and complaining about invisible imperfections, Mercy faced her locker to wiggle out of her sports bra under cover of the practice jersey. In the beginning, the girls ribbed her—*Think you're so hot you gotta hide the goods, Louis?* But Mercy held strong, never offering an excuse for her choices, and after a while, her rituals went unremarked.

Now Illa watches Mercy wrap her arms around her torso for warmth against the frigid water, hair forming a cragged black boundary against the vestigial wings of her shoulder blades. Illa can see the map of blue veins just beneath the moon-colored skin of her back. Mercy holds her face up to the showerhead, her long limbs water-glazed and gleaming. A pulse of longing shakes Illa, followed by a deeper rush of illicit thrill. She swallows. *Dyke lesbo gaywad.* These are words the girls use on each other, teasingly, as they swat and josh each other in the locker room. Annie would call Illa these things and worse if she caught her there gaping, and Illa wouldn't be able to defend herself. Despite the risk, Illa wants to stay, waiting until Mercy turns around so that she might witness the dark hollows of Mercy's violin hips, her flat, shadowless stomach, the rise of her small perfect breasts.

Mercy reaches for the faucet, which squeals in protest as she turns it off. Holding her breath, Illa dashes toward the door, elation and shame and curiosity knocking around inside her.

# MERCY

When three-thirty arrives, hollers ricochet up and down the hallways. Lockers smash shut with a satisfying metallic crunch. In a distant corner, someone's blasting Alice Cooper. Goodbyes chase me down the hallway: Bye, Mercy; Later, Mers! See ya, hoss! Have a great summer, stay sweet, girl! The clamor gives me a headache.

When I pass her in the hall, Brittny Wood invites me to the tie-up later; she and some others are going to loop their daddies' bass boats together in the fat part of the bayou, drink Bud, and look at the stars. I bet it's nice floating out there with the moon on the water.

For a moment while I walk, I'm overwhelmed by sadness; I stop by the window and pretend to wave to someone so I can recover myself. I don't know why I'm concerned, the halls are practically empty now. Everyone is already in the parking lot below, where they're celebrating noisily. Charmaine has walked these halls, maybe even stood in this exact spot, looking out over the student lot toward the football field. Sure, I've thought about my mother hundreds of times,

but only in an abstract way. Reading her letter has made her real in a
way she wasn't before.

"Don't you have something better to do on the last day of school
than stare out windows, girl?"

I turn to find Coach smiling at me. In my throat, a choking sensation, and then I'm doing the worst possible thing, crying in front
of Jodi Martin. I try to cover my face with my hands, but it's too late,
tears drip from my chin, my nose is snotty, I'm a mess.

Without asking what's wrong, Coach takes me in her arms and
hugs me close. Her Lady Rays polo shirt smells freshly laundered.
After all this time working together, we've never hugged, not like
this, and I realize she's softer than I imagined she would be. I lean
in to her and she pats my back, running her hands awkwardly
over my shoulders. Already I feel the relief that comes with spent
tears.

Careful not to meet her eyes, I step away, wiping my nose with the
back of my hand. "Sorry," I say. "I don't know what came over me."

"Didn't think you were going to miss me *that* much," she jokes,
grinning. She's got such a nice, genuine smile; I wish she'd use it
more.

I think about the letter in my bag. I can't tell Maw Maw about it,
but what about Coach? When did she start working at Port Sabine?
Early eighties, wasn't it? I doubt she would have crossed paths with
my mom, but maybe she heard things about Charmaine and could
tell me about her.

"My mother . . ." I start, fumbling for the right words. "I . . . Did
you . . ."

But the look on her face shuts me up, her eyes gone stormy at the
word *mother.*

"What is it, Mercy?" she presses. "Did something happen?"

"It's nothing," I say. "I guess I just miss her sometimes. It's stupid . . ."

"No, it isn't," she says. "It's natural, Mers." A pause. "But you're doing fine, hon. Remember that. Your grandmother has done a lot for you. She loves you." She chucks me on the chin with her knuckles.

I manage a smile, the skin of my cheeks tight from the dried tears. That's when I remember Annie. I glance at the clock: 4:03. I was supposed to meet her fifteen minutes ago. "Annie's waiting for me," I say.

Coach glowers. "You make that girl behave herself this summer."

I'm tired at the thought of corralling Annie for three long months, but I nod anyway. "Have a great summer, Coach."

"You, too, hoss."


I find Annie with Lennox behind the portables. His arms encircle her waist, hands running along the strip of lower back revealed by her upward-creeping shirt. They're so tuned in to each other, they don't hear me approach, and for a second, I watch them kiss. I'm ashamed for her, that she'd let herself be handled so publicly by a man who won't be her husband. They look like animals, their heads jerking from side to side as they try to devour each other's face. She buries her fingers in his Afro, yanking his hair a little.

She sees me through slitted eyes but promptly closes them again, keeps on kissing. After a minute, I clear my throat. "Ready?" I ask. More kissing, this time with wet sucking noises, like a boot being yanked from the mud. Finally, she squirms out of Lennox's arms.

"Going to get chicken-drunk," she says, brushing her hand against his cheek. "Later, Len!"

After catching the end of their performance, I'm embarrassed to meet Lennox's eyes, but I give a stiff wave before we lope across the grass toward the parking lot. We drive to Hunan Palace, a Chinese buffet a couple towns over. The place is empty, the food glistening under heat lamps. It smells of grease and garlic and burned sugar.

Atonal music trickles out of a bulky black speaker on the floor in a corner. We don't come here for the atmosphere; we come here to get chicken-drunk, as Annie says.

Silently, we take up the warm white plastic plates from the end of the buffet. Then, with workmanlike dedication, we fill them until we can no longer see the red bamboo pattern along the edges. Onto our plates we pile a cushion of fried rice dotted with egg and peas, then carve out holes for General Tso's chicken, sesame shrimp, beef with broccoli, chow mein, and lo mein. I shore up the pooling sauces with an egg roll dam, add a couple crab Rangoon and fried pork dumplings. In a corner booth, we lean over the food and start inhaling it. From a table by the kitchen, the bored waiters watch us. A toddler wearing nothing but a diaper plays on the rug at the waiters' feet.

This is our last-day-of-school ritual. A couple years back, Annie started it to celebrate the end of Coach's meal plan, or at least the "technical" end of the plan; we know she expects us to keep to it through the summer so we don't chunk up. Looking at Annie slurping noodles, I consider telling her about Charmaine's letter but hesitate. It shames me to see my mother's pathetic story written out, black ink on a white page. So instead I smile at Annie across the table, spoon up silky mouthfuls of egg drop soup, growing my belly taut with each bite. For a little while, there's a strange relief in the discomfort of being stuffed to popping, drowsy and warm and full up.

After I drop Annie, groaning and ripping belches, back at home, I drive up LeBlanc Avenue. Past the Market Basket, where yellow police tape is the only reminder of the morning's drama, the football stadium rises, its tall light posts angled over the field like chrome flowers.

Hopping the perimeter fence, I start a slow jog down the straightaway in front of the home stands. The humid air is wet on my face.

From the interstate, the sound of traffic arrives, muffled, steady. In my stomach, the undigested food sloshes with each footfall. Around and around the track I go, not fast but moving, until I lose count of the laps. Eventually, the sun dips behind the horizon, casting in pinks and oranges the veil of smog from the refinery. Feeling purged, I lie down in the middle of the football field, the grass damp and fragrant at my back. Around me, the chorus of crickets, a quickening in the air as night falls. Tomorrow is almost here, the first wide-open day of summer.

Watching the late afternoon turn to evening, I'm struck by a sudden sense of loss, knowing that each sunset like this is moving us closer to the end. Is it possible that in a few months, this sweet-smelling earth will be scorched beyond recognition? That soon I will have to leave behind this body that has given me so much? Lying there, I poke my belly, feel the resistance of the muscles. I wrap my arms across my chest, a hand on each bicep, thinking of the hours I have spent lifting weights, working this flesh to strength. Quickly, I do a couple of leg lifts, thighs and calves pressed together like a mermaid's tail, heels tapping the ground before springing up again. The acidic gift of muscles at work. When I try to picture myself bodiless in heaven, I see my soul like a white cloud, naked and ordinary, in a sky full of them.

Secretly, I want Maw Maw to be wrong. There's too much I haven't had a chance to do, not just winning State, but graduating, going to college, kissing a boy, falling in love. You need a body to do those things, you need a world like this one. *Look, Lord,* I pray. *Look at that sunset. A world still capable of such things can't deserve to end, not yet.* Even as I think the words, though, I know that this small moment of beauty is rooted in ugliness, the refinery chemicals the reason for the sky's riotous light.

On the way past school, I stop into the Market Basket to buy some bottled water. The caution tape snaps in the wind. Inside, the cashier sits behind the register reading *Rolling Stone.*

"Looked a little crazy over here earlier," I say, placing two water bottles on the counter. "What was the commotion about?"

"Ain't you seen it yet?" he asks, ringing me up. "It's on every news channel here to Dallas." He shakes the remote control in the direction of the muted television over his head. "The *Today* show even called wanting details, but something like this happens, a man don't want to go on about it. My manager's about ready to fire all of us for the bad press, like it's my fault that baby got dumped here."

"Excuse me?" I say, thinking I must not have heard him right. "A baby?"

"Cops called it a fetus, but Richie said it looked like a baby to him, little arms and legs and toes and everything. No bigger than a grapefruit, stuck in a beer case in the dumpster."

The store's air-conditioning against my sweaty skin sets me shivering. "Was it alive?"

"Nope," he says. "They don't know how long it's been dead for or what killed it. Some doc has to take a look."

The room is too bright, dizzying; I sway a step, knocking into a display of chips. The colorful bags scatter across the floor.

"You okay?" he asks. "Need a smoke? Hell. *I* need one. I just keep picturing it, all tiny . . ." He shakes his head like he's trying to jolt the memory loose. Scooting past me, he moves toward the door. "Don't forget to pay for those." He indicates the waters. Cradling them in the crook of my arm, I leave a five on the counter. It's too much, but what does that matter now? Someone has dumped a baby in the trash. *Forget what I said about what this world deserves, Lord. We deserve nothing.*

Before church, Maw Maw and I tune the radio to Hoakum and Pursifull to hear what people are saying about the LeBlanc Avenue baby. Lyle mentions a tip line that the police department has set up, and Bud Lee says the medical examiner will have his report ready in about a week.

"The report will determine whether the woman who left the baby will face murder charges," Lyle says. "So stay tuned, folks, because you better believe we're going to follow this story. I mean, our town's had its share of bad press, what with the explosion and all, but you ask me, this is worse. We are going to do everything we can to bring the woman who did this to justice."

Maw Maw switches the radio off, uptilts her chin. "Got to ready ourselves," she murmurs. "It's close now." Crickets screech beyond the porch lights. She drinks from her glass of sweet tea, ice cubes clinking as she sips. "We'll pray that baby to heaven tonight."

"Yes ma'am." She doesn't need to tell me to pray; since I learned the news, I haven't stopped.

"Mercy, *ma fille,* remember *les feux follets?* Will o' the wisps?" She pauses as if waiting for an answer, but I know she's only collecting herself to tell the story I've heard dozens of times. "There was a traveler through the swamp who one evening saw a light like a floating candle appear before him. He was tired, and the night in its blackness stretched long before him, so do you know what he did? He followed the light. Followed it into the darkest part of the swamp, where he could hear the gators thrashing and snapping their jaws. They could smell him, but mostly, they could smell that he was lost. Still, he followed the light that floated like a ghostly candle, moving and bobbing through the lowlands. He tried to stay close to the light, but each time he walked faster, the light drew farther away, until finally, he could no longer see the light at all. He was pitiful lost, *ma fille.* What was the man to do? But he remembered a story he'd heard in a tavern on the road, a story of will-o'-the-wisps that led travelers astray. He carried a knife, and remembering the story, he thrust the knife into the heart of the night, into the black soil of the swamp.

"Suddenly, the light appeared again, but this time it grew bigger and bigger as it came closer to him and his blade, stuck as it was in the night's heart. Scared, the man hid behind a tree and watched. Soon the light was just above the blade, and with a flash like lightning, it spun around the blade, around and around, and he heard a terrible scream, a child's scream. The traveler fell over from the blinding light, and when he stood up, it was daytime and the day birds were calling their sweet songs. In sunlight, he knew exactly which way was west, the direction he had been traveling. He pulled his knife from the ground and was surprised to find it covered in bright red blood. He wiped the blood off with his shirttail.

"For *les feux follets* are the souls of unbaptized babes, *ma fille,* and they haunt those who wander the swamps and forests. With a knife to the heart of the night, the traveler had released the children out of purgatory, out of their ghostly state, and into hell." She looks at me over her glass, her long fingers wrapped around it thoughtfully. "Pray for that baby, but say a prayer for yourself, too, *ma fille.*" I can see by the light of the hurricane lamp propped on the floor that her eyes are glistening.

I've never seen her eyes wetted except by full sun. I stand from my chair and walk toward her, but she shoos me away, dabbing at the corners of her eyes.

"You were so close to being one of those pitiful creatures," she says.

"What do you mean?"

"I bargained for your soul, child." She takes a long draw from her glass, and in the quiet, I can hear her swallow. "She was going to get rid of you, had an appointment at a clinic in Houston. For a thousand dollars, she agreed to keep clean and bring you to term. Marry Witness, too, so you wouldn't be born a bastard. I couldn't allow her to put that burden on you right from the start."

The truth lands like a punch: if Charmaine had her way, I'd have been nothing more than cells scraped off her womb by some doctor.

To know what your life is worth to your mother and that it is a dollar amount. The physical pain of the news surprises me, the way it roots between my ribs.

Maw Maw sniffles softly. "There is no greater evil in the world than a wrong done to a child," she says, and I wonder if she's thinking of me or the LeBlanc baby. "I'm scared for this town." She looks ahead into the night that is just starting to come alive, sounds sharpened by the blanket of darkness. "With every sin comes retribution."

As we pull into the gravel parking lot at church, kids charge back and forth in a game of tag, illuminated by the wobbly headlights of arriving cars. I'm glad to be here in this familiar place. More than the stilt house, which feels lonesome sometimes, this white clapboard church is home.

Weeks after Paw Paw Gaspard died and Charmaine hitched out, we left the Catholic church and joined up here. *Abandoned you and killed her own father, did that woman,* Maw Maw says. I was still a baby in a Moses basket, and the way she tells it, she needed God direct, not on a priest party line. She'd heard about a nameless church lodged in a copse of warty toothache trees outside of town, how the pastor knew to fear the devil as much as love the Lord, and how the Lord called on people right there during the service. After losing half her family, that was the kind of faith she was after, so she swaddled me up and drove out to see what was what. Maw Maw had her first vision that day, birds falling out of the sky. The next morning, that Sands tanker ran aground and leaked millions of gallons of oil into the Gulf, the worst spill in history. Thousands of white egrets and blue herons and gulls died glued to rocks or drowned by sludgy water. Thousands more died of starvation because they couldn't fly to hunt with their blackened wings.

Inside the church, there's the familiar piney smell of wood soap and, faintly, coffee from the kitchen that sits just off the worship room. Maw Maw wags her finger impatiently in the direction of our pew, and I hustle past the other worshippers to take a seat. Usually people are animated before services, but today the room has the subdued feel of a funeral service. The heaviness in the air that death brings. News of the baby has hit everyone hard.

Maw Maw and I sit, room enough for another body between us, and she bows her head in prayer. Because I've spent years crammed in a locker room with nine other girls, pinballing up against their bodies, sharing clothes and sweat and menstrual cycles, I understand her need for space. Tonight I'm glad of the distance because of Charmaine's letter. I'm scared to think what Maw Maw would see if she laid hands on me. I picture Charmaine rising from my blood like a summoned ghost. *That woman,* the one who was ready to hand my soul to the devil. I close my eyes to pray thoughts of her away, but instead of the peace of darkness, I see that tiny bloodied corpse, arms stiff with death, reaching upward for deliverance.

I look around to see if anyone else has seen what I have. A few rows back, someone is groaning softly. It feels wrong to look at people's faces while they pray, they're so vulnerable. Some are open-mouthed, some are pinched in concentration, many sway gently, that quiet dance you do as you find the rhythm of your prayer. Nothing out of the ordinary, but that heaviness I felt when we walked in seems worse, the air before a storm. Briefly, I lock eyes with Marilee Warren, a girl from my grade. She looks beseechingly at me, her large green eyes striking against her black dress. It's not just any black dress, I realize then. It's the shapeless sackcloth that girls wear when they've been caught violating the promise of chastity made at their purity ceremony. I feel a fluttering in my gut, imagining what it is she's done. If she's already wearing the dress, it won't be secret for long.

Maw Maw follows my gaze to Marilee and clucks her tongue.

"They let her go around in those dancing-girl costumes. Hypocrisy in the parent breeds hypocrisy in the child."

Pastor Parris clears his voice and a hush descends on the room. "Let us pray," he says. "Lord, today evil has shown its face among us. Today we have learned of a baby treated like common trash, a life tossed out as if your greatest gift had no value. A child who could not speak to defend itself, who could not lift a finger to fight for its life. Only the truly evil would treat the defenseless so cruelly!"

I think of Charmaine, how she would have dissolved me before my heart even had a chance to form. Once you're firmly rooted in this world, it's strange to consider that it might have been otherwise.

Pastor Parris continues: "I want all women of childbearing age to stand up." He watches us expectantly. "Come on, now. No one's in trouble. But I want every woman between the ages of thirteen and forty to please stand."

We're slow to follow his order. After a pause, a few women, mothers with babies on their hips and some of the older married women, stand. Arms crossed over chests, they shift nervously from foot to foot.

"Go on, Mercy child, you've got nothing to hide," Maw Maw says. Reluctantly, I get to my feet. Those still seated look around at us, eyebrows raised over questioning eyes. How many of these people know who my mother is and what she's capable of? *Daughter of a whore, must be one herself.* Mrs. Warren prods her daughter, and when Marilee rises, everyone stares at her, standing there in that ugly dress. They know what it means, and a whisper travels through the congregation as the sight registers with them. I feel sorry for Marilee, she looks so small and pale, swathed in the telltale black cotton.

"Take a look at these women," Pastor Parris continues. "Your wives, sisters, daughters, friends. While I'm certain that none of them is responsible for what happened to that child, I want to make an important point." He pauses for effect, walks to the front of the stage, and looks from left to right, nodding at each row of people. The pastor's a nervous man with cornmeal-colored skin, a swatch of steel-wool hair, and darting pale eyes, as if he can see the angels and demons he says are battling in the air around us. Though I'd never tell Maw Maw, I don't like him. He relies on the pulpit too much, something to lift him above the rest of us, and there's dark talk about why he left his church in Nacogdoches, some girl hurt during a cure.

At last he starts up again: "That point is this: when a child suffers, all of us must bear the guilt and shame of it, all of us are tainted. Let us remember, too, we are all of us sinners, no one is immune to evil."

*Amen amen amen,* people chorus. A chill chases down my neck, causing me to jerk my head back. A voice: *Speak for me.* Mouth open, a low note escapes, *Uhhhh,* like the start of a hymn. People shift around me. I hear Maw Maw's voice, "Child, what—" *Pay them no mind. Speak for me.*

Eyes closed, heart and head up to heaven, arms at my sides. I don't recognize this voice singing, but I feel its vibrations in my throat, it can only be mine. Sounds like the language of a far-off land, but it makes perfect sense to me. The child, too, must understand. I know with clarity it's a girl. I tell her she's loved, that she contains all the innocence of the world in her child-heart, and for that, her place in heaven is already secured. I tell her the Lord waits for her.

No bigger than a grapefruit. I raise my arms, cup my hands overhead. The flow of words bubbling up like a spring. Strange sounds that sift through my ears, so I have to translate myself. I don't feel scared. I put my trust in God, and I speak louder.

*We are sisters, you and me. You think no one understands, but I do.* Pastor Parris's voice, "Yes, Mercy, let the spirit of the Lord fill you, speak His message."

*Find the one who did this.* Something pushing from inside my skull, little jackhammer hands against the bone of my nose, behind my eyes. Shouting now, chin jerking up, up to send the words higher, farther, that everyone might hear and obey. *Find the one who did this.* Someone's hand—Maw Maw's?—on my wrist, but I shake it off.

After a while, a minute, an hour, the words dry up, my mouth is empty. This time the silence a blanket around my shoulders, God-given. Closed eyes bathed in darkness, the tiny, reaching corpse gone. I think of *les feux follets,* my words a knife to the heart of the night, only this time, instead of hell, the baby's soul has been released into heaven, I know it has.

When I open my eyes, everyone is turned toward me. Some are praying in low voices. A few women wipe tears from their cheeks. Legs shaking like I've run a fast mile, I swoon backward and the bench hits me at the knees.

"The gift of tongues!" Pastor Parris says, reaching for my forehead. Someone shouts: "She's falling, catch her!" Time slows: the curtain of Sue Chessly's auburn hair filtering the light; the deep scar in the pine bench in front of me; at last, the concrete of the floor cold against my cheek. Then: nothing.

# ILLA

LLA DOESN'T WANT to go downstairs. It will mean seeing Mama—no, *smelling* her—and being forced to confront the fact that in the last week, for reasons unknown, her mother has stopped bathing herself. When they heard about the baby on the news last night, Illa was horrified to realize she was glad for the distraction the grisly discovery provided. So long as the world delivered new crises, Illa and Mama wouldn't need to address the small one developing in their house.

The midmorning sun has already rendered Illa's bedroom stuffy, and soon it will be unbearable, the heat rising as if even physics is in conspiracy against her. How is it they have managed to survive with nothing but a single window unit in the kitchen to take the punch out of the bruising Texas summer?

She pushes open a window, hoping for a breeze, but all she gets is the unfiltered smell of the refinery, which hulks just beyond the tree line. Sometimes Mama sits on the front porch sniffing the air, trying to identify the chemicals. *That's benzene,* she'd say. *That's toluene. That's nitrogen oxide.*

*Smell of money, my ass,* Illa thinks. Money, real money, smells like the cosmetics floor of the Dillard's department store in Houston—spicy perfumes with ingredients like sandalwood and saddle leather, fresh-cut day lilies, marble floors mopped to a mirrored shine with citrusy cleaner. Often Illa thinks of Mama's settlement money sitting in that Houston bank, a million dollars, and dreams of all the things they could buy with it. Four years of college, for starters. Smaller things, too: nice clothes to fit Mama's new, larger body instead of just Walmart sweatpants; that pair of tan and turquoise boots Illa saw in the display window of Buck's; a real nurse to help Mama so that Illa could move into the college dorms next year. But Mama refuses to touch the money, claiming she let Sands buy her too easy.

About a year after the explosion, around the time when Mama, under pressure from her lawyer, settled with Sands, she was arrested for trespassing on refinery property. Furious and regretful over the settlement, wanting to make some kind of statement, she'd called the paper, then wheeled herself two miles to the refinery docks and started ranting that Sands got away with murder, that the Occupational Safety and Health Administration fine was a joke, and that Beau Putnam and the rest of the Dallas suits should go to criminal court for gross negligence.

After the arrest and the story in the paper, people started calling Illa and her mother the Strange Starks. It didn't help Mama's case that some folks in town viewed Beau as a hero for pulling people, including Mama, out of the wreckage before the first responders arrived. The Port Sabine *Flare* ran a front-page photograph of him cradling her like a bridegroom, emerging from behind a curtain of smoke and flame. *Refinery manager Beau Putnam pulls his secretary, Meg Stark, to safety.* The Occupational Safety and Health Administration and Chemical Safety Board and internal reports cited only "organizational failings." OSHA handed down the largest fine in its history, but Mama said it was pennies to Sands, which pulled in billions every year; that of course they would go on pumping oil in a death trap, when forty-seven lives could be bought that cheap.

Illa has failed to convince Mama many times that they needed the settlement money, so every Friday, she pockets her twenty-dollar allowance and tries to adjust her dreams to fit reality. After graduation, maybe she can get a part-time secretarial job, leave the house for a while each day, and earn some extra cash. Maybe she can scrape together enough to rent one of those sagging Craftsman cottages off the downtown strip so at least she'll have some time alone, eight or nine hours to pretend she has a life of her own.

Illa slides the window shut and latches it. With the air smelling perpetually of rotten eggs, it's easy to attribute the new odor in the house to some refinery project. But whenever Mama wheels past her, Illa has to hold her breath against the stench, which doesn't waft in Mama's wake so much as knock into Illa's nostrils like a swift uppercut, a dense mix of sweat and piss that reminds Illa of the Salvation Army men's shelter on Rangeline, or the backyard petting zoo in Orange that Mama took her to once when she was too small to be put off by stink or by small, mangy farm animals kept in cages. Back when she and Mama still spent time together. Back when Mama still left the house.

Illa hasn't been able to bring herself to ask her mother what's wrong, because it frightens her to consider the possibilities in any detail. From Mama, she has learned that so much can go wrong with a body. Pushing the wheelchair, doing errands, driving Mama to her doctors' appointments, even trimming toenails—these are tasks Illa has grown accustomed to. She has not, however, seen her mother's naked body, even when it was beautiful: a courtesy every parent owes a child, in Illa's opinion. But the violent new funk trailing behind Mama threatens to breach this last remaining boundary of decorum. Either Mama can no longer bathe herself or she's lost the will to, meaning Illa will have to intervene.

Illa pulls on a pair of jeans, noting with satisfaction that they seem looser this week. The jeans are already a size zero. What if she shrinks below that? Is there a size subzero, a denim category for the less-than-nothings? It would be a PR nightmare for clothing brands, all those self-esteemy parents in a tizzy over the message being sent to their shrinking daughters. Thankfully, Mama isn't one of those parents; she's too caught up in her own body woes to concern herself with her daughter's. Which is just fine with Illa. Because so what if she wants to be light as cotton candy, a puff of cloud that can soar on the wind? What is so wrong with wanting to be small? It means you're that much closer to invisibility, and invisibility can be a superpower. Her entire life, Illa has relied on it to protect herself. So long as she kept under the radar, no one could see to hurt her.

Mama calls from the base of the stairs: "Illa?"

"Yeah?"

"You coming down? I need my shot."

"Yup," she says, mildly annoyed to be rushed on what is, after all, the first day of her summer vacation. Still, she knows the shot is time-sensitive; how often has Dr. Lawrence warned her to be sure to administer the shots at the same time every day, speaking slowly like she's a little girl or perhaps a nonnative English speaker? Meanwhile, she's never missed a dose, has been a damned shot-giving machine.

She slips through the bedroom door and jogs down the steps, where Mama waits for her at the base of the stairs. Taking hold of the wheelchair's handles, she pushes Mama toward the kitchen. The television is tuned to one of those morning news shows where the anchors wear jaunty skirt suits and talk about fad diets and celebrity books. When Mama talks about these smiling women, she uses their first names as if they're personal friends.

"Come here, girl," Mama says, pulling Illa into the hard plastic arm of the wheelchair in her version of a hug. That's when Illa gets a sour whiff, the unmistakable smell of an unwashed body.

"Ma, stop." Illa squirms free in knee-jerk distaste.

"Ah, yes," Mama says. "Can't be taken for a mama's girl."

"Right," Illa says, pulling a grapefruit from the fridge and slicing it open with a serrated knife. She remarks the pleasing tug of the knife's teeth against the fruit's peel and wonders if this will be the most satisfying thing she does all day. During the summer, her allowance goes up to cover the extra hours she works, but it isn't enough to compensate for the boredom. These endless summer days, just her and Mama, the clock on the wall ticking away the seconds, the card games abandoned for long naps from which they both wake grumpy and dry-mouthed.

"They're talking about that baby," Mama says, pointing at the TV. "Turn it up."

Sure enough, one of the anchors, the blond one, is standing in front of a map of Texas, pointing to the little red dot in the southeastern corner of the state. Illa finds the remote and cranks the volume.

"Some of you will remember a couple years ago when we reported on the baby born at the prom in New Jersey left in the trash by its mother, who kept on partying. Well, we have a story almost as horrifying, this time out of Texas. Yesterday a fetus was discovered stuffed into a beer box in a convenience-store dumpster . . ."

The woman goes on to say that the discovery has shocked Port Sabine, a *deeply religious, severely economically depressed swampland presided over by the sprawling Sands Oil refinery, the fourth largest in the nation.* She rattles off some depressing statistics about unemployment, teen pregnancy, poverty, and pollution. "This isn't the first time the town has known tragedy," the anchor starts, doing that weird frown-smile they must learn in newscaster school when they're trying to reflect gravitas. On the screen, the photo of the crumbling Pleasure Pier with its decrepit carousel and sagging Ferris wheel is replaced by that all-too-familiar shaky home-video footage that ran on every news station in the wake of the disaster. Into the gray February sky the fireball roars, billowing a hundred feet up, the force of the blast knocking the amateur cameraman on his ass. Illa gropes for the remote, trying to shut out the terrible whooshing sound that must roam through Mama's nightmares. Mama covers her ears and folds forward as if trying to duck and cover. *Three years ago this February, Port Sabine got hit by one of the worst industrial disasters in U.S. history . . .*

Illa clicks off the set, then blurts: "Mama, I think it's time for a bath." Anything is better than seeing her mother reminded of that hellish day, even the shame that shadows her face now. Though it cracks Illa's heart to see her like this, she's thankful for that look. It reassures her that Mama hasn't lost pride altogether—that somewhere inside the folds of flesh that cling to her like the layers of a failed cake, the woman she once was still exists.

"I'll need your help," Mama says, sighing.

"Yes ma'am," she says officiously, glad to be able to steer Mama away from the TV. In the bathroom, Illa plugs the drain and opens the hot-water tap.

"You can go out and I'll get myself ready," Mama says. "It's really just the lowering down that I need help with."

"Sure," Illa says, slipping back out the door and pulling it closed behind her.

Her mother's body, with its bear-in-winter metabolism, its cascades of pale flesh that she seems doomed to wear like some great, cushiony straitjacket, baffles and embarrasses Illa, so it thrills her to witness, day in and day out at the gym, bodies that work. With their rangy arms and loping legs ending in mean little calves, the girls on the basketball team are another species altogether. When they're on the court, they are serious and strong. After the games, people talk to them and about them like they matter.

Illa knocks on the bathroom door. "Ready?"

"Okay," comes Mama's muffled voice. "I'm ready."

Illa takes a breath, pushes open the door. *Don't close your eyes,* she admonishes herself. Mama would be able to see her flinch in the mirror. Her mother has situated herself at the lip of the bathtub and looks poised to dive in. Rising pale and broad above the blue plastic back of the chair, her shoulders melt into bulging upper arms, which are demarcated by a dark seam where the two seas of flesh meet.

"If you want to stand up, I'll pull the chair back and get you under the arms," Illa instructs. Wordlessly, her mother rises, and Illa shifts into position. She wants to avoid seeing the contours of Mama's deformed body, but she rubbernecks, steals a glance downward. On Mama's left hip and buttock, a bruise large and purple as a slab of steak spreads outward, sustained perhaps during her last attempt at a bath. Her legs are a mass of pink and red scar tissue from the burns. Illa chokes down a gasp. In all the trips to the doctor, through all the shots administered and medicine doled out, Illa has never seen the ruined legs. The sight speaks of suffering so intense that Illa feels a stab of sympathy pain shoot through her femurs. Spontaneous tears form at the corners of her eyes.

"Illa?" Mama says, bringing her back to the task at hand.

"Sorry," she says. Pressing into the soft flesh of Mama's back, she positions her arms like bars beneath the armpits, and together they move the single step to the tub. She can tell Mama is trying not to lean all her weight on her, but even so, Illa strains beneath the heft, face growing hot from exertion as Mama lifts first one leg and then the next into the water. Bracing her back against the strain, Illa helps her mother into a squat, and from there, Mama sinks into the water. She lets out a deep sigh, and Illa moves quickly past the sink, back toward the door.

"I'll call you when I'm done," Mama says.

"All right," Illa says over her shoulder. "I'll finish making your breakfast in the meantime."

"Not feeling hungry, I said."

"But Dr. Lawrence says—"

"That man says a lot of things."

"Okay," she yields. Odd that her mother would refuse food, but Illa doesn't want to get into a fight on her first day of full-time work. It would cast a pall over an already bleak summer. "I'll get you a change of clothes, then," she says, a little too loud.

After emerging into the hallway, Illa wanders to her mother's closet. When she kneels to rummage in the dresser for a shirt, her eyes wander to the shoe boxes in the corner. After Mama gave up on the physical therapy, she went through the house and collected all the old pictures of herself and hid them here, a kind of graveyard for her former self. She also stashed away her yearbooks, anything that reminded her of who she was. Illa missed the photos; she had been proud and a little envious of her mother's intelligent, hawkish good looks. The deep-set Mediterranean eyes and fine, high forehead over which she side-swept her straight dark hair. Illa had thought her mother's body was just as a woman's should be—not wiry and boy-ish, like Illa's, but voluptuous in a way that was both maternal and secretive.

Taking a seat on the floor of the closet, Illa slides a yearbook out from under the shoe boxes. She flips to the index to see where her mother appears in the book and is somewhat surprised by the long list of page numbers. She knew her mother had been well liked, but the number of times Mama appeared in the book suggests a level of popularity Illa can't believe belonged to someone related to her. One by one, she thumbs through the photos, most of which are blurry and crowded with other kids. A group outside the Pelican Club, one of the all-night roadhouse dance halls over the state line; kids cheering at the edge of the Red Dump while someone slides down the

mud bank and into the mucky water below; Mama posing coquett-
ishly, hand over her mouth in mock fear, next to a ten-foot gator that
someone caught and killed. Seeing the ease with which Mama nav-
igated high school life gives Illa a flash of that old pride; she keeps
turning the pages.

Buried in a section called "Junior Life" is a photo of Mama and
Charmaine Boudreaux, Mercy Louis's long-gone mother. They're at
the beach, arms slung over each other's shoulders, the Gulf spread out
like mercury behind them. Mama wears a white two-piece, her hair
wild with the salt wind, the lids of her eyes drifting to half-mast, giving her a sleepy, sexy quality. Next to Mama's Brigitte Bardot, Charmaine is well scrubbed and guileless, a chambray shirtdress falling
slackly around her thin frame, face turned toward Mama adoringly.
The image makes Illa's heart beat fast. Was her mother friends with
Mercy's mom, or were they just standing near each other by chance
when the photographer passed by, the picture capturing a closeness
that never existed?

Illa decides to ask her mother, even if it might pain her to look at the
photo. Maybe Mama needs to be reminded of how strong and beautiful she once was so she'll have something to work toward. Remembering why she's in the closet in the first place, Illa stands to choose
out a skirt. As she flips through the hangers, her hand lingers over the
only serious outfit her mother still owns, a black jersey-knit dress with
three-quarter sleeves that she wears whenever she leaves the house.
In the past six months, there have been three such trips: two to the
doctor's office, and one more recently, to last winter's memorial service marking the third anniversary of the refinery explosion. Tensing
in her chair, Illa waited for her mother to cause some kind of a scene,
but instead, Mama sat quietly in the shadow of the Praying Hands
memorial with the other people who'd been injured that day, listening
as Mayor Sanchez read out the names of the dead while the rest of the
town looked on, heads hung in memory or prayer.

At the end of the ceremony, Mama remarked that Sands hadn't even bothered to send a representative. "See, Illa?" she said. "This is why I can't touch that money. Company pays everyone off, and then they can pretend like it never happened. If they started putting those suits in jail, you bet Sands would start giving a damn about safety." And Illa wanted to say that no, actually, she *didn't* see, didn't understand for a second why Mama wouldn't use the money her agony had earned her and that they needed so bad. But there was no talking to her; she possessed the stubborn righteousness of the badly wronged.

What would happen if Illa took the dress to her now, demanded that she put it on, and then drove her downtown? Where would they go? Was there a place left in town where Illa could bear to be seen with her mother? Mama hadn't died in the explosion, not technically. Her heart still beat inside her body. Her brown hair still grew thick to her shoulders. She still insisted on holding Illa's hand when they watched rented horror movies together. Initially elated over her mother's survival, Illa hadn't acknowledged the change in her mother's personality. Only when it became clear that Mama didn't intend to resume the physical therapy to try to walk again did Illa have to face the truth that while her mother hadn't died in the blast, she hadn't emerged fully alive, either.

"Illa?" her mother calls now from the bathroom.

Illa exhales. "Coming," she answers, leaving the black dress on the hanger but tucking the yearbook under her arm. In the bathroom, she sets it on the counter next to the sink. She helps Mama maneuver from the tub back into the wheelchair, then angles her mother's arms through the sleeves of her bathrobe. Once Mama is comfortable and clothed, Illa asks: "Were you and Charmaine Boudreaux friends?"

"Why? Who's been talking to you?" Her voice is defensive, and Illa notices she's gripping the wheelchair's armrests so firmly that the veins in her hands stand out.

"No one, I just saw that photo in the yearbook." Mama relaxes her grip on the chair. Illa hesitates but then forges ahead. "So, were you? Friends?"

"We were," Mama says. "Some people would say we were good friends."

Illa smiles to herself; this seems like the best news. Like maybe because of this history, she and Mercy are destined to be close. "That photo in the yearbook. Why didn't you ever tell me? You've heard me talk about Mercy. You know she's on the team."

"I . . . I don't know . . ." Mama stutters. "I guess I just never thought of it . . . it's been such a long time . . ."

"What was her deal?" For years, Illa's wanted to know more about Mercy, and all along, Mama's had the inside scoop on the girl's mysterious mother. "What was she like? Was she nice?"

"Nice? It was more than that. Charmaine was gentle. That's how I'd put it. People thought she was weird. Well, she *was*. It was like she'd been spit out of a time-travel machine. She had an old-fashioned quality to her. But that's what I *liked*. She was different from other people." In the mirror, Illa can see Mama smiling with the memory. "She could be funny, too. Char wasn't anybody's fool, even if she was naive about some things. She didn't go out of her way to make people try to like her, just kept to herself, mostly."

"When did y'all become friends?"

"My senior year, I guess? Which would've been Charmaine's sophomore year. Me and some of the other kids, we were kind of beach bums. That's where Char and I first met, at the beach. She saw us and came over and started talking about what we'd seen that morning, if there had been any dolphin sightings, and when the tide had gone out. The surfers in the group were real in tune with the water, so they got into it with her, talking about the weather, full moons and the tide, how it affected the chop. She knew a lot. God, I remember that day so clear. Someone offered her a cigarette and she shook her head at the same time as she reached for it, which made all of us laugh." Her face hardens. "I knew she was Evelia's girl, but I didn't really know what that meant, not then. I took her to a couple parties. We'd get to talking, and pretty soon she was telling me all kinds of stuff, the way girls do, I suppose."

"Like what, Mama?" Illa asks, greedy for Charmaine's secrets.

Mama tenses again. "It wasn't fair, her going away all of a sudden like that," she says, voice rising. Putting a hand to her mouth, she turns away, shoulders moving with silent sobs.

Surprised by the violence of her mother's reaction, Illa says gently, "It's okay," even though she has no idea what's wrong. She wants to continue probing about Charmaine, but she understands that would be cruel. She vows to bring up the subject in the future, once her mother has gotten over this fit of nostalgia, or whatever it is.

After a couple minutes, Mama collects herself, but her bottom lip quivers. Her expression, previously wistful, is now opaque. "I thank you kindly for your help," she says. "I'll be in my room if you need me." She motions Illa out of the way, then wheels herself out of the bathroom and down the hall.

# MERCY

—————

"'M KIDNAPPING YOU," Annie says when I answer the door Monday morning. She's wearing oversize red heart-shaped sunglasses, the halter strings of a turquoise bikini pulled tight behind her neck. Her skin gleams with suntan oil and smells of coconut. A red hibiscus flower tucked behind her ear brings some order to her muss of blond hair, frizzy from humidity. Crowned by the fan of banana plants growing by the stairs, she is summer incarnate. Looking at her, I can practically taste the salt of the Gulf.

"We're going to Crystal Beach. Grab your suit."

"All right, all right," I say, deciding to forsake the day's workout. Maybe the beach will shake me from this haze I'm in. "Wait here." She pulls out a menthol cigarette, puts it between her glossed lips, and makes to light it. *"Annie,"* I hiss.

She grins at me. "Just trying to keep you sharp."

She claps her hands, motioning me off the gallery and back inside the cool dark of the house. I scurry to the bedroom, where I throw my suit and a towel into a canvas bag. Maw Maw's still asleep, so I leave a note for her on the kitchen table. Ripping down the road in Annie's Mustang, radio blasting, I feel better. There's something healing about the beach. Dipping your head below the surf, listening to the waves whisper promises carried from other shores, letting the sun burn away the skin of who you were yesterday to make you new.

Since Friday I've been grinding my teeth over the message I delivered in church: *Find the one who did this.* I can't stop thinking of Charmaine, as if she's the one responsible for the baby, her letter and apology meant for that little one and not me. For some reason, this makes it easier to think about her.

I peer out my window at the sky unfolding to the horizon. It's shimmering blue like glazed china. Later there will be storms, thunder bouldering down from quick-forming cloud banks, sheets of sudden rain that will scatter swimmers and picnickers. I love summer showers, the warm bath of rain, the loamy scent of the washed earth afterward. As a child, I relied on the parents of friends to take me to the beach, since Maw Maw found the sight of women in bathing suits to be vulgar. Because of this, the shore has always held the special magic of something rationed, even now that I can drive myself whenever I like.

This early in the morning, the peninsula road is empty. We pass dozens of brightly painted vacation homes, all built up on stilts. At a gas station we stop to buy supplies. Annie grabs Cheetos and Funyuns, Dr Pepper and Skittles. Trying to stick to the meal plan, I pick cold-cut sandwiches in triangles of plastic, a package of peanuts, bottled water.

"Oh, oh, hold up," Annie says before the guy can ring us up. He watches us from eyes like black beads pressed into the smooth white egg of his face. She takes a pair of pink-rimmed cat's-eye sunglasses from the rack on the counter and slips them on. "I'm so getting these for you," she says, tossing the glasses onto the counter. "Remember my tenth birthday? At the roller rink? The sock-hop theme? My mom got those glasses for everyone, remember? Man, we looked cute as fuck."

She pays for everything—when we're together, she always pays, says she needs help wasting her daddy's money. She hands the sunglasses to me, then breezes out the door. I follow her, sliding the glasses over my nose. They pinch a little, but I'll wear them in honor of Mrs. Putnam, back when she was happy. Annie used to be, too. *Here come Miss Silly and Mademoiselle Serious*, Mrs. Putnam used to say.

Eventually, Annie parks on the shoulder and scrambles out of the car. After making sure no one's coming, I struggle into my bathing suit, a ragged black one-piece I've had for ages, then pull my shorts back on. Once outside the car, I can hear the sighing of the waves, the call of gulls as they ride the updraft of wind off the water. From the sandbank, tall grass blows silver-green, changing direction with the snaking breeze.

Racing to crest the dune that separates the road from the beach, Annie squeals like a child. I follow behind, heart wild with blood, feet sinking deep into the warm sand. My flip-flops slip off along the way, but the sand feels so good against my toes that I don't care. At the top, we pause to take in the view, the water a muted blue, broken only by a few orange buoys that mark the end of the swimming area. The beach is empty but for a fisherman casting off a distant jetty.

"Last one in has to do a hundred clean-and-jerks!" Annie shouts, barreling down the dune, all legs and arms. I'm right behind her, and when she pauses to strip off shorts and T-shirt at the water's edge, I overtake her, running full-throttle into the surf. "No fair!" she shrieks.

"Prude's advantage!" I holler over my shoulder. I keep running, legs churning up foam, until the tug of the water gets to be too much. Then I throw my arms out and dive, and there it is, the beautiful quiet of losing gravity and all the sharp sounds that travel by air. I go limp and let the current carry me. When I run out of air, I surface with a gasp. Annie joins me and we swim out as far as we dare, then float on our backs for a while. In earth science, we learned that the sky isn't actually blue, its color a trick of light scattering as it passes through the atmosphere. Sometimes science ruins things. I wish I could unlearn this, but once a mystery is gone, it's gone.

While we're toweling off, I notice a red stripe stretching from Annie's right shoulder blade to her middle back, a belt-wide welt. I've seen these wounds on her before, in the locker room. I walk up behind her and ever so lightly kiss the outer ridge of the mark by her shoulder, then pull her into a hug. In my arms I feel her stiffen and then go soft, a sigh escaping to mingle with the sea breeze.

"I love you, Annie," I breathe into her back, feeling the sentiment so powerfully that I imagine the words radiating beneath her skin.

"Love you, too, Mers." She reaches back and scratches the top of my head, then clears her throat and shimmies away from me. "I'm starving," she says, tearing into the bag of Cheetos. "The water sucks the juice out of you."

I sit down to eat my peanuts. The grit of their salt mixes with the sand on my skin in a pleasing way, so that I rub my hand back and forth on my wrist just to feel the sensation. After we finish eating, we lie back on our towels, the day's heat building around us. We pace ourselves, take swim breaks when it gets to be too much, when we find ourselves starting to breathe through it like we're distance runners. Gradually, the beach starts to fill up, families spilling out of vacation homes and station wagons, boys knee-deep in the surf tossing footballs. When they pass by, they ogle, and for a moment I'm proud of the way we must look to these boys, beautiful and strong, the Gulf of Mexico stretched out at our feet like an offering. They know we're athletes, they can see it in the cut of our arms, the lines of our quads, even when we're at rest. If we were walking down the beach, they would remark on our strut, the gait we've perfected entering other teams' gymnasiums, the one that announces we are there to win, that we believe bone-deep we are the baddest ballers around. *Cocky,* we've been called, and I wouldn't disagree. You don't win championships by apologizing for yourself the way some girls feel the need to do. I have guarded such girls, girls with good fundamentals who lack the killer instinct. Blood roars in my ears when I realize my luck, I have eaten them alive, and God help me, but I enjoyed doing it.

After cruising by a couple times, a pod of guys stands over us, the long shadows cast by their tall bodies cutting through the sand. My heart thumps with the threat of them, they are little bombs of hormones and intent, there's something so honest about them and their needy, gawky bodies. But that bald need scares me, too, especially when I'm the object of it.

As usual, Annie is unfazed. She props herself up on her elbows and lowers her sunglasses to the tip of her nose. I see her movie-star body, the turquoise suit stretched tight across her hips, her Rapunzel hair, the way even her belly button winking out at them seems flirtatious, and for a moment my faith in her falters; she will accept their advances, she won't protect me like she always does. But then she speaks: "Dudes, you're in our sun," she says, flopping back down on the towel and turning over onto her belly as if hoping the red stripe on her back will scare them off.

"How about a couple beers," one of them says. "Need to cool you off, y'all are sizzling."

Annie rolls back over and holds up a hand; the boy places a silver can into it. *"Grazie,"* she says, popping the top and taking a sip, nestling the can into the sand next to her.

"What about you?" a blond one with a blotchy face says to me. "You want some?"

I keep my mouth shut tight. If I don't, I might just say yes. There have been times before when I've wanted to say yes. With bite in her voice, Maw Maw says I have a face like an invitation. I pray: *Get thee behind me, Satan!*

"Boys, don't take this the wrong way, but be dears and piss off?" Annie says.

"Whatever," the dark one says. "Tease."

"Not responsible for every boner, sorry."

With a kick that sends sand spraying away from us, the boys continue down the beach. I exhale back onto the towel. Annie takes my hand and kisses the knuckles. Now we're even.

On the way back into town, Annie steers us into the Market Basket lot. It's late afternoon now, my body lazy with sun. I don't want to be here but don't have the energy to protest.

"I need some Tic-Tacs," she says, cupping her hand in front of her mouth and exhaling. "Ever since that baby, Beau's been a Nazi." She looks at me. "You know he actually had the gall to ask me if *I* did it? Like suddenly, just because I have a uterus, I'm a criminal." She snorts indignantly. "Can you believe it?"

Actually, I can. Over the years, I've lost count of how many boys Annie has slept with. I don't even know if *she* knows the exact number. *Slut,* some kids call her, though never to her face. Beau Putnam is a lot of things, but he's not a fool.

"You've got to be kidding me," she says. I realize that I haven't been quick enough to agree with her.

"No, no, what an idiot," I say ardently, trying to make up for my mistake, but it's too late. Already she's out of the car. She slams the door, and I watch as she crosses the parking lot, legs scissoring angrily. Staring across at the dumpster, I see that a makeshift memorial for the baby has gone up, a pile of stuffed animals and a ring of candles. Someone has hung a handwritten sign on the dumpster: At 24 weeks, I could breathe outside the womb. How do *you* define homicide?

I don't really believe Annie did it, do I? She goes to that clinic in Houston to get pills, ever since the Walmart refused her. But I remember her confession in the parking lot: *I'm so fucking* hard. *Everything breaks against me.*

---

OVER BREAKFAST THE next morning, Maw Maw says that Beau Putnam called and told her he'll be at church tonight.

"Whatever for?" I ask. The Putnams are fair-weathers, going to All Hallows for Christmas, Easter, and the occasional baptism so Beau can schmooze with the biggest congregation in town. As Annie puts it, her daddy prays only to the dollar.

"Said his soul needs some polishing up." Maw Maw sniffs. "Says he wants to talk to me about something."

Maw Maw dislikes the Putnams, Annie in particular; she disapproves of the tight jeans and dyed hair. If Maw Maw guessed at half the secrets I keep for Annie, she would take me straight to the river, rebaptize me, and forbid me seeing her again. As it is, Maw Maw only says, *Don't know why you spend so much time with that girl.* If I told her that I'm trying to save Annie, or that Annie's love for me is forceful and steady as the sun, would she understand then?

Up at the football field, running stairs with Annie later that afternoon, I broach the subject during a break, trying to make sense of it.

Doubled over gasping for breath, she says, "Dad's going to run for mayor. Election's in November." She spits onto the pavement, where the heat evaporates it immediately. "He's planning to put on his pious face and visit every church in town as part of his campaign. Wants to be governor one day." She straightens up, stretching her hands overhead. "He'll need a miracle to win. You know, we still get skinned critters on the front porch." She looks at me and wrinkles her nose. "Before the memorial service last February, someone left a tiny jewelry box on the front step. Lourdes opened it, and for the longest time, we couldn't figure out what the hell we were looking at, pearls or what. But then I saw it, this dark spot in the center of one. It was a filling. They were teeth, Mercy. From the site."

I swallow, feel the sweat trickling down my neck. "Pray for the dead," I say.

"And fight like hell for the living," she says, tearing at a fingernail with her teeth.

"Maybe he wants to be mayor so he can make amends," I say. "Help people."

She looks at me like I'm mule-stupid. "We Putnams watch out for ourselves," she says.

As the old Lincoln groans down the road to church, Maw Maw glances at me through the rearview mirror, eyes serious. "Bet it's the Loup Garou ball tonight," she says. "By the looks of the moon. Lives by the blood of sinners, Tee Mercy, the devil prowling around in the skin of man."

The Loup Garou—body of a man, head of a wolf—is one of Maw Maw's favorite tales.

"He'll be taking babies tonight," she says in the exaggerated voice she uses for her stories, so I can never tell just how much of it she believes. "Stalking into bedrooms of new mamas, waking them, asking permission to take their babes. Better not be drunk or otherwise compromised, because you might just say yes, and then your baby's lost forever."

Maybe the Loup Garou caught the LeBlanc Avenue baby's mother by surprise, stole the child away, and left her in the dumpster. Maybe the baby's mama, sick with grief, wandered out of town never to return.

At church, Beau Putnam has situated himself near the main door as a kind of unofficial greeter. His silver hair sits thick over his lined forehead, his tanned face handsome in the way of newsmen and politicians. Someone, probably Lourdes, has ironed his Wranglers; there's a crease down the front. Fancy ostrich-skin boots peek out from beneath the cuff of his jeans.

"Where's Annie?" I ask as I pass inside.

"Ladies' room," he says before turning his attention to Maw Maw. "Something important I'd like to talk to you about, Ms. Boudreaux."

Though I'm curious to hear what he says, Maw Maw gives me a sharp look, so I make for the washroom to find Annie. Before I reach the entrance, she emerges, frowning when she sees her father with Maw Maw.

"What are those two up to?" she asks.

I shrug. "No clue."

She eyes me suspiciously. "You better tell."

"For real, I don't know," I protest.

Before Annie can say anything more, Maw Maw strides over, gives us a strange smile, then takes me by the elbow and leads me to our usual spot. After the sermon, Pastor Parris invites Beau to the platform, but Beau doesn't say what I thought he would—nothing about his campaign for mayor, no catchy slogan for us to latch on to. "I just got off the phone with Chief McKinney," he says. "And the medical examiner said that baby took breath outside the womb." A woman exclaims and a murmur ripples through the crowd. A few people stand to pray, arms upraised, calling out to Jesus. I feel nauseated. I want to close my eyes and pray, too, but after Friday, I'm afraid of what I might see.

Beau clasps his hands, purses his lips, and dips his nose toward his thumbs, waiting for his words to sink in. Then he announces that he is offering a reward of ten thousand dollars to anyone who has solid evidence leading to the capture of *the baby killer.*

"I don't know about y'all, but it makes me sick to see my hometown trashed on the national news." He shakes his head. "We have got to come together as a community and find the person responsible for this heinous act. We've got to show the country that we're a town of honest, hardworking people, that we raise good girls, and that we don't accept this kind of behavior. Only way we can do that is if we catch who did this."

Before he leaves the pulpit, he invites everyone to Annie's Purity Ball. I startle at the words. *What?* He says Maw Maw will be in charge of planning it, and he nods graciously in our direction; Maw Maw beams back at him. It's a service she and the Purity Coalition perform for the daughters of the town's believers, though some families opt for a quieter purity ceremony instead of a ball, fathers bestowing promise rings to daughters in exchange for a pledge of abstinence until marriage. Beau Putnam doesn't do anything quietly, though.

From my place near the front of the room, I turn around, scan for Annie. The look on her face tells me that she's as shocked by this news as I am. It's late for a Purity Ball—Annie just turned seventeen. And there's the issue of her reputation. We're taught that it's never too late to commit to abstinence, but I wonder if Annie can uphold the promise, or if she even wants to make it.

Maw Maw takes my hand across the pew. "Finally, that girl's going to raise herself up to your level," she says.

I smile. Even though the idea of a ball for Annie is odd, I'm relieved, glad, even. For years, I've loved someone who continues to damn herself. Do you know what that does to a heart? Only look into Maw Maw's ruined face to know for sure. As we make to leave the church, I see Annie at the cookie table. I wave and start to approach, but she scowls, then turns her back to me and moves to the end of the table. From the way she stands there—arms crossed, jaw set—I can feel the fury burning off her in little waves, smudging her hard edges. I can't tell if she's angry with me or the world, but I know that she needs space, so I turn toward the door. Outside, the sound of a distant chain saw, a plane passing far overhead. I wonder how I can convince Annie to wear the white gown and accept the ring, and, most of all, to keep the promise she'll make before God and the town.

————————

THAT NIGHT I can't sleep. Every time I close my eyes, I see Charmaine. Sometimes it's the lonesome woman from the photo, and sometimes it's the woman from Maw Maw's stories, the one who keeps bad company and has scars that crater the skin around her mouth like the surface of the moon. To clear the images away, I visualize my free-throw ritual: place right foot slightly ahead of left, line up right elbow directly above knee, bounce ball twice, hard, backspin it once, cock wrist and balance ball off the palm, just under nose, then arc, release, follow through. Swish. And again. Swish. Again. Again. Again.

My alarm clock glows eleven o'clock when I hear Maw Maw clearing her throat in the hall. It's miles past her bedtime. Perhaps a vision has jolted her from sleep. The night's silence delivers sounds from the hall so clear, I don't need to move to know what she's doing: dialing the phone, which sits in the hall halfway between her room and mine. Quietly, I slide to the door, butt down, feet wide in my best defensive crouch to avoid creaking the boards. I could stay like this for hours, my quads volcanic rock, alive with burn inside.

I listen at the crack of the door.

"I'm not going to let her play," she whispers. Pause. "I got a bad feeling, gut-deep, is why." Pause. I realize she means basketball, and that she must be talking to Coach, and my stomach drops somewhere between my haunches. "What with this baby, I think it's best to keep the girl close, I keep seeing girls falling . . ." Pause. "Don't you patronize me, you know my visions are a gift from the Lord." Pause. "She goes where I say she goes." Pause. "Hmph. Obviously concerned you enough to wait a week to tell me." Pause. "No, I don't think twice about it. That's why it's called faith, not doubt, Jodi. Starting to regret ever getting you involved, though." Pause. "You don't know that, only the Lord can know how it would've gone." Pause. "You're bluffing, you'd never . . ." Pause. "Fine, but only because I'm a woman of my word."

The soft click of the receiver returned to its place. The shuffling of slippered feet. The thunk of a door closing. Back in bed, sheets cool against tingling thighs, I wonder if Maw Maw would really forbid me to play.

Through the empty stretch of deep night, I don't sleep a lick, instead reading and rereading Charmaine's letter. By dawn, I can recite it top to bottom. *Maybe I will come to your game just to see who you have grown into. You don't need to talk to me if you don't want.*

But see: there is a world of difference between *want* and *need*.

---

IN THE NEWSPAPER the next morning, there's a color photo of the memorial at the dumpster. The headline reads, MEDICAL EX-AMINER SAYS BABY DOE BORN ALIVE, DEATH RULED NEONATICIDE. I sit down at the kitchen table to skim the story.

> Two days after the discovery of a fetus in the dumpster of the Market Basket convenience store on LeBlanc Avenue, the autopsy results are in. Medical examiner Tony Reina says there is evidence that the fetus, approximately twenty-four weeks old, was born alive before perishing due to high levels of the ulcer medication misoprostol found in its system. Dr. Reina says that the baby died about one week ago, judging by signs of decay found on the body.

I take the newspaper back to my room, sit down at the desk, and write a letter to Charmaine. I don't put a salutation because any endearment, even her name, seems too kind, and I'm in no mood for kindnesses.

> *I already know all I need to know about you. Maw Maw*
> *has told me everything. I know that you would've been*
> *no better than this girl, would've killed me if you could.*
> *You say you want to get to know me but that is a privilege*
> *for the people who love me. You say you want to learn all*
> *about me as if it will all be good and pretty, just because*
> *I'm Mercy Louis and in the newspapers up in Austin. But*
> *I can tell you it is not all good, it is sometimes ugly. If I*
> *were you, I'd be scared to learn all about me. Please, leave*
> *me alone, let me try to be good, or at least better than you.*

Hand trembling, I cut out the article and fold it into the envelope next to my note. From Maw Maw's sewing drawer in the hallway, I sneak a stamp. At the post office, I drop the letter down the slot. In my chest, a loosening like a bad cough breaking.

---

FOR A WEEK, I can't get through to Annie, though I call her every day. Finally, I go to the house, peer through the beveled glass of the towering front doors. When Lourdes answers, she tells me apologetically that Annie isn't feeling well. But then Annie appears, teeth flashing like I'm a bone she wants to gnaw. Lourdes blushes at the lie she's been made to tell and then scuttles away. Annie stares as if waiting for an explanation, eyebrows raised, mouth pursed. I've seen this look before. In fact, it's the look that Annie directs at most everyone else, a fearsome mix of anger and contempt and haughtiness. In the silence, I hear Goldie, the family retriever, barking from her pen in the backyard, the nattering of mockingbirds, the hiss of sprinklers.

"First chance you get and you sell me down the river," Annie says.

"What?" I say.

She crosses her arms over her chest. "Don't play dumb. You've always wanted me to be someone different. So you and Beau and Evelia planned to throw me a little party, whitewash the dirty girl."

She has a way of saying a thing with such sneering conviction that it becomes truth.

"Annie, I'd never—"

"You think I did it, that's what this is about. You and Beau both."

"No, I don't—"

"I don't want to hear it!" she bellows toward the ceiling, the veins in her neck rising beneath her skin, tiny trapped rivers of blood. When she looks at me again, her eyes glisten. "You were all I had, Mercy."

Then she slams the door so hard, the brass knocker gives a single clap. She thinks I've told her secrets. And why should she trust that I haven't? I've judged her a thousand times, spent hours praying for her salvation. *At last,* I thought when Beau announced the Purity Ball. *Someone else to help save her.*

# ILLA

As soon as Mama is in bed these summer nights, Illa flees the house. She gets in the car, cranks the AC, and heads for the seawall. She turns over in her mind the conversation about Charmaine, the knowledge of her mother's friendship with Mercy's mom warming her. But it also makes her sad. If Charmaine had stayed, maybe Illa and Mercy would have grown up playing together. Maybe instead of Annie, Illa would be the friend Mercy couldn't live without.

She wanders without a particular destination in mind, her school-issued Canon tucked comfortingly in the passenger seat. Dozens of times, she parks the Accord and scrambles outside to capture a promising shot: brown pelicans in V-formation cruising low over the water, watermelon-colored thickets of oleander tall as houses, the abandoned Pleasure Pier ablaze with a violent sunset, a fisherman in a floppy hat casting line from the end of a jetty, a smoky bank of thunderheads piling up at the horizon, the Gulf churning from the pull of a coming storm. The photo contest deadline is still a couple of weeks away; she probably won't be able to get a great shot, but she hasn't given up entirely. It's something to do, at least.

One evening, Janis Joplin singing about heartbreak on the radio, Illa ventures away from the coast into the industrial maze that is downtown Port Sabine. *Blighted,* a magazine had dubbed the downtown after the explosion. The word stuck with Illa so that whenever anything bad happened, she blamed it on Port Sabine. Like the terrible fight she had with Mama after Jay left them. "Good riddance," Illa said of her stepdad, a pit bull of a man, all shoulder and no hip. Her mother snarled: "You don't have any idea what it means to be just another bitch without a man in this town." The bite of the curse lingered in the air, shocking Illa because her mother usually spoke with a hushed gentleness, as if inside a library or church. She shook her head, a thin line of snot dangling from her reddened nose. "I was alone when your daddy died. I've seen what that life is like. You know what I remember about those days? Food stamps and bad men and a job so hard it nearly killed me." She paused. "You're thirteen, though. You'll understand soon enough."

To escape, Illa went for a bike ride through the neighborhood. After a few minutes, she was pedaling down deserted streets, darkened windows like eye sockets in the wan faces of paint-peeling homes, grass grown knee-high over concrete paths leading to locked front doors. Even the streetlamps stood lightless in some places, the city having cut power to the empty blocks. Illa stopped pedaling, brought her feet down on either side of the bike. For a minute, the sounds of her breathing filled the air, but soon even that faded against the silence. In the months since the explosion, to cope with the fines, the refinery had laid off hundreds of workers. Illa's eighth-grade class had shrunk to half its size. She looked down the street and counted the real estate signs that had popped up on lawns: eleven in total, the families gone before the houses sold because the market was bust. Everyone was leaving, not just Jay, and Illa had the feeling that she and Mama were being left behind.

*How did Janis manage to get out?* Illa wonders as she steers the Accord farther inland. Did it require months of saving and planning, or did she just steal some of her mama's money and get on a bus? Maybe she's not the best model for escape, though, her tragic end somehow foretold by her bad beginnings in these swamplands.

Driving past Park Terrace with her window rolled down, Illa sees people playing ball on the park's old cracked court. When she rolls to a stop at a traffic light, she looks closer and sees that it isn't just people but Mercy Louis, summoned from an overactive corner of Illa's imagination, charging up and down the court as if she owns the night. As Illa idles at the light listening to the banter echoing up from the court, she considers driving into the park to catch some of the game. She scans the crowd for Annie's telltale blond ponytail; no way will Illa venture down there if Annie Putnam is lurking about. When the light changes, the driver on her tail blasts the horn.

"All right, all right," she mutters, goosing the Accord so it leaps forward into the intersection. Better not to venture down. She'd be radically out of place sitting alongside the players' girlfriends, the pretty, brash Chicanas and black girls whose neon tank tops she can just make out in her rearview mirror, bright dots moving like Christmas lights in the dusky air.

Illa decides to go to Sonic for a diet limeade. Something about the roller-skating carhops and chemically bright, unnaturally sweet beverages cheers her, and she can scope out her classmates from the safety of the darkened car. In Port Sabine, Sonic is the place to promenade, strut, preen. Rising ninth-graders with dreams of high school dominance make their debuts at the drive-in, the girls done up like pageant contestants, wobbly in too-high wedge heels, the boys in ball caps and shit kickers.

Illa places her order, then slumps low in the seat to watch the social pantomime unfold. There is something predictable and easy about the way girls throw their french fries at boys whose shoulders seem perpetually raised in the posture of the offending male—*what'd I say?* The girls are masters of pouting and feigning injury. This Sonic dinner theater makes Illa feel at once superior and wretched. She doesn't want admission into the Sonic crowd—these are the girls who "get into trouble" and then get stuck in Port Sabine; each year a couple of big-bellied girls are banished to the pregnancy trailer to get their GEDs, and those are the ones who don't drop out altogether. *The fruits of abstinence-only sex ed,* Lennox says sardonically. But she's begun to feel that she would give almost anything to have one of the students recognize her and call her over. Do they even know a name to call her by other than Strange Stark?

On this particular Wednesday, the crowd is entirely female except for Ronald Tucker, a tenth-grade pipsqueak with a squishy, child-like face who might as well be one of the girls for all the attention they pay him. Illa recognizes most of the crew—Abby Williams and Marilee Warren and some nameless freshmen members of the Stingarette drill team who are doing their utmost to look as much like each other as possible. Without boys around, the girls are restless, looking past each other, surveying the parking lot for traces of testosterone, tossing hot-curled hair, rubbing glossed lips together to keep them wet and shining.

Over the drone of idling engines, snatches of conversation land near enough for Illa to hear: " . . . such a fucking joke . . . think she's fooling . . . dunno, sometime in August . . . Annie Putnam is such a . . ."

At the mention of Annie's name, Illa sits up, straining to hear more, but it's hopeless with the big four-by-four trucks growling on either side of her. Soon, though, the truck-driving bubbas get their colas and burgers and disappear back onto the highway, taillights glowing red in retreat. With only the crickets and the skid of roller skates on concrete to compete with, the girls' high-pitched voices carry piercingly through the night.

"I'm going to go just to see her try to keep a straight face when she's saying the pledge."

"Hate to break it to old Beauregard, but Annie's given away her *gift* so many times she's like the fucking Santa of sex," Abby says.

"Not even a monthlong purity festival could change the color of that girl's soul."

"Now, y'all, stop," Marilee says cajolingly. "She's not a bad *person*."

"Annie's not a person," Abby says. "She's a snake."

"Whatever, it's a good excuse to eat free steak," Ronald says. "I'll pretend Annie's the Virgin Mary if it means I get me some filet."

"You're probably not even invited," one of the younger girls says.

"Whole town's invited, at least all the high school families," Ronald says. "Invitations go out this week."

"Oh, joy," Abby says, picking intently at a scab on her knee.

Illa's confused. A Purity Ball for *Annie?* Annie isn't a Sonic girl—probably sees herself as too cool for it—but anyone with eyes in her head can see that Annie has a body and knows how to use it. Her bedroom eyes, the way she slinks hippily through the hallways.

A carhop skates up to Illa's window, balancing a diet limeade the size of a small child on her tray. Illa pays, tells the girl to keep the change. Annie is a lot of things, but she isn't a bullshitter, so why this farce of a ball? Has Mercy finally converted her best friend? The thought sends jealousy frothing through Illa.

"Think Annie'll join the virgin club, too?" Abby says. "Now that Marilee's been demoted, maybe Annie can be treasurer."

"Oooooh, busted," Ronald says.

"Shut up, Abby," Marilee says.

"What? You're damaged goods now, sweetie. Want to be a hypocrite, too?"

"You said you weren't going to bring it up," Marilee stutters. "You said you forgave me . . ."

"Yeah, well, I changed my mind." Abby gives Marilee a steely look. "Should've thought twice before messing with Wyatt if you cared what I thought. Not to mention being dumb enough to get caught."

Marilee stalks off toward the street, stumbling in her high heels, face pinched. Illa puts the car in reverse, then loops around the parking lot and back onto the road. As she passes Marilee, she considers giving her a ride but stops herself. Better not to get involved. Her only interaction with Marilee was at a virgin club meeting last spring when she handed Illa a flyer about *how to be a crusader against the abortion genocide*. Illa had gone to the meeting to see if Mercy would be there, but she wasn't, and the president, Tiffany Barnes, spent the bulk of the lunch hour taking roll. Apparently, the most important part of the True Love Waits club was showing up.

Illa surprised herself by returning to a couple more meetings, hoping that a club dedicated to abstinence would involve at least a *little* talk about sex. It didn't, but Illa took some comfort in being surrounded by other girls who were just as inexperienced as she was. After roll call, Tiffany opened by quoting Matthew, *I tell you that anyone who looks at a woman lustfully has already committed adultery with her in his heart.* One of the girls asked how you know if you're looking *lustfully* or just looking, and Tiffany described how lust felt: your heart would beat fast, you'd feel tingly or short of breath. You might start focusing on the person's body, imagining yourself touching him. *Fight those thoughts!* she warned. *They're dangerous because they could lead to action!*

Illa thinks of all the times she's watched Mercy—on the court, in the locker room, in class, that day in the shower—heart thumping like a bass drum, stomach fluttery to the point of sickness. And what about Lennox? They talk all the time, but whenever he leans near her to scrutinize something in the rough draft of the paper pasted on the layout board, she has to grip her pen extra tight to keep her hand from shaking. Whenever she tries to let her feelings blossom into fantasies, just to see where they'll take her, she freezes up. Not from squeamishness but simply because she doesn't technically know how a crush is supposed to transition into something more—a date, a kiss, *sex*. How do people go from behaving normally to ripping each other's clothes off? There's something inherently confusing in the logistics of it. She's overthinking it, and that's her problem: she doesn't know how to just *act*.

Fat raindrops plash against the windshield, unsettling its coat of dust. Somewhere over the Gulf, thunder speaks. Through the window, the air smells of wet asphalt and earth. If the whole town is invited to Annie's ball, that means Mama, too. While Illa doubts her mother will want to go—she hasn't wanted to do anything social in the last three years—Illa can't risk the slim chance that Mama will accept the invitation. She usually lets Mama check the mail, since doing so guarantees she'll see sunlight once a day, but Illa decides that for the next few weeks, she'll get to the mailbox first in case the invitation lands. That way, she can squirrel it away upstairs to ensure she won't have to roll Mama into that party in front of the whole town.

———

EACH MORNING ILLA watches for the mailman's white car. As soon as he drives away, she beelines for the mailbox, the sun a rebuke against her pale skin. On these short walks, she dreams of living in a cooler place, maybe in the mountains, someplace where a cold front doesn't warrant mention in the supermarket checkout line. At first, the mail yields nothing of interest—junk ads, coupon pages, medical and utility bills. But on the third day, a standard white envelope materializes, hand-addressed to Mama in messy script and bearing a stamp with bluebonnets on it. The return address is a post office box in Austin. Hovering in the entryway of the house, Illa examines the envelope carefully. Who is in Austin, and what do they want with Mama? After the explosion, she let her old friendships wither like the yellowing photographs in the closet.

"We get anything good?" Mama asks, wheeling into the hall.

"Depends on what this is," Illa says, handing over the letter.

Mama eyes it, then slips her finger under the envelope's flap. As she scans the letter, a bewildered look chases across her face.

"So . . . ?" Illa says. "Who's it from?"

"No one you know," she says distractedly, looking past Illa and out the front door. Before Illa can ask more questions, Mama spins around and wheels into the kitchen, where a minute later Illa hears the static click of the television turning on, then the muffled dings and applause of *Jeopardy!*

---

AFTER LUNCH, WHILE Mama naps, Illa goes up to school to develop her photos. The whole area is a ghost town except for a handful of pro-life college students who are holding vigil in front of the Market Basket. They arrived on a bus the day after the medical examiner determined that the baby was born alive. Mostly, they sit in lawn chairs with graphic posters of aborted fetuses propped against their knees. Occasionally, when a car passes by or someone ventures into the convenience store, a girl with bobbed black hair stands up to shout things through a megaphone. Illa is glad that at this distance she can't hear what the girl's saying, because she looks seriously pissed. The black-haired girl and her angry cohort are at odds with the lazy heat of summertime.

Illa knows the mother will be tracked and tried like a murderer based on the findings of the medical examiner's report. She wonders if it's one of her classmates, perhaps one of the chubby girls whose body could hide that kind of secret for months. It seems like the kind of desperate act only a young woman could commit, someone without options or knowledge of options. *Murderer.* It doesn't seem like the right word for the situation, somehow. At the end of the article about the medical examiner's report, there was a sentence about how the ulcer drug, when taken in excess of the recommended dosage, could cause not only fetal demise but also severe cramps and heavy bleeding. The police already searched County Hospital and a handful of other clinics to see if anyone checked in with those symptoms, but so far they haven't found any leads. Illa imagines the girl squatting in the woods behind the Market Basket, groaning in agony. To know something is dying inside you, to feel that sickening ache. Illa hopes the girl, whoever she is, has found someplace clean and quiet, far from these angry college girls and their lurid signs that would remind her of that pain.

One afternoon as Illa is parking her car in the student lot, she sees Lucille Cloud and her dog sprawled out on a blanket in front of the Mr. Good Deals. The wind off the Gulf carries the rotten sweetness of gardenia. From where Illa sits, they appear to be snoozing, a broad straw hat pulled partway over Lucille's face. There's no mistaking her, not with that giant hound by her side or the long dreadlocked hair spread out behind her. Illa wonders how Lucille can stand to be out in the heat before remembering that she doesn't have the luxury of air-conditioning at her cabin, and that maybe even the word *cabin* is too luxurious for the cinder-block-and-soda-bottle structure, crowned with blue FEMA tarp, that Lucille calls home.

Illa went there once, a few months after the refinery disaster, hoping Lucille might give her a magical potion that would make Mama's legs strong again, or even something to startle her out of depression. On a hazy Saturday afternoon in May, she set out by bicycle. No way was she going there close to dark—she didn't believe about all the reported Lucifer sightings, but the woods made her jumpy; there were plenty of other devils who did business out there, she knew that much from listening to the police scanner that Lennox kept on in the journalism room. The shanty listed against a tree not a hundred yards from the Century Oak. Illa spotted a sizable herb garden set back in a clearing where the midday sun slanted through the tops of the trees.

As she approached the cabin, Illa was surprised to find her hands shaking. In town, Lucille sparked all manner of loose talk—that she worshipped Satan, making animal sacrifices to him on a full moon; that she was descended from a long line of Indian witch doctors and had the power to hex you and ruin your life; that, as revenge for her people's displacement, she lured white men out to her cabin, had sex with them, drugged them, then robbed them blind. What Illa discovered that day, though, was not a sex-addled freak but a young woman so poor she ate gator gar barbecued over a small fire just outside the cabin's entrance. That was how Illa found her, stinking of beer, crouched over the fire, turning gar flesh on a spit made of cypress branches. When Illa told Lucille about her problem, Lucille said it sounded like maybe the explosion had damaged Mama's spirit, and she gave her a jar of dried St.-John's-wort, which could be made into a tea to ease depression. When she spoke, she slurred ever so slightly.

Illa pressed her to help with Mama's legs because she'd heard Lucille could cure people of just about anything. At that, Lucille had taken a drink from a chipped mug and said, "So now I'm supposed to work miracles? You probably think this is an ancient Attakappa burial ground, and that I'm here to guard it from the white devils. Or that I give ten-dollar blow jobs to high school boys? Judging by how many punks come creeping around here, that seems to be the most popular one."

Illa felt sheepish for believing the gossip, so to atone for her mistake, she asked Lucille what her story was. "Got tired of all the drunks and pervs on the rez. And I like the ocean. I try to get by doing natural medicines like my aunt made." Lucille offered Illa some gar, which she politely declined. Lucille smiled, ripped off a chunk of meat with her stained teeth. "Now I get why the medicine men were always so quiet back home. They knew too much about everybody's business." She smiled down at her hands. "People tell you things they'd never talk to a doctor about, even if they could afford to go, which most of them can't." She sucks her teeth and laughs, her molars dark with rot. Despite her soiled clothes and matted hair, Lucille was pretty, with large hazel eyes and smooth olive skin. "Speaking of getting by," Lucille said, "that'll be five dollars."

Sitting in the parking lot, Illa frowns, remembering her naïveté. That was back when she felt hopeful about Mama's future and her own. Since Illa parked, Lucille hasn't moved. Illa wonders if the girl's drunk or maybe sick. Where are her mom and dad? Does she have any friends? Illa feels a flash of pity for Lucille. But then who is Illa to feel sorry for anyone? Mama is all that distances Illa from Lucille's fate.

Once inside the school building, Illa sneaks past the administration area, glides down the silent hallways and into the journalism room. She likes being in the empty school building. Striding alone across the rotunda where students gather before school, she imagines them looking up from their conversations to watch as she passes by, arm in arm with Mercy, head back, laughing at some private joke.

When she gets to the journalism room, Lennox is sitting at a computer. He looks up and raises a hand in greeting.

"Is the world still ending in seven months?" she teases, thinking fleetingly of Mercy's order to *live to meet the end without dread*. Maybe she just meant death, though Illa didn't know many teenagers who thought so concretely about the subject.

"You jest, Stark, but we'll see who's laughing come January first.

Ten bucks says you're sitting in my kitchen begging for Vienna sausages."

"Don't tell me you're stockpiling food."

"I'm not stockpiling." He laughs. "I just have an impressive collection of nonperishable goods. How do you think I feed a family of four on five bucks a night?"

Last spring, Lennox started obsessively tracking news stories and message boards about Y2K, which seemed a little out there, but his dad's cancer had come back, and Lennox probably needed someplace to channel his anxiety. In a way, the millennial uproar was perfect. If chaos was coming for everyone in six months, then maybe it made it easier to accept the prognosis that his father had about that much time to live.

"I've got a surprise for you," he says. *For you.* The words make her shiver. From beneath the computer desk, he produces a small cooler. "Refreshments."

"Nice," Illa says.

"To the Prrrraying Hands," he says, speaking in a bad British accent, comically rolling the "r." "Let us retire to the Hands and take in a view of the estate, shall we?"

"Dork," she says, laughing. "Sure. Never been up there."

"Come on."

She wonders how many calories are in a can of beer. At home, she tries not to drink anything but water. He picks up the cooler and goes out into the hall, looking left and right theatrically before tiptoeing forward. The city built the Praying Hands statue in memorial to the victims of the refinery explosion. The Hands sit beseechingly just off the highway, in the shadow of the refinery towers, 110 tons of carved concrete, forty feet tall, set atop a man-made hill. At sea level, they make for a formidable landmark. Illa has heard of students, possibly subversive, probably stoned, climbing into the deep bowl where the heels of the hands meet.

"Let's take my truck, I've got a ladder in the bed," he says as they make their way out to the parking lot and into his truck. Lucille lies unmoving on the sidewalk.

"Should we check on her?" she asks, pointing in Lucille's direction.

"Probably just sleeping off a bender," he says. "Plus, that dog scares the shit out of me."

She nods agreement. Windows down, they roar through the mid-afternoon stillness. Her excitement at being in this unremarkable social situation—going to drink beer with a friend—shames her. Before the explosion, she'd never felt especially lonely because she'd had her mother. When Mama would arrive home from work, they'd take two sweating glasses of sweet tea out to the sagging Adirondack chairs on the concrete block they called, grandiosely, "the terrace," and sip their tea while revealing each little mundane detail of their days.

Near the Hands, there's a short fence at the base of the hill, which Lennox clears easily before helping her over. Shouldering the ladder and hauling the cooler, he powers up the hill toward the statue, which in full sunlight is a brilliant white that shocks her eyes. When they're both inside the sheltering cave of the Hands, Lennox pulls the ladder up behind them. From where she sits peering through the slit formed by the Hands' two pinkies, Illa can see the sprawl of the downtown grid, the curve of the seawall, the sleepy port where a huge red cargo ship sits, and finally, the sea with its undulant waves winking like spilled coins.

"Wow," she says. "I don't know if I'd call it beautiful, but there's something about being up this high."

"Here." He cracks a Shiner and hands it to her. The bottle is icy against her palm. "Cheers. To Pit Sabine."

"Our beloved hometown."

"The place of our provenance." When he talks, the stud in his tongue glints like a filling. For a moment, she sees him with his head between Annie's thighs. Illa is inexperienced, but even she's heard what those studs are for. Sometimes a first kiss seems as distant as the moon, first love even further. And now, thanks to the LeBlanc baby case, all of it seems dangerous.

"What doesn't kill us makes us stronger." Lennox stomps a sneakered foot against the statue. "But if you're already dead, you're shit out of luck." Bitterness has threaded its way into his voice. He pops open his beer and they clink bottles. The beer is more sensation than flavor, moving down her throat and hitting her bloodstream fast. The word *dead* brings tears to her eyes. In her anger, she often forgets that Mama could be just that. She blinks back the wetness. The refinery smokestacks belch white smoke that drifts overhead on the sluggish breeze, disappearing into the absorbent sky.

"How's your pops?" she asks.

"Furious," he says. "Literally shaking mad. He's worried about what we'll do when he's gone." He inhales slowly, and Illa can tell he's trying not to cry. "I keep thinking if he really only has six months to live, we should be doing things. Like our days should be special or something. But the problem is, I can't really wrap my head around it."

"It must seem pretty unreal," she says.

"Most days it's all I can do to open a can of chili for the kids, do my homework, help them with theirs. While he's just sitting there, mad as hell, watching us do this shit that means nothing."

"That sucks," she says. It's all she can come up with in the face of such awfulness. Maybe it's morbid, but one of the reasons she feels close to Lennox is because she knows he understands when she talks about Mama, though the difference is that Mama lives like she wants to die, while Mr. McBaine is ready to set the world on fire in order to keep breathing.

"I can't believe that asshole thinks he can win an election in this town."

"Who?" she asks.

"Who do you think?" He sucks his teeth. "Mr. Big Shot."

She thinks for a second. "Beau Putnam?"

"Annie told me. He'll announce at the 'Purity Ball.'" He makes air quotes as he says it. "What a crock." It all makes sense now, she thinks. Beau needs Annie to play golden girl at the Purity Ball so he can win in November. "You can see the GB apartments from here. You know how many times we change our air filters?" He pauses. "Once a week. We take them out and they're black as coal. Sanchez at least pays lip service to change, but it still doesn't mean shit happens. You think Beau Putnam's going to watchdog his own company? You think he gives a shit for the black folk on the Fenceline? For all the ignorant suckers like my dad who worked for twenty years at the plant only to end up with a death sentence?"

"Sands must be backing him."

"Annie says he wants to be governor one day, and pity the fool who gets in his way. *He'd kill a man for that kind of power,* that's what she said."

Illa decides not to tell Mama; the news will cut her to the core. Beau will make a public announcement soon, she's sure. Why not give her mother a few more weeks of ignorance? She watches the distant ship channel, the waves whipped to frothy peaks by the warm wind. She drinks the beer down in three long gulps, puts her hand out for another. Lennox opens two fresh bottles, then hands one to her before sitting down beside her. This close, she's aware of the warmth of his body, the bready smell of his sweat, the movement of muscles in his lean arms, which makes a fat pink scar just below his elbow dance.

"You could get some great pictures up here," he says.

"Left my camera back in the room." She places her hands flush against the cool concrete of the sculpture. *Danger, danger,* she thinks. The heat and beer have made her unaccustomed body slack and dreamy. With drunken boldness, she studies his profile: broad jaw, blunt, square nose, pillowy lips, a somewhat outsize ear, wild dark eyebrow parenthetical over amber eye, honey skin, a shadow of stubble. A shiver starts in her groin, moving down her legs to her toes. Panicked, she looks away, fixating on the red ship now gliding slowly out of the harbor. This is the feeling that makes girls into fools, makes them pine for boys like a body misses a bone. His thigh brushes hers and she shies away. No one ever regrets staying in control.

"Beau Putnam has to get his," Lennox says. "I'd give my left nut to be the guy who gives it to him." He sets his bottle on its side and lets it clatter down the concrete slope and disappear over the edge. The length of a breath, then the sound of shattering glass.

"How are things with Annie?" She can barely speak the words. From Lennox's silence, she senses that even this question is the wrong one and that no amount of beer will make it right.

"Beau caught us together a couple weeks ago. He called her *nigger lover.*" He spits over the edge of the Hands. "The man's scary when he's mad. I didn't want to leave her there alone with him raging like that, but there's no arguing with two hundred and fifty pounds of pissed-off beef."

"You think he hit her?"

"Don't think he read her a bedtime story."

Illa feels sewn to her spot. In the tiny openings between the Hands' fingers, she can see gulls coasting on the wind, snowy heads trained downward looking for food, their shrill calls accusing. A hiss as he levies another beer cap. She swallows, her throat dry from beery sugar.

"Man, Annie ran off the rails when her dad announced that stupid ball. She even stopped talking to Mercy. Thought she had something to do with it."

Illa sits up. "But they're still friends, right?" She wants the answer to be no. With Annie around, it would be harder for Illa to find her way into Mercy's circle. Even though she knows she could be a better friend to Mercy than Annie Putnam—hell, a nutria rat could do the job better. Illa just needs a chance.

"No idea. Annie's not really the talkie type. Not with me at least."

"Sorry," Illa says again, feeling doltish.

"You ask me, it's stupid of her to wrong Mercy that way, after all the girl's done for her. It's bad news for everyone."

"What does that mean?" Illa asks. "Why?"

He takes a slug of beer. "Without Mercy around, Annie's a ticking time bomb."

# MERCY

ANNIE'S PURITY BALL is set for August, just before school starts, and Maw Maw has been busy with preparations. *Just in time,* she says. *Now the girl won't burn come December.* The women of the Purity Coalition are excited about the ball; they're glad to have such a high-profile family in for the cause. To start with, there's the budget—more than most weddings in town—and the coalition, made up of a dozen women from different churches around town, hopes it'll bring in lots of people.

How strange that Maw Maw now has more contact with the Putnam family than me. With each day that passes, I miss Annie more and more. That early-summer day with her at Crystal Beach, that perfect day, seems distant as a dream. We've fought before, but we've never gone more than a day without seeing each other. Without her, I wake disoriented, waiting on a phone call telling me to meet her at the field house or the gym or the seawall for a run through the soft sand. But the call doesn't come, so instead I try the Putnam house. Every morning I call first thing, only to have Lourdes tell me that Annie isn't feeling well and can't come to the phone.

To try to take my mind off of her absence, I throw myself into training. I go early to the track before it gets too hot, but even at six a.m., you can feel the day sitting on your shoulders while you run. I start in the dark, do ten four-hundred-meter sprints with two minutes recovery time between. Some days I run hills, sprinting the incline, feeling my hamstrings harden into steel bands before jogging back down the hill to do it again. By the time I finish, the sky is an ecstatic pink, clouds spread out like orange petticoats, the Gulf beginning to reveal itself on the horizon. Sweat-soaked and spent, I like to lie on the nubbly surface of the track and watch the day take shape. There is something satisfying about disciplining the body in this way; the completion of each punishing routine leaves me happy in the knowledge that, come the season, my feet will be winged.

Every other morning, I go into the field house to do weights. The place is built of cinder blocks so it keeps cool, and I don't mind the smell of stale sweat. Coach Martin would kill me if she knew I was working without a spot, but what can I do, with the other girls on the road playing AAU all summer? Alone with only the sound of plates clanging together between sets, I can count the beats of my heart. Clean-and-jerks, squats, wall sits, bench presses, pull-ups: I work my arms lean and strong, my calves into tight pistons. I talk to myself, count out loud, yell to get the last push like the guys do.

Evenings, I play pickup at Park Terrace, down near the shuttered elementary school. The first night at the playground, I'm nervous. I haven't played a real game since the semi, because afterward, even the smell of the gym made me anxious. When Marcus Drab passes the ball to me so we can shoot for teams, he ribs me: "Show me you're not all hype, Miss Mercy." He's six-five, skin the color of caramel sauce and eyes just the same, his mama a Creole from an island she returned to without him long ago. When he slips the ball in the basket, his fingertips caress the rim. "She my lady, gotta be gentle," he says, and the other boys say *Oooooeeee* as if they're in pain. I starfish my hands onto either side of the ball, squeeze hard; the leather surface has a pleasing tackiness. I dribble once, twice, bend at the knee, my arm arcing up. It is so quiet you can hear my fingernails drag on the surface just before the ball releases into the air. Then: *swish*. Such a soothing sound for a rough-and-tumble game. *My body remembers*. Standing here, I feel such a warming flood of relief that my legs noodle, threaten to go out. Marcus breaks the silence, snapping me back to the moment: "Thas right, there the Black Angel, she all *walk*, no *talk*, and she on *my* team!"

On that court with these boys, my game returns, and gratitude sharpens my play. After the semi, I was scared my touch was gone forever, but here I see that I just had a bad game.

At Park Terrace, I forget about Charmaine and Annie, the Le-Blanc Avenue baby, and the coming Rapture. I remember only the feel of the ball in my hand and what it's like to fly. Playing good ball is like total freedom and total control, two opposing wires fused together to make me electric. And oh, I love to shock these boys. After I hit a three, Marcus crosses his wrists at his chest, flutters his hands like a dove taking flight. "Dang, snowflake," he says. "Dang."

Insects form clouds around the park lights as they flicker on. Cheers echo from the nearby baseball diamond where boys play American Legion, the announcer's baritone like a muffled blues horn, ball against bat ringing out like the sound of summer. Young women push strollers by, laughter bubbling up into the air around them. There are girls who come to watch us most nights, black and Mexican girls I recognize from school, Fenceline girls I never talk to because we're in different crowds. They wear candy-colored halter tops, jean shorts that end just below their butt cheeks; they jeer at the boys, say sassy things when a shot is missed, join the chorus of shouting when someone blocks a shot.

I know it's an act; that later, the candy girls will pair off with the boys and sneak away to dark, cool places—cars, movie theaters—

and in private, they will go soft, giggling, whispering sweet words that the boys will store up to remember later, when they're alone. I wonder what it's like to have a boyfriend. In church, we aren't allowed. When we're ready to marry, we go through a father-guided courtship. I'm supposed to start mine after graduation, but if Maw Maw is right, there'll be none of that. I guess it's better to die a virgin, anyway, a real bride of Christ.

Here on the blacktop, this street ball is pure joy, the games ritual chaos, all pumping legs, swiping arms, forward-tilted bodies; I give myself up to the glorious mess of it, and I remember something I forgot in the struggle to earn hardware for Coach's trophy case: this game is *fun*. And I'm *great* at it. Quick first step, sure shot, fast hands. Yep, yep. These summer nights I feel God all around us, watching our bodies do these miraculous things. Though I'd never say so, I know Maw Maw's wrong about basketball, that it doesn't distract from the Lord but proves the potential of our flying bodies, built in His image.

At night I struggle to sleep. My body doesn't want to stop moving, even for a second. I'm hungry to play. Now that I have my game back, I start to dream about college again, the word *scholarship* a luxurious sigh. Sometimes, during breaks in play when I catch my breath, gulp down Gatorade, marvel at the shadow-shapes the trees make against the darkening sky, I catch myself wondering about Charmaine, if she got that letter I sent and what she thought about it. *Forget Charmaine,* I think just as quick. *She is as nothing to you now as she ever was, a letter is no better than a story; neither is flesh, neither is warmth.* Still, I remember how her letter blazed through me, leaving my heart bald as a flame-eaten hilltop.

One night when I get home from scrimmaging, my skin wet with the warm rain that has started falling, I hover by the phone, considering a call to Coach. I want to reassure her that I won't let her down again, not after everything she's done for me—the hours of game tape analyzed, the highlight reel she put together and sent off to dozens of college coaches. And then the follow-up phone calls, the update letters written to include each milestone I reached, each school or district record broken. Outside, the rain insists against the window and steam rises from the pavement, veiling the fresh darkness. *Why do you do it?* I asked her last spring, a few weeks before State. *Spend all this time, when you've got classes to teach and your own life to attend to?* We'd finished a team dinner at her house, and as the other girls filed out, she'd gestured for me to stay. *Because praying's not going to get you this scholarship, Mercy,* she said. *You need boots on the ground for the dirty work. That's me, that's my job. When your kind of talent comes along . . .* She whistled. *Boy howdy. As a coach, you just kind of wake up and go, Okay, this girl is going to be a big part of my life from now until she goes to college, I'm going to do whatever it takes to make sure she gets where she needs to go. And you thank your lucky stars.*

I remember that night as I stand by the phone, and tears gather at the corners of my eyes. With effort, I blink them back, eventually walking away without picking up the receiver. I'll get to that place with her again, I'm sure of it; prove that her time and trust weren't wasted.

---

AT PARK TERRACE, people drop by the playground to watch us play, neighborhood boys dreaming of varsity, the candy girls, old men playing checkers who want to remember what it was like to be young. When Travis Salter first appears, I don't make much of it. Still, the way the boy moves catches my attention. He's tall, not thick-shouldered like the ballers but slender, and I swear, he *glides.* He has this guitar, and whenever one of the candy girls yells an insult at a player, Travis puts it to music, harmonizing with her yowling until the whole row of girls is busted up laughing. He must be angling for one of the Candies, with their suntan-oiled legs and big summertime hair cascading around their faces.

One night when I've got the hot hand, I float to the bucket and drop in a delicate layup for the win, despite the hulking boys who, flailing, try to keep the ball from its destiny—*thump, swoosh.* I whoop and say something obnoxious to Hector Hernandez, the guy guarding me. He has a blockish face covered in acne scars. As the words leave my mouth, I catch sight of Travis, who's got this grin on his face like he's enjoying the moment as much as I am. I stare a little too long, I guess, because Marcus starts in with the teasing: "Angel face got a *crush,* oooooh." But Marcus is soon distracted by one of the Candies, and I scurry to where my things are piled up at the edge of the court. When I look up again, Travis is standing over me.

"Hey," he says.

"Yeah?" I say defensively. Dadgummit, but where is Annie Putnam when I need her most?

Lord forgive me, but I'm weak. I look up and take in Travis's face. He's got a wide, expressive mouth, a dimple splitting his chin. Hastily, I glance down at my gym bag, pretending to dig for something. But then I look up again, feeling like Lot's wife, waiting to be turned to salt for my staring. Instead, there's just this strange sensation, my whole body the beating wing of a butterfly.

"Mercy Louis, I know I'm not the first to say it, but you're a natural," he says.

I take off my soaking socks, slide into rubber flip-flops. "Thanks," I say, still a little out of breath. He's not a jock, so I don't see much of him around school, but I know of him the way I know about everyone in my class. Each spring, he's playing a new instrument in a new band at the talent show, and every year, his band wins with some song he's written. *Emo,* Annie says, pretending to shove her finger down her throat—but I always found the music good-sad, like a happy memory recalled.

The boys have cleared out; even when they're on my team, they don't like to stick around too long if I've been the one to have the last word.

"You don't look happy when you play," Travis says.

"Supposed to smile pretty taking an elbow?"

"You don't look unhappy, either."

"God gives you a gift, you don't spit on Him with unhappiness."

"You sure it's God? You look devilish out there sometimes." I swear he winks, and though I'm not the kind of girl to giggle, I nearly do, it strikes me as so corny. "You look like . . ." He pauses. "Like you're in pain, a little. Your brow creases up . . ."

"Focus . . ."

" . . . you purse your lips until there's almost nothing left of them . . ."

"Not out there modeling lipstick."

" . . . which is kind of a shame, because your lips are your best feature."

A wave of feeling close to nausea in the pit of my stomach. I look up and meet his eyes.

"I'm good, so I do it," I say. "All glory to Him for my gifts."

"Fair enough," he says. "But the best part of watching you play is the love you bring to the game, I think. That intensity. Like I said, not happiness or unhappiness. Just a look that says this is what you were born to do. It's not a game with you. It's an art."

He looks at the ground as if nervous about how his words will land. Softly against my skin, I want to tell him. It takes a minute for me to absorb all these sweet things said at once. We walk without speaking for a few minutes, but I wouldn't call it silence; the night birds are chirruping the coming darkness. Travis slaps at mosquitoes and fingers a few lazy chords on his guitar. The frog noise is rich and rhythmic. At the edge of the park, he stops me.

"You didn't have that look on your face when you played the

semis last year," he says. "There was something different about you from the minute you took the court."

"You were at the game?" I ask.

He laughs. "Whole town was at that game." He waits, watching me, and I'm embarrassed. Here I was, bragging on myself and my "gift" when this boy's seen the semi. I wait for his leveling remark, something along the lines of *Well, you can't be perfect all the time.* Instead, he says: "You know the Longfellow poem about Evangeline and Gabriel?" The first answer that comes to mind is unkind—*Yes, you fool, I'm Cajun generations back, can trace my roots to Nova Scotia. I know that sap Longfellow's poem as well as I know the Lord's Prayer.* But I like walking close to him—the absent way he hums, the way he accepts my postgame need for quiet to calm my blood—so I quash that response and say instead: "The star-crossed lovers."

"I know this isn't really their tree." He gestures at a big oak, its branches like shadowy fingers reaching to the sky. "Even the one in Louisiana isn't theirs. They just say they're buried there to get the tourists to show up. But I like their story. All that wandering to find a single person."

Maw Maw doesn't tell the story because she thinks it glorifies fluffy notions of romance. *Had to drag your mama kicking and screaming to the altar so you'd be born legitimate,* she says. *Wouldn't allow for that kind of burden on a child. I made her say her vows like a Christian woman so there'd be no taint of the bastard on you.* Charmaine and Witness split up after my birth, Witness disappearing onto an offshore rig, Charmaine wandering east in a haze of booze and dope. No, I don't suppose Maw Maw and I put much stock in stories about rosy-cheeked lovers.

"What about scary stories?" I say. "If you like scary ones, Maw Maw's got about fifty different versions of the Loup Garou. Probably why I never broke any rules as a kid. I was scared half to death of waking up with a werewolf at my bedside."

He laughs, then looks up into the reaching boughs of the old oak tree. "Some corn ball at the Port Sabine tourist office wrote in the brochure that the wind through the tree makes the noise of the reunited lovers' laughter."

"Oh, brother," I say. "Isn't the wind through the trees nice enough all on its own?"

"Yeah," he says. "I suppose it is."

He stands too close, looks at me too long. Though the wind blows hard off the Gulf, I don't hear laughter in the trees, only Maw Maw's commandment: *No boys get the privilege of your flesh, not ever, until you're wearing white.*

"Good night, Mercy," he says. "I'll see you around."

" 'Night, Travis."

---

THAT NIGHT I write Annie a letter, again explaining that I knew nothing of her father's plan for the Purity Ball. Inside the envelope, I place my favorite snapshot of the two of us. It's seventh grade, and we're in a photo booth at the Beaumont mall, goofing for the camera. In the shot, Annie's face has an innocence to it I haven't seen in years. I drive to her house, ring the bell. The foyer's dark, but the light of the television flickers against the sliding glass doors of the living room. I knock, wait, then ring again, but nobody comes to the door. After a few more minutes, I prop the letter on the front step. "I miss you, Annie," I say to the moon before getting back into the car.

---

AT THE PARK the next night, Travis approaches me again. He moves with the jointy fluidity of a big cat. With his flip-flops and sun-streaked hair, he looks like he lives at the beach, and I wonder if he ever hangs out with the surfers down at the pier, smoking dope around bonfires and falling asleep in the sand. When you've lived in a small town your whole life, you start thinking you know everything about everyone, but all I really know about Travis is that he's got a gravelly singing voice that surprised me the first time I heard it. It seemed like such a *man's* voice coming out of that skinny boy. He invites me to hang out sometime, and I say no, I really can't, sorry.

I wanted so much to say yes. Because I want to know that feeling again, the one where my whole body is a butterfly wing.

———————

THE SECOND AND third time he asks me to hang out, I say no, and I feel good, strong. But his face. That face like a stick in the ribs, demanding attention. And the words. More than the looks, I can't get enough of the words. When I see him at the park, I try to will myself indifferent, but when he gets close, I go into a lather; this animal me doesn't listen very well, won't take her eyes off the boy. The fourth time he asks, I nod, eyes cast down, as if by not voicing my agreement, I can escape blame. "Is that a yes?" he asks. When I don't answer, he tells me to meet him at the boardwalk day after tomorrow.

Two days later, we stand out front of the Pleasure Pier, which closed up when Mama Charmaine was still a girl. Behind us, the rusting Ferris wheel rises, and the carousel, with its salt-bloated, decapitated horses, sits motionless. They are specters of a boom time that ended before we were born. The bay water murmurs, the gulls dive and peck along the shore. On the air, the rotted smell of decomposing seaweed, which sits on the beach behind curtains of gnats. We plop down on one of the sagging benches facing the water. He's brought along a plastic grocery bag, and from it, he pulls out a take-out clamshell.

"I thought we ought to have the right food for the boardwalk," he says, handing me a still-warm funnel cake wrapped in a napkin. The smell of the fried dough gets my saliva going. "Fresh from Ed's."

"Are you trying to bribe me with sweets?" I say.

"I'd say sweets for the sweet, only I've seen you on the court, and you aren't going for Miss Congeniality."

Before taking a bite, I think of Coach's meal plan. I shouldn't eat this, but Travis looks so eager to please, and it smells delicious, so I take a big bite, the powdered sugar dusting my lips. "Oh, good grief," I say between bites. "I'll say *please* and *thank you* on the court from now on if it means more of these."

"You been playing hard to get for weeks, and all I had to do was buy you a donut? Could have saved me a few hard nights, girl." He grins, tears a piece off his cake. "I haven't noticed your sidekick around much these days. You two have a fight?"

"Annie?" I smile at the idea of her as my sidekick; when we're together, I feel like the tagalong. "I guess she's mad at me."

"What the heck for?"

I pause; I don't want to talk about the Purity Ball, not with Travis, who wouldn't understand. "I don't know," I lie. "I miss her. Wrote her a letter and everything."

"She didn't respond to a letter?" He whistles. "That's cold. But tell you the truth, I'm kinda glad. Y'all were pretty unapproachable as a tag team."

"Really?"

"Annie Putnam, you kidding?" He grins. "When I saw you alone at the park, I thought I better make my move."

"Because my bodyguard was off-duty?" I say playfully, but I know he's right. If Annie had been at Park Terrace, I wouldn't be here now.

"Here," he says, suddenly bashful. He slides headphones over my ears. On his Discman, he plays a recording of a basketball poem from a CD he found at the library. It's by a Louisiana poet named Yusef Komunyakaa, a black man with a voice like Moses:

> *In the roundhouse*
> *Labyrinth our bodies*
> *Created, we could almost*
> *Last forever, poised in midair*
> *Like storybook sea monsters.*

"I love it," I say. "That's how it feels sometimes. Epic." I tilt my head to one side. "So you just had this basketball poem tucked in your back pocket for a rainy day?"

"Mighta done a little sleuthing." He smiles wide so I can see his wolfish incisors, which sets me keening for something I can't identify. Slipping his hand behind my neck, he starts at my left ear. At first he's polite, peckish. I watch the sea as the sun meets the horizon in a fiery line, throwing up rays like the arms of a drowning man. But then a shift, and he turns his whole body toward me, his pelvis pressed gently against my hip. I shiver somewhere deep.

He fits his mouth to the curve where my neck meets my shoulders. He smells insanely good, like I don't know what. Just good. I should tell him to stop, but I don't. When his lips overlap mine, it feels as if he is coaxing my heart out of my chest. When his hand brushes my nipple, though, a wave of shame overtakes me. *I am the daughter of a nothing whore.*

"Stop," I say, and he does.

"Sorry," he says. "It's just, I really like you."

I smile. "Me, too."

I want to ask him: *Would you still like me if we were just two souls meeting, bodiless, in space?* That's how I imagine God loves. We pick our way to the end of a jetty, find a flat rock to sit on. Afterward, he drives me home in the dark, the air thick with insects. He idles at the corner, out of sight of the stilt house, gives me a peck of the cheek.

In the bathroom mirror, I notice that the skin around my mouth is pinkish from the friction of Travis's stubble. I brush my teeth, gargle twice. The taste of his tongue persists.

At the vanity, I sit down and draw out Charmaine's letter. I wonder if years ago she sat in this same room marveling over the tobacco taste of Witness's mouth. After she gave herself to him in sin, did she dampen this desk with her tears?

Striking a match from the box I keep for my candles, I hold the flame close to the paper, the curls of smoke sharp in my nostrils. The match burns so close to my fingers that I have to shake it out.

I can't destroy the letter. I need it to remind me what not to become.

O VER THE NEXT couple days, Illa continues to check the
mail. While the Purity Ball invitation fails to arrive, a couple
more of the chicken-scratch epistles land and are spirited away by
Mama to parts unknown. With each letter, Illa's curiosity grows, so
that by the time the third one arrives, she barely notices the invitation to the Purity Ball beneath it in the stack. Mama is napping in
the kitchen, the afternoon silence heavy and close through the house.
*What if I just have a peek?* Illa thinks.

Before she can consider the consequences, she rushes to her room,
taking the stairs two at a time so that when she lands on the bed,
she's breathing hard, temples pulsing with blood.

She looks over the invitation to the ball, which is made out to Ms.
Meg Stark and Miss Illa Stark, just as she feared. She skims it for
details, then buries it at the bottom of a desk drawer. It's overkill, she
knows, but if Mama sees the invitation and insists on going with her,
it would be like the funeral of that French president where his wife
and mistress stood side by side at his grave. Over the years, Illa has
taken pains to ensure that the two spheres of her life—basketball,
Mama—never overlapped.

Holding one of the mystery letters, she tears the envelope along the seam, unfolds the sheet of paper. Given free rein over a blank page, the handwriting expands into something loopier. The salutation takes Illa by the throat: *Dear Mercy.* How has she come to be holding a piece of private correspondence meant for Mercy Louis? Maybe the mailman had made a mistake and dropped the letter in their box by accident; she flips the envelope back over to confirm the address. 3156 Galvez Street, Port Sabine, Texas. Apparently, the letter's in the right place, but that only adds to Illa's confusion. She reads it:

> *Dear Mercy,*
> *There was something I used to do when you were small,*
> *when I was still a mess with the dope. Believe me, when*
> *you're unemployed and zonked out of your head, you have*
> *a lot of time alone with your thoughts, what fried bits of*
> *them there are left, that is. Anyway. I would picture your*
> *face as I remembered it—your baby face with its squishy*
> *nose and serious blue eyes (you didn't have eyebrows at*
> *first, just these huge staring eyes). And I'd try to fast-*
> *forward in time, like those nature videos that show a flower*
> *growing from a seed, to try and picture what you looked*
> *like at different ages. I think mostly I just substituted my*
> *face from when I was a child, which is cheating but it was*
> *the best I could do. I don't have much of an imagination.*
>
> *Of course, I did this on my best days, when I could*
> *think straight enough. I'll admit it, there were bad days,*
> *really bad days, when I didn't think of you, or much of*
> *anything. Days I was barely alive. I lost weeks, maybe*
> *years, that way but I try not to think about it too much.*
> *Shame and regret are already close friends of mine.*
>
> *Love true,*
>
> *C. Ω.*

C. B. must be Charmaine Boudreaux, Mercy's mother. So the rumors are true, the drug stuff, at least. In a small town, it's hard to tell fact from fiction, the apocryphal making the rounds alongside the God's honest until they're indistinguishable and both cited like gospel.

Why are these letters coming to Galvez Street? Illa wonders, listening for sounds from the kitchen, rustlings to indicate Mama is awake. Nothing. On tiptoe, she makes her way down the stairs, past the kitchen where Mama naps, and into the bedroom, where she suspects the other letters reside. Inside, the room is dark and smells of unwashed sheets; Illa makes a mental note to strip the bed later. She opens the blinds, the sudden daylight catching dust motes on their soundless descent. If her mother is trying to hide the letters, she hasn't done a great job—they're stacked neatly on her bedside table. Next to them sits a mother-of-pearl letter opener. So Mama has already opened the letters and read them like dog-eared paperbacks before bed.

Why would Mama withhold this correspondence from a girl who's probably starved for news of her mother? It seems perverse; Illa decides to deliver the letters to Mercy at Park Terrace that night. Finally, a good excuse to show up at the park. And she knows Annie won't be there because of the fight Lennox told her about.

———————

THAT EVENING, THE letters tucked neatly in the side pocket of her camera bag, Illa ventures to the Park Terrace basketball court. She waits until after the sun sets, a silvery twilight wrapping her in protective shadow. At the edge of the park, bulrushes and cattails announce the beginnings of the salt marsh that stretches from there to Chocolate Bayou. Illa watches a pair of redwing blackbirds feint and dodge as they dance in and out of the reeds.

Before she can see the court, she hears its familiar sounds—the

scuff and squeak of sneakers, the clanging of ball against rim, players conversing in their language of grunts, shouts, whistles, claps.
And then there they are, nine boys and Mercy carving up the air
under the streetlights.

With possibility fizzing in her bones, Illa walks to the wooden
benches that flank the court and starts to take pictures, trying to
look purposeful. A few of the girls cock their tweezed eyebrows at
her, gold hoops flashing, but they don't say anything.

"It's for a contest," Illa murmurs in the direction of the girls, but
they've already trained their eyes back on the court.

"What contest?"

She turns to see who's spoken. It's Travis Salter, sitting on a patch
of grass, legs splayed in a V in front of him, torso propped up by
kickstand arms dug into the ground.

"Some scholarship thing," she says. "For sports photography."

"Cool," he says. He's an exceedingly *long* human being, she notes,
so much that it's almost comical, which has always inclined her to
like him.

"I guess," she says, shrugging, trying to sound bored even though
what she wants to say is *Yes, it is cool, really, really cool!* She knows
that saying anything fervently is an invitation for mocking.

During a break in play, Mercy sees her and waves. The gesture
bolsters Illa's confidence. As the game continues, she paces the sideline, bringing the Canon to her face and following Mercy as she
moves. She looks leonine, crouched low and slapping the cement
tauntingly on D, fluid and confident on offense. What a change
from the semifinal, when she was wound so tight that Illa thought
she might go flying off the court and into the stands.

After the game, the players and the gold-hoop girls stand
around in semicircles that break apart and re-form into various social compounds. Illa sees Travis unfurl his long body and start to

sidle across the court. Illa has never seen anyone *sidle,* though she has long liked the word. His gunboat Chuck Taylors are stripped of their laces and flap loudly against the concrete as he walks. Across his back, he's slung a guitar, which bumps against him with each step.

Almost too late, she realizes he's walking toward Mercy, who sits on a bench unlacing her sneakers. Crap. If they start talking, Illa might miss her window. *Go,* she commands herself.

"Mercy!" she exclaims too loudly, so that the kids at the sideline pause to see what's going on. At the sound of her name, Mercy jerks her head around. "Can you come here a sec?" Illa says, quieter this time. She feels herself blushing aggressively. Mercy stands and trots toward Illa, nodding at Travis as she passes. He flips his guitar around to the front and starts strumming it absentmindedly.

"Long time, no see," Mercy says. "How you been, girl?" Sweat drips off her chin, slicks her dark hair to her head. She dabs at her forehead with a sweatband she wears around her wrist, but there's no stanching the flow; the heat lingers well after sunset, stored up in the pavement and cars to be released slowly over the night hours. At dawn, it will still be eighty-five degrees and ninety-nine percent humidity.

"Good, good," Illa says distractedly. "Here, I have something for you." She fumbles in her bag for the letters, holding them out as if they can explain themselves. Mercy glances down, eyes lingering on the envelopes for a half second before meeting Illa's gaze. "Why'd you bring those here?" she hisses, stepping toward Illa.

"If you're wondering why they're open—"

"I'm not wondering about them at all," she says. Out of the corner of her eye, Illa notices Travis watching them. "Those letters don't exist."

"But your mom—" Illa continues.

"My mom nothing, you don't know *piss-all* about my mama."

"I'm sorry . . ." Illa says helplessly, still holding the letters out. She's not sure what she's apologizing for, but she's ready to say anything to stymie Mercy's anger.

"You didn't read them, did you?"

"No, of course not, no," Illa lies. "That's why I was bringing them to you, I thought you'd want to—"

"Everything all right?" Travis says, coming up behind Mercy. She grabs for the letters, but not before he sees them. "What's that?"

Mercy glares at Illa, jaw set, eyes flashing. "Nothing," she grumbles. Travis doesn't look convinced, but Mercy makes it clear the subject is closed. They look at Illa, Travis with concern, Mercy with such stark animosity that it makes Illa want to cry. What has she done wrong?

"I . . . I was just going," she manages, shoving the letters back in her bag before turning and tripping her way out of the park, hot tears streaking down her face.

———————

ON THE CAR ride home, sobs leave Illa gasping for air. She's spent her entire life trying to avoid conflict—trying to avoid being noticed at all. If not for Mama and the stolen letters, the fight with Mercy never would have happened.

Illa made a mistake by going to Park Terrace; it's obvious now that Mercy wants nothing to do with Charmaine. How could Illa have known? She thought she was doing Mercy a favor. And Charmaine wanted so badly to connect with her daughter. The letters bled a raw truth that made Illa ache while reading them.

Back at the house, Illa bangs through the front door; she's on the hunt. It's late, past nine o'clock, which means Mama's already in bed. Illa doesn't care; if she could wake the whole neighborhood, she would. She's spent years of her life looking after a woman who should have been looking after *her*. And now Mama has gone and mucked up Illa's chance to ever befriend Mercy. Come September, the year will start, unfolding in blocks of hours and days and weeks, and it will be lonely as any other year, except that when it ends in May, that will be it. There'll be no more basketball, no more team, no more Lennox and his stories and beer, no more darkroom. After graduation, it's going to be Illa and Mama together in the house on Galvez Street until one of them dies.

Bursting into the bedroom, Illa switches on the overhead light. It shines ruthlessly on her mother, who groans from where she's curled beneath the comforter.

"You're a freak, you know that?" Illa says, the consonance of *freak* satisfying in her mouth. She sees Mama shift toward the sound of her voice, but she doesn't come out from beneath the covers, as if Illa is a nightmare that will dematerialize if Mama keeps her eyes shut tight enough.

"Do you know what it's like to be ashamed of your mother every hour of every waking day?" Illa shouts, panting with exertion.

Slowly, Mama's head turtles out from her cave. "Illa—"

"No, no, shut up," Illa says, pacing in front of the door. "I'm sick of listening to your excuses. Other people lost things that day, Mama, and you don't see them just *giving up,* just throwing in the fucking towel! Christ, Lennox's dad is actually *going to die* in six months, and he's in a *rage* because of it, because he's not ready to go."

"Illa, what's got into you?"

"The letters, Mama, Mercy's letters."

Mama struggles to sit up, squinting against the harsh light. Her wide-necked nightgown has slipped down one shoulder, revealing a slab of pale flesh.

"How do you know about those letters?"

"It'd be so easy if I just let you keep playing your sick little games, whatever they're about."

"So you read them?"

"I opened one and figured out pretty fast it wasn't meant for you, so I found the rest of them and gave them to their goddamned owner!"

"Illa, you weren't—"

"No, *you* weren't supposed to go reading Mercy's mail, but you *did,* and now everything's fucked."

"I was supposed to hold the letters until Mercy came to get them, Charmaine asked me to."

"But you *read* them." She waits for Mama to deny it, hoping her mother hasn't been pathetic enough to pore over a teenage girl's letters, but Mama keeps silent, her eyes fixed on the floor, chest laboring with each wheezy breath. Then Illa says what she has long thought but never been cruel enough to utter aloud: "Everyone thinks I'm a weirdo because of you. I never had a chance at a regular life, you made shit sure a that!"

Mama flinches as if Illa has chucked acid on her, and Illa feels a twinge of regret. But there's no turning back from the truth; it lies between them in the room, continuing to do damage, like one of those bullets designed to mangle flesh on its journey to the bone.

———

AFTER THE FIGHT with Mercy at Park Terrace, Illa reads the other letters. She knows she's a hypocrite but that's not enough to stop her, because when she reads Charmaine's letters, she feels ushered into Mercy's inner circle. After reading them over several times, Illa understands why Mercy wants to pretend they don't exist. Charmaine's need for her daughter rips through the page.

In the weeks that follow, two more of Charmaine's letters arrive. Both times Illa reads them as soon as she closes the bedroom door behind her. A few times Illa finds herself choked with emotion over the hurt that belongs to this woman. Though she wants to be angry with Charmaine for abandoning Mercy, Illa feels a conservative but unmistakable sympathy taking root. Charmaine doesn't dodge blame or make excuses for her behavior, nor does she disguise her reason for writing. Illa admires anyone with the guts to ask for something she doesn't deserve. That kind of audacity is grounded in desire so deep a person stops caring about means or odds, shame or embarrassment. It makes Illa sad to know that Charmaine's letters will go unread by Mercy; she commits them to memory so they won't be wasted. One of them contains a cryptic warning that raises the hair on Illa's neck:

> *Mercy, I hope you'll hear this: if you ever feel unsafe at home, go find someone you trust. Just please, get out of there.*

Illa wants to find Mercy and ask if everything is okay, but she knows that she is the last person Mercy wants to see. Evelia seemed wacky, with her visions and her wild eyes, but was she dangerous? What exactly happened to Charmaine in that stilt house at the edge of the bayou?

# MERCY

CHARMAINE IS A weed that grows back no matter how many times I take it out at the roots. She must've seen my one letter as encouragement; it was foolish of me to send it.

Poor Illa, wisp of a thing, bringing those letters to the park like she was doing me a favor. I terrorized her, even scared myself a little bit. *Nobody likes an angry woman.* And Travis Salter standing right there, close enough to hear everything.

I continue to train and play every day, hoping I can make myself tired enough that I don't have the energy to think about Charmaine. Now in addition to basketball, I also think of Travis. This new pressure at the chest. At church we're taught to be careful not to fall in love with a man until we're ready for marriage, so we can give our whole heart to our husband. *Every time you love and lose, you give away another piece of your heart,* Pastor Parris says. *Do you want to stand before your husband on your wedding day with nothing but an empty shell where your heart should be?*

Sometimes I think guiltily of Coach, the stipend she pays to Maw Maw to make sure I stay sharp over the summer. *True champions aren't well rounded,* she says. *They have a single-minded focus on their goals, and that makes them the best.* I should stop this nonsense with Travis today, I know better. And yet a part of me wonders, what if this is my only chance for love on this earth, in this lifetime? *Love,* the word strange and delicious on my tongue.

We see each other almost every day, except for the afternoons he works at the auto shop downtown. He can't call the house because of Maw Maw, so we make plans every night at Park Terrace, after I'm finished playing. He continues to woo me with sweets, his mother's bread pudding thick with raisins and swimming in bourbon sauce, carrot cake with cream cheese frosting made by his sister, pecan sandy cookies, sweet potato pie from the Boxcar, chocolates from the drugstore; we try to guess the filling before biting into them glee-fully, kissing each other with chocolate-cherry mouths, and I think of the Song of Solomon, *Your lips drop sweetness as the honeycomb, my bride; milk and honey are under your tongue.* I'm the happiest I've ever been; I didn't know a person could feel like this outside of church, dreamy and complete.

Over our days together, I begin to discover the secret things in him, like how much he loves words—so much that he's got a whole wall filled with them in his bedroom at home, which he shows me one sticky afternoon, the heat like a third person between us, bully-ing. As he walks me through his house, we wipe away sweat with the heels of our hands, blink it out of our eyes. It's a nice old house, roomy and full of light, the pine floors knotted and uneven but gleaming with wax, the furniture and curtains in shades of green and yellow and cream. There are sturdy bookcases, a series of framed charcoal drawings of life unfolding in a foreign village, a colorful woven tap-estry encased behind glass. An antique map of Texas beckons from over the fireplace, which is filled with half-melted burgundy candles. On the coffee table are more books in teetering stacks, some cracked open at the spine. Out a large picture window, I can see an old oak with low-hanging branches, hummingbird feeders hanging like

Christmas ornaments. A tall man—perhaps even taller than Travis—is mowing the lawn, a broad straw hat flopping with each step. I recognize him as Travis's father. He spies us through the window and waves.

Except for the homey untidiness, the house could be from a catalog. I guess you never know what you want until you see it, because yearning clutches at my heart now—it's so different from the stilt house, where I keep quiet as I can so I don't disturb Maw Maw. He's got two younger sisters, one gangly girl I've seen around school from time to time, striking for her height and white-blond hair, and one still at the middle school. They have names like money, Alexandra and Sophia.

Travis's bedroom is dark, done up in boy colors—hunter green, navy, maroon—and filled with the faded smell of his cologne. When he shows me the wall where he's carved or pasted song lyrics and funny bits of conversations he's heard, he's proud but also embarrassed. "No one ever comes in here," he says by way of excuse; it makes me feel privileged. There are some snippets of poems and lines from books, and it creates a mishmash that makes his room seem cozy and smart, like it's having an artsy conversation with itself. On the wall, Allen Ginsberg, Hunter S. Thompson, Jean-Paul Sartre, Bob Dylan, and Trent Reznor have pride of place. Even the lamp talks, its shade plastered with newspaper headlines he's cut up to say things like *Nuns with guns* and *Planet Earth resigns in disgust*.

"Nice lamp," I say. It *is* nice, simply because it belongs to him, but he thinks I'm joking and says, "Yeah, about that . . . remnant of the eighth-grade me . . ." I can tell by his expression that he's rethinking the idea to bring me here, glancing around nervously at this space that represents his private self, just to make sure it won't embarrass him more.

"No, really, it's great," I say, quick to try to reassure him, thinking, *Everything about you is great,* but knowing I can't come out and say that.

"As you can see, I'm a card-carrying member of the Sensitive Boy Club."

"Your secret's safe with me," I say, edging close to him so he puts an arm around me. I nuzzle in to his chest and wrap my arms around his narrow hips, let him stroke my hair and kiss the crown of my head until I start to get drowsy. I imagine us standing here like trees entangled on a riverbank until days turn into weeks, then months, legs intertwining like roots, arms like branches. Water, air, sun, and touch, that's all we'd need to live.

When we leave his room, his mom is just getting home from the store. She peeks at us over the edges of the brown paper sacks balancing on her hips. "Howdy," she says, brushing a strand of honey-colored hair back from her forehead. She's wearing scarlet linen pants and a tunic heavy with dozens of tiny clouded mirrors that reflect light onto the ceiling and walls like a disco ball. From her ears swing filigreed silver earrings. "I'm Sylvie." She puts out her hand, which is pale and china-delicate, laden with chunky rings. I take it in mine, conscious of the calluses spread over my palms from the weight machines. The words *hippy-dippy* float up to me from the part of my brain that stores random facts about people in our town. Yes, of course, this is *Sylvie,* the *hippy-dippy* artist type who spends all day in her garage making pots out of coils of clay that she stains in outrageous colors, then sells at the Beaumont farmers market. The one who *refuses to marry her children's father even though it means those kids will grow up bastards* . . . *That* Sylvie. The *crazy pot lady.* I've heard people gossip about her but never connected her to Travis because she doesn't have the same last name. Instantly, I sense that she is a woman who takes herself seriously, even if the town doesn't. She's older, too, maybe halfway between Maw Maw and Charmaine.

"Ma, this is Mercy Louis," Travis says, placing fingertips at my elbow in a shy attempt at gallantry.

"It is, isn't it?" she says, putting her bags down on the kitchen table. She smiles at me, and I see where he gets it; it's as if she's swallowed a lightbulb. I like her instantly, something in the toothy openness of the smile. Then, unexpectedly, she draws me in to a hug; she smells of lavender and the sun, her skin warm against mine. When she pulls back, she holds me at arm's length. "I read all about you in the papers. Good God, but you're pretty."

"Mom," Travis protests.

"What? I'm an artist," she says. "I can't help it, I like beauty."

"You make *pots*," he says.

"My pots are beautiful," she says, aping injury.

"They really are," I volunteer.

"I'll make you one," she says cheerfully as she starts putting away the groceries. On the kitchen island, she forms little pyramids of tomatoes, yellow peppers, green apples. "You'll have to come to my studio to sit for it, though."

"It's a *pot*, not a portrait," Travis says. He looks horrified by the idea of me spending time alone with his mother.

"But for Mercy's pot to truly be *Mercy's pot*, I have to at least talk to the girl a little, get to know who she is and what she's about. I can't make a pot out of thin air." She turns to me for support. "So will you? Sit for me sometime?" The sun coming through the kitchen window catches the gold flecks in her green eyes, making them glitter.

"Absolutely."

"Fine, Mercy can sit for her pot," Travis says with a shake of the head, bugging his eyes at his mom in a playful way that tells me they only pretend to goad each other, that there is huge affection between them.

"Wonderful," sings Sylvie as she moves around the kitchen putting things away. My first reaction is one of happiness—it's fun to be part of this—but then I feel a swarm of jealousy. How good it must feel to be *known*. Sometimes it feels like the girl who lives at home with Maw Maw is a different person from the real me.

"We're gonna go now, before Mercy decides she likes you more than me," Travis says.

"Impossible, my son," Sylvie says. "You're the most eminently likable person I know."

"Thanks for the endorsement, Mom." Flustered, he runs a hand through his hair. "We're going to leave now and maybe never come back."

"It's a wild world out there," she says, washing an apple and biting into it.

"Sounds good to me," he says.

"Life on the road is a lot less glamorous than it sounds, Mercy, don't let him talk you into anything. I lived in the back of a converted van in Mexico for about six months—"

"Aaaaand we're out," says Travis, shepherding me toward the door. "Later!" he says with finality.

"Fare thee well," Sylvie says.

"Nice to meet you, Mrs. . . . ," I say, hesitating because I can't remember her last name—only that it's different from Travis's.

"Leger, But just call me Sylvie."

"Bye, Sylvie," I say, embarrassed. She's strange and fascinating, this woman with the gobs of silver jewelry and her own last name.

"Your mom's cool," I say to Travis as we climb back into his truck.

"She actually is," he says. "I'm glad you got to meet her, even if it means I can now hold what remains of my dignity in a commemorative shot glass."

As we drive away, the noon sun seepy as the yolk of an egg, I flash-forward, fantasizing about time after school spent around that kitchen island, talking to Sylvie, feeling her happiness rub off on me. Out the window, the heat plays tricks with the air so it shimmers like an oil slick. I think how much like houses people are—there's our curb appeal, what the whole world can see of us, and then there are the hidden chambers behind the facade, rooms and rooms inside us where we store up all the things that are too private or tender or shameful or mysterious to share with anyone. Today Travis has shown me into one of his interior rooms, given me a part of his secret self. He loves words so much he's made a wall of them; he loves his mother. I realize how excited I am to learn more about this boy and his family. This must be one of the biggest gifts of love, the process of discovery, finding worlds upon worlds inside the other person, his soul a hall of mirrors stretching inward forever.

But now I have another reason to be wary of Travis. I know he'll want to venture into the dusty back rooms of me, where the furniture is covered in white sheets, where no one's been for years. "Hey, drop me here, will you?" I say.

"Isn't it a little far? The heat . . ."

"Don't worry about me."

"Suit yourself."

I give him my best smile.

"Damn. I just want to—"

"Don't take the Lord's name."

"Only word for your kind of gorgeous."

"Blasphemer and flatterer, huh? Two kinds of trouble."

"What, me?"

"See you soon."

"Not soon enough."

I roll my eyes, slam the door, pretend to be huffy as I walk in the direction of the stilt house. When I'm sure he's turned the corner and can no longer see me, I double back and head toward Galvez Street. Outside Illa's house, an overgrown white oleander offers me cover. I wonder if more letters have arrived and why Charmaine sent them care of the Starks. I stand there until sweat has soaked every bit of my clothes and I can no longer smell the medicinal scent of the oleander leaves. After a while, I turn back toward the stilt house.

———————

BECAUSE I LIKE Travis so much, I want to give him things. He loves words the way I love basketball, so for him I steal Maw Maw's stories. I make her retell them so I can record them in secret while we sit on the screened-in gallery and listen to bugs hit the zapper. I'll never be as good at tale-telling as she is—somehow the stories aren't the same in English—so although I know them all by heart, I want Travis to hear *her* versions. Between sips of sweet tea, she speaks to me, the nasally notes of her Cajun French hanging between us. There is a slow quality to her style, time for the words to bloom in your mind's eye. When she tells tales, the characters become so vivid they inhabit the space around us: sly Lapin and dopey Bouki, the ethereal *feux follets,* the Loup Garou. It is easy to imagine them living in the darkness beyond the porch, where dry land gives way to a soggy forest of cypress, palm, and lacey pine that runs to the Louisiana border.

I want Travis to know this part of my history; that my family tree extends to parts far north, that my people made an exodus out of Nova Scotia like the Hebrews out of Egypt; that I have people at all. Meeting Sylvie today felt like another clue to his true self. How sad that he can never meet Maw Maw and come to appreciate her as I do. She's a hard woman, but I owe my life to her.

I write a list of my reasons for spending time with him, because I like the tidiness of lists, and because I need convincing:

1. I like the smell of his shampoo.
2. I like that he likes the corny story of Evangeline.

3. I like his pale eyes clear as creek water.
4. I like his strong hands with their too-large thumbs.
5. I like the way he watches me play ball.
6. I like the way he reminds me that what I feel for the game is love.
7. I like him.

In return, Travis gives me poetry and songs and simple warmth that seems miles away from the exhausting fusion Annie and I shared. After the first slipup on the boardwalk, I got control of the animal me; I showed Travis my promise ring and told him we deserved better than blind groping. He said he could respect that because my body was only a small part of what he loved about me.

At night as I sweat to sleep, frogs noisy beyond the window, I think of Annie. How easily she believed that I took her secrets to Beau. Yet here I am with her last confession still rustling black-feathered on the branches of my heart. *I have kept your secrets so long, Annie,* I think, willing the truth to her. *I still do.*

———

ONE JULY DAY, Travis and I listen to the recording of Jean l'Ours et la Fille du Roi while digging out a frozen watermelon by the river. The flesh is red and icy, its juice dripping down his bare chest like blood. We've spread an old quilt on the grassy slope of the bank, its gingham faded from washing. From where we sit, we spit the black seeds into the river, and I wonder if a watermelon vine will take root in the swamp and produce great bulbous fruit for the gator gars to pierce with their snouts.

The recording crackles to life, and Maw Maw sounds like a preacher at the pulpit, her voice dipping and rising for emphasis. I stretch myself out on my stomach, rest my head on a forearm, and close my eyes so I can focus on the words. Travis doesn't know

French, but I make him listen anyway, to hear the beauty of the sounds, the flow of each syllable into the next, like river water over rocks. After we listen once, we play it again, and I translate each line the best I can:

> *The king was rich, swimming in treasure. He was a jealous man, and it made him cruel. He had a daughter that the people of his kingdom called the Jolie Blonde, for her hair like sunshine, her eyes pale as the morning sky. He had always told the good people of his kingdom that suitors would have to win her, she was that precious to him.*
>
> *There was a young man, not exactly handsome but with a special kind of face you remembered. He was named Jean l'Ours, John the Bear, and one day he became neighbors with the jealous king. Jean l'Ours was a successful man with huge, able hands. He had to have the best of everything.*

I tell him about John the Bear stealing upon the Jolie Blonde while she bathed, and asking her to marry him though he had never seen her before, and how she told John she had to be won, not asked. I tell him about the hog auction that John the Bear arranged, so he could beat the king with his fine-looking hogs, and the five-hundred-mile race, and the hurricane he called up to stop the king's man from beating his own. I smile as I tell him the good news: that Jean l'Ours won the king's daughter, and that the king gave up his castle and huge bags of rubies, too.

"Your Maw Maw's kind of like the king," he says, rolling over on his back. "She guards you like he guards his daughter."

"She just wants to protect me."

"But do you need protection? You're what, seventeen now?"

"Eighteen in October."

"Eighteen in October." He sniffed. "If I met your grandma, maybe she'd see I'm a good guy."

"You know that's impossible."

"Do you think there's something wrong in what we're doing?"

*No one gets the privilege of your flesh until you're wearing white.* The answer is yes.

He continues: "Do you like being around me?"

"Of course."

"Do I make you happy?"

"Travis, don't . . ."

"What? I'm just trying to make a point. We should be allowed to be around people who make us happy."

If he knew how much Maw Maw lost when Charmaine coupled with Witness and then left us both, he wouldn't preach like he does. For a while, I keep quiet, twisting the ring around on my finger.

"Just because something is good doesn't make it right," I say at last.

He nods, but I can tell he doesn't agree. Instead, he changes the subject. "I dig these stories." He catches a drop of sweat from his upper lip with his tongue. "But I want to hear a real story. A story about you." He pauses and looks at me with his serious sea-glass eyes. "If I'm going to love you, I need to know what you're about."

*Love.* It's the first time anyone besides Annie has said that word to me. *Love.* In his mouth, it's got the glow of a worn gold ring. I hear it from Maw Maw when we read Scripture together: *God is love. Love is patient.* But it's different then, chilled and silvery, not meant for me.

"Basketball's the only good story I have," I say. He wouldn't love me if he knew the trash I was born out of. The truth is like fish. When people ask for it, they usually don't want it eyes and all. Playfully, he flings his arm around my shoulders, pulls in close, and buries his nose near my armpit. He whistles, *Woooeeee.*

"Quit!" I say.

He draws back. "How did I end up with the princess of Port Sabine?" His mouth crooks in a half-smile. "I am but a humble minstrel with no rubies or hogs."

I laugh. "Oh, Lord help us."

He grins. I reach out and touch his ear, studying it; even ears are interesting to me now, because Travis has them. It looks so delicate and exposed peeking from beneath his shaggy sand-colored hair. The lobe is soft between my fingers, and for some reason, touching it makes me want to cry.

"It's okay to want things, to take something for yourself now and then," he says. "There's so much pleasure in the world. Watermelon, for starters." He spits a seed with impressive force, and we watch it alight on the river. *Pleasure.* I don't like the word, the sound of it like a cat's purr. "I wasn't kidding before," he continues. "I feel lucky to know you." *But you don't,* I want to say. *I've given you stories because there's so much truth I can't tell you.* "And I do love you, Mercy."

He's close to me, and when I shut my eyes to his searching gaze, I realize I'm trembling. "I better go," I say, gathering my things and dashing up the bank. He calls out to me, but I don't look back, just jog home barefoot, trailing the muddy quilt.

––––––––––

THE NEXT MORNING when I wake up, I feel a tingling in my right arm like pins and needles. I slide to the edge of the bed and dangle my legs down the side, massaging my arm hard to get the blood flowing. I get a sneezy feeling and then the overpowering urge to thrust the arm straight down, so I do, again and again and again, my forearm thunking softly against the bed. I grit my teeth, will the arm to stillness. But again it thumps downward, *one two three.*

All I can think is *Shit, my shooting hand.* I stand and windmill both arms hard, then pull each one across my chest in a stretch. I wait for the weird feeling, but nothing happens. My breath comes in short gasps. Is it flu? Dehydration? A muscle spasm? I get those in season when I work my body to the bone. *It's just a spasm. Breathe. Relax.*

Again my arm thumps down, *one two three.* Quick breath, too quick, panic like spilled ice water spreading through, making me shake. *Breathe. Breathe.* Darkness at the edge of the room, the ceiling suddenly lower, pressing down. I look toward the door for Maw Maw. *Help me.* When my eyes pass over the silver pool of mirror, a face stares back.

*Her* face.

Charmaine, lips black with burn, parted, saying something I can't hear. *Shut up, shut up!* I press my fists into my eyes and rub, and when I stop, the face is gone.

Reaching for the water glass on my bedside table, I misjudge the distance and knock it to the floor, where it shatters.

"Mercy?" Maw Maw calls from down the hall. "What in heaven's name is going on in there?"

"Nothing," I say weakly. "Dropped something."

What I want to say is *Help me, Maw Maw. I'm afraid.* But I can't. I remember her call to Coach that night. I know she's looking for any excuse to keep me from playing ball. *Breathe.* I place my hands in the puddle of water on the floor, careful to avoid the broken glass, and bring them to my cheeks. The cool wetness against my skin brings me back to earth.

If Annie were here, she'd tell me to get up, stretch it out, and get over myself. She would tell me everything is okay and remind me of all the times our bodies have revealed their limits when we push them—through sprained ankles and torn ligaments and broken fingers, asthma attacks and vomiting and concussions.

There's no one here to direct me, though, so I'll have to make my own instructions. I reach for my notebook and write, white-knuckling the pen to stop my hand from shaking:

1. Put on your khaki shorts with the blue Gap T-shirt.
2. Brush your hair and teeth.
3. Go to the kitchen.
4. Eat egg-white omelette.
5. Lift weights (legs, today).
6. Make 200 shots.
7. Get rid of the letter and photo.

I read through the list. Just looking at the instructions, I feel a sense of calm returning. I make a mental note to take it easier at Park Terrace, to drink more water and stretch better after games. Everyone knows the heat makes people crazy.

# ILLA

_____
_____

EVERY EVENING DURING dinner, Illa and Mama watch the news together, and Illa feels relieved for how it fills the cavernous silence that has developed between them since the fight over Mercy's letters. There is something comforting about TV news anchors, Illa decides. Even when they're telling you horrible things, they look so put together, bringing order to the chaotic world they're forced, regretfully, to inform you about. When they say that strangely sterile word, _neonaticide,_ it sounds like science, like it could almost make sense.

"This is Joe Hartman, and he owns the Market Basket at the corner of LeBlanc and Main," says a male anchor with a well-coiffed pouf of hair. "The baby was found in the dumpster behind his store, just across the street from the high school. As we heard from Detective LaCroix at the press conference earlier today, an employee of Mr. Hartman's who was working the night that police speculate the baby was left recently gave a statement to the police. It may be the closest we'll come to eyewitness testimony in this complicated case. Joe, tell us what your employee saw that night."

"He couldn't see real good, Bill, but he told the detectives he heard something around one a.m. We got bulletproof glass on the windows, so it can get pretty foggy, but he told the detectives he thought he saw a young girl in one a them hooded sweatshirts by the bathrooms. But like I said, he had a hell of a time seeing clear through the glass."

"And how old was the girl? Did he say?"

"Thought she mighta been around fifteen, sixteen, but you know how it is with women, you get teenagers looking like they're thirty and grandmas who look the same way. Hard to tell."

"And what color was the sweatshirt, did you say, Joe?"

"Told Detective LaCroix it was one a them navy and gold sweatshirts like all the high school kids wear."

"Thank you for the information, Joe. I'm sure everyone in town is grateful to your employee for keeping an eye out."

While the anchors try to maintain a neutral tone when reporting on the story, their furrowed brows the only indication that they have feelings on the matter, the townspeople they interview are less objective. "That girl better hope I don't meet her in a dark alley someday," one woman says. Another says, "I hear there's a special reckoning for baby killers down at Henley." The protestor with the short black hair says she hopes that lawmakers will do what's right and pass the parental notification law *because maybe advice from a mom or dad could have prevented this kind of tragedy.* One policeman mentions the large amount of blood at the scene and speculates that perhaps the mother hemorrhaged and passed away; he says they've stopped checking the hospitals and are now searching morgue records. Finally, Beau Putnam comes on, talking about the demonic nature of the crime and the reward he's offering for any tips leading to the capture of the killer. Mama asks Illa to change the channel, and she does.

"What's he frothing at the mouth about that baby for?" Mama says. "He wouldn't part with a cent of his money unless he stood to gain something by it."

"No idea," Illa replies. Then she remembers what Lennox said about Beau's plan to run for mayor, that he'll need a miracle to win. Maybe the LeBlanc tragedy is Beau Putnam's twisted version of a miracle.

––––––––

AFTER DINNER, ILLA goes for a drive. The tension between her and Mama is crazy-making. As she drives, she thinks that this is how they will lose each other, slowly, like Pangaea breaking into the continents.

Passing Park Terrace, emptied of players for the day, Illa remembers that at least one good thing came of that awful night in June when she and Mercy fought. Finally, Illa got her contest shot, a singular image of Mercy dancing in celebration after a baseline-to-baseline drive, tongue out, eyes wide with disbelief at her own physical genius. *Euphoric sport.* Hell, yes. Everything about the picture— the framing, the saturated sunset colors, the glint of the metal net against the darkness of the surrounding trees—was perfect.

From the darkroom, Illa had shouted with joy as the shot emerged from the murk of developing fluid and Lennox had hurried in to see what was wrong. *Dude,* he'd said. *Excellent shot. So tight.* From him, the highest possible praise. At the eleventh hour, she stuffed the photo into an envelope and mailed it express to 4 Times Square. She also kept a copy in her backpack so she could look at it from time to time, because seeing it made her feel proud and happy, and she needed a little of that this summer. The contest website said they'd notify winners by February.

After that evening's news story, she feels drawn to the crime scene, so she drives to the Market Basket lot and snaps a few photos from her car window. The college students positioned near the dumpster barely blink as she clicks away, probably inured by the media bombardment from earlier in the summer.

Cruising away from the convenience store, she sees that the street has been blanketed with posters. They are simple and striking, black letters on a white background, and they hang alongside the colorful flyers advertising Zydeco and country bands at the Pelican Club and the Rodair. HELP US FIND HER, $10,000 REWARD FOR INFORMATION IN LEBLANC BABY CASE, they read.

Illa pulls to the curb, grabs her camera, and takes half a dozen snaps of one of the signs, taped crookedly inside the window of a payday loan place. After a couple of minutes, a man appears behind the door, where he hovers, arms crossed over his chest, until she replaces the cap on her lens and slides back into her car. She glances in the rearview mirror and sees that he has come out onto the sidewalk and is staring after her. She sees him writing something on his palm, probably her plate number, and wonders if, once inside, he'll phone the tip line with the information.

———————

AS THE NEWS of the reward spreads, and after the eyewitness report, the tip line sees a surge in calls. Messages spring up on church marquees: WHEN YOU ARRIVE AT THE GATES, WILL YOU BE ABLE TO TELL HIM YOU PROTECTED THE UNBORN? and ABORTION IS MURDER and LORD, PRESERVE THE VIRTUE OF THE GIRLS OF PORT SABINE. Mayor Sanchez says the town is engaged in a robust investigation, but that in cases like these, barring better physical evidence, it's very difficult to find the perpetrator. Beau Putnam responds by saying that Sanchez is soft on crime. Because the local news channels love both a political dogfight and a loose cannon, they return to Beau again and again, until it's almost as if he's the official spokesman for the case. Even though Beau hasn't announced his candidacy, people start rallying around him. They're unhappy with the slow progress on the case. They want assurances that it will be solved, and Beau is ready with the strong words they want to hear.

Illa watches as fear grows its tendrils through the girls of Port Sabine. At Sonic, she overhears rumors about girls called in to the station for questioning, about rape and broken condoms and so-and-so who thought his cousin might have been pregnant but then never had a baby. When girls talk about the case, crunching ice from their empty Styrofoam cups, they seem ill at ease, dropping their voices low and looking over their shoulders as if to catch someone watching them.

You were always watched, Illa wants to tell them. In your bikinis at the river, at the Sonic, cruising the seawall hanging out of your friend's car, tanned arms held aloft, shrieking with joy. All over this town, people watch you because you're young and radiant, and you make them desire things: to touch you, to be you. Or at least to be as free as you.

One night, when a sophomore named Katie Dirks skates up to deliver Illa's diet cherry limeade, some tubby punk in a Ford truck heckles her, invoking the LeBlanc baby, her mother, her short shorts and nice ass. As the girl counts out Illa's change, she says: "You'd think being a girl was the fucking crime."

---

RETURNING FROM THE pharmacy one Tuesday in late July, Illa pulls alongside the curb in front of the house. Lingering by the car, not wanting to go inside just yet, she takes stock of the neighborhood. The homes on Galvez Street are modest but neatly kept, with crepe myrtle blooming decadently from every yard, the roots of ancient pecan trees coming up through the sidewalk like the tentacles of sea monsters. Farther down the street, someone is grilling, the scent of singed meat carrying on the torpid breeze. Illa's house sits on a large corner lot, partially hidden from view of the street by oaks, palms, banana trees, and a tropical thicket of hibiscus and oleander bushes. A tall wrought-iron fence separates the yard from Mr. Alvarez's, and bamboo runs wild along the barrier.

The family who lived there before them had abandoned the house; they'd fallen months behind on the mortgage, and Mama bought it cheap at auction back when she drew a paycheck from the refinery. *Two stories, Illa,* her mother stressed to her when they pulled up in front of the house for the first time. With its paint-bare cedarwood planks made gray by weather and neglect, and a turret that was righteously out of place among the clapboard ranch styles, the house on Galvez Street looked to Illa like something out of a Tim Burton movie—haunted, whimsical, and completely unsuited to daily life. And since the day Mama could no longer move up and down the stairs she'd been so proud to own, it carries the whiff of tragedy.

Illa finds Mama in the kitchen looking shifty-eyed. "Hey," she says, surveying the room.

"Hello!" Mama says too cheerily. She smiles broadly, but there's something wrong—one of her teeth is black. Illa leans in to get a better look. She's pretty sure it's Oreo cookie. She goes to the sink, opens the cabinet door beneath it, and looks into the trash can.

"Illa?" Mama says.

Illa moves toward the door to the garage.

"Sweetie?" Mama calls after her.

Illa unties the full trash bag that sits waiting to be put out come trash day, and sure enough, there's the telltale blue of an Oreo bag. Two, actually, both empty. But how did Mama manage to get them when she doesn't even drive?

Back inside, Illa washes her hands. "You know you're not sup-posed to eat that junk." She can't bring herself to look at her mother, so she speaks to her own distorted reflection in the faucet.

"I just treat myself every once in a while, I didn't eat it all at once . . ."

"Where'd you get it?"

"That's none of your business."

"Goddammit, Mama, if that's not my business, I don't know what is, seeing as I'm the one trying to keep you alive, and that trash bag is chock-full of things that'll kill you."

Her mother looks at the floor. "Your life would be easier if I were dead," she says, folding her hands in front of her and staring at them.

"My life would be easier if I had a *mother*. Sometimes you act like you've forgotten that you were one of the lucky ones that day."

"You haven't got a shred of love left for me," Mama says, her breathing uneven from holding back tears.

"Mama . . ."

"You've saved it all up for a girl who doesn't even know your name."

Illa looks at her sharply. "What are you talking about?"

"I saw the photo in your backpack, Illa. And you never shut up about her during the season."

"How dare you look through—"

"Take my advice and don't waste your time on Mercy Louis. No use loving a girl raised by Evelia Boudreaux." Mama dabs at her runny nose, her pale skin pearlescent from sweat.

"You're just jealous of Mercy," Illa says. "That's why you never told me about Charmaine or the letters. That's why you read all of them."

"I read them looking for the apology Charmaine owes me!" Mama says. "I'm sick of feeling like shit every time I think about her."

"If Charmaine's mad at you, she probably has a damned good reason."

"Don't go talking about things you know nothing about. It was Evelia who crushed Char. By the time that woman got finished with her, the girl was the walking dead."

Mama's words remind Illa of Charmaine's warning to Mercy in the letter: *Get out of that house.* Eager for whatever information

Mama has, Illa swallows her indignation and asks: "What do you mean, *crushed* her?"

But Mama, injured by the pointed exchange, ignores the question. "I'll need my insulin," she says.

Illa sighs, exasperated. "What's the point?"

"Illa, please . . ."

"No, really. What's the point, Mama, when you're obviously hell-bent on staying put in that chair."

"You know I can't do the shot without you," Mama says quietly.

Illa has more than a minute; she has an hour, an evening, a day, weeks, years, her whole frigging life, to spend nursing Mama. This is her sorry destiny.

"You never even tried to get out of the chair," Illa says. "Insurance covered everything, all the physical therapy. Mr. Alvarez drove you there every day. All you had to do was show up."

From the cupboard to the left of the sink, Illa pulls out the insulin kit, then yanks open the fridge to grab a vial. She washes her hands, then swabs the top of the vial and sticks the needle in it. Mama lifts her shirtsleeve to expose the stippled white flesh of her upper arm. Illa jams in the needle, too hard, judging by the way Mama sucks air between her teeth.

"Beau Putnam is going to run for mayor," Illa says. "He'll announce at the Purity Ball."

The look on Mama's face wavers somewhere between pain and surprise. After a long pause, Mama says, "He's just arrogant enough to do that, isn't he?" Then a mirthless laugh. "Thinks he's untouchable, and why should he believe any different? If I'd gotten away with murder and managed to hang on to my fortune in the meantime, I'd think I was bulletproof, too."

Illa thinks of Annie Putnam, the haughty upward tilt of her chin, the way successes accumulate around her, her friendship with Mercy, the dozens of teachers and students—boys, especially—vying for her attention. Is it luck that allows people like the Putnams to thrive? Or is it fate, the inevitable result of their ruthlessness?

"You know they never found any evidence of wrongdoing on Beau's part, Mama," Illa says, regaining her composure. She doesn't like defending Beau, but she likes Mama's victimhood even less.

"Don't think OSHA looked too hard after it was clear that Sands would pay its way out of the mess . . . the idea that they could put a price tag on my legs, all those plaintiffs' attorneys happy with any settlement they could get . . ."

"But Mama," Illa says. "You're alive. At least you're alive."

The newscaster's voice fills the silence until Mama, staring out the window, says, "Is that what this is?"

# MERCY

—————   —————

SOMETHING IS WRONG with my arm. After the episode in my room, I made sure to stretch every day, massage
it with Icy Hot. I even put a heating pad to it after games. But the
bad feeling came back and my arm went wild again. Cold showers,
hot showers, bench presses, wind sprints. No matter what I try, the
sneezy feeling returns to set my arm jerking. I mean, it's not contin-
uous, the twitching, it only comes on a few times a day. But when it
does, it lasts minutes. It frightens me.

The past few nights, I've avoided Park Terrace. I can't play ball
like this. If the tics struck during a game, word might get out that
Mercy Louis has lost her touch. Even in summer, scouts have eyes
and ears everywhere, especially the playgrounds. After the semifinal,
I've got to be careful; Coach says I have only one more shot with this
season, and I've got to be perfect.

Because Travis and I usually meet up at the park, I haven't seen
him lately, either. Maybe it's for the best. Perhaps this affliction is
God's way of telling me to give up the boy.

A FEW DAYS before Annie's Purity Ball, I see Witness Louis coming out of the pool hall on LeBlanc Avenue. What's he doing hanging around? I squint to see him better. The constant sun of the rig has aged him, though he's no more than forty. It's been years, but I'd know that face anywhere. Handsome, in a hard-living way. Nose belonging to a richer man, someone descended from nobility, maybe—straight and thin. Eyes green and shrewd. Severe hairline. He's just as tall and ropy as before, but he's lost the crazed look that made me cry out when he grabbed me at the door those years ago.

He's with another man whose pants hang precariously beneath his big belly, whose bald head glows red with sunburn. Next to this round man, Witness looks gaunt. *Dad,* I think now, though I've never called him that. It just pops into my head, and immediately, I feel foolish.

There's a poster of the team taped to the saloon door, and I wonder if he noticed my name and picture there when he went in. I cross the street like I have somewhere to be.

"Hi, Witness," I say.

He stares at me, his eyes bleary from drink. I see a hint of recognition take root there.

"Hello, sweetheart," he says, then lights a cigarette.

His friend leers at me.

"Hi," I say again. I realize I don't have much to say to this man, so I ask the only thing that pops into my mind. "Do you know who I am?"

He laughs. "Sure I do," he says, kicking at the sidewalk with the scuffed toe of his work boot.

*Liar,* I think.

"Who, then?" I press, steeling myself for the worst.

"Girlie, you got a boyfriend?" the round man asks. He laughs, then spits, chaw-dark saliva clinging to his chin.

"Hell, Darryl, this here's my daughter." Witness smiles at me.

"What you need, hon? Need some cash?" Before I can answer, he reaches in his pocket, pulls a twenty-dollar bill from his wallet.

"Wit, you ain't got no daughter, or the devil hisself has titties."

I wait for Witness to correct the man, but he just grins and spits.

"No," I say, flustered. "No, thank you." This sets the two of them laughing and as I walk away, the fat man wolf-whistles after me.

---

PARK TERRACE IS empty this time of day; it's too deadly hot for basketball. As I dribble, the ball can't hit my palm hard enough. *Hell with finesse,* I think; I want to smash something. Lines from the poem Travis and I listened to on our first date come back to me:

> *When Sonny Boy's mama died*
> *He played nonstop all day, so hard*
> *Our backboard splintered.*

At the elbow, I hoist the ball overhead and launch it at the backboard. It bangs hard and ricochets back to half-court. I chase it down, take two big dribbles, jump-stop on the opposite elbow, shoot. Repeat. Repeat. Repeat. My body goes slippery with sweat; I'm not breathing so much as growling.

I play until I vomit onto the cedar chips at the court's edge. I feel faint, all the liquid drained out of me—sweat and tears and bile. But I keep going, squaring up for an eighteen-footer. Just before releasing the shot, I get that strange feeling from before, and the shot swings way wide, as if I'm not aiming at all. Then the downward thrusts in my arm start again, *one two.*

I chase my rebound, hoist up another shot that flies wide again. This time I have to stop because my shooting arm is so painfully tight. The ball rolls under a bench staked in the cedar chips. I follow but don't pick it up, instead collapsing on the bench.

In the afternoon's stillness hangs the question I can no longer avoid, which comes in rhythm with my gasping: *What. On. Earth. Is. Happening. To. Me.*

---

AFTER THIS AFTERNOON, I'm desperate for company. I need to tell someone about Witness, about my arm. At Annie's house, I try the gate, but the old code no longer works. When I buzz the house, no one answers.

I pound the steering wheel in frustration. "Come on, Annie!" I shout out the car window. "I *need* you!"

Staring up at the house, I see a curtain flutter on the third floor. Mrs. Putnam. What does she think of the Purity Ball, the LeBlanc baby? Does she even know about these things, or is she so cut off that news no longer filters up to her?

Out of options, I wind up sitting next to Travis on the riverbank, my bare toes pressed into the cool mud. For now, my arm has stopped its haunted-house act. He tells me how much he missed me, strokes my hair as I lean in to him.

After a time, I tell Travis about Witness. I think: *You asked for my story, so here is just one ugly part of it.* For a long while, Travis doesn't say anything, just holds me close. I'm worried my arm will start up again, but for now it's still. Through his thin white undershirt, I feel the heat of his chest, imagine his heart pumping the blood that allows him to hold me, to form the words *I'm so sorry.* My tears have made the fabric of his shirt transparent in places.

"What are you sorry for?" I ask, speaking into his chest. I don't want to look up, to remove my cheek from this warmth. "It's got nothing to do with you." I think of that word, *sorry,* in Charmaine's letter. From her it's not enough; from Travis it's too much. Useless thing.

"Because you deserve better, Mercy," he says. "You deserve the best."

"I need you closer to me," I say.

"Closer than this?" He laughs.

"Yes," I say. "Closer."

Despite the heat, I'm shivering. If Maw Maw is right, and all of this will come to an end in just a few months—the river, this town, Witness, Charmaine, basketball—then, God forgive me, but I cannot go a day longer without love; if my time is almost at an end, then please, let me revel in this boy who loves me. I am only a daughter of Eve, after all.

Travis grabs my shoulder and, quicklike, spins me over so that I am just under his face. I catch my breath, stare into the clean cavities of his nostrils. The blue twilight spreads out behind him. Eyes darting in their sockets, he studies my face. "Are you sure?"

"You're the best thing I have," I say.

"I love you," he says. "So much."

"Say it again."

"I love you." He thrusts his nose in the air and howls: "I love you!"

"Softer."

Near my ear, the warm whisper like a tickle: "I love you."

I want to say it back but can't; when I go to speak, I only goggle up at him like a fool, surprised by my own muteness. Maybe people are like apple trees; I read somewhere that they need years of care before they bear fruit. Can Travis love me for the time it takes me to learn how to do this?

I feel the sharp protrusions of his hip bones, the heat of his belly. My bones are liquid over the ground. Slowly, he sinks in to me. I feel the mounds of grass beneath the quilt pressing into my back. *Closer, closer.* I wrap my arms around him and pull hard until I feel his whole weight crushing me. His skin smells of sweat and salt and something else, the sweetness of pine needles baked in the sun. Our breathing becomes matched. Then I kiss him, pushing my tongue into his mouth. I press my face up into the concave space between his chest muscles, where I can feel the warmth of his blood beneath his skin. I never want to let go.

"Come on, come with me," Travis says. Quickly, we climb into his truck and speed away, leaving our bodies' indention in the riverbank. I try not to think. He drives us exactly where I hoped he would, into the great silence of the forest, with its hushed and hidden places. We park a mile in, beneath a curtain of kudzu. Travis rolls down the windows, turns off the ignition. Together, we clamber onto the rear bench. He strips off my mesh shorts, then my shirt.

Sitting back a moment, he tilts his head to one side. He has a funny expression on his face. What's the matter? I wonder, suddenly self-conscious. He shakes his head slowly. Then, because I can't bear it anymore, I ask him what's wrong.

"Wrong?" he says. "It's just . . . look at you." He places one of his big hands on each of my shoulders, then runs his fingers along my collarbone until his hands meet at my sternum. I shiver. "You're *ripped.*"

His face shines with admiration. In one easy movement, he pulls his T-shirt over his head, grabbing at the back of the collar. He may be skinny, but he's got nice arms, his torso washboard-flat and smooth. Taking my right hand and kissing it, he stretches my arm out long, makes like he's appraising it. "So this is the golden arm," he declares. "The one that scored all twelve hundred and eighty-seven of your career points?"

My poor stupid arm. For a minute, I'd almost forgotten about it. I fold it tight to me like it's a wounded animal. I pray that it won't start twitching in front of Travis.

"Come here," he says, pulling me into the V of his legs so my back is to his belly. The warmth of his breath against my hair, the whisper of kisses on my ear, along my shoulder. Where his skin meets mine, a borderline that threatens to go up in flames. His hardness against my rear. One word runs through my head: *want want want want.* It's a hollow word, a nasal cave of longing, everything else lost in its void. I am the word, nauseated with desire, emptied of all other feeling. His hand fits between my legs. With his fingers, he presses against my crotch. I feel my wetness against his skin and wonder if I will stain the car's upholstery. Forever, no matter what else passed between us, he would have my smell. I arch back and his other hand finds my breast. He groans softly.

Then, with urgency, he turns me around, pushes me flat against the seat. We kiss deeply, a hint of spearmint gum on his breath. *More,* I think. Or perhaps I say it, because he pauses and pulls away.

"Wait," he says. "Wait a second."

From his pocket, he gets his wallet, then slides something out. He unzips, and that's when I see what it is. A condom. He tears it open and starts to put it on. Something in me recoils at this. *Condom.* The word has seemed dirty to me since ninth-grade health class, when Mrs. Ancelet told us, *Don't trust boys who keep condoms within easy reach. It doesn't mean they're prepared; it means they're sleeping around.* Now what we're doing seems cheap. I panic, not wanting to lose the intensity from before.

"Don't," I say, putting my hand on his. He looks confused. "The condom. Just . . . it's okay."

He looks confused. "What do you mean?"

"I'm on the pill," I lie. "Because of my skin medication." I try to recall the name of Brittny's acne stuff. "Accutane."

"Oh," he says. "But what about . . . "

*"Please,* Travis," I plead. "I need you close to me *now."*

He slides into me, a look of astonishment on his face. Briefly, there's pain, not sharp but a dull tugging. My hands move with his narrow hips, I can feel him at the deepest part of me. *Union,* a round, full word, so much better than *want.*

Afterward, my thighs are sticky with blood; Travis cleans them with a kerchief he keeps in his back pocket, dampening the cloth with water from my thermos and rubbing it in soft circles. When he finishes, he kisses me down there, and then we lie sandwiched together on the seat for a spell. He hums a song I don't know, his voice a deep, pleasing vibration.

"I didn't want to pull out like that," he says. "But I thought I should."

"Mmmm," I say, lost in a pleasant fog.

"Damned if I know which way is north anymore," he says after a while, laughing.

*Sorry sorry sorry sorry,* I think. Everyone else is, why not me, too? It is so easy to say.

*"We are beautiful and dangerous,"* he says after a while, using the words of the Louisiana poet, tracing his finger along the curve of my waist. *Dangerous to whom?* I wonder. I'm uneasy. We're skin to skin but we're separate bodies once again, the feeling of completion gone. I remember Witness outside the pool hall, the way he dangled money between thumb and forefinger, the way he laughed at me, and I'm sunk low. This is what *they* did, he and Charmaine. *Sorry sorry sorry sorry.*

I go to open the door for some fresh air, but my hand freezes when I see her staring at me through the steamy window—Lucille Cloud. I cry out, scramble to depress the door's lock. When our eyes meet again, a smile hovers on her face.

"Shit," Travis says. "Where'd she come from?"

"Shhh," I hush him, pulling my shirt down over my head. I shimmy back into my shorts, hoping the dark is enough to keep Lucille from seeing too much. "Her cabin must be somewhere nearby."

She knocks on the window slowly, deliberately, *knock knock knock.* I can hear her dog whining on the other side of the door.

"Let's get out of here," Travis says.

He dislodges his shirt from between the bench and seat back, then propels himself behind the wheel. A fumbling for keys, then the engine sputters to life. Lucille steps back from the car as the tires spin in the mud before catching. At last the car bolts forward. As we gain some distance, I look back. Lucille is rooted to the same spot, watching us drive away. The dog howls, a baleful sound that makes me shiver. Exhaling, I climb into the front seat next to Travis.

Once we're well away from the spot, he says, "Sorry that Nutter Butter had to go and ruin things."

He puts his hand over mine and gives a squeeze, but he's right, the night is ruined. Any tenderness from our lovemaking has disappeared into the yellow moon like everything stolen or lost or forgotten. Guilt hangs on my heart. For a breath of pleasure, I have shed my innocence. I think of the times I've judged Annie and Charmaine, and here I am, not a bit different. All Maw Maw's teachings, all my hours in church and in prayer, and how easily I gave in. *Shame shame shame,* the car scolds as it rumbles over the ruts in the forest floor. I roll down the window for a breeze. After a while, lights appear through the trees.

"Look, it's the refinery," he says, pointing through the windshield. "Come to guide us home. Can't escape that place." He glances at me with his sideways smile, the light of the dashboard illuminating his face. We drive and drive, following those lights, which appear through the branches of the trees like fireflies, the only other light the shine of our headlights on the forest floor. Occasionally, they catch the eyes of creatures in the scrub and make them glow like lit matches.

I'm tired from my morning workout, from Witness and the sun, from sex, drained by what we've done. I feel the tiny particles of guilt, shame, and regret rising like sand fleas in a swarm around my organs. The truck noses through the broad darkness of the forest.

Soon the lights disappear. When we finally come out of the trees, we are several miles too far east, out by the old Garrison homestead. *Strange,* I think. Two kids born and raised in Port Sabine getting lost in territory we know like our own faces. I think of Maw Maw's story of the *feux follets,* the ghost lights, and wonder if what we saw wasn't the refinery at all but the glimmerings of that poor baby's unbaptized soul trying to find its way to heaven.

Maw Maw says that the devil's business is easy, it is the Lord's work that is hard. And it's true. What I did with Travis tonight was easy. Our bodies spoke to each other in a language that came so naturally, we mistook it for truth. At home, I curl into bed and start to cry. At first I cry for the baby, but soon I'm grieving for myself, for the letter that reminds me of all that I've lost, for what I've given away tonight. I open my mouth wide into the pillow so Maw Maw doesn't hear.

———

THE DAY OF Annie's Purity Ball arrives. She's still not speaking to me, but I hope that when she sees me up close, she'll realize that my friendship is worth more to her than the moral high ground.

The summer has given me more secrets than I can bear: Charmaine, my arm, Travis. When I try to pray for help, I feel false and wretched, like I have no right to ask for anything.

And now I understand how Annie has felt all this time, with no one to turn to but me. I hope she can put aside her anger and be my confessor as I was hers. I'll force the matter if I have to, corner her in a bathroom stall until she'll look me in the face. She's bigger than me, but I've always beaten her one-on-one, which is what makes our friendship possible in the first place. She has nothing but contempt for the people she beats, and she beats everyone at everything. Except me.

I put on the white dress I wore for my purity ceremony three years ago. Taking stock of myself in the mirror, I barely recognize the girl staring back. I feel far from the person I was at the start of the summer, the one blessed by the Holy Spirit with the gift of tongues, who promised her grandmother she wouldn't let trouble find her. The dress, with its white flounces and frills, feels childish next to my face, aged by this knowledge I shouldn't yet have. I tear off the dress and shove it under the bed, donning instead the navy sheath I keep for funerals.

But when Maw Maw sees me, she sends me back to my room to change, despite my protests that the dress is too small. When she secures the final pearl button at the top of the neck, I feel choked. I cough, tug at the collar. The tulle petticoat is scratchy against my legs. Still, I know there's no arguing the matter. I slip on my shell-pink shoes and climb into the Lincoln. There are faded stickers on the glove compartment, placed there by Charmaine when she was a girl. Only these shreds of evidence prove she was ever here at all.

Inside the gym, clusters of white balloons are tied to the backs of white plastic folding chairs, and white sheets bunch beneath the legs of cafeteria tables, which have been covered in white tablecloths. It looks like some kind of Winter Wonderland–themed prom, or maybe an insane asylum. Someone's hired a harpist, and the music floats through the air. On a projector screen, childhood photos of Annie flash up. She's scarcely recognizable to me behind the dusting of freckles and carefree grins. I notice that the photos don't show her past the age of twelve or so. They are all pre-painted-on-jeans-and-navel-ring Annie.

Maw Maw looks at me. "Who you are in this dress is more important than who you are in that uniform that everyone makes so much of."

"Yes ma'am," I say, cheeks hot with shame. I don't deserve this dress anymore, or this ring. Twisting the gold band on my finger, I get the prickly feeling and try to breathe through it, folding my arms over my chest. Temporarily, it seems to work.

I think back to Marilee Warren at church on the last day of school, how shrunken she looked in the black modesty dress. If I were brave, I would deliver myself to Pastor Parris now so that he could give me the dress to wear for everyone to see. The black angel, fallen.

Folks have started to find their name cards and sit down, the women dressed in white and ivory and cream, the men stiff in their cheap collared shirts and wide ties. We pass Mrs. Ancelet, the health teacher, sitting with the girls of the True Love Waits club. "Ceremony's fixing to start," Maw Maw says. Like an anxious wedding planner, she clutches a program listing the order of events, which she shows to me now: punch and appetizers first, then the ring ceremony and dance, then dinner. "Annie's probably in the bridal suite," she continues. *Bridal* because she's becoming a bride of Christ. "Go on and go see her, see if she needs any help getting fixed up."

Relieved to have an excuse to get away from the crowd, I head toward the bridal suite, which is just the locker room counter with the addition of a folding chair, a plug-in makeup mirror, and a hair dryer. On my way there, I spot Illa Stark standing alone at the edge of the collapsed bleachers. She's clutching a Dixie cup of punch, her eyes roaming the room. When she sees me, she startles, her owlish eyes grown even larger.

"Hey, Mercy," she says.

"What's up, Illa?"

She looks so tiny in her baggy white linen pants and jacket, like she's a head atop a wire mannequin. Looking at her in these shabby clothes, I feel bad for my outburst at the park.

"Hey," she says. "I wanted to apologize about what happened at Park Terrace. It was none of my business, and—"

"Don't give it another thought," I say. "Please. Just forget you ever saw those stupid letters."

"Okay," she says, looking at the floor, then back up at me. "You have a good summer?"

I consider this routine question, which to me, coming at this moment, seems important. "I wouldn't call it good," I say. "It was . . . complicated."

She laughs. "I know what you mean." She bounces slightly on the balls of her feet so that some of her punch splashes out of the cup and onto the hardwood. She kneels to mop it up. When she stands, she looks like she wants to say something more, her mouth parted.

"What is it, Illa?"

"Nothing." She stares into her cup. "It's nothing." She laughs nervously. "Hope Coach didn't see me spill, she'd tan my hide."

"See you in school," I say.

"See ya."

I'm not sure what I expect to find in the locker room—Annie with dyed black hair, wearing some shredded Goth dress, or perhaps no Annie at all—but it's certainly not this: she is sitting upright in a cap-sleeved antique white ball gown, applying pink cream blusher to the apples of her cheeks, her blond hair twisted into a sleek chignon punctuated with a pearl brooch. Through the mirror, our eyes meet and she smiles. I feel a physical pull toward her, like someone reunited with a long-lost twin.

"Hey, kiddo," she says. From her affectionate tone, I know I've been forgiven.

"You look beautiful."

"You know what they say." She smooths some stray hairs back into place. "The higher the hair, the closer to God." She grins.

"You're an idiot," I say. "You know that, right?"

"Believe me, I know it," she says. "I lost the plot there for a little while." Unconsciously, she brushes a hand across her collarbone, and I notice a crosshatching of welty pink scars peeking above the bodice of her dress, covered in cake makeup.

I wrap my arms around her shoulders and bury my face in her neck. When I look up, she has tears in her eyes. "I missed you, you fool," I say.

"I'm a stubborn bitch," she says. "Don't know how I thought I could live without you."

"You should have called," I say.

"Mers, it was . . . It got real bad." She dabs at her eyes, trying not to smudge the mascara. "I was so upset after dad announced the ball, I raged for weeks." She shakes her head. "Last week I hit bottom. Got wasted and took one of Dad's guns out of the safe." She pauses. "It was so bad I actually prayed. I started thinking maybe this ball wasn't such a stupid idea after all."

The door creaks and footsteps sound in the hall. BobbyAnn Baker, one of the officers of the Purity Coalition, peeks around the bank of bathroom stalls. "You almost ready?" she asks, smiling at Annie.

Annie glances at me and nods. "Just another minute."

"So long as it's not much more than that," BobbyAnn cautions. "You got one eager daddy out there, waiting for his little girl's promise." She beams, then disappears back down the hallway.

Annie rolls her eyes, a strangely comforting throwback to her old self. "Like this is anything more than leverage for Dad," she says.

"Your ma here?" I ask.

"No. Too much commotion for her nerves."

I try to find words of encouragement, but I don't have the energy for lies today. Annie takes my hands in hers. *Now is when I will tell her everything,* I think. Already, my heart feels lighter. But then she continues.

"I'm not going through all this for him. It's just, after this summer, I'm resolved to be good. I have to be good. Or at least better. But Mercy," she says, her eyes pleading. "I'm going to need you more than ever. To keep me on track. You'll be, like, my sponsor."

"Okay," I say.

"You look freaked out," she says. "It won't be hard. Just keep being your perfect self. I will be your disciple."

"Wow, Annie," I say, feeling woozy. "This is . . ."

Just like that, Travis's name disappears from my mouth. After the years I've spent hoping Annie would embrace the Lord and be saved, I can't sully the moment with talk of my sins.

"Come on, I expected at least a smile." She stands up, fluffs the full skirt of the gown. She looks as beautiful and virtuous as a Disney princess. I feel like I'm going to hurl.

"What about Lennox?" I ask.

"I broke it off," she says. "Honest to God, I think the boy was relieved. I mean, he loves me, but I think I scare him a little."

"I'm happy for you," I say. "Really."

"I'm going to get my act together. This whole stupid ball is my promise to *you,* Mercy. That I'm going to be the friend you deserve. This year I'm going to be *good.*" She hugs me, but I can barely manage to squeeze her back. *I'm not the person you think I am,* I want to say. "I'm so sorry about this summer," she says. Then, smiling: "How did you survive two and a half months without me?"

I feel awful, like I've betrayed her by being so happy with Travis while she was slicing up her skin in misery. "You better get out there," I say, giving her a peck on the cheek. Holding hands, we walk into the gym. When people see Annie, they stand up and clap. I take a seat at Maw Maw's table while Annie continues to the flower-banked platform at the front of the room, where Beau waits with Pastor Parris. The harpist has stopped playing for the vows, which have been typed up and placed on the tables so people can read along as Annie recites them.

"Welcome, everyone," Pastor Parris says. "We are gathered together today for a truly special occasion: to celebrate a young woman's commitment to lead a chaste life until she finds the man with whom Christ intends to yoke her." He clears his throat. "But this ceremony is about more than celebration. Let it also serve as a reminder that this commitment to chastity is a remarkable one, and that it is not shared by all the young women of our town. In the face of this summer's tragedy on LeBlanc Avenue, it's important to take the time to celebrate this commitment and to remember the dangers that exist outside of the chaste life."

I reach under the petticoat to drag my nails along my itchy legs, but that brings no relief. In these layers of tulle and satin, I feel like I might catch fire. He continues: "I would like to use this occasion to remind all of us how easy it is to be tainted by those around us who insist on a life of sin. I urge you to be on your guard with your neighbors. In John 6:70, Christ says, 'Have I not chosen you, the twelve, yet one of you is the devil!' It is His prophesy of Judas, and oh, it is a dreadful thing to be a devil and to sit down at the Lord's table, yet it happens every day. Somewhere the mother of that child is sitting down to dinner. Is she at your table? I urge you to take stock of your household. Christ knows our devils, though we may not. Pray for His guidance in identifying evildoers, and if you cannot help them, cast them from your lives and be warned: we are none so strong that we can afford to knowingly comingle with those who would see us brought low."

Staring at the hem of my dress, dirty from dragging on the ground, I remember Charmaine's ghostly face in the mirror when I was first struck by the twitching. I try to pray but can't form the words. Pastor Parris begins the vows.

PASTOR PARRIS: Hear, oh Lord, in this sacred hour, on this holy ground, our commitment to You and each other. Lord be

glorified as Anne Putnam commits. Believing that true love
waits—

ANNIE: Believing that true love waits—

PASTOR PARRIS: I make a commitment to God, myself, my family.

ANNIE: I make a commitment to God, myself, my family.

PASTOR PARRIS: To my friends, my future mate, and my future
children to a lifetime of purity.

ANNIE: To my friends, my future mate, and my future children
to a lifetime of purity.

PASTOR PARRIS: Including sexual abstinence from this day until
the day I enter a biblical marriage relationship.

ANNIE: Including sexual abstinence from this day until the day I
enter a biblical marriage relationship.

PASTOR PARRIS: May this ring be a reminder of your commitment
to purity.

He waits as Beau slides the ring onto Annie's finger, then
continues.

PASTOR PARRIS: It was given to you by someone who loves you
and supports you in this commitment. Wear it with the
knowledge that your purity is for God's glory. On your
wedding night, you are to give this ring to your spouse as a
celebration of promises given and promises kept. May it also
be a symbol of your continued sexual purity and the provision
found in the gift of your spouse.

Beau leans in to embrace Annie, who lets herself be held stiffly for
a few seconds before breaking away. When Annie turns toward us
to accept our applause, I notice the earlier serenity is gone from her
face, replaced by a dazed expression, her blue eyes large and search-

ing, her eyebrows raised as if in amazement at what she's done. My arm bumps once, twice against the bottom of the table, tinkling the ice in the glasses. Thankfully, all eyes are on Annie.

"Praise be to God," Maw Maw says.

Usually, I find comfort in church and ceremony—the familiar words spoken or sung, the feeling that God hovers somewhere nearby as we call His name. Today, though, I hear only *promises given and promises kept* and think, *How worthless and common a thing is a promise broken.* The world needs no ceremonies to commemorate them, for they are the rule and not the exception. When a server places a plate of food in front of me, I push it away; the sight of the chicken-fried steak swimming in gravy makes my stomach lurch.

"Mercy," someone says. I look up to see Coach Martin.

"Coach," I say, standing.

"No, no," she says. "Sit. Eat."

I sit but leave the food untouched. She eyes my plate, and I know what she's thinking. "I've pretty much been sticking to the team menu," I lie, thinking of all the junk food I've eaten with Travis, the burgers and shakes and funnel cakes, his mom's bread pudding and carrot cake.

She waves my words away. "By this point, I should be able to trust you to know what's good for yourself. It's okay to have a little grease in the summertime. Should burn off by the first practice." Her left eye winks almost imperceptibly. "Speaking of summertime," she goes on, taking a seat in a chair next to mine, "yours been good? Been eating, sleeping, and dreaming ball?"

"Absolutely," I say. Another lie. I've been eating, sleeping, and dreaming Travis.

"It takes total commitment, Mercy," she says. "But you know that. You know firsthand what happens when we let ourselves lose focus."

"Yes ma'am," I say.

Her face is stern; she pats my hand, which is closed tight around my dinner knife."I know how bad you want it, Mers," she says. "I trust you. You're my girl, and I'll do anything for you, understand? This year we're going to make it happen." Her eyes are determined, her brows kinked. She stands. "I'll see you in school next week." As she turns to go, she thumps me on the back, and the punch sloshes in my stomach. I exhale and push my plate back. The cream gravy has congealed on the cold meat. Around me, people busy themselves eating. *None of you care a flip about Annie,* I think. During dessert, Beau announces his candidacy for mayor.

"You just have to take one look at that beautiful girl of mine, wearing that white dress and that ring which signifies her covenant with God, to truly understand what this town is capable of. Whether it's on the basketball court or at these celebrations, our girls represent what we stand for. I promise you, we're going to catch the woman who put a stain on this town's reputation. From this point forward, only good things for Port Sabine!"

When he's done, I make for the door fast, waiting for Maw Maw in the car. I wonder how much Beau paid someone to come up with that slogan. I pull at the neckline of my dress, which seems to have shrunk a size in the last two hours. People stream out of the gym, but I pitch the seat all the way back and lie down so they can't see me through the windows. I'm so tired—tired of trying to be twice as good as other girls, tired of running from my fate. Even when I was perfect, I didn't gain anything by it—no state trophy, not a single person who really loved me. Even Annie's love is tainted by her huge need for me.

There's only one person who truly sees who I am and gives me the love I need. Travis. Just thinking about him melts me farther into the hot vinyl of the passenger seat.

THAT NIGHT, AFTER Maw Maw is asleep, I sneak out to Travis, jimmying the back window and dropping to the soft ground below. At the dock behind the house, we launch my skiff, paddling until we're far enough up the bayou to start the motor without waking Maw Maw. We fix a strobe to the bow and cruise through the inky water, cutting around stumps and thick patches of water hyacinths and lilies, the blooms closed up tight, awaiting the morning sun. Overhead, lacy pines and live oaks hung with ball moss block out the fingernail moon.

As we glide along, the strobe catches the eyes of a Seth peering out from the lily pads, the ancient curve of its skull just visible above the waterline. I shiver and scoot closer to Travis on the bench. A fisherman landed a twelve-footer in Bull Bayou last summer, shot it, and pulled it into his boat, but as he went to tag it, the gator knocked the man into the water, flipped the boat, and made its escape. Which means the creature still skulks somewhere in these waters.

"You know we've got more variety and quantity of poisonous snakes here than in any other place in the U.S.?" Travis whispers. "We got copperheads, coral snakes, water moccasins, three different kind of rattlesnake."

"Shush now," I say. "Tell me something good."

He moves his hand to my thigh, his fingers tracing an invisible pattern on my bare skin. "I love you," he says.

"*Again,*" I say, leaning back and dragging my fingers through the water.

"Mercy Louis, I love you so much, it might up and give me a heart attack."

The symphony of crickets, the croaking bass notes of the bull-frogs, his words transformed from a sound into an object that catches in my throat, drops into my chest.

"I love you, too," I whisper. The words feel right on my tongue, round and declarative and perfect, crumbling into sweetness like one of Sylvie's pecan sandies. He beams.

"How was the ball?" he asks.

I sigh. "It was awful. Just awful."

"Because of us?"

"At first, yeah, but then it was other stuff. Annie seems so fragile, and the way she *needs* me . . . it's a lot to deal with."

"She went the whole summer without you, and now all of a sudden she needs you again?"

"Yeah," I say. "It's like she wants me to be her watchdog." I lean in to him and let myself go soft.

"Sounds like you get a lot out of the bargain."

"Sarcasm doesn't become you, Mr. Salter." I run my hand along the knob of his anklebone, feel the soft elevation of veins there. "And then I saw Coach, and whenever she's around, I just feel so . . . never mind. I shouldn't complain, not after all she's done for me."

"That woman scares the crap out of me," he says. "I can't imagine what it's like playing for her."

"She's been like a mother to me," I say. "I don't know where I'd be without her and Maw Maw . . ." My voice cracks; I swallow hard, pinch the skin of my inner arm. "If you had any idea what my real mother was like . . ."

I cover my face with my hands, ashamed. Travis folds me into his arms. My hiccupping breath, his shushing, two more sounds in this loud, living night. "Baby baby baby," he whispers. "It's all right, it'll be okay."

*But how can you be sure?* I want to demand. *You don't know the truth of my life, you don't know anything about me, really.*

Once I calm down, he asks me what's wrong, and I say can we talk about it some other time. He nods because he's gentle like that, and also because I've scared him with my tears, I can tell by the graveness of his expression.

We're at the place where the bayou meets the Sabine River, so he cuts the motor and we drift for a spell in the open water, the moon visible now that we're out from beneath the trees.

"Tell me another story," he says. The boat moves with the water's gentle ripples, the cadence slow like a poem we're living inside. Travis moves to the opposite end of the boat, sets his feet on the wooden slat where I sit. I rest a hand on the thin ankle tucked inside his oversize sneaker. His ankle is rough with hair, and I think how personal it is to rest my hand there, on skin no one else touches.

"I'm tired of stories," I say. "You never know what's true or not."

Moon shadow plays on his face. His eyes are closed, his breathing steady. From somewhere farther up the river's mouth, the splash of a fish. I kneel in the bottom of the boat and move carefully to his side—I don't want to send us into the river reeds tickling the bottom of the boat. Burrowing into the warmth of him, I rest my head on his chest. He's put on cologne, a familiar smell I've come to love. He kisses me, and for a minute, we've escaped everything, Maw Maw and Annie and Coach and Charmaine; we float on the river, an island of us.

"Okay," he says. "You want happy?"

"After tonight?" I sigh. "I really do."

"You want fun?"

His enthusiasm is catching; I nod. Yes, yes. I want happy and fun. To think it was this easy all along: he offers, I accept.

"Smart girl." He reaches out and touches my cheek. "I know a place." We row for a while, passing beneath a stretch of highway where shadowy figures by the pylons cast lines in the darkness. Music echoes faintly across the water. Soon a small structure becomes visible through the trees, bathed in the light of dozens of neon signs advertising Lone Star and Shiner and Miller Lite. As we get closer, I see a small illuminated blue and white sign that reads RODAIR CLUB. Of course I've heard of it, the place is legendary. And there's no way

I'm supposed to be here, a dance hall on a Saturday night, where people two-step and make out and drink beer.

"What you hear is Steve Riley and the Mamou Playboys," Travis says. "Wish I could play the squeeze box like those guys. For dancing? Oooh, mama."

"I've never danced," I say, my nerves alight with the danger.

He looks at me, eyes wide with astonishment. "And you call yourself Cajun?" He hoots. "Girl, they're going to revoke your membership."

I shrug. "Maw Maw doesn't allow it."

"What about prom? You were on the court last year, so I know for a fact you were there."

"You know those are dances in name only."

He exhales loudly, *shhhhhiii*. His mouth is crookedy; I want to kiss it, so I do. Drawing back, I tell him I don't even like to dance, so why make a fuss about it?

"Ah, but how can you know you don't like it if you've never *done* it?" He's proud of his point, punctuates it by jabbing his finger in my direction.

"Look, it is what it is."

"First time for everything," he says. "Come on. Good Cajun music. The best. Ms. Boudreaux would have to approve of that. I'll give you some time to think it over. Here."

He takes two Tupperware containers from the plastic bag he brought on board. Inside, there's leftover boudin and fried crawdads, their skins blistery with cayenne. We eat greedily, and when we kiss, our lips burn with the pepper. From inside, the accordion wheezes, and I can hear boot heels stomping the floor, the occasional whoop from the crowd. Past the open front door, bodies spin by, whirling flashes of color.

"All right," I say, licking the last of the peppery grease from my fingers. "Take me dancing." Across the parking lot we walk, hand in hand, our feet crunching the oyster-shell gravel. On the outside, the place is shabby, like it's been cobbled together from scrap lumber. Inside, it's warmth and noise. Women in red lipstick, their hair teased up and shining, dance with men in Wranglers and pointy boots. The room smells of sour beer and fried things. Behind an ancient cash register, a woman with hair straight out of the sixties rings people up. Though we are on the wrong side of twenty-one, nobody gives us a second look; I don't see anyone from school, and people from church would never come here.

On the dance floor, another woman, head tilted back with laughter that can be heard over the sounds of the band, wears silver moccasins, and when she dances, her feet are a lightning blur. The men corkscrew their hips, shuffle their feet, twirl the women, the whole place so alive with movement, I can't help but tap my foot. The jumble of voices joke-telling, gossiping, cursing, promising, flirting. A man with a dimpled chin croons in plaintive French, the music pure heartbreak, and for a minute, I think of Maw Maw telling stories, I can conjure her pauses, the precise way she stresses a word. But because tonight my instructions are to *have fun,* I bury the thought.

Before I have time to protest, Travis grabs my hand and pulls me onto the floor, where the crowd parts momentarily before swallowing us into its circle. I have no idea what I'm doing, but it's of no consequence because Travis has good rhythm and, with a focused look, establishes us in a simple two-step, *one-two-two, one-two-two,* a hand at my waist, the other clasping mine tight, his sandy hair flopping with each step, the pearl buttons on his shirt glinting under the lights. We spin around and around the floor. Sometimes he lifts me clean off it, and I can't help myself, I laugh and laugh; something about moving like this, encircled by his arms, hair flying, turns me into one of the people whooping, *whooooo,* my cry melting into the crowd. In this moment I'm more in love with Travis than ever, and I wonder if what he said is true, if it's possible to die of love. It feels like a crashing wave and I'm tumbling around inside.

It's almost criminal when the band pauses to tune up fiddles and banjos and guitars and sip bourbon before moving on to the next song, their faces shiny with sweat. Slowly, we come down from our high, grinning like maniacs.

"See what you been missing, Louis?" he says before leaning in for a quick kiss.

"Good Lord," I say. "It's almost better than basketball."

"You want a beer?" he asks.

Because this is a night for new things, I nod, my whole body tingling. He returns with two icy cans of Lone Star, already popped, and we cheers before tilting them back and glugging, the liquid bubbly down my throat, my brain frozen by its cold. I wait for the roof to blow off the club, the hand of the Almighty swooping in to shake some sense into me, but nothing happens. I know it doesn't work that way; He's not a babysitter, like Annie wants me to be. He gave us free will, and the rest is up to us. But why make being good so hard? Why make a beer so delicious? Why make sex so very *very*? Forgive me, Lord, but it seems mean.

Soon the music starts up and we're off again, my head foggy from the beer, the lights bleeding together in a pleasing blur. We stay for hours. When the club closes, we pour out into the parking lot with the rest of the diehards, where we stare at the star-bright August sky. Necks craned upward, we try and fail to identify constellations, collapsing into each other with laughter, and I feel simultaneously that our lives will go on forever and that we will never be able to re-create this feeling ever again; it is too perfect.

Back in the boat, we drift far out into the water until the lights of the Rodair are no longer visible. Quietly, gently, for we are exhausted, Travis works over my neck, the cayenne on his tongue making my skin tingle. He unhooks my bra, pulls my shirt over my head, and looks at me. Carefully, he takes my nipple into his mouth, first one, then the next, and my body becomes flame, orange and dancing.

When we dock the boat out back of the stilt house, it's nearly three o'clock in the morning, the moon no longer jaundiced and sultry through the trees but white and high over the water. Travis gives me a leg up onto the balcony and, still wobbly from the beer, I hoist myself the rest of the way—it takes me three tries to get a toehold, grunting and grimacing all the while. Below me, I hear Travis laugh. Peering down at him, I raise my finger to my lips, *hush,* and shoo him away. He takes off running.

Though I don't want the night to end, I know I can't maintain this elation even if I try. Better to go to bed with the evening fizzing in my blood, the memories—for they are already that, memories—still dazzling. I turn to go inside.

And there is Maw Maw, ghostly behind the glass door in her long white nightgown, her eyes, nostrils, and mouth black holes in her pale face. The night swallows my scream.

"Do it," she says. "Do it this instant!"

I'm kneeling in front of the toilet, toothbrush in hand, the tile floor hard against my bare knees.

"Purge yourself, or I'll do it for you." The sobs come hard, tears and mucus pooling in my throat, a headache building behind my eyes under the bathroom's harsh dressing room bulbs. Moving behind me, she grabs my hair. "Have you forgotten what you come from, girl?" Gives a yank. "Easiest thing the devil ever did to gain a soul was give a person the demon alcohol, 'cause it does his job for him." She nudges my hand so that the tip of the toothbrush handle touches my lips. "Have the nerve to come home *chockay* like this, then you got to be willing to right a wrong. Now do it."

This is how the night ends, me with my head in a toilet bowl, heaving up what remains of the three Lone Stars and the boudin, the smells of bleach and vomit in my nose.

"Who were you with?" she asks.

"Annie," I gasp. "I was with Annie."

She leaves before I finish gagging myself. I do it again, and a third time, just to be sure I've gotten it all out, this sin that comes in rivers of sick.

# ILLA

THE FIRST DAY of school arrives in a blaze of stultifying heat that bubbles the tarred streets. It is nothing if not anti-climactic. Illa parks in the same assigned spot in the student lot, enters through the same double doors, passes the same tittering clusters of freshmen girls. Okay, maybe the girls are technically different, these ones fresh out of middle school, but they ignore Illa as handily as the last batch. The worst sameness of all is that Annie and Mercy are friends again; Illa could tell by watching them at the Purity Ball, their closeness in evidence through the conspiratorial looks and gestures and touches that have always defined them.

Whatever spark of hope Illa had that this year would be different is now extinguished. How can she compete with Annie Putnam, dark goddess, destroyer of mortal girls? Illa spends the rest of the day stewing over the fact that these hallways that had seemed so full of promise over the summer are now filled with people who don't give a damn for her dreams, people who don't need her other than to serve them—to take their homecoming and prom photos for the newspaper, to bring them water bottles and towels when they get subbed out. Senior year, she knows, is merely the fourth out of four required to earn her high school degree, and it will be made up of 180 days more or less like this one, which is to say, dull as dirt. Droopily, she makes her way from class to class, her whole body a resigned sigh.

The day would have been a complete wash if Illa hadn't run into Lennox in the parking lot after school, reflective aviators perched on his nose, curly hair teased up in a 'fro.

"Hey," he says. "A bunch of us are going to hit up the Death of Summer party at the Hotel Sabine tonight. Want to come? It's supposed to be crazy."

"And I look like someone to whom *crazy* would appeal?" Illa says.

"Come on, I know you're one of those chicks with a secret identity. You're, like, a burlesque dancer or a raver or an international chess champion on the side. Anyone who appears to be as straight as you always has a side gig." He grins.

"Illa Stark, PI," she says. "You found me out."

"Seriously, though, you coming to the party?"

"Sure," she says. "Is this thing really in the Hotel Sabine?"

The hotel closed after the explosion, when layoffs and sanctions brought business to a standstill. Now all the windows are busted out, the rooms transformed into terrariums by the flora that took root in the molding carpet.

"Yup, nine o'clock. It'll be like *The Shining,* ghosts mixing drinks, all kinds of spooky stuff."

"All work and no play, et cetera," Illa says.

"Let's hope no one goes murderously batshit."

On the way home, she cranks the radio; it doesn't matter what's on so long as it's loud. Is it possible to break your face smiling? Briefly, she considers stopping in the Shop 'n Save to buy one of those black spiral date books, just so she can write down the date and time of the party. Finally, she has somewhere to be. Maybe senior year won't be so terrible after all.

THAT NIGHT ILLA finds herself wondering, how does one get ready for a party? Not a stupid Purity Ball, where all the girls dress like cream puffs, but a *real* party. What do girls wear? It's not as if she has any girlie outfits to choose from, but she wants to be prepared for just how out of place she'll look in her Rocky Mountains and boots.

She studies her face in the mirror and decides that while she'd call herself passable before pretty, hers is not a face to be ashamed of: large brown eyes intersected by the straight bridge of a pointy nose that is counterbalanced by a wide mouth built of thin lips, all set in a round face like a child might draw atop the stick figures in her first family portrait. On many occasions she has compared herself unfavorably to an owl startled from its perch, comforting herself with the knowledge that owls appear both wise and ferocious, that they are birds of prey. She'd like to claim the owl as some kind of totem animal, but she knows that in truth, she's more field sparrow than owl.

Illa searches under Mama's sink for makeup. She's heard people remark on the mysterious transformations, both good and bad, undergone by girls over the summer, so maybe this is the night she will convince the jury of her peers that she has emerged from summer's fire smelted into someone interesting.

There beneath the pipes is a trove of dusty fragrance bottles and old lipsticks that smell of wax, accoutrements that speak of a hopeful femininity that neither she nor her mother practice. As Illa roots among the discarded compacts and stubby eyeliner pencils and half-empty blush pots, she realizes she has no idea what she's looking for, just a collection of words and vague notions picked up from paging through women's magazines at the doctor's office: *foundation smoky eye bold lip neutral palette.*

Eventually, she settles on a tube of plum-colored lipstick that looks brand new. As she presses it to her lips, she wonders for what occasion Mama purchased it originally. What secret desires made her lift that vivid shade from the drugstore shelf? Clumsily, Illa fills in her lower lip, then her Cupid's bow. Using a square of toilet paper, she does some damage control and then assesses herself in the mirror. The color makes her look older and happier. Does she appear to be someone capable of having fun, but not a dangerous amount? That's a quality Mercy probably looks for in a friend.

"You look nice," Mama says when Illa arrives downstairs. The television is on low, a sitcom with bad lighting. "You want me to do some eye makeup on you? Got to get gussied proper for a party. I used to be real good at eyes. When we went out dancing, all my girlfriends made me do theirs."

It's a peace offering, the most Mama has said to her since the binge episode.

"Sure," Illa replies.

"Let me get my gear," Mama says excitedly, wheeling to her bedroom and returning with a fistful of supplies. "Here, sit." She points to the dining chair and Illa takes a seat. "How about a dramatic eye with black liner? That was always my go-to. Can't go wrong with a classic."

"Whatever you think," Illa says. If it's horrible, she can always wipe it off in the car. Mama tells her to close her eyes, and she does, feeling her mother's fingertips skim her hairline and eyebrows like she's readying a canvas. The snap of plastic shadow containers opening, Mama's careful breathing as she leans close to Illa in order to get the right angle, the makeup brush dabbing against her skin in short, sure strokes. There's something luxurious about having another person touch your face, Illa thinks. She feels coddled, fussed over, for the first time in so long. It reminds her of when she was a little girl sick with a cold, tucked under blankets, Mama stroking her hair, kissing her hot forehead. Though Illa wants to follow up about Charmaine, she knows it would ruin the moment, so she holds her tongue. It's been so long since she and Mama have been together in a room like this, actually enjoying each other's company.

"Okay, now open." Mama leans back to examine her handiwork, nodding her approval. "Now for liner and mascara."

On the TV, a beautiful brunette brings a beer to a disheveled guy sitting on a couch, then says something with a smirk. With the volume this low, their voices are subaqueous, indistinct. The laugh track bleats on.

"Don't go crazy, I don't want to look like I'm trying too hard."

"Oh, honey, your mama knows makeup. Look up," she orders, running a pencil along Illa's lower lid, smudging the top outer corner with the edge of her thumb. "That's always the thing, making it look easy-breezy, even if you spent an hour in front of the mirror." She unscrews the top of the mascara, plunges it in and out of the tube, then rubs the brush against the tube's edge to wipe off the excess. "Look down."

It tickles a little as Mama tugs the brush along Illa's lashes, and she giggles. Mama giggles, too, before admonishing Illa to *hold still, for Pete's sake, or I'm going to put your eye out.* After fiddling with the finished product a minute, she sends Illa to the bathroom to judge the results. Expecting the worst, Illa is astonished to see that she looks pretty and even a touch mysterious.

"I love it!" Illa calls, leaning close to the mirror to examine this unfamiliar face. No response, just the sound of the TV turned up loud. Walking back into the kitchen, Illa says, "It's . . . just, wow." But Mama holds up her hand for quiet. She's staring at the television, where a reporter stands in front of the Market Basket, gesticulating.

"They found something in the woods," Mama says without taking her eyes off the screen. "A Port Sabine High School football sweatshirt. The blood's a match to the baby." She looks at Illa. "Chief McKinney says they'll focus the investigation on the school now."

SINCE THE EXODUS out of Port Sabine following the explosion, the warehouses, gambling halls, and saloons erected downtown during the boom stand empty, stripped of raw materials—bricks and windowpanes, copper piping and roof tiles. From this graveyard of buildings, the Hotel Sabine rises thirteen stories, its pocked facade like a relic of some war-torn place, the once manicured grounds now wild with weeds. Illa hears about petty crimes committed in the blighted hotel—arson and drug deals, homeless people arrested for vagrancy.

From the front, all the windows are dark, and briefly, she wonders if Lennox has played a prank on her. But as she pulls her car around back, she sees light flickering behind a dark sheet that billows from a fifth-floor window, hears a pulsing bass line. Grabbing her camera off the passenger seat, she gets out and walks quickly to the door. She feels like a radical going to some underground meeting. Someone has put a Mexican saint candle just inside the front door, which is propped open by a rubber flip-flop. Illa hesitates at the threshold. Across the street, the canal leading to the bay ripples in the muddy light of the rising moon. She's glad she decided to bring her camera along. If no one talks to her, she can avoid feeling like a doof by hiding behind it.

The stairwell is bathed in darkness. Clutching the cold metal railing for guidance, she huffs up the five flights of stairs. On the landing of the fifth floor, another saint candle glows, and when she opens the door, the hallway blazes with dozens more. The music is loud now, some shouty hip-hop song. The party occupies a large ballroom, revelers' shadows moving against the white walls. From the doorway, she looks for Lennox or Mercy. At this distance she can't distinguish faces, so she shoulders her way in, happy for the flanking bodies and candlelight. The room smells earthy, like the forest after a rain, a breeze fluttering the bottom edge of the bedsheet pinned over the room's only window. There are clusters of beach chairs scattered throughout the room.

"Here!" someone shouts above the din, thrusting a cold beer into her hand. She pops the top, takes a sip; it's bitter, cheap-tasting, but she drinks it down. Immediately, she feels safer, like she could float here anonymously for hours, drinking and swaying to the music. It's strange to see her classmates out of context like this, ungoverned by the school bell's directives or Mr. Long's surveillance. There's Travis Salter, Port Sabine High's resident beatnik poet, his guitar propped next to him. It surprises Illa to see Tiffany Barnes, her dirty-blond hair curled stiffly into twee ringlets.

Next to Tiffany stand Chole Gomez and Corinne Wolcott, Chole lip-synching animatedly to the song, her short dark ponytail whipping back and forth in time to the music. Looking around, Illa notices that people wear slightly different faces from those they put on for school, their expressions excitable, alert. She wonders if they've heard the news about the sweatshirt, and if that's to blame for the frisson of tension in the air. Or maybe all high school parties feel this way, thrilling but limned with danger.

The drill team girls, Abby Williams, Marilee Warren, and Mackenzie Wolcott, Corinne's twin sister, sit in a corner surveying the partygoers. They are like specters against the dark brick of the wall. Marilee's bare, lotioned shoulders look wet in the low light, a silver cross winking between her collarbones, a thick chestnut braid coiled over her shoulder. Instinctively, Illa raises her camera and, after checking that the flash is off, snaps a few quick photos, *click click click*. The act makes her feel powerful, as if these girls are performing for her, dancing, singing, flirting, and drinking in service to her art.

She decides to be the unofficial party photographer; she will find small moments of beauty and capture them. She's so tired of ugliness. Even her face, which she has grown so sick of looking at over the last few months, is fresher tonight. She rubs her lips together, enjoying the sticky feeling of the lipstick. With a long draw, she finishes her beer, places the empty atop the Tetris-like sculpture of cans someone has started. She wants to find Mercy; in the ballroom's dim light, her exquisiteness would be just muted enough to be believable. As Illa turns to make a pass around the room, she collides with Lennox, sending beer down his shirt. "Sorry!" she says. "Sorry about that."

"Happy to see you, too," he says with a laugh. Travis Salter passes them, and the two boys do the dude nod. "Leaving already?" Lennox asks her.

"Nah," she says. "I'm just going to check out what's happening around the room." She raises her camera as if in explanation. "This is wild. Fashion photogs pay good money to build sets this weird."

"Here," he says, reaching into the pocket of his cargo pants and pulling out a slim silver flask. "Mezcal for courage." She takes the flask from him and tips it back; the tequila burns down her throat, leaving a smoky aftertaste of forest fire. As she hands back the flask, she notices he's studying her face. "You look different," he says.

She puts a hand to her cheek, then quickly removes it. "Thanks?" she says uncertainly.

"I mean you look nice. Pretty."

She hopes the plum lipstick hasn't been discontinued, because now she wants to buy a dozen tubes of it. "Okay," she says before chiding herself for her stupid response. Now he probably thinks she's full of herself.

"You hear about the sweatshirt?" he asks.

"Yeah."

"Shit's about to get real. If anyone wasn't blaming y'all before, they are now."

*Y'all.* Sometimes she forgets she's one of them, a teenage girl. She hasn't even kissed a boy, how can she possibly be implicated?

"Can I ask you a favor?" he says.

"Sure, yeah."

"Check in on me every once in a while, okay? Annie's pretty wasted, and when she gets like this, she leaves no survivors. I mean, even though we're broken up and all . . ." He looks around to make sure no one's listening. "She's like catnip or something."

Illa's heart flip-flops. They broke up! "I don't know if I'm the one you want to call for backup. When you're dealing with Capone, you need the FBI, not the municipal police."

He chuckles. "Still, you got my back?"

"Always," she says.

She turns away from him to follow the celestial blur of candles lining the wall. Did Lennox break up with Annie, or was it the other way around? The answer matters, somehow. *Click click,* she takes a knee to get a good shot of one of the illumined saints. She wanders for a while, nodding hello to people who pass her in the darkness. She avoids the corners, where intertwined couples throw up monstrous eight-legged shadows. Soon she finds herself back out in the hallway, the dance beats absorbed by dozens of yards of damp carpet, the runway of candlelight gone. The doors are all closed except for the one on the end, cracked just enough for a wedge of light to emerge onto the carpet. As she approaches, she hears voices speaking in urgent cadences. Curious, she pushes the door open slightly and peeks in.

Perched on the windowsill facing each other are Mercy Louis and Travis Salter; her arms are folded protectively across her stomach, one leg dangling down the wall, the other tucked beneath her. She sniffs and then rubs under her eyes; she's crying. Travis sits cross-legged, one hand gripping the window frame for balance, his whole body leaned forward. Behind them, the canal glimmers, the wind-carved troughs in the water's surface alive with moonlight.

"But that doesn't mean we have to break up," Travis says. "I'm so sorry for what happened, but I just want to help. I want to be here for you."

Mercy doesn't look at him while he speaks, instead staring out the window. A white curtain billows over their heads like the sail of a ship. Up that high, they appear suspended in air.

"I'm beyond help," Mercy says, pulling back from him.

"But we love each other. Whatever we did, we did out of love. If you'll just let me help . . ."

"You don't understand," she says. "You're the *problem,* not the solution."

Quietly, Illa steps back from the door. As she hovers in the darkness, Travis says something else, but she can't make it out. Pressing her back against the wall to steady herself, she exhales. Mercy and Travis, dating. Or at least they *had* been up until a minute ago. Feeling bad for eavesdropping, she starts to retrace her steps down the hallway when she notices someone coming toward her. She doesn't see who it is until it's too late to duck and cover: Annie Putnam, beer in hand, standing so close that Illa can smell her yeasty breath, poorly masked by the peppermint gum she smacks loudly.

"Who's that?" Annie says, slurring slightly, wrinkling her nose in a squint.

"Illa."

"Oh," she says, sounding disappointed. "I'm looking for Mercy. She abandoned me, and I *need* her. I told her to come right back and not leave me *alone.* You seen her?"

"Yeah," Illa says, relieved that she knows the answer to Annie's question. "She's in the room at the end of the hall."

"Of course you know where she is, you little stalker." Annie sways forward slightly. "What the hell is she doing all the way down there"—beer sloshes from the can onto the carpet—"when she *knows* I need her close. It's a *party*. It's like my *Kryptonite*. There are boys *everywhere*." With each word, she grows more emphatic.

"I'm sorry," Illa ventures nervously, hoping it's what Annie wants to hear. But Annie pushes past, tottering into the blackness on her towering heels. Too late, Illa remembers Lennox's warning: *When she gets like this, she leaves no survivors.* A feeling of dread settles in Illa's stomach. *Come back,* Illa wants to say to Annie, who lingers in the open doorway before exclaiming loudly, "What the fuck? Mercy, what the *fuck* is this?"

The washing-machine rumble of voices too low to make out.

"*Mercy,*" Annie whines. "Your *boyfriend*, for God's sake?"

More garbled voices, then the sound of shushing.

"Don't *shush* me!" Annie shouts. "Please don't treat me like an idiot. How long has this been going on, anyway?"

A pause before an inaudible answer.

"Oh my God, you've been keeping this a secret from me for months? How can I be your best friend if you don't tell me *anything*? At the ball, we agreed to be closer than *ever*!"

*What have I done?* Illa wonders. It unnerves her to hear Annie Putnam so vulnerable, almost unhinged.

"You're all I have, Mers," Annie continues. "You're all I *have*. I *need* you, like, *right now*."

And then finally, Annie's crying, a muffled decrescendo overlapping with Mercy's maternal shushing. Illa darts back toward the ballroom. Dizzy from the alcohol and the scene she's just witnessed, she catches the doorframe to steady herself. A few girls are dancing to "Gangsta's Paradise"; guys are clustered around the boom box, riffling through the pile of CDs. Just then Abby Williams shoves by, clutching a giant Market Basket soda cup rattling with ice. She's wearing the black sheet from the window like a cape, and it fans out behind her as she beelines to Marilee, who is dancing next to Wyatt Bell, arms overhead, face tipped upward, hips grinding. In the dim light, Illa can just make out Abby's silhouette as she upends her Coke on Marilee's head. Marilee squeals and shrinks down, her soggy braid whipping back and forth as she shakes the liquid off.

"What the hell?" Wyatt says. Coke drips from the sleeves of his shirt.

"Fuck you, Wyatt!" Abby shouts.

"You're such a witch," Marilee squeaks. "That baby's probably your fault."

Abby darts to the window, where she hops nimbly onto the ledge, the fingertips of her left hand gripping the top of the frame, her right hand clutching the sheet. She looks like a superhero about to take flight. Someone cuts the music and the partiers go quiet.

"Abby, get down from there," Wyatt says, suddenly serious.

Illa finds Lennox standing in a corner, brow knitted in concern.

"Take it back!" Abby shrieks. "Take it back right fucking now!"

"Come on, Abby," Wyatt says, starting toward the windowsill.

"Don't fucking touch me or I swear, I'm jumping," Abby says over her shoulder.

Illa feels a hand warm at her waist. Lennox, watching the scene intently, has put his arm around her as if to protect her from what's happening. He pulls her closer, so that her cheek brushes his sleeve. He smells of shaving cream and dryer sheets. She pictures him doing the laundry at the apartment, separating his kid sister's and brother's whites and colors, and her chest swells.

"Abby, please," Marilee says. "I'm sorry, I didn't mean it."

"You don't care about me, don't even pretend like you care about me!"

"I was just—" Wyatt says.

"Just what?" Abby says. "I suppose you were going to marry us both, too? I know that's the only way you got Marilee into bed." Marilee puts her face in her hands and starts to cry, which seems to soften Abby. "I should've known better than to trust either of you assholes."

"Don't kill yourself!" Marilee pleads.

Abby jumps down from the ledge, pulls the sheet tight around her body. "Go to hell," she says, trying to muster what remains of her dignity. She stalks to the doorway through a gauntlet of onlookers and disappears. Someone cranks the music. Illa is afraid to move because then Lennox would let go of her and the moment would end, so she wills herself statue-still. Instead of backing away, Lennox faces her, putting both arms around her waist and pulling her tight to him, his forearms firm at her back, guiding her in to him so that soon they are swaying like one body, the bass resonating through them, directing their hips. His hands move to her ass, and he dips his head so they're cheek to cheek and then mouth to mouth, his lips warm, his tongue probing gently, and Illa feels like the wax pooling beneath the dancing flame in the saint candles, hot to the touch, reflecting a miraculous light.

On the drive home from the party, Illa tries to resurrect the moment with Lennox, that feeling in her stomach, the mammoth hunger to be closer and take more. It was so exquisite and terrifying that the memory seems not like a shadow of the lived experience but close to the experience itself. Turning off Main onto Galvez, she has to pull the car over and close her eyes. She feels a strong sense of melancholy, because she knows that even in her jubilation, she's lost something, the chance to be seventeen and kissing a boy for the first time.

With that kiss, she feels as if she's staked a flag to claim her place in the world. But now she knows she'll have to be ready to ricochet off others—to get a Coke dumped over her head, to jump from a window; to love and fight and fail. It all seems so painful, yet she's certain there will be no prize if she makes it to the end with an unmarked heart. So she mutters one of her ersatz prayers, this time to Venus, which shines like a diamond beauty mark on the face of the sky: *This year, let me see what my heart can bear. Break it if you must.*

———

THE DAY AFTER the sweatshirt was discovered in the woods, the Market Basket is again a media circus, busy with talking heads from what seems like every local news station in Texas and a few from Louisiana. Illa can see their bleached teeth, smell the hair spray from a hundred yards out. A few of them try to come onto school property to talk to the students, but Veryl Johnson, the parking lot attendant, shoos them back across the street. Near the dumpster, people holding candles and poster boards scrawled with Bible verses sit vigil alongside the angry college students. They are all crisis tourists who've come not on a pilgrimage made for their own salvation, as at Lourdes or the Dead Sea, but as a kind of widdershins journey of faith to save the girls of Port Sabine.

On the sidewalk lining the student lot, a deep-voiced preacher hollers. He wears business-casual attire, his face a withered raisin beneath sun-bleached hair. As students walk by, his voice rises in a throaty vibrato: "You who dress like whores, you who dress like common sluts in the way of this fallen country, may the Lord God bring righteous punishment on you! You will know punishment for this, rutting like dogs outside the sacrament of marriage, without the blessing of your Lord! A baby has died for your ways, and now you will be seized by God's judgment until you repent! Worry not about your precious computers and bank accounts but about your souls, for in a few months, Jesus Christ will return and take the righteous with Him and leave the rest to burn! Repent, you sinners!"

Illa's not a believer, but as she passes this man, his condemnation makes her feel blushingly glad of her androgynous cargo pants and baggy top. Such a funny thing, shame, that in the scramble to avoid it, you forget who has the right to shame you in the first place. For her, for all the girls of Port Sabine High, it is not this perma-tanned man sweating in his cheap suit, and yet they shrink from him as if they are guilty of these sins and worse.

From time to time during the day, Illa looks out the windows lining the senior hallway to assess the scene across the street, the news vans that come and go, the police car that remains in place, its headlights tuned on the high school, watchful. Principal Long calls a mandatory meeting of all the school's girls, in order to discuss the new development in the LeBlanc Avenue case. When the bell rings to signal last period, Illa exits Physics and lets herself be borne alone on the tide of girls heading for the gym—the nobodies and the somebodies, the smart-mouthed and the shy, the big-breasted and the prepubescent, the lost girls and the confident ones. Nearby, a piercing laugh that goes on too long, until someone shushes the offender. Girls loud-talk about their weekends to demonstrate nonchalance, but Illa knows they're scared. She knows this because *she's* scared, and she's only made it to first base a single time.

It takes several minutes for the crowd to filter into the bleachers. How strange to gather like this, she thinks, just the girls. The last time they were brought together en masse was in fifth grade, when they watched a video called *Changing Bodies, Changing Selves,* and then it was only Illa's grade, not the whole school. Illa remembers Mrs. Darnell, one of the fifth-grade teachers, standing next to the VCR after the tape ended, saying, *Your life will change forever when you experience menarche, girls. You'll be women then, and you can expect people to treat you differently. Don't be afraid. It is a blessing, but it comes with many expectations.*

*But how will people know?* one girl asked. *If the bleeding is on the inside, how will they know to treat me different?* Mrs. Darnell just smiled a knowing smile and said, *Not to worry, dear. It will be obvious.* When she got her period at twelve, Illa spent the week terrified that every boy in school knew, bloodhounds on the scent of her hapless, maxi-pad-wearing rabbit.

Illa finds Mercy in the crowd and sits a row behind her. She looks pale and unhappy, her hair pulled back so tightly that Illa can see the skin puckering at the temples. It's the end of the day; gone are the sweet smells of vanilla lotions and berry body sprays from the morning, replaced by a more essential *themness.* It reminds Illa of the locker room after a tough practice, when the girls peel off their drenched clothing and walk around like hard-run derby horses, the small room filling with animal smells, the sour pheromones of sweat and blood and adrenaline.

On the gym floor, someone has erected a projector screen. Mrs. Ancelet, the health teacher, stands next to Mr. Long. Standing beside Mr. Long and Mrs. Ancelet, Chief McKinney practically dances, shifting his weight from foot to foot. Just then Annie Putnam jogs through the gym doors and bounds up the bleachers, where she slides in next to Mercy. Glancing over her shoulder, she catches sight of Illa and narrows her eyes. *Has she heard about me and Lennox?* Illa wonders.

Illa shifts her weight forward to try to hear their conversation over the noise of 250 girls whispering, sniffling, coughing.

"Chief looks like he's about to piss himself," Annie says.

Mercy manages a wan smile, which quickly fades back into the perfect architecture of her face. "I feel sick over this whole thing," she says.

"Everyone's so broken up about the baby, what about the mother? I mean, she was obviously too scared or poor to go to a real hospital . . ."

"I can't talk about this," Mercy says, massaging her right temple as if she has a headache.

"You brought it up," Annie says.

Mr. Long raises both hands and motions for silence. "Girls, girls, shhhhhh," he says, tapping the cordless mic. "By now, you've probably heard about new evidence they discovered in the marsh behind the Market Basket." They nod. Of course they've heard, the whole town has talked of nothing else for two days. "I thought we would take this opportunity to go over what happened. We'll let Chief McKinney take the lead."

McKinney's speech is brief. He asks them to come talk to him or call the hotline if they know anything about the incident. He says they aren't in trouble, but does he think they're stupid? They know that emergency meetings called by the principal mean *someone* is in trouble. A crime has been committed, he says, and if they know anything, they're obliged to say. Not to seem too obvious, but have any of their friends been pregnant lately? Or gained weight over the last few months? Maybe they know someone who used to wear tight clothing but suddenly started to wear sweats? What about someone who's been depressed or not really herself lately?

"He just described pretty much every teenage girl ever," someone behind Illa mumbles.

"We have a potential eyewitness," Chief McKinney says, continuing to move back and forth on the balls of his feet like a prizefighter. "And he's given us cause to believe the culprit is a young woman around your age. That, coupled with the football sweatshirt, means that we are fairly certain it's a girl at this school."

Illa's skin prickles as a murmur sweeps through the bleachers.

"Any questions?" The chief scans the room. "You in the red sweatshirt," he says, pointing to someone behind Illa. She strains to see who is brave or stupid enough to draw attention to herself at that moment. It's Ginny Collier, a junior, one of those smart-ass girls with colored streaks in her hair and big boobs that she hides beneath Alice in Chains and Korn T-shirts.

"Uh, yeah, Chief. I got a couple questions, the first being, wasn't it a football sweatshirt, so, like, why aren't all the football players here listening to this?"

"That's an excellent question," he says, nodding. "In any investigation, we've got to start at the beginning, and when you're dealing with a baby, the mama is always the beginning."

"And the second thing is, well, what if you just had a really shitty summer and ate Snickers all the time and got real fat but don't have nothing to do with that baby?"

Some snorts and stifled laughter.

"If you'll come see me after the assembly . . ." Chief said, his face flushed.

Ginny points a few rows in front of her. "Like Kelsey White up there, I mean, she can't help it, she's just big-boned . . ." The ensuing exclamations and groans drown her out, and in two quick leaps, Kelsey is in Ginny's face, her belly spilling over too-tight jeans as she lunges at her accuser.

"Girls!" Mr. Long hollers, but he's too far away to prevent Ginny's bloodied nose and the crimson handprint across Kelsey's pockmarked cheek. Once he does pry them apart, he admonishes them by saying that was no way for young ladies to behave, to which Ginny replies that as far as she can see, weren't none of them in that room ladies, just some titless girls. "Another word and you'll get corporal, I guarantee it," he says, so she sullenly allows herself be led down the steps to the floor and escorted out of the gym by Mrs. Ancelet.

Mercy stands abruptly and starts picking her way down the bleachers. Girls seated nearby stare after her.

"Wait a sec," Annie calls after her. "Mers!"

Illa wants to follow Mercy but stays seated, afraid of what Annie might say. Principal Long dismisses them to last period. On her way out, Illa stops in the locker room to see if Mercy has taken refuge there. The lights are off, the clock on the wall ticks loudly. She's about to walk through the door that leads back to the varsity lockers when Mercy shoulders through it, right arm crossed over her chest with the hand clamped on her left elbow like she's nursing an injury. Avoiding Illa's eyes, Mercy nods, then disappears into the gym. As the varsity door closes, the breath of air it releases smells strongly of vomit. When Illa checks the bathroom, one of the toilets is still running, the bowl filling with fresh water.

---

OVER THE NEXT weeks, Illa busies herself with schoolwork, trying to keep her mind occupied until the season starts. Since the party, things have been awkward with Lennox. When he sees her, he goes into formal editor mode, talking about event coverage and editorial content. He's painstakingly earnest, as if she might misread irony as flirtation. But what did she expect? That she'd show up to the journalism room the next day to a five-course meal served by candlelight in the darkroom? It was a party, they'd had too much tequila, and Abby threatening to throw herself out the window had made everyone overemotional. Lennox's response was a sentimental one, and Illa is glad, because now she has the memory of that night, which glows like a golden egg hidden deep within her. What's interesting is that she's most disappointed over their lost camaraderie, the easy rapport they developed over the last several years working together. He was her only real friend, and now she might have screwed that up.

Still, from time to time, she finds herself overcome by the urge to fold herself into him again and take his tongue into her mouth, friendship be damned. When she gets this feeling, she exits to the darkroom to wait it out, chewing the inside of her cheek, trying not to imagine what would happen if he followed her, the way their naked bodies would look in the room's red light, the way his bare skin would feel against hers. God, she can't wait for college, when hopefully she can just get drunk and let a semi-stranger unburden her of her virginity. She's so confused, she can't even decide if she'd rather kiss Lennox or Mercy, for fuck's sake.

Around school, girls are wary of each other. Illa notices less PDA in the hallways, fewer dress-code violations. There are a few odd incidents, which Lennox reports in the "In Brief" section of *The Wave*. Medication starts to disappear from the nurse's office, first just the harmless stuff—ibuprofen and acetaminophen—but later, the prescription meds from the locked drawer where Mrs. Ancelet keeps them on hand for the students with various diagnoses—Ritalin and Vicodin and Xanax and Prozac.

In the bathrooms and the parking lot, girl fights break out with such regularity that Ms. Custer, the school counselor, takes to patrolling the grounds. More than once, Illa sees her walking back to her office between two sulky offenders, a hand placed on each girl's back. One morning in mid-September, Illa hears a rumor that Chief McKinney, after a series of false tips and skimpy leads, has begun calling girls in for questioning. Or, rather, one girl: Marilee Warren.

"I'd be so totally freaked out," Illa hears a girl say from the bank of lockers next to hers as she gathers her books for morning classes.

"I know," another girl answers. "Such a shame. She's so *pretty,* too. Now her life's ruined."

"They're just questioning her, nerd."

"Lucinda Warren got herself knocked up and thrown in the pregnancy trailer a few years back. Who knew being a slut was genetic?"

"Wonder who it'll be next."

"My money's on Annie Putnam. Everyone knows that Purity Ball was a sham. I mean, come *on*! If you have to spend that much money to prove your virginity, something's fucked."

"Yeah, and now she's all *I'm such a good girl,* and *I've got the certificate from the pussy police.*"

"*Good* meaning she only gives head now."

"You are such a bitch."

Laughter as the girls' voices grow fainter down the hallway.

---

"I CALLED DETECTIVE LaCroix to find out what's going on with the hotline," Lennox says when Illa arrives in the journalism room later that afternoon. "He said they got a lot of false leads from over three hundred calls but that five contained good information."

*Three hundred* calls. In a town of ten thousand people, the number is shockingly high.

"Did he give names?" she asks.

Lennox shakes his head. "Said he couldn't comment on specifics."

"What about the rest of the tips?"

"Backbiting, finger-pointing. *So-and-so's a ho bag, just ask X boy. I know so-and-so is having sex, I saw a condom fall out of her backpack.* Women calling in neighbor girls they've caught making out in cars. People in this town seem to think that wearing a miniskirt and eyeliner counts as evidence."

"They feeling pressure to solve the case before the election?"

"He got a little defensive when I asked." Lennox exaggerates his accent in an approximation of Hamp LaCroix's. "*We put the pressure on ourselves, election or no. You put that in your article. I want people in this town to know we're serious about our jobs, but we got to do things the right way, not rely on a bunch of he-said, she-said.*"

"I hardly think that's the problem," Illa says. "If anything, girls feel like the cops are going to show up at any minute to cuff them and drag them away."

———————

IN EARLY OCTOBER, Coach calls her "refresher class." She doesn't waste time with housekeeping, just gets straight to the point and reminds the girls what's considered in-season contraband: cigarettes, drugs, booze, and boys. Hers are not empty threats, she reminds them. As if they need reminding. Sometimes she and Coach Thibodeaux case the hallways wielding yardsticks pinched from a classroom, waiting to catch Annie or Keisha or Melissa mooning over some boy so they can wedge a yardstick between the offenders.

"From now until March, no one's allowed inside your personal bubble of space except the girl you're guarding," Coach says. "I don't want to see a single one of my girls draped over some boy like a one-legged hooker at last call, hear?" She smirks. "This year, I even got the law on my side. Y'all are better off putting on a wimple and acting like nuns, way things are going."

The girls, normally jocular, don't so much as cough.

After lunch, Illa dumps the contents of her tray in the trash and wanders in the direction of her next class. When she passes through the senior hallway, she notices a disturbance at one of the lockers. A large group of students swarms around Abby Williams, who's pacing a short strip of hallway, her face blotchy with tears.

"What the fuck is that?" Abby wails. "I mean, who the fuck *does* something like that?"

Illa strains to see what has caused the commotion. Peering over the shoulders of her classmates, she catches sight of the offending locker. Someone has written BABYKILLING CUNT in permanent marker, along with a crude caricature of Abby sporting devil horns. Below the scrawled message is a graphic photo of a bloody fetus. Illa ducks away from the crowd and finds the nearest drinking fountain, where she takes several gulps of water, then splashes some on her face, trying to erase what she's seen.

———————

ILLA REREADS CHARMAINE'S letters until she's memorized everything about them, down to the zip code on the envelope. As she moves through her days, the lines float through her head. *Get out of there, go find someone you trust.* Even if Mercy hasn't personally shared the information with Illa, it's as if she is destined to have it in order to help protect Mercy. But from what, exactly?

———————

SOON IT'S BASKETBALL season. The first weeks of practices go well; the team is strong and focused. Most of the girls played summer league, so when they step onto the court, it's as if they've never left. Mercy looks game-ready, running plays from the top of the key, driving past defenders with such ease that Coach Martin stops play to make the defense run lines.

"Got a bunch of sleepwalkers on the job," she says. "Mercy pay you to make her look good? That it? Nike making sneakers out of bowling balls now?"

At one point, Annie fires a missile of a pass to Mercy at close range; the ball speeds through her fingertips and thumps her hard in the chest. When Mercy looks askance at Annie, rubbing the spot where the ball hit, Annie says sorry, but it's obvious she doesn't mean it. Illa remembers their argument at the party, Annie's bitterness over being left out about Travis. Nobody seems to think much of the pass, though, and practice continues. Coach seems almost jovial, ribbing the girls rather than talking to them in her usual lockjaw shorthand. The school board is set to announce the new Jodi Martin athletic complex at the first game that Friday.

After practice, Illa squirrels away in the equipment closet, pulling boxes of uniforms and warm-ups so she can wash out the summer mustiness. Flipping open the cardboard flaps, she buries her hands elbow-deep in the cool nylon of the jerseys, closes her hands around fistfuls of navy fabric. Beyond the door, the slow rhythm of a couple of basketballs being indolently dribbled. She breathes in the smell of the leather balls and mineral concrete and dank old uniforms and thinks *happiness*. She's sure the game will save them all by helping the town remember that it loves its girls.

# MERCY

THE STENCH CHOKES me awake, a fist of burlap down my throat. Still foggy from dreams, I thrash off the bed. The impact clears my head.

Living in a refinery town my whole life has prepared me for wretched odors, but this is the worst I can remember. When I stand up, I sway a little, my head filled with a dull ache like I've been wearing a headband for too long.

I stand and walk to the window. Drawing back the thin yellow curtain, I look toward the tree line, half expecting to see a fireball rising over the tops of the live oak trees like the day of the explosion, but there's only the same dozen plumes of smoke. I try breathing through my mouth, but it's no better, the smell so thick I can taste it on my tongue. Across town in that room covered with words, Travis is waking up. I pray he has an easier time of it than I did.

Today is my birthday. I am eighteen years old. A legal adult, but I don't feel like it. Before Travis and I broke up, Sylvie said that come October, she'd make me a 1-2-3-4 cake with pineapple and coconut, like she does for all her kids on their birthdays. I wonder if Travis remembers that today is my birthday, or if he's forgotten about me and moved on. I told him don't bother getting in touch, I won't return his calls. I made so many mistakes this summer, but when school started, I knew I did what was right. I don't guess loneliness knows the difference between right and wrong, though.

I remember the night of the Rodair: I never felt worse in my life. That's when I decided I had to break up with Travis. Snuck out to the Hotel Sabine to do it, but that's the last sneaking around I've done. I don't feel good or healed or anything like that, but at least I don't feel as bad as I did that night.

Charmaine has sent a cheap drugstore birthday card with a hokey message on the outside. When school started back up in August, so did the letters. They come in care of the front office, like the first one. She's wrong in the head, I've decided. Why else would she keep writing when she knows I'll never write back?

I read the letters just to confirm she's got a screw loose. Or maybe I'm trying to prove something to myself. But her notes still pierce me. I am the carnival lady in the leotard spinning on a wheel while she throws daggers in my direction. Only difference is, she isn't trying to miss; she aims straight for the heart. I will keep reading them, waiting for the day when I can open one and feel nothing at all. Then I'll know I've beaten her.

I pick up one of the recent letters off the vanity and reread it:

> *There are two sides to every story, I only want to tell*
> *mine. You are now older than I was when I had you. I*
> *was scared. I wasn't ready to love anyone. When you were*
> *born, you were so pure I was terrified I would drop you,*
> *mess you up. But that wasn't why I got wrecked and had*
> *to let you go. Someday I'll tell you, when I don't have*
> *to write it in a letter. The dope helped me forget your fat*

*little sweet-smelling body, the way it felt to nurse you. You
didn't cry when I left, you weren't old enough to know.
They say that attachment stuff happens later, once kids
realize what leaving means. The day I left, I just slipped
out the door like I was going to get milk, and you didn't
bat an eye.*

Practice is in an hour, first game's tomorrow. I decide I'm ready to
read the card. Here is what Charmaine says to me on my birthday:

*I have a dream most every night. It is you and me in a
diner and you reach your hand across the table and let me
hold it and when I touch it, it is like plugging something
into a socket—I feel a spark like electricity and then all
the love you've deserved these years flows out of me and
into you and when you let go I feel tired but so happy I
wake myself up because otherwise I might die of happiness
and I know you're not supposed to let yourself die in your
dreams. Please meet me Mercy. I just want to hold your
hand and see your face is all.*

And for the first time, she leaves a phone number. It messes with
your head to hurt over someone you don't even know. Seems I can't
get away from the fact that eighteen years and a day ago, I lived inside this person, neighbor to her heart and lungs.

The only phone in the stilt house is halfway down the hallway,
between my bedroom and the living room, on a rickety wooden
stand that trembles each time the phone rings. I creep to it, listening
for Maw Maw between steps. But she's still asleep, nothing but silence from her room.

I hold the receiver to my ear as if the dial tone will give me instructions. It's early yet. Is Charmaine asleep, too? I dial slowly, waiting as

each button sticks and pops up again. As the phone rings, I remember late nights on the bus back from away games in middle school, girls talking breathlessly in the dark about phoning boys—searching for words to say to them, the pauses when they could hear the whistling of the boys' breath. Some even wrote down questions to ask so they'd remember when nerves wiped their memories clean, writing *like* and *so* and *um* into the question so it would sound authentic, spontaneous. *Silly girls,* I thought at the time, and yet here I am, wishing I had a script of some sort.

The ringing clicks over and my heart flips, but it's just an answering machine. Not her voice, just some robot. *Please leave a message.* So I do. I tell her I don't believe I owe her anything, that the sooner she stops these selfish letters, the sooner I can forget about her. "You made your choice, now you got to live with it. Don't contact me again."

On my way out the door, Maw Maw calls to me to wait: "This stench . . ." she pauses. "I fear a dark tiding, Tee Mercy. Remember Isaiah, when God punished the women of Jerusalem for their vanity and pride by replacing their perfume with putrefaction. That baby has brought a curse on this town, mark it."

"It's my birthday, Maw Maw," I say, feeling like a child, but I need someone other than Charmaine to recognize the fact.

"Pray for that baby. Pray for yourself."

I'm late for practice. As I drive, my right hand goes stiff, refuses to close over the gearshift. I press my fingers against my jaw, extend the wrist in a stretch, shake the hand hard, then will my fingers to close over the stick. They do, but then the sneezy feeling comes on, my hand thrusting down once, twice, three times.

*Please, God, no.* When the light changes, the car glides forward in neutral, nosing toward the canal. A blue Chevy coming fast from the other direction honks as it flies past. *Dear Lord, help me, I place my life in your hands, please. I did wrong, but I repent. I gave him up, I want to be pure again. Forgive me!*

I grab the clutch and grind into gear, whipping back onto the road.

# ILLA

THURSDAY ARRIVES. ILLA hums as she prepares breakfast: egg whites and a grapefruit half for Mama, oatmeal for
her. It's the day before opening night, also Mercy's birthday. Illa
has the day circled in red on the calendar hanging in her room.
Nothing—not even the putrid smell from the refinery—can
dampen her mood today.

Good Lord, but the air is nasty. Illa imagines one of those green
cartoon clouds of stink settling over Port Sabine. She switches on
the television to see if there's any news about the stench, but a blond
woman is smiling and pointing to a weather map like nothing is out
of the ordinary.

Illa sets the eggs on the table, then spoons up a few mouthfuls of
oats, enough to get her to lunch without too much cramping. Kids in
class give her weird looks if her stomach gets too rumbly.

"Ma, breakfast," she calls.

When Mama wheels out of her bedroom, she's disheveled, her
nightgown stuck beneath her right thigh, exposing the scar-mangled
calves. Illa looks away and says, "Morning," grabbing her backpack.

"Team dinner tonight, so don't wait for me—I put some dinner fixings in the fridge for you."

"You smell that?"

"Sure," Illa answers. "Bet all of Mexico can smell it, too."

"Illa, honey, I was wondering . . . I've been feeling under the weather, and this smell's got me a little anxious . . ."

"Ma, call Mr. Alvarez if you need anything, but I've got to go or I'll be late for practice." She gives her mother a quick kiss on the cheek. "I'll see you tonight . . ."

"Okay," Mama says.

"Don't wait up!" she shouts over her shoulder, racing down the path to her car. She purposely leaves the front door ajar so that when Mama goes to close it, she'll see the green lawn and blue sky and red oleander, and perhaps miss it a little bit, this world she has forsaken.

———————

IN PRECALCULUS, LAYNIE Hibbard comes in wearing a blue surgical mask over her nose and mouth. Illa feels sorry for her because the other students roll their eyes behind her back. Midway through class, Laynie gets up to sharpen her pencil, but before she makes it to the sharpener, her knees buckle and she goes down. Someone gasps and Mrs. Maxey runs to her. Already Laynie has regained consciousness. Groggily, she sits up, eyes glassy.

Rubbing Laynie's back with one hand, Mrs. Maxey waves Nancy Cobb over with the other. "Walk her to the nurse's office, would you, Nancy?"

Mrs. Maxey asks Laynie if she remembered to eat breakfast that morning.

"I don't feel good," Laynie says.

Mrs. Williams frowns. "Just go on to the nurse. She'll get you fixed up."

"What about tonight's assignment?" Laynie asks.

"Don't worry about that now. You can do makeup work later, if need be."

When the bell rings a half hour later, students shoot out of their chairs and down the hall, where Illa can hear them buzzing about Laynie. *Bet she's knocked up,* someone says. *Maybe the LeBlanc baby was hers! No way. She's just looking for attention.*

When Illa passes the nurse's office at the end of the day, there's a line of people stretching down the hallway, including Nancy Cobb. Illa counts nine girls and one boy sitting on the linoleum, some holding wet cloths to their foreheads, some clutching sick bags. Since the refinery blast, Illa has felt connected to Nancy, a pudgy, dark-haired girl who lost both parents in the explosion. At school, she often looks as miserable as Illa feels.

"What's going on?" Illa asks Nancy.

"I feel sick to my stomach," Nancy says. "And dizzy." She leans back against the wall, clutches her stomach like she's in pain.

"What about the rest of them?" She spots Marilee Warren in the line.

"They shoulda let us stay home today," Nancy says. "Aunt Carol said it wasn't safe."

"Yeah, but what did the nurse say?" Illa's nervous. What if one of the players gets sick?

"She told me to go home and rest and I'd feel better in the morning."

———

AT COACH'S HOUSE for the team dinner, the girls are subdued as they pass plates of food around the table. Normally at team meals, the mood is buoyant, the girls ribbing one another, psyching themselves up for the coming game by recounting funny stories involving past victories. Tonight, though, they're on edge. Illa sits wedged between Keisha and Brittny, whose bony shoulder Illa has to lean around to see when Mercy starts to tell a story about last year's Holiday Classic tournament in Corpus Christi, something about Annie and an all-you-can-eat seafood buffet, but Annie cuts her off: "Heard that one about a million times already."

Like kids with bickering parents, the players can feel the tension between Annie and Mercy, and they're probably wondering what it will mean for them tomorrow. For years, Annie has shared Mercy with an entire town; can one boy really make that much difference? But even in that brief moment at the Hotel Sabine, Illa could feel the intensity of Mercy's feelings for Travis.

At the end of the meal, the coaches go into the kitchen to wash up and drink their good-luck Scotch, which they put in coffee, thinking they're being clever.

"You hear the chief hauled in Lucille?" Chole says after the water in the kitchen sink starts.

"For the baby?" Corinne asks.

"Duh," Chole says.

"Chief best watch himself," Keisha says, coughing into her arm. "He question her good enough, gonna wind up with half the town's secrets."

"If she's got all those potions, don't you think she'd know how to keep herself from getting in a *family way*?" Brittny asks.

"Maybe it was one of her potions that killed the poor thing," Corinne says. "I've heard the talk about those 'cures.'" She uses her fingers to put quotation marks around the word. Keisha is coughing harder now; Jasmine gets up to refill her water glass.

"Maybe it was some kind of sacrifice," Chole says. "Some Comanche shit or something."

"Lucille's Attakappa," Illa says.

"Whatever, they've all got their weird rituals," Chole says.

"And Catholics don't?" Annie says.

"I only go to All Hallows because Tia and Tio would send me back to Juárez if I didn't. They're mad strict." She turns to Keisha, who's coughing violently now. "Dude, you okay?"

Keisha shakes her head, flapping her hand in front of her mouth like she's trying to get air. In the silence of the stalled conversation, Illa can hear her wheezing.

"Coach!" Mercy shouts. "Asthma attack!"

From the kitchen, the sounds of banging drawers. Mercy motions the girls to give Keisha space, so they get up from the table and move to the edge of the den. Annie rifles through Keisha's backpack, then runs her inhaler to the table. Keisha's eyes are wide with fear, tears glistening at the corners.

Coach flies to her side, clutching a brown paper sack. "Here, hon," she says. "I need you to breathe into this." She puts the bag to Keisha's mouth and holds it there. "Breathe, honey. Slow down. Breathe."

Illa has never been so thankful for Coach's steady voice and fearlessness. Gradually, Keisha's breathing slows and she removes the bag. She draws two quick puffs from her inhaler, tears streaming down her cheeks.

"It's okay, sweetheart," Coach says, rubbing her back. "You're fine. Everything's going to be fine."

———

THE NEXT MORNING when Illa gets up, Mama is still in bed, a sign that she's sunk into one of her depressions. When Mama gets like this, Illa usually tries to take special care with her, bringing breakfast to her in bed, reading aloud articles from the morning paper. But Illa has little patience for her mother's moods, what with the season opener that night and everything falling to shit. It doesn't seem to matter what precautions Illa takes, though; Mama's melancholy bleeds into Illa's psychic space.

Once the season gets going, Mama tends to be grumpy. *Just wish I saw more of my girl,* she'll say when Illa gets home late from away games. Illa has to bite her tongue to keep from reminding her mother that, if not for basketball, Illa would see nothing *but* Mama, and any armchair psychologist could tell you that wasn't healthy for a girl. Pocketing the note, she grabs her backpack and bangs out the front door into the sunshine.

As she cruises toward the student lot, Illa notices a small crowd gathering in front of the Mr. Good Deals. A local news van is already jammed up against the curb. Approaching the crowd, Illa sees a dog sprawled out on the pavement, blood trickling into the gutter beside it. People have left a semicircle of space around the beast, as if afraid it will leap from beyond the grave to savage them. When Illa gets out of the car, she sees it's Lucille Cloud's dog, still lying on the dirty woven blanket Lucille puts out for it every day when she sets up her wares. Illa gags at the pulped bits of brain smeared out around the carcass.

"Already dead by the time Hartman got to it," a man wearing oil-stained coveralls says.

"He see who done it?" another man asks.

"Didn't see, but he says between that baby and this, he's ready to close up shop."

"You ask me, it serves the girl right for coming back here to sell her junk so close to a crime scene. Disrespectful, is what it is."

A diminutive news anchor in a mauve skirt suit has buttressed herself against the front wall of the Mr. Good Deals to deliver a report. Illa wanders in as close as she can without being conspicuous.

"Good morning, Luke," the anchor says into the camera, hanging heavily on the first syllable of *morning* and pressing the earpiece farther into her right ear. "For the second time in two months, I'm here at the corner of LeBlanc and Main to report on an unsettling incident. Early this morning, a large German shepherd–mix dog was found shot through the head on the sidewalk. There were no witnesses, but the dog appears to be the same animal that belonged to the woman who sold home remedies and jewelry here on this sidewalk, Lucille Cloud. Cloud was interviewed and released by detectives yesterday evening, probably around the same time the animal was shot."

Illa checks her watch. It's almost seven o'clock, time for walk-throughs. She cuts across the student lot toward the gym, wondering where Lucille is and if she's okay. The LeBlanc baby is making people nuts. Illa passes through the gym doors, which are covered in posters promoting that night's building dedication: JOIN US TO HONOR LIVING LEGEND JODI MARTIN!

Inside, the girls are gathered in a circle by the bleachers, balls on their hips. Everyone but Annie, whose presence Illa always registers instinctively, the cheetah to her gazelle. The girls look distressed. Corinne Wolcott is crying, Brittny rubbing her back.

"So who's going to start, then?" Corinne sobs.

"Didn't you hear Coach?" Chole answers. "She said don't worry about it, so I say we don't worry about it."

"Don't worry about it? Don't worry about it?" Corinne parrots hysterically. "Easy for her to say, no one's arresting *her*!"

"She's not under arrest, C," Mercy says. "They're just asking questions."

"I thought they were questioning Lucille," Brittny says. "I thought Lucille did it."

"Don't you read the paper?" Chole says. "They released her yesterday. Nothing to arrest her for. She had some kind of alibi for the night they think the baby was dumped."

"Someone shot her dog this morning," Illa says. "In front of Mr. Good Deals."

"God in heaven," Corinne gasps, her tears starting afresh.

Brittny looks like she's on the verge of crying, too. "That poor animal. What is *wrong* with people?"

"Poor dog? Poor Lucille. Poor Annie!" Chole tugs at the hem of her penny. "Shit is getting out of hand."

"Couldn't the police wait a few days to talk to Annie?" Keisha asks. "It's opening night!"

"This is all that cholo Sanchez's fault, man," Brandye says. "Election's next week, he just trying to shake things up because he losing."

"Who cares about the election? *We* can't win without Annie," Jasmine says, bouncing the ball hard with both hands. "For real."

"This is bigger than basketball," Mercy says quietly. "Bigger than all of us."

Illa wants to know more, but just then the buzzer goes, and Coach Thibodeaux slams out of the office. "Think y'all are going to get the *W* sitting on your rear ends?" she yells. "Let's go!"

On the court, the girls play nervous, rattled by the morning's news. They flub bank shots, throw passes into the arms of defenders, forget in-bound plays. In a team as tight as theirs, their moves synced carefully as clocks through hours of practice, a player doing her hair differently on game day is enough to throw them off. Annie's absence is like sand in the gears.

Afterward, Coach Thibodeaux tries to rally them in the huddle: "I'll start by saying we're literally lucky to be here today, in this gym right now. They were ready to call off school because of the stink, but we reminded him about UIL rules. Y'all need at least half a day in the classroom in order to play tonight. So let's not take anything for granted; let's remember everything we've overcome, the large and small, to get *right here* today." She stomps her foot for emphasis. "Annie *will* be back, you heard Coach. You're prepared for this. Your bodies are ready, they know what to do. You know what we say: losing is a failure of the mind. So you take the rest of the day today and get your minds right." She scans the huddle to drive home the point that she isn't being rhetorical. "Scouts'll be here tonight. You owe it to Mercy to bring your head. This is her chance, so let's get Mercy some papers to sign. After all she's done for us the past three seasons, we owe it to her. Don't we?"

"Yes ma'am," the girls say.

"Don't we?"

"Yes ma'am!"

"Bring it in."

In the locker room, Illa learns that Detective LaCroix showed up outside the gym that morning and asked Annie if she wouldn't mind answering a few questions related to the Baby Doe case. Annie declined to call Beau or talk to Coach, just got in the car with La-Croix and sped off. When the girls got inside and told Coach what had happened, she said nobody, not the police, not the president of the United States, was going to keep her starting forward out of the lineup on opening night. Before hustling out the door, she threatened to kick their asses off the team if news of Annie's trouble traveled farther than the locker room.

Sure enough, Annie is back at school in time for first period, AP Government, the interview postponed until Monday.

———————

THE CHAOS OF opening night: a gym so packed it vibrates, the warm-up music loud enough for Illa to feel the bass rattling her spleen. People who can't find a seat in the bleachers line up five deep at the corners of the court, which the officials allow because it is opening night at Port Sabine and they don't dare cross Jodi Martin by sending any of the fans home. Students have made glittery banners on butcher paper, which they wave overhead: Lady Rays Show No Mercy and The Road to State Goes Through Port Sabine.

An older woman wearing a navy Port Sabine High School sweat-shirt like the one they found behind the Market Basket holds up a neon-green poster board that says GOD BLESS THAT BABY AND OUR GIRLS in lopsided black bubble letters.

The girls come tearing out of the locker room in a blur of navy and yellow, their snap-down warm-up pants flapping around their legs. A roar goes up from the crowd. Everyone wants to be close to the girls. Because she's captain, Mercy's out front. As the girls fly past the bench, Coach Martin slaps their hands and shoulders. Watching Mercy warm up, Illa sees how she owns each step but without arrogance, inviting you to be proud of her.

Illa spots Lennox looking in her direction from the senior section and her belly goes warm. Is he looking at her or past her, to Annie? She pencils in the lineup with a shaking hand and gives it to the scorekeeper, then turns her attention to Mercy, who has set her feet to take a three-point shot. When she releases the ball, she lets out a half-strangled, bestial cry, her shooting arm flopping down awkwardly. Instead of arcing into the air and landing with a swish, the ball rockets into the crowd of bystanders gathered along the gym wall, a full forty-five degrees southeast of the bucket. Mercy hesitates before turning to the people hit by her errant ball and clapping her hands twice to indicate she wants the ball back, as if she meant to pass it to them all along. Illa knows the leather balls can get slippery if sweat gets on them, so she jogs onto the court with a washcloth to wipe down Mercy's ball.

"Sucks when that happens," Illa says as she works the cloth over the ball.

Mercy nods. "Thanks, Illa."

The next song comes on, and the girls continue their warm-up routine. Mercy takes another shot; it looks solid but barely reaches the rim, glancing off the side. She chases her own rebound and positions herself at her favorite spot on the three-point line, just north of the key. Backspinning the ball to herself, she receives it between her hands, then launches another massive air ball.

Illa wonders if she's pulled a muscle. Mercy, embarrassed, looks to Coach Martin, who's facedown in her playbook, oblivious. By now, the other girls have stopped their warm-ups, and Annie races over to put an arm around Mercy's shoulders. With that gesture, Illa can see the trouble more clearly: Mercy's upper body is jerking spasmodically, Annie's body both absorbing and deflecting the movement, revealing the freak contractions of Mercy's arm. The game clock reads two minutes and twenty seconds to tip-off.

"Coach," Illa says, pointing to Mercy.

It takes Coach a few seconds to register what's happening, but when she does, she runs onto the court and tries to shield her player. There's an operatic twist to Mercy's lips as her head thrusts back. Once more, that pained cry issues from a jaw wrenched open too wide. The crowd goes silent. After an agonizing minute, when Coach and Annie seem to be deciding if they should touch Mercy, they steer her into the locker room, and Annie goes to the officials with a message: *Give us five minutes.* Then she grabs a bottle of Gatorade and follows in the direction of Mercy and Coach.

In a situation like this, you expect to see concerned parents bolt onto the court, but Evelia has never come to a game, not even the state tournament. It saddens Illa that Mercy is in there with Annie and Coach. Chole stares at the locker room door, then throws up a shot, trying to keep her rhythm going. Corinne and Brandye do the same, while the others head to the bench to stretch and catch their breath. Fifteen minutes pass; the crowd grows restless. The warm-up CD has ended, but someone starts it over from the beginning so that "Sweet Home Alabama" blares out a second time. It elicits no clapping or singing from the stands this time, its rollicking chorus in stark contrast to the grim atmosphere of the gym.

When the locker room door opens and Coach Martin steps out,

people cheer, but the noise dies quickly when they realize she's alone. Jodi claps several times, raising hands overhead to urge people to stand up, trying to salvage the home court advantage. Reluctantly, people get to their feet, but their enthusiasm has soured. They are moviegoers at a premiere where the headliner has failed to show. They will not be satisfied unless Mercy Louis takes the court.

"Let's play ball," Coach says, nodding at the refs. "Keisha, you're in for Louis. Wood, you'll play the three spot tonight."

Brittny looks terrified, but she nods, then licks her palms and swipes them across the bottoms of her shoes.

"Huddle up," Coach says.

Illa ventures quietly, "What about Mercy? Is she going to be okay?"

"I look like a fortune-teller to you, Stark?" Coach snaps.

"No ma'am."

She pauses, sniffs. "We got a game to win. Hands in!" The girls comply, layering their hands into the huddle. "Mental toughness on three. One, two, three . . ."

"MENTAL TOUGHNESS!"

After tip-off, Coach Martin leans in to whisper to Coach Thibodeaux, then slips off the end of the bench and back into the locker room. A couple of minutes into the game, the Lady Rays already down, Illa sees Coach emerge, her broad back turned to the court as she makes her way toward the gym door, slowly, struggling to move. It's then that Illa notices a pair of long legs dangling over Coach's right arm, black hair cascading off her left. It's Mercy being carried away like a rag doll.

# PART II

*Remember, until an hour before the Devil fell,*
*God thought him beautiful in heaven.*

—ARTHUR MILLER, *THE CRUCIBLE*

# MERCY

───────────

"STOP THAT," COACH says in the locker room, where my right hand slaps against my knee, palm up, the *thwack* of skin hitting skin a clean sound in the silence. *Stop that, stop that,* I tell my hand, but it doesn't listen. Coach paces the room, keeping her distance. As she moves, her nylon windpants tell me *shush shush shush.* After a minute, she grabs my hand and presses it firmly to my leg, so that I feel my knuckles dig into the muscle of my thigh, shifting it on the bone. "*Stop,*" she says.

I'm desperate to do what she asks of me, but when she removes her hand, mine rockets upward again. *I'm trying, I swear,* I want to explain, but I'm an actor in a badly dubbed film; someone has taped over my words with funny sounds that aren't mine. *Huh huh huh,* come the noises from my mouth. *Help me, please God, help me, Coach, anyone, help!*

"Come on, don't do this to me," she says.

*It's not me doing it,* I want to say. *This is not my body, get me out!* Annie comes in and Coach steps toward the door, then back to me, an awkward waltz.

"I brought some Gatorade," Annie says.

"You see what you can do with her," Coach says.

Annie sits down behind me on the bench, threads her arms under mine, and clasps her hands at my stomach. She puts a leg on either side of my hips, her pelvis curved into me like we are stacked dishes.

"A *hug?*" Coach bellows. "Get up, Putnam." I feel Annie's shoulder move away from mine; she's being peeled from me. "Give her space, she needs *space.*" There's a seed of panic in Coach's voice.

But Annie lays her head against me and squeezes tighter. I'm so relieved by her familiar warmth. *Flap flap flap* goes my hand. *Flap flap flap.*

"We got to get her to a doctor," Coach says. "I'll tell Thibodeaux."

I try to pray, but my words are scrambled, the familiar phrases undone. I hear the door sigh shut behind Coach as she leaves. In the hallway, Beau's loud voice sounds.

"Of course he's come to check on you," Annie says, grunting a laugh. "If you were his daughter, you'd win him an election."

"Travis," I say. "Get Travis." It takes such effort to speak; I'm buried beneath a dune, each word fighting its way to air.

"No," Annie says. "You broke up, remember? I'm here, Mers, I'm here." She breathes into my back. Then, quietly: *"What is happening to you?"*

When Coach returns, she smuggles us out the gym's back entrance; I'm carried like a child, my legs crooked over her forearm, my right arm windmilling at the elbow, churning the night air into nothing. She places me in the passenger seat of her Explorer gently, like I'm a valuable vase or perhaps a stick of dynamite. Annie climbs in the backseat as the car shudders to life. Through the night we drive. I feel as if I'm in a car in one of those old black-and-white movies, wooden sets depicting the countryside flying past the window as we stay still. *This is not my body, I'm not here, I'm not moving.* Tiny me in the cave of this disobedient body, shouting up toward daylight. Before I took that shot, I felt a tickle, a premonition of the coming spasm. A split second when my body told me *hang on* because there was no stopping what was coming.

As we drive, I will my flapping hand to stay in my lap, but it rises up and up and up, spring-loaded. *This is not my body,* I want to say again, but I realize: I feel the smooth leather of the seat, the swing of the forearm on its invisible up-down track, I recognize the wrist. This is my body, but I am no longer in charge of it. A sudden press of panic. I clench and unclench my left hand, my good hand, watch the blue veins ripple in my wrist. As we pull into the circle drive in front of the ER, Coach tells Annie to stay with me, that she's going to get Evelia who didn't pick up the phone when she called earlier. *She's asleep, don't wake her for this,* I want to say. *Huh huh huh* is what comes out instead.

Annie guides me out of the passenger seat, pulls my good arm around her neck. Together, we hobble through the sliding doors. Inside, we're given a wheelchair and I'm told to sit in it. A round, dark-haired man hovers over me as we roll down a white hallway. He tells me his name is Dr. Elgin and that I'm not to worry about a thing, they'll take care of me.

"You're Mercy Louis, aren't you?" he says, smiling. "I recognize you from the papers. Want to tell me what's wrong, Mercy?" My eyes must tell stories I can't, because Dr. Elgin says, "Mercy, can you answer me? Just say yes or no."

*Oh, Dr. Elgin, I want to, I want to answer yes or no. Please don't get the wrong idea about me, I'm a good girl, and you've requested something of me in a slow, kindly way that makes me think you have young children at home. I wonder what their names are, what your wife looks like. I bet you're a good father. If I answer you, will you take me home to meet your family? Will you speak gently to me, ask me easy questions I can answer? I will be your most obedient daughter.*

All I can do is shake my head no. Touching my shoulder, he says again that they will take care of me. Gratitude spreads like a hot drink warming my insides. Soon I'm in a room with Dr. Elgin and two nurses in brightly colored scrubs. He asks if I've taken any pills, if I've been feeling sick lately, if I have a headache, if I think I've eaten something bad, if I have a history of seizures or spells. His breath smells like tomato soup. I shake my head no to all questions.

"We were warming up for the game like usual," Annie offers. "And Mercy started to have some kind of attack."

I want to tell him my version, but I'm not sure what it is. The moments following that shot are a blank; one minute I felt the bass line of the warm-up music rivering through me alongside the adrenaline, and the next, I was back in the locker room with Coach, my hand a hooked fish flopping in the bottom of a boat.

"What kind of attack?" Dr. Elgin asks.

"Her arm started flapping like it's doing now, and there was something freaky with her jaw. And the weird noises . . ."

"Did she fall down and hit her head? Did she have something that looked like a seizure?" he probes. "Where her body started to jerk around and her eyes rolled up?"

"No, nothing like that. Just a bunch of air balls and then the hand and stuff."

"And she hasn't been sick lately? Feverish? No vomiting?"

"Not that I know of."

He turns to me and I shake my head, confirming what Annie has said.

"Annie, you'll come with me. Mercy, rest here with Edie"—Dr. Elgin indicates the nurse in purple scrubs—"while we wait for your grandmother. Take some deep breaths and try to relax, and we'll talk more about what's happening once the others get here, okay?"

"But I need to stay with her," Annie says. "She needs me . . ."

"We're not sure exactly what Mercy needs right now," Dr. Elgin says sternly. "But we know that she needs to rest. Come with me, please."

"But Doctor, you don't understand, we're never apart, she really, *really* needs me to stay with her." She pauses, a desperate look on her face. "Don't you, Mers?"

I can't bring myself to nod. He motions her out the door; she follows him, sighing petulantly before disappearing into the hallway. I barely have time to exhale before they are both back in the room, close on the heels of Maw Maw and Coach.

"See?" Coach says, pointing at me for Maw Maw's benefit. "See her arm?" I can't say I've ever seen Jodi Martin scared, but she looks it now, tugging at her ear, biting her lip.

"Hmm," Maw Maw replies, eyeing me.

"What's the matter with her?" Coach asks Dr. Elgin.

*Huh huh huh,* I say as if on cue.

"We're going to do a couple tests on Mercy to try and figure that out," Dr. Elgin says. "Whenever we have a patient who has a spell like this, we want to make sure that the brain looks healthy and that there hasn't been any damage to it. As soon as we can get Mercy an appointment with a neurologist, we'll do an EEG and an MRI to try and see whether it's a neurologic problem that's causing the movements. That will teach us what to do to help. Right now we're going to do a urine test to check for infection or the presence of any substances that might have triggered the symptoms."

"Are you suggesting drug use?" Coach asks defensively.

"We just want to cover all of our bases. Sometimes we can only determine what it is by figuring out what it isn't."

"I can assure you, this girl's kept her body clean as a whistle, we make sure of that."

I remember the beer fizzing down my throat, the stickiness of my thighs that night in the forest. *I'm not clean, I'm filthy.*

"We . . . ?" he asks.

"The coaches, the team . . ." Coach responds. "I run a tight ship."

He pauses. "All the same, it's a test we'll perform." He turns to me. "Have you had any injuries to your head lately? Anything that might have led to a concussion or other form of brain trauma?" I shake my head no. "And have you ever had a seizure or spell of any kind before?" Again I shake my head before remembering how I spoke in tongues at church last summer, falling to the floor in rapture. I'm not sure that counts, and besides, I haven't been filled with the spirit since that day. "What about family?" the doctor asks. "Anyone in your family have a history of seizures?" I start to shake my head but realize I don't know the answer. Perhaps Witness is an epileptic, Charmaine a chronic fainter. I remember my phone call yesterday, the message I left on Charmaine's machine. *No, I don't know my family history, Doctor. I've never even heard my mother's voice.* I look to Maw Maw for help.

"No sir," Maw Maw says firmly. "I'm healthy as a horse; it's just me and the girl at home."

"Are you the biological mother?" he presses.

"Grandmother." She sniffs.

"What about the parents, then?"

"What they got, no medicine can cure," she says, but he's not satisfied.

"Meaning?"

"Meaning their bodies are healthy but their souls are sick, sir."

"Hmm," he says, writing something on his clipboard. "Was Mercy premature at birth?"

"Praise the Lord, no," Maw Maw says.

Dr. Elgin instructs me to leave a urine sample in the small bathroom off the hallway. I don't want to; Travis and I were only together twice; still, I'm scared of what the test will reveal. I go to the restroom and leave the sample anyway. To refuse would raise suspicion.

Once I'm back in the room, Dr. Elgin says, "Just as soon as those results come back, barring anything unusual, we'll send Mercy home to get some rest . . ."

"I don't think we should leave till we figure this thing out," Coach says.

The doctor clasps his hands in front of him, the clipboard flat against his belly. "I wish it were that simple, but it's going to take some time . . ."

"When can she do the tests? Look at the girl, she needs help right *now.*" She paces to the window in agitation. "We've got a game on Tuesday, and this girl is everything to that team."

Dr. Elgin purses his lips into a tight smile that produces a stress dimple on his lower left cheek.

"She seems a little better since warm-ups," Annie offers.

Maw Maw turns to her as if registering her presence for the first time. "What's she doing in here?" Maw Maw asks the doctor, pointing at Annie.

Flummoxed by this turn, he says, "I thought she was a friend of the patient?"

"Friend, my foot," Maw Maw spits. She turns to Annie. "You get out. Mercy don't need your kind of influence right now. I know all about the summer, you getting Mercy drunk on the night you made your promise to your daddy and the town. Shameful!"

"Now, ladies . . ." Dr. Elgin says, but he might as well be furniture for the heed they pay him.

"You're wrong, Evelia," Annie says. "She's never drunk a drop around me. Mercy, come on, tell her. Come *on*." I'm frozen, though, my words retreating further down my throat.

"You're a devilish girl," Maw Maw says, jabbing a finger at Annie. "I won't have you corrupting her."

"What, because Mercy's so perfect?" Annie's face is bright red. "You think you know everything about her." *Don't, Annie, please.* I make my eyes wide, pleading, but she's not looking at me.

"Get out," Maw Maw says.

I feel a sudden sharp pain explode inside my legs. I slide from the bed straight to my knees before listing left. My cheek meets the cold ground, where I roll onto my back. From here, I can see the stars flickering dimly out the room's single window. Now I'm glad to be a tiny version of me stowed at the bottom of this cavernous body, far away from these others. I want to stay here forever, drinking starshine.

"Jesus Christ," Coach says.

Maw Maw cringes. "Jodi, mind yourself," she snaps.

I blink up at Dr. Elgin's concerned face. He's saying something, but to my ears it comes out staticky. Am I dying? For a flash, I hope the answer is yes. Maw Maw is unafraid of death; she knows she'll be secure in heaven when her time comes. She doesn't rush to me. *The Lord don't make mistakes.* If I sleep for a hundred years, wake cradled in the roots of a tree where the hospital once was, all of these people will be dead, these troubles past. I'm exhausted, my body slack against the floor except for my right arm, which pulses against the air, flexing and relaxing. I feel again that sensation of movement I haven't ordered up, gathered in the muscle just under the skin. Hands under me, but I make myself deadweight; I don't want to be lifted back into that scene.

"Edie, clear these people out," Dr. Elgin says. *But but,* they say. Their voices grow faint. The door closes. In the quiet of the room, I hear Dr. Elgin breathing.

"Mercy," he says after a time. "They're gone. It's just you and me now. Will you open your eyes and sit up for me?"

For minutes that stretch on like hours, I don't move, but he waits with me. Slowly, I rise to sitting, then open my eyes. On the floor across from me, he pretzels his legs in front of him like a kindergartener.

"Your coach was right about one thing," he says. "You're clean as a whistle, according to your urine test." *Thank God.* "Anything you want to share with me, Mercy? Anything you can think of that might help us get this figured out for you? Any questions we should be asking?" His eyes are large and chocolaty, warm as a horse's. *There's plenty to ask,* I think. *Like how can a mother abandon her baby? And why do we betray the people who have been most generous with us? How can we tell the difference between love and lust? And can we return to innocence after we've sinned?*

I hope hard that on Monday, the neurologist will give me a diagnosis and prescription. *Anything you want to share with me?* Dr. Elgin asked. But I need a savior, not a doctor.

We schedule a Monday appointment with the neurologist. When I'm discharged, it's after midnight. Annie, still seething over Maw Maw's accusation, glowers at her as we make our way through the crowded waiting room. We're near the door when I see Travis seated in a far corner, his ball cap pulled low over his eyes. He spots us but doesn't get up; he knows he shouldn't be here. Though I want nothing more than to feel his arms around me, I walk faster, hoping Annie doesn't see him. But it's too late.

"There's your problem, Evelia," Annie says, halting our group as she points to Travis. She looks triumphantly at Maw Maw. My body screams with indignation, but it comes out as pathetic grunts. *It wasn't your secret to tell, Annie!* Travis must sense what's happening, because he comes toward us.

"Who's this?" Coach says.

"Mercy's *boyfriend*," Annie says. "See, y'all think I'm the problem, but—"

"Annie, shut your mouth," Travis says.

But her words are bricks tossed through glass, no chance for salvage. Under the hospital lights, surrounded by Coach and Maw Maw, Travis looks boyish, and for a moment I see us as they do: naive kids fooled by our hormones into thinking what we had something real.

"Not anymore," Coach says. "Fun and games are over, kids." On her face is a new expression: anger edged with disgust. She continues, "Do you know until tonight I've never missed a game in twenty-two years of coaching?" She looks at me. "Mercy, I thought we had an understanding. You told me you wanted this, so I've been busting my ass on the phone with scouts hours a day, swearing by my good name you have more in you—"

"Excuse me," Travis says, but Coach won't be stopped.

"I groveled *in the dirt* to get some of those scouts to take a second look at you, and now I learn that instead of doing *your* part, you been running around canoodling with mister here all summer?"

"There'll be none of that talk about Mercy," Maw Maw says.

"What?" Coach turns to look at her. "You're living in the wrong century, Evelia. I made the mistake of thinking your girl was different, wanted something more for herself than a baby by eighteen."

"Excuse us for having a *life* outside basketball—" Annie starts but Travis interrupts.

"Mercy *is* different. She's different from you, is the problem." He waves his hand at Maw Maw and Coach. "Both of you. You love her so long as she's your little robot . . ."

*Huh huh huh.* My head goes gauzy. "Well" is all Maw Maw says, looking at me impassively, as if she's expected this all along.

"We'll go now," Coach decides.

"Is Mercy okay?" Travis asks as Coach ushers Maw Maw, Annie, and me outside.

They ignore him. Annie tries to take hold of my hand, but I move away from her. How stupid I've been, keeping her secrets all these years, and at the first opportunity, she spills mine. As we near the Explorer, I see a man leaning against the passenger door. He looks familiar, but I can't place him.

"Evening, folks," the man says. He turns to me. "Mercy, that was quite an exit tonight."

"You want a busted nose, Gatlin?" Coach says.

Now I know who he is—Russell Gatlin, sports reporter for the *Flare*.

"Just want a quote or two, Coach."

"I don't give a good goddamn what you want."

"Jodi," Maw Maw scolds.

"What's the matter, Mercy?" Russell says. "What'd the docs tell you?"

"That's none of your business," Coach says.

Russell scribbles in a tiny notebook. "What's going on with your arm there?"

"Don't talk, Mercy," Coach says.

*Huh huh huh.*

"Excuse me?" Russell says.

"Piss off," Annie says.

"Get in the car, ladies," Coach says, opening the back door.

"What's the diagnosis?" Russell asks.

He's looking me over as if my body might give away more clues.

"Hush now, Mercy," Maw Maw says.

"Don't answer him," Coach warns again.

All those hours together in the hospital, and they never realized I haven't said a word.

BACK FROM THE hospital, Maw Maw sits at the edge of my bed. *She doesn't know everything,* I remind myself, pulling the blanket to my chin. *She still believes in me.* Even Annie, for all her jealousy, doesn't know how far I fell this summer. Nobody does, and that gives me hope that I can make things right and get back to who I was before.

Then I remember Lucille Cloud that first night in the forest. How much did she see before she knocked on the window?

My arm refuses to stay tucked, worming its way out from beneath the blanket. Maw Maw regards it like it's a snake crawled up on the porch. Still, she takes hold of my wrist, turning my hand palm up and caressing the skin there. She runs her elegant fingers carefully over the raised veins. "Let me read you, child," she says. "We've got to know what's coming." I think of Travis and me in the back of his truck, sweat-slick and panting. *It's the future she sees,* I remind myself. And her hand feels so good; I raise my arm and bring both of our hands to my cheek, kissing the base of her palm. I open her fingers from where they encircle my wrist and place her palm flat on my forehead. Closing my eyes, I move her hand over my temple, down my cheek to my throat. These hands that bathed me as a baby, fed me pea mush and changed me when I was wet. The love lives in her works, in all the drudgery of raising me up. She sheltered me, fed and clothed me, guided me in faith, why can't that be enough? What good are three words, anyway, when words are so slippery?

"My little one," she says, moving her other hand up to cup my face. "My Tee Mercy."

She kisses my eyes and promises she won't leave me behind at the end, that no matter what it is I've done, she will make sure I take my place with her in heaven. Then she's quiet, letting her hands absorb the story from my bones and blood. Several minutes pass, my body a coiled spring. Maw Maw's eyelids flutter, she moans softly, her mouth twitches as if in a dream. Finally, she opens her eyes. "Lord help us," she says.

"What is it, Maw Maw?" My first words in hours, fear-driven.

"Protect these girls, Lord," she says, gaze cast heavenward. "They know not what they do."

"What do you see?" I ask.

"I understand it now, that vision I been having for so long, all those girls on the floor." She's squeezing my wrist so hard it hurts, but when I try to wiggle free, she holds tighter. "I see it clearly, Mercy girl. You're the first to fall, but you won't be the last. The devil is walking Port Sabine, a curse on this town for the soul of an innocent." At last she releases me, and I rub at the red skin. "Guard your heart, Mercy, a pure heart is the strongest weapon against evil. We were warned of these tribulations, that darkness would descend to test believers and strike down the sinners before Jesus returns. This sickness is a test. Is your faith strong enough, Mercy girl? Is your heart pure?"

"Yes, Maw Maw!"

She grips my hands in hers. She prays for the town, for the LeBlanc Avenue baby, for the girls. Last of all she prays for me, that God will protect me from the curse brought down on us by that baby, that He will keep my heart pure so that I can join Him in heaven soon.

When she finishes praying, she withdraws her hands. "Best keep to the house."

"Yes, Maw Maw," I say.

At the door, she turns and says, "Remember, no matter what the doctors say Monday, it's the Lord who heals. *The righteous person may have many troubles, but the Lord delivers him from them all.*"

I don't tell her that my prayers are scattered out in my head like so many Scrabble letters, that I have only this strange unlanguage now. *Huh huh huh.* I can't help but hope that on Monday the doctors will fix my arm so I can keep playing. If I miss many more games, my chance at a scholarship will be lost.

When I can no longer hear Maw Maw's footfalls in the hall, I slip out of bed and move for the stack of letters in my desk drawer. Finally, I will do what I should have done back in May—toss Charmaine's letters and card in the trash. I draw them out and look at them. Charmaine is only paper and ink, and she slips easily through my fingers and into the trash. Maw Maw is the only family I've ever known; she is a rough mother but a good one. Outside, a car glides by, shushing the din off the bayou. My hand lingers over the photograph, the face that tells me, fair or not, what I will look like as a woman. I thrust it to the bottom of the trash, reminding myself that physical likeness is the most superficial bond.

---

IN THE MORNING, Maw Maw tells me to stay in bed and rest, then goes to church. For a long while, I lie still, waiting for another spasm, but nothing happens. I decide to go to practice because I can't afford to miss it if I want to play Tuesday.

In the kitchen, the morning paper is wrapped in plastic on the counter. I unfold it to put next to Maw Maw's place setting, but the headline stops me short: MYSTERY ILLNESS DOWNS LADY RAYS' TOP PLAYER. And in smaller print, *Louis rushed to hospital as team falls to St. Pete's.* I feel my cheeks flush. Now the whole town will be watching me, waiting to see what happens next.

As I walk into the gym, Coach sees me; she looks surprised but pleased.

"How you feeling this morning?" she asks.

"Fine," I say. "Really, honestly fine." I'm glad to notice my voice is back.

"You had any more of those fits?"

"Not yet, thank God. I feel totally fine, I swear. But Maw Maw told me I need to rest . . ." I pause, not wanting to reveal too much; Coach wouldn't understand if I told her about Maw Maw's latest prophecy. "She'd be upset if she knew I was here."

"Let me worry about your grandmother," Coach says. "You focus on you."

"Okay," I say.

Yes, though I'm scared of defying Maw Maw, I'm not ready to give up on basketball yet. I will leave Travis, cast off Annie, toss Charmaine's letters, pray most every waking hour, but I can't give up basketball. I recall the loose-limbed joy of summer ball, how I danced baseline to baseline in the dusk, too fast for even the mosquitoes. The game restored me once, maybe it will again.

In the locker room, I dress out—navy mesh shorts and gold T-shirt, navy pinny so old the stenciled number has peeled clean away. On the court, a few of the girls hug me like we haven't seen each other in years. Even Illa Stark comes out from behind the video camera and shyly pats me on the shoulder, asking how I'm doing. Before I can answer, Corinne blurts: "So what happened last night?"

"I just got a little light-headed," I say. "Probably didn't drink enough water."

"What was with that article in the *Flare*?" Chole asks. "That guy made it seem like you were dying."

"Slow news day, I guess," I say. "I'll be okay."

"*Mystery illness,* like it's *The National Enquirer,*" Keisha says. "Next they be saying you got abducted by aliens."

"Town can't make up its mind about us girls," Chole says. "We're criminal bitches or we're poor sweet sick babies. I say fuck 'em." She swings an arm in front of her face like she's waving away a bad smell. "But dude, seriously, you okay?"

"What's up with your arm?" Brittny says.

"If that were any of your business, she might've told y'all already," Annie snaps.

"Shut up, Annie," I say.

"Oooooh, snap!" Jasmine says. Annie steps to her, arm cocked, and Jasmine gets right back in her face. At six-two, Jasmine towers over Annie. "What? What? Come on, Putnam. Hit me. Think I'm scared of your honky ass?"

"Knock it off, Jazz," Zion says.

"Yeah, it ain't worth it," Jasmine says, turning away.

"What is *wrong* with y'all?" I snap. "We are a *team,* we've got to act like it. It's been a tough couple days, but we're the Port Sabine Lady Rays. Let's show some pride." I turn back to Brittny. "I'm going to the doctor on Monday. They're going to give me some meds, fix me up good. I'll play Tuesday night."

"Good, chica," Chole says, slapping my shoulder. "We need you. Obviously. *Especially* if they're going to arrest Annie on Monday."

She hoots, but no one else is laughing. Surprisingly, Annie doesn't answer, just heads for a bucket and starts a Wooden drill, jumping block to block, nailing dink shots. I've never known Annie to turn the other cheek. This police thing must have her jittery, even if it *is* political, like everyone says.

"Don't joke about that," says Corinne. "Stop joking about that baby. Everybody!"

"Kill me for trying to get a laugh," Chole says. "Everyone's so uptight. We all just need to fucking *chill*. Can't play this game tight."

We scatter out to warm up. At a side hoop, I toss the ball up against the backboard, jump for the rebound, and throw up a shot while still hovering midair. No precision required here, just enough skill to bank it in. My heart thumps to life, sweat springs up on my skin. I abandon myself to the drill.

After what Annie did yesterday, it's hard to summon pity for her over the police stuff. I think of her vault of a bedroom with its hotel art on the walls, sheets so soft you'd swear they were spun on tiny fairy looms. I picture the velvety campus lawns that she'll sunbathe on after graduation, the parties she'll go to, the boys who will love her regardless of how selfish she is, because she's Annie and being with her will make them feel immortal. It's funny, but we've shared everything for so long that somewhere along the way, I forgot we didn't share destinies. She has money, and she will go where that money takes her, which will be far away from here.

Maybe that's why she never understood why I followed Coach's rules to the letter—because that was the path to a scholarship. Now that we're seniors, I can no longer ignore how different we've become. Perhaps we've always been different, and I was a fool, imagining real friendship where only a child's affection existed.

By the time Coach emerges from her office, I'm warm and ready. With each minute that my arm cooperates, I feel more confident that I'll be okay.

But when I take the court with the other girls, my arm goes stiff, thrusting down once, then twice. I angle my body so they can't see, shaking out my arm.

Coach blows the whistle and we start a scrimmage drill; in the first couple minutes, I toss up a few threes, none of which makes it to the rim. When it becomes obvious I don't have my shot back, Coach moves me to defense. I pump my arms and legs hard when I run, trying to feel the old magic of movement, that feeling of flying from baseline to baseline. But because I'm hyperaware of my gimp arm, my reflexes aren't sharp, so I let easy passes go by, and I can't stop even the slower girls from breaking past me to the bucket. The weird feeling arrives every few minutes, and I have to pause to thrust my arm down, one-two-three. The other girls stop to gawk. I face away from them, trying to swallow my despair.

"Louis, get some water, rest your legs," Coach Martin says quietly when it gets too pathetic. "Freeman, you're in."

As I jog off the court, my throat closes up. I shake my head hard, left to right, my neck popping. Jogging in place, I try to seem nonchalant, as if I could be subbed back in any second, as if my season and future don't depend on this freak arm.

Halfway through practice, the girls are running three-on-two, two-on-one when all of a sudden, Annie collapses on the wing, knees buckling, her legs disappearing under her. She sits there a beat before her head starts to twitch, jerking down so her ear nearly touches her left shoulder, then back up, then two jerks down. I pause my jogging to watch. Is she really doing this?

Chole's the first one at her side. "Get up, yo," she says, holding out a hand, but Annie stays put.

Coach narrows her eyes to slits as if she's trying to make out something on a horizon we can't see. "Wood, you're in," she says.

*She's faking!* I want to scream. Brittny walks to where Annie sits, wide-eyed and mute.

"Walk it off, Putnam," Coach says to Annie, whose head is still jerking to the left, *one-two, one-two.* Coach reaches down to help her up, but Annie doesn't move. "You want out of practice this bad, hit the showers, I don't give a damn."

The other girls look to me as if for an explanation, but I don't want to be associated with what's happening on the court. She can't let me do a single thing on my own, not even get sick. How could I forget? Any drama in this life belongs to *her.* Watching Annie sit like a deer that's had its legs shot out from under it, I try to decide whether to offer help or retreat to the locker room. I have to admit that the fear on her face seems real. *You're the first to fall, but you won't be the last,* Maw Maw said. My skin is clammy with dried sweat, the gym's air-conditioning suddenly too cold. *No.* This isn't the sign of a curse, only another one of Annie's cons. Finally, Annie breaks the silence with two words: *Help me.*

After Chole and Corinne shoulder Annie off the court, she begs me to stay with her until Beau can get there. I agree, mostly because I want to watch her up close, catch her doing something that would prove she's hoaxing. Practice is over, the other girls dispersed into the late-autumn afternoon. Annie and I sit in Coach's office, facing each other without making eye contact. She looks embarrassed, periodically rocked by a neck twitch. "Shit," she says. "Mers, I'm scared."

I want to say, *You could stop this if you wanted to.* But silence is so much easier. Coach doesn't take her eyes off her ancient laptop, where she's configuring defensive plays for Tuesday's game. Her right hand is a claw over the mouse, she's gripping it that hard. Since she found out about Travis last night, she won't look at me.

When Beau arrives at the gym, he storms into the office, already checking his watch. He tilts back his Stetson. "Now, will somebody kindly explain to me just what the problem is?"

It's the week before the election, and he's likely missing some schmoozy lunch to be here.

"She's having muscle spasms," I say, pointing to her jerking head. *Allegedly.*

"And you called me about this because . . . ?" He looks at Coach.

I may be angry with Annie, but Beau's lack of concern proves that two parents under the same roof doesn't always add up to a whole person who gives a crap.

"It means I've probably got whatever Mercy's got," Annie says with exasperation.

Beau raises an eyebrow at me. "And what is it that Mercy's got, specifically? Paper never did put a name to it."

"We need a doctor," Annie says. "Can't you see that? I mean, look at us!"

She's right that we make for an unsetting pair, our bodies periodically jerky as zombies.

"Take them to the doctor, Beau," Coach says. "I need my leading scorer and rebounder for Tuesday."

"But I'm booked solid—" he starts.

"Figure it out, you're the parent here."

"I'll take them," he says reluctantly. "But we can't have any more stories in the paper."

"We all got things at stake here, Beauregard," Coach says. "Ain't going to lose a game on account of keeping up appearances. Besides"—she looks at us—"they're our girls, and whatever this is, they need help."

I feel grateful to see that she still cares, despite all the trouble I've caused. "I've got the name of the neurologist," I offer. Let the doctors prove that Annie's faking. I hand the card Dr. Elgin gave me to Beau, and he dials the number, speaks with an on-call nurse who says we should come to the hospital immediately and Dr. Joel will meet us.

"Best ring Evelia," Beau says.

It's eleven o'clock, she'll be getting home from church and will wonder where I am. "Will you call and explain?" I ask Coach. She has a knack for convincing Maw Maw to see things her way.

"You bet," she says. "Now go get yourself well." The words sound cheerful, but she's got a sad look to her face, apology pooling behind her eyes. I shuffle out the door to my car and follow Beau's Tahoe to the hospital.

———

MAW MAW STEERS the Lincoln into the hospital lot, parks, then totters toward the bench where I've been waiting, trying and failing to control my skittery arm. She's losing her hip to arthritis, will probably need it replaced soon. In the raw morning light, she looks sickly. Her scuffed brown handbag swings like a pendulum at her side, her short legs wrapped against the chill in thick wool tights. Without a word, she takes my hand, her grip viselike. She turns and starts to pull me back toward the car. I trip forward a few steps.

"Maw Maw . . ."

"Shush."

"I've got an appointment," I say. "Where are we going?"

"You're not safe here." She keeps yanking me forward. "They can't protect you."

*Huh huh huh.*

"Maybe they can figure this out, give me some medicine that might help . . ."

"Nothing can help you now but the Lord."

"But just in case . . ."

She stops, spins to face me; there's a wild light in her eyes.

"Annie's been taken, too," Maw Maw says. "It is just as I've prophesied, God help us." She lets go of my hand, clasps her hands together, and looks skyward. "Lord, forgive us for that murdered child! Don't abandon us!" She doubles forward in a coughing fit, hacking until I begin to fear she'll die right here in the parking lot.

"Breathe, Maw Maw," I say, touching her shoulder. "Breathe."

A man and woman holding the hands of a small boy eye us warily before scurrying to their car. On the force of the wind, the weather is changing, jagged gray clouds scudding in, a fine rain misting our faces.

"I'm all right," Maw Maw rasps. "It's not me I'm worried for, Tee Mercy. I only want to protect you in these final months."

"Let's go inside," I say. "I'll get you some water."

"We should be at home kneeling in prayer."

Her eyes dart with a rabbity anxiety. Inside, we find a bench by the nurses' station, and I fetch a paper cup of lukewarm water. While she sips and catches her breath, I hold her hand. Passersby startle at my grunts as if I've insulted them.

"I'm scared, Maw Maw." She presses the back of my hand to her cheek, and I think maybe she could love me in spite of everything, Travis and the letters and all the secrets I've kept. "We're already here," I say. "Can I just see what the doctor says? They might give me medicine."

"Won't give you no medicine." She shakes her head with a certainty that angers me. She's been wrong before, thought the Linzer baby would be healthy, but it came to Mrs. Linzer blue, stillborn; she could be wrong about this.

"You don't want me to play anymore," I say. "I heard you on the phone with Coach last summer. You've been looking for an excuse. You hate the game, you always have."

She clucks her tongue. "Basketball's the least of my concerns, Tee Mercy."

"Well, it's not the least of *mine*," I say. "And this guy's a doctor, a brain doctor. He's going to help me."

"The doctor won't do a thing for you. He *can't*. But if you need to hear it from a stranger to believe it, so be it."

Once the hours of tests have been completed, we four sit in the hospital room awaiting results, Beau, Annie, Maw Maw, and me. Though weary, I'm filled with manic energy; we're so close to an answer that each minute spent waiting feels like it's been stretched into a fourth dimension. Finally, Dr. Joel returns, a stack of papers in his hands. He tells us that our brains look healthy on MRI, that the EEGs are normal, that our *spells* aren't related to brain malfunction, which is a good thing. When Beau presses him for a diagnosis, he says that with cases like this, it's often a process of elimination, and we can now eliminate brain damage, epilepsy, tumors.

"But can't you give me a prescription?" I ask. "Look at my arm! I'm sick. I need help!" Panic blooms in my gut.

"Unfortunately, there's no treatment I can administer at this time, because you are healthy, according to the tests."

I glance at Maw Maw, but her eyes are on the floor, hands clasped in front of her. She was right, the doctor can't save me, not in time for Tuesday's game.

Dr. Joel looks at me and Annie with sympathetic eyes. "I'm sure these spells are scary. These kinds of physiological symptoms can force us to slow down and take a good look at our lives . . ." He pauses to pull a business card from his pocket and suspend it in the middle of our small circle. "I suggest you call this woman, Dr. Frances Ducharme."

Beau snatches the card, scrutinizes it. "A headshrinker?" he says.

"So you think we're nuts, Doctor?" Annie asks. She's trying to sound tough, sarcastic, but I remember how often she's turned to me after a confession to ask, *Am I crazy?* I know she's thinking of Mrs. Putnam shut up in her satiny bedroom, and she's frightened.

"No, I don't, Annie," the doctor says. "But there are forces within and without us, acting on our body and mind. What I know is that Dr. Ducharme can provide people with the tools to deal with those things that lie within us."

At this, Maw Maw breaks her silence. "Funny," she says. "When I was a girl, that role belonged to Jesus Christ."

Dr. Joel chortles, but Maw Maw looks at him with raised brows, withering his laughter.

"Why don't you just lock us up and give us shock treatment, like the olden days," Annie says. "Not too olden, though. *Daddy* had it done to Mama when she had her breakdown, didn't you?" *Daddy* like she's cussing.

"Hold your tongue, Anne," Beau snarls.

"Once you realized keeping her locked in the castle was making her a little loony, right?"

Beau's face goes purple; I can see a blood vessel pulsing in his veiny eye.

"Annie," Dr. Joel says in such a measured way that the word falls like a blanket over the fire that has just ignited between father and daughter.

"We're *sick*," Annie says, turning back to Dr. Joel. "We need medicine."

"The man just said you weren't sick," Beau says. "He doesn't have time for your poor-little-rich-girl act, so you're going to have to shape up and start—"

"Start what, *Dad*?" she says. "Start behaving like a mayor's daughter? Like a governor's daughter? Maybe if you weren't running, I wouldn't be getting called in by the police!"

"Don't fool yourself, Anne Elizabeth," Beau says. "I already called Sanchez on it, but he denied pulling a stunt, and I believe him. You're getting called in because you're a whore and everyone in this town knows it." Annie looks stricken. He turns back to Dr. Joel. "I *expect* you practice doctor/patient confidentiality."

Annie jumps off the examination table and flees. Nobody says a word to stop her.

"We thank you for your time, Doc," Beau says. "You've given us all the information we need." He's recovered his politician's glibness. "Let's go, Evelia." He puts a sheltering arm around her and escorts her to the door. She goes without a word because she has no questions for the doctor; he has confirmed what she knew all along.

"Goodbye," I say to Dr. Joel.

The others are already in the hallway, but I hesitate. I don't want to leave, because what waits for me outside the door is too dark to contemplate. But then Dr. Joel pats me on the shoulder, tells me to try and get some rest, and that the whole town's proud of me, no matter what happens.

# ILLA

AT THE HOSPITAL, Illa hides out in the cafeteria. From there, she can see the entrance that Mercy and Annie will have to pass through in order to leave. She knows she's taking a risk by being there, especially if Annie sees her, but at this point she's so thoroughly freaked by what has happened in the last twenty-four hours that she's willing to brave Annie's barbs to find out what's wrong with the girls.

Restless, Illa wanders the food line, examining the hard-tack biscuits and lumpy gravy, the mound of powdered eggs forming a dark boogery crust under the heat lamp's orange rings. She should eat something—already the day has a fever-dream quality from lack of sleep and sustenance—but she takes a weird pleasure in denying herself, as if this act of fasting can somehow cure Mercy and fix everything. Back at the table, she half watches the news, some PR robot from the refinery who wants to reassure everyone that nothing out of the ordinary has happened at the plant to cause the smell and they should just go about their daily lives.

When Illa sees Annie, dressed in a hospital gown, walk into the women's restroom at the far end of the cafeteria, she contemplates diving beneath the Formica table but doesn't. Even though Annie will give her a hard time for asking, Illa has to know how Mercy is doing, and at this point, Annie is the only person who can tell her, so she walks past the other bedraggled diners to the restroom.

The door opens on silent hinges to reveal a corridor of stalls, at the end of which is a bank of clay-colored sinks. Annie has ducked her head near one of the faucets and is splashing water on her face. Afterward, she stands with both hands on the counter's edge, her head sunk below her shoulders, so that from a certain angle, it looks like she's been decapitated. She kicks the tiled wall beneath the counter, hard. *One-two one-two,* her head bobs to the right. *One-two one-two.* "Stop it stop it stop it stop it," Annie growls.

Instinctively, Illa takes a step toward Annie. It's upsetting to watch someone in a bad state like this, even someone upon whom you have wished a mild kind of harm—stubbed toe, failing grade, pinkeye, bad-hair day. The physical antics are unsettling, but it's the inhuman cry that sends Illa scrambling out of hiding to where Annie squats, head between the knees, breathing hard. Unsure what to do, Illa waits for Annie to look up and notice her, but a minute passes and Annie doesn't stir from her position. *Huh,* Annie says finally, head jerking up. She loses her balance and falls backward onto the floor, where she sits, stunned, legs splayed out in front of her like a little kid. She looks around the empty bathroom, her face scrunched, crinkling the skin around her right eye, mouth a rictus of terror. It's unclear whether she's registered Illa's presence.

"Annie, do you need help?" Illa asks. "Should I get someone?"

Annie's expression morphs from fear to surprise, and she blinks repeatedly. Struggling to stand, she eventually regains her footing. From somewhere outside comes the tomcat whinging of a siren.

"How long have you been there?" Annie asks, her eyes wet and unfocused.

"Not long," Illa lies. "I just . . . You should get help."

*One-two one-two* bobbles Annie's head.

"Fu . . . Fuck off," Annie stutters. "Just fuck off."

"I was just wondering," Illa ventures. "Is Mercy—"

"LEAVE OR I'LL CALL THE COPS ON YOU, STALKER!" Annie bellows, this time stomping her sneakered foot threateningly in Illa's direction. *One-two one-two.*

Illa backs quickly out of the room. She needs air. Darting through the doors leading to the parking lot, she flinches against the watery light. The cold front that arrived last night wraps its icy shawl of breeze around her. In her thin T-shirt, she shivers violently. Watching first Mercy and then Annie taken by these strange spells, she's felt so helpless. She needs a task, something simple she can start and finish. She decides to go to the gym and do the laundry left over from that morning's truncated practice.

She takes a few woozy steps toward the car, then feels her knees buckle. *I'm fainting,* she thinks just before crumpling to the pavement. She's out only a few seconds, at least that's what the guy hovering over her says. She recognizes him as the reporter from the *Flare* who covers the basketball games.

"It's like you knew you were going down," he says. "Your head fell against your arm. It was a close call. Whew." Reaching out a hand to help her up, he asks if she's okay.

"It's been a long day," she says, taking his hand and standing. She's so tired that the guy looks fuzzy around the edges.

"It's only eleven o'clock."

"That's what I mean."

"How's Mercy doing?" he asks.

"I only saw Annie."

"Were you at the practice when Annie collapsed?"

"Yes, yeah . . ."

"I heard she went down like a ton of bricks. I got Wood and Gomez on the record about it. They were pretty shook up. What's your name?"

"Illa," she says.

"You're the manager, I recognize you now." He pauses. "You fainted. Are you sick, too? Is Mercy contagious? Are there more sick girls besides you and Annie?"

"I'm not sick," she says peevishly. "I'm just tired, that's all." She's confused; he's confusing her. She wants to get to the gym, throw the practice jerseys into the wash, then sit with her back against the warm, rumbling machine until she falls asleep.

"I've got to go," she says, stepping around him and into the car. She starts the motor but idles there, watching until he returns to his vehicle and drives away. Just before she puts the car in gear, she sees Evelia and Annie walk out. Illa sinks herself lower into the seat. Beau comes next, followed by Mercy. They've been released from the hospital; that's a good sign. And Mercy is walking on her own; but it's *how* she walks that catches Illa's attention. A kind of hobble-skip, apparently adopted to help counterbalance the swinging arm. As Mercy makes her way across the lot, she grimaces periodically.

Beau and Annie roar out of the lot in his black Tahoe. When Mercy and Evelia pull out, Illa glides after the Lincoln, making sure to leave some distance between the cars. They head east toward Chocolate Bayou and the stilt house. Once arrived, Illa parks halfway down the block in the encompassing shadow of an ancient cypress, hunching below the dash. She sees Evelia usher Mercy inside. The woman looks up and down the block as if she can feel herself being watched, then shuts the door after them. Illa's skin prickles. What, exactly, is going on? She decides to wait there to see if she can find out.

# MERCY

---

AT HOME, MAW MAW watches as I change into my pajamas and get under the covers. She tells me I'm to fast, pray, and rest, and that she will join me in this period of cleansing.

"We've got much work to do, hard work, to fend off these demons that want your body. No school this week. Need to keep you away from those other girls. So long as the killer walks unpunished through this town, more girls will fall."

She tells me she's going up to the church for an emergency meeting with Pastor Parris so she can tell him about her latest vision and call on him to harness the prayers of the congregation. As soon as I hear the Lincoln sputter away, I slip out of bed. I believe in the power of prayer, but I'm running out of time. If Maw Maw's right and this is a curse, there's only one person left who might be able to help me get back on the court. Lucille Cloud.

No time to change out of pajamas. I tuck the money I've been saving for new Jordans into the elastic waistband of the pants, then slide behind the wheel of the Accord and race for the woods. As I drive, a verse from Leviticus runs through my head: *I will set my face against anyone who turns to mediums and spiritists to prostitute them-selves by following them, and I will cut him off from their people.* But I'm cut off already. I ache for Travis but can't go to him. Annie betrayed me. Maw Maw thinks she can pray me to healing but doesn't know I'm not pure anymore.

It's dusky beneath the canopy of trees, the Century Oak tall and broad in the middle of a small clearing. I think of Lucille's hound shot dead yesterday, and I'm glad he's not there to announce my arrival. I get out of the car and notice immediately the eerie, suffocating silence of the woods. Inland away from the Gulf breeze, the smell from the refinery is so overpowering, I hold my shirt over my nose.

"Well, well, well," Lucille says when she pulls open the door to her cabin to find me standing there in my plaid flannels. "Look who's come from Grandma's house to visit the Big Bad Wolf."

*Huh huh huh.* I must look desperate, because Lucille doesn't make another smart remark, only pushes her tangled hair out of her intense little fox face and stares at my arm. Though she isn't much older than me, her face speaks of centuries I haven't lived through. Perhaps it's being alone, or living at the mercy of the elements, or perhaps it's as they say: that she's a witch who's not in her early twenties but is well over three hundred years old, born in this territory's lawless age, when the Gulf foamed red with the blood of Indians and settlers alike, when Jean Lafitte's pirates ruled.

Lucille raises a toothpick to her mouth, and I shy away from her hand, thinking she means to hit me. She ignores my jumpiness, sucking on the toothpick. "What's going on here?" she asks, indicating my arm. She steps toward me.

"Don't . . ." I say, sidestepping her advance.

She puts her hands up. "Fine by me, but I don't imagine you came out here to chew the fat."

I shake my head. "I . . . I need help."

She assesses me before continuing. "The police searched this place upside down for the stuff that killed the baby. They wanted names of all the girls who've ever bought anything from me." She laughs bitterly. "Like I keep a log or something." She looks at me, suddenly serious. "If I help you, you've got to get Evelia off my back. I don't want them troubling me again. All's I want is to get left alone."

"I'll make sure she leaves you alone," I promise, knowing that if I mention Lucille's name to Maw Maw, she'll take it as proof the devil's won me.

"Let me take a look, hon," she says. To my surprise, she doesn't start with the arm, instead checking my glands, pulse, temperature, examining my tongue, my irises. Finally, she takes my arm in her hands and holds it away from her like it's a bone she's excavated. "You been to see a doc yet?" she says at last.

I tell her about the doctors and tests, how they didn't find anything wrong. She nods and steps back, still assessing me. Then, because I feel as if I might burst if I don't, I ask what she can give me to make it go away so I can play come Tuesday. She goes to a plywood shelf nailed into the trunk of the tree and pulls down a red lacquered box, sorting through its contents until she finds what she's looking for: a purple stone encased in thin wiring, hanging from a leather strip. She holds it out to me. "It's a protector amulet," she says. "An amethyst."

Reluctantly, I take it. "Don't you have some herbs or something? I need something strong . . ."

"Hon, all your vitals are good, you got the standing heart rate of a marathoner. You ask me, I think it's the negative energy of all these—"

"You don't understand." I pace the narrow cabin, the amethyst swinging as I walk. "I can't . . . This is just *a necklace*."

"Mercy, listen to me," she says. "It's not just a necklace. It's a blessed stone, but you have to really *believe*."

"Don't you talk to me about belief!" I'm crying now, filled with despair.

"I think you better go," she says, pushing past me to open the door.

As I leave, our fingers touch; I feel a sharp shock and draw back. On the wind, a gamey scent, pungent and sickening. Some unseen animal moves in the underbrush.

"If you're going to take the stone, you have to pay me for it."

Still clutching the necklace, I reach for the wad of cash in my waistband, scatter the bills on the dirt. It was a mistake to come here. I stumble back toward the car. My hand's shaking so bad I can't fit the key in the lock. The sneezy feeling, then an attack, my arm flapping *one-two-three*. I howl up toward the treetops, hurl the necklace away. This arm! *This damned arm.* I squeeze myself hard at the wrist, dig my nails into the skin, clench my teeth until I'm sure they will fall from my mouth like bits of smashed porcelain.

If this arm must move, I'll move it! *I'll* move it! Again and again and again, I swing the arm against the side of the car, and Lord it feels good, this dull pain in the meat of me. *Thump thump thump.* Eyes closed, I swing it so hard and fast that there's no time for the flapping; *I* control *you; I* control *you.*

Someone's arms around my shoulders, holding tight. I keep my eyes shut.

"It's okay, Mercy. You're okay. You're okay. Let's sit. *Shhhh.* Sit, now."

I let myself be guided to the ground, my arm numb but still. I curl into the lap in front of me. When I finally look up, there's Illa, her thin face so near I can see the texture of her freckles. She takes my hand in hers, strokes my hair.

"Will you stay with me, please stay just a few minutes?" I ask.

"Of course, Mercy."

"Is there anyone else here?"

"No, no one. Just me."

"But it feels like there's someone else. I feel someone breathing."

"It's just me, Mercy. I promise."

"I need help, Illa. Please, stay close."

She squeezes my hand, hard. "I can do that. I can definitely do that, Mercy."

"I'm all alone."

"I'm here, Mercy. I'm here for you."

"You're not scared?"

"Of you? No. Never."

"That you might catch whatever it is I've got."

"I'm not scared."

"I am, Illa. I'm terrified."

———————

THAT NIGHT THE tics get so bad they keep me awake. They come on every few minutes, shuddering through me, making my jaw clench and my whole body tighten while the arm does its freak thing.

After I hear Maw Maw's door close for the night, I wander into the kitchen, fill a gallon bag with ice, and set it heavy on my wrist. For a minute it feels good, but then with one swift jerk, the bag slides off my arm and onto the table. In the living room, I lie on the carpet and wedge my arm under the couch. But when another round of tics start, the pain is too much. After I pull my arm out, there's a dark red line where the wooden frame dug into the flesh of my upper arm.

I give up trying to stop the fits and lie back on the floor. The hardness of the surface feels good at my back. I want the peace of sleep so bad, but my churning mind and body won't allow it. What was Illa doing in the forest? In the moment, I'd been so grateful for her calming presence, her familiar face, but thinking on it now, it makes no sense. Still, she stayed with me until I felt better, and then she drove me home, where I showed her how to sneak up the back way and she boosted me to the balcony. Before we said goodbye, I made her swear not to tell a soul, and she said she would never. I believe her; she hasn't told anyone about Charmaine's letters.

It's strange that this person I've never thought much about now knows so much about me, but there's something in Illa that makes me trust her. A gentleness you don't find in many people. She takes such care with everything she does, folding our uniforms into crisp rectangles, winding bandages around ankles. With a label maker she borrowed from the faculty lounge, she put our names on the water bottles so we wouldn't share germs and get sick, and on game days, she makes glittery signs for our lockers. I hear she's a nurse to her mama, which is refreshing somehow; most girls are *me me me* all the time. After her kindness in the forest, I feel bad for never truly noticing her before, but she's so *small,* and she ghosts in and out of the locker room, never really participating. When she put her hands to my face to wipe the tears away, I was almost surprised to realize she was flesh and blood like the rest of us.

I must have fallen asleep, because Sunday morning arrives with Maw Maw squatting beside me, telling me *wake up, wake up,* asking if I'm all right. She brings me water, and I'm careful to take it with my left hand so it doesn't spill.

Maw Maw tells me that after talking to Pastor Parris yesterday evening and giving it some thought, she's decided to withdraw me from school. "Only two months till Judgment Day. We've got to get you right before then. Pastor Parris has a plan, but he needs to do the proper preparations."

"What preparations? What's the plan?"

I'm hopeful but wary. I recall the girl in Nacogdoches, the one whose dress supposedly caught fire.

"When I have the details, I'll surely share them," she says, taking my empty glass back to the kitchen.

So it's all but settled now. There won't be four more years of ball; there won't even be one more game. Just two more months on this earth. This can't be how it ends, though, everything is happening too fast. *Please, slow down, I need more time,* I beg, though I don't know who I'm pleading with now that I can't pray. *One-two-three,* my arm flops down.

I haul myself up onto the couch. "Let me tell Coach in person. At least let me do that."

There should be a ceremony to mark the end of basketball, the death of this thing I've loved so long. Like so many things, however, it will slip away without fanfare.

"Come straight home after, don't tarry," Maw Maw answers. "We must take care when the devil walks abroad."

Soon I'm blasting down residential streets until I hit the seawall. During the season, Coach practically lives at the gym on weekends, reviewing game tape or devising plays, so I head for the school to find her.

It's all over now; I must try to forget the girl I was, the one who was beautiful and dangerous, who could bring herself to imagine all the glories of the world but only with a basketball in her hands. I pass the turnoff to Travis's house; the happiness of the summer seems so distant, another land I traveled to once. If what we had was only lust, then why do thoughts of him linger and deepen far past the first physical pulse of my body in response to his memory?

But if I hope to rise to heaven with Maw Maw in two months' time, I have to stop this thinking. Though she didn't say the word, it hung heavy between us: *hell*. Without intervention, the destiny of sinners like me.

On the far side of the bay, the Praying Hands rise white against the blue sea. From here it looks as though they are begging something of the refinery, negotiating for the souls of the dead.

Raised voices on the radio catch my attention " . . . election's a week from Tuesday, Beau, you still promising to get the case solved before then?" Beau Putnam answers that, as a matter of fact, he just got off the phone with Chief McKinney, who's going to give any high school girl who wants to clear her name once and for all the chance to voluntarily submit a DNA sample this Wednesday morning. They've already got it worked out with the school board, because everyone wants to see this case solved.

"A source says your daughter was supposed to be questioned first thing Monday," the interviewer says. "But they've postponed it."

After a couple false starts, Beau recovers enough to say that the whole town went to Annie's Purity Ball this summer and can testify to his daughter's commitment to remaining intact until marriage, but that yes, certainly, she plans to cooperate with the investigation if the chief deems it necessary.

"I understand the interview got postponed because your daughter is sick right now. Y'all were seen leaving the hospital on Saturday . . ."

"Well, the doctors have told us that they're healthy, so it's really nothing to get worked up about."

"But Jodi Martin's told the *Flare* that Mercy and Annie won't play in Tuesday's game. According to the story that ran Saturday, Mercy has physical tics that make it too hard to play. The town wants to know, Mr. Putnam, what's wrong with the girls? What's made your girl so sick she can't cooperate with the law?"

"Tell you what, I believe that's a question for Mercy Louis," Beau says.

*No,* I think reflexively. *No, no, no.*

He continues, "Annie was a happy girl until Mercy went down. What I can say for sure is that she'd follow Mercy off a cliff. She idolizes Mercy. Hell, this whole town does."

"Mr. Putnam, what about the talk that it's the refinery poisoning our youngsters? There's been extra flaring lately, a bunch of kids up at the school feeling dizzy and such. Could that have something to do with your daughter's illness? We know Sands has given a lot of money to your campaign, so how does that make you feel . . ."

I swerve into the gym lot and dash out of the car. Down the steps, through the doors, into the gym where I knock on Coach's door. No answer. This time I bang hard.

"Coach, it's Mercy," I shout through the door. *Bang bang bang.* "Please, Coach!" Still nothing. I fall to my knees and rest my head on the door. The pressure feels good, all my frantic thoughts dispersing into the wood. "Coach," I whimper.

Someone says: "She's not here."

I glance around to find Illa Stark standing behind me, arms laden with uniforms.

"I know," I say, getting to my feet. Trying to gather my wits, I smooth my hair behind my ears.

"She was here earlier, but she went home." She looks apologetic. "Is there anything I can do?"

I shake my head no. *One-two-three.* I clutch my arm, embarrassed.

"Do you have a minute?" she asks. "I have something I think you should see."

The journalism room smells faintly of cigarette smoke and stale french fries. Illa walks me into the darkroom, and I appreciate its dimness for the cover it gives me and my arm.

"Here," she says, pushing a photo across the counter toward me.

When I see it, I remember the exact moment, the salty warmth of sweat as it streamed down my face and into my mouth, the explosive aftershocks of having driven full court, weaving through a forest of swatting arms and knocking Dawaun Brown on his rear end somewhere near the bucket as I laid in the most delicate kiss of a shot, *thump swish*. In the photo, I'm raging with happiness and pride.

"I entered this in a contest, I hope that doesn't weird you out," she says. "The theme was 'Euphoric Sport.'"

The words snare my heart, and just like that, I'm crying, tears sheeting down my face. *Euphoric.* I was, once.

"Hey, hey," she says, kneading my shoulder with awkward little pushes. "I didn't mean for you to get upset. I thought it might help you feel better."

We sit side by side on the floor as I try to catch my breath. Eventually, I ask: "How do you get back to a feeling? You can't just buy a ticket." I wag my head back and forth.

"You'll get back there," she says. "You've hit a rough patch, but come Tuesday, remember this picture. I can make you a copy, if you—"

"I'm not playing Tuesday," I interrupt. "I have to quit the team."

"What? Why? You can't give up, you'll get better, I know you will!"

"No point talking about it, it's already been decided. My grandmother . . ." I consider telling her the truth—that Maw Maw thinks I might be possessed, that the world is going to end in two months, so I need to focus on saving my soul—but I know it'll sound crazy to a nonbeliever, so I just say, "My grandmother wants me to focus on healing."

"But what about . . ."

"It's a done deal." I'm short with her, but she's making it worse; she can't make any argument I haven't already thought of myself.

"Want a Coke?" she asks, resignation in her voice. "There's a mini-fridge we keep stocked for when we go to press."

"Sure," I say, and we push back into the classroom's yellow light.

She starts to hand me a Dr Pepper, then remembers my arm and pops it open for me and hands it over. "Do you miss her?" she asks.

*Huh huh huh.* I don't have to ask who she means. I run my finger along the cold ridge of the Coke can; I press the pad of my finger into the sharp metal of the tab until I draw blood, then put it in my mouth and suck.

"Never knew her, how could I miss her?" I say, polishing off the Dr Pepper and clinking the empty can against the desk. "Don't know the first thing about her. Favorite food, favorite color, when her birthday is."

"It seems like she misses you."

"How would you know?"

"There were a few more letters over the summer . . ." she stutters, looking sheepish. "I . . . I read them . . . Please don't be mad at me, I just felt so bad that there were these letters to you that you'd never read . . . Don't be mad, Mercy, I couldn't take it if I made you mad at me again."

She says this fast, like I might not understand the words if she just speeds through them; she curves her body inward like a comma. She's waiting for me to lose it like I did at Park Terrace last summer, but if I lose any more, I'll disappear.

"Yeah, I miss her," I say at last. "I miss her every single day. Even before she wrote to me, I missed her." I bite my tongue, pinch my inner arm, anything to keep from crying again. "So why did Charmaine send the letters to *your* house?"

Illa stands and walks to the other side of the room, where she examines a line of books shelved there before pulling one off.

"They keep the yearbook archive in here," she says, thrusting one at me, the 1980 *Stingaree Jubilee,* laminate peeling back from the mustard-yellow cover. When I hesitate to take the yearbook from her, Illa flips it open to a dog-eared page. "Here," she says. "Look. Our moms were friends back in the day. That's why we got the letters, I guess."

On a page titled "Junior Life," there's a photo of two young women standing on a beach, their arms thrown around each other in the casual posture of close friends. Illa's mom looks like the cat that ate the canary; Charmaine is round-cheeked, sunburned, a string bean of a girl. I see myself in the shape of her calves, her elfin ears. Maw Maw must have been horrified as I grew to look more like my mother with each passing year.

"What does your mom say about her?" I ask.

"Not much," she says. "I just found out they were friends this summer, and when I asked her about it, she got upset."

I want to get back in the car and drive to Illa's house to excavate Meg Stark's memories, every last one. Getting upset over Charmaine Boudreaux is something we have in common.

"You want to see what your mother looked like as a freshman?" Illa asks, fetching another of the books from the shelf. "Go on. There's an index of students at the back, you just look up the name and it tells you where in the book a person's mentioned."

Hands shaking, I flip to the back of the book and run my finger down the row of *B*s until I find *Boudreaux, Charmaine*. Pages thirty-eight, fifty-three, sixty-seven. I turn to the first page, but I'm unprepared; freshman Charmaine is so young, her face squishy as a baby's, all cheek and lip. She wears a blouse with a Peter Pan collar, her grin guileless. She is not trying to act older than she is, like so many girls in high school. She is fourteen, and it shows. Beneath her photo is a quote by Ralph Waldo Emerson: *Live in the sunshine, swim the sea, drink the wild air,* as well as a list of her interests: church, movies, summer, basketball. *Basketball?*

I have pictured her with a crack pipe in her mouth, under a raw-

boned man working his mean hips hard; I have pictured her emaci-
ated and wild-eyed from the drugs, stumbling down the streets of
New Orleans in torn stockings. Never have I pictured her capable of
doing anything as disciplined as squaring up for a shot. What happened to her between this photograph and her years wandering the
purgatory of Maw Maw's stories?

In the car on the way back to the stilt house, I remember what
Charmaine wrote: *There are two sides to every story, I only want to
tell mine.* Maw Maw never mentioned that Charmaine played basketball, though surely she must've known it would give me a nip of
happiness. Is this the reason Maw Maw hates the game and refuses
to watch me play? What else has she left out about Charmaine?

When I arrive home, I expect Maw Maw to lecture me about
being out too long, but she doesn't even register my entrance. She
stands frozen by the telephone, receiver dangling from her hand, the
phone's busy signal beeping angrily.

"Maw Maw?" I say quietly, not wanting to startle her. She looks
at me foggily, preoccupied. "What is it?"

"That was Jodi Martin," she says. "Two more girls have been
taken."

# ILLA

AFTER MERCY LEAVES the journalism room, Illa guns it to a ramshackle roadhouse that sits on a lip of the bayou, orders a bourbon, and sucks it down, grateful for its spirit-shocking burn. She has just had the longest conversation of her life with Mercy Louis, and she needs to recover.

The roadhouse is not the type of place where a person's age matters much—everyone looks life-worn, herself included, and that's as good as legal. From a darkened corner, she hears the sound of coins dropping into the jukebox, and then George Jones singing "He Stopped Loving Her Today." At the bar, a few men sit slumped over their beers. From across the room, the cracking of pool balls. Smoke makes a haze of the air. For the first time in a long while, Illa finds that she's hungry. Starving, in fact. It's such an alien sensation that at first she mistakes it for cramps.

From the barkeep, she orders a burger with grilled onions and pickles. It arrives on a single square of waxed paper translucent with grease. She wolfs it down in three bites and decides it is possibly the best thing she's ever eaten; she orders another one and dispatches it with the same efficiency. To round out the meal, she gets a bag of potato chips and eats every last one, down to the salty crumbs at the bottom of the bag, which she collects by pressing her forefinger to them and licking them off.

It is her first real meal in days. Her hair has begun to fall out in clumps; she didn't get her period last month. She does not want to be lighter than air anymore; in a world that can bring down even the strongest girls among them—Mercy, Annie—making yourself deliberately insubstantial seems foolish.

For years Mercy's power existed in her beauty, talent, strength, and goodness. Now Illa understands that wretchedness, too, is a form of power, because seeing Mercy like this rocks Illa with an overwhelming desire to do whatever is necessary to get Mercy healthy. Guiltily, she thinks back to the summer when she hoped that Mercy might one day need her the way that other girls on the team did. She never imagined a situation this dire, only thought that perhaps Mercy would develop shin splints or something so Illa might have the opportunity to minister to her and perhaps, through those ministrations, befriend her.

Remembering Mercy's desperation in the forest and her great sadness earlier today, Illa is suddenly glad of her ability to meet people's needs, honed over years of caring for Mama and managing the team. Even if helping Mercy means she will go back to being a superstar with no desire to talk to Illa ever again. Illa will do that, sacrifice this newfound, prayed-for closeness if Mercy can just be herself again, powerful, shimmering, triumphant.

That afternoon Mercy confessed that she missed Charmaine every day. Yet she stubbornly refused to respond to her mother's letters and still thinks of the woman as the enemy. Illa admits that Charmaine doesn't have much going for her other than a few badly punctuated but earnest letters, sent years too late. Still, Illa has a soft spot for Charmaine, something about the blunt honesty of the letters and the adoring look on her face in that yearbook photo with Mama. Whenever

Illa turned to the photo over the summer, that look made her proud of her mother. And it made her want to love her better. She failed, though. With Mama, she continued to be impatient and churlish, shaming her mother when she should have helped her. If Charmaine Boudreaux deserved a second chance after being gone seventeen years, then surely Mama did, too.

Illa finds a sticky pay phone in the hall by the bathrooms, dials information, and asks for Boudreaux, Charmaine, of Austin. No luck. What about Boudreaux, C? Still nothing. She scribbles down the numbers of the six Boudreauxs listed, gets change, and calls them. Two lines have been disconnected, one leads her to an answering machine for a Tuff Boudreaux, and the other three have never heard of Charmaine. Back at the bar, she asks the bartender for a piece of paper and pen. He has to hunt in back, but he returns clutching a Howard Johnson clicker pen and a yellow sheet of paper torn jaggedly from a pad. "Any chance you've got a stamp and envelope back there, too?" she asks. "I can pay you cash." To her surprise, he doesn't scoff or reproach her, just leaves and reappears with a Forever stamp and a coffee-stained envelope. "Thanks a lot," she says, sliding a dollar toward him.

He waves it away. "Anyone writing a letter in a bar needs whatever help I can give 'em," he says, wiping down the counter with a yellowing rag.

Illa has Charmaine's address memorized from the summer, the PO box and zip. On the yellow sheet, Illa writes,

> *Don't panic, but Mercy is sick, and I think she needs you, though she'll kill me if she ever finds out about this letter . . .*

When she finishes writing, she folds the paper in threes, slides it into the envelope, and carefully writes out Charmaine's name and address. She affixes the stamp and then pushes the envelope to arm's length, wary of what she's done. She orders a ginger ale. For as long as it takes her to drink the soda, Illa can pretend she hasn't just defied Mercy's most ardent wish. While she knows it will probably reach its destination in a day or two, she wants to give fate or chance or whatever the opportunity to intervene, if it cares to.

From the jukebox, Johnny Cash sings about Sunday mornings coming down, a mournful song well suited to a roadhouse bar on a stormy Monday night when all the world seems to be going to shit. Illa finishes the ginger ale, folds the letter into her pocket, and pays her tab. Back outside, rain dampens her face, steam rising from the low, wet country lining the highway. Thunder unfolds through the trees. After depositing the letter in the postbox, Illa pulls into the driveway on Galvez. She sees the upstairs light come on in Mr. Alvarez's house. She presses her cheek to the cool glass of the window, her head swimming a bit, her belly warm and full. Rain blurs the windshield, cocooning her inside the car. She thinks of Mercy's stricken face during warm-ups that Friday night, the arhythmic dance of Annie's disobedient body in the hospital bathroom. What *is* happening to the girls? And can it spread?

---

COACH TELLS THE team about Corinne Wolcott before practice Monday morning. According to Mrs. Wolcott, Corinne woke up Sunday morning with a bad stutter and can barely talk.

"They're at the doctor now," Coach says. "But it's likely Corinne won't play in tomorrow's game."

Brittny mentions that Corinne's twin sister, Mackenzie, is sick, too, that it started with stiffness in the neck that traveled down her back and left her bedridden.

"Actually," Brittny says, "the doctor is making a house call because Mackenzie *can't even move.* I hope I don't catch it." She shudders. "I spent Saturday night over there, we were drinking out of the same water bottle. What if it's meningitis? A couple years ago some kids at my sister's college got it. They got real stiff necks like Mackenzie, fevers, and headaches. One of them almost died."

"No one's dying," Coach says. "That's enough of that kind of talk."

"What about Mercy and Annie?" Zion asks. "When are they going to be able to play again?"

"Not sure just yet," Coach says. "We've got to give them some time to recover, but you know those two, they're fighters. They'll be back."

Has Mercy not told Coach the news about leaving the team? Maybe she lost her nerve. After practice, Illa decides to let Coach know so that maybe she can talk some sense into Evelia. Mercy said it was useless to try to change her grandmother's mind, but people have a hard time saying no to Jodi Martin.

"What is it, Stark?" Coach says when she finds Illa waiting at her office door.

"It's Mercy, Coach. She was up here yesterday looking for you, I thought she told you already, but I guess not . . ."

"Spit it out, what's going on?"

"Evelia isn't going to let her play ball."

"I know, she already told me about tomorrow's game."

"Not just tomorrow's game. She's not going to let her play the rest of the *season.* She's withdrawing her from school today."

Coach's face puckers like she's tasted something sour. "We'll see about that," she says.

"You going to go over there now?" Illa says, glad to have a bulldog like Coach fighting for Mercy.

"I got class," Coach says distractedly. "But I'll take care of it first thing after school." Then she squeezes Illa's shoulder, smiles, and simply says, "Thank you."

By lunch, the whole school knows about Annie and the Wolcotts. Nancy Cobb and Laynie Hibbard are home sick, too. In the cafeteria line, at the tables, by the Coke machines in the courtyard, everyone is talking about one of two things: the mystery illness or last night's radio announcement about the voluntary DNA testing later that week. Students buzz down the hallways, atoms of anxiety fusing with one another to form dangerous compounds.

*Meningitis,* someone whispers over a lunch tray. *They call it the kissing disease. It's crazy contagious. Dude, if Annie Putnam has a kissing disease, the whole school is doomed!* Laughter and hissing. *Shit's real, y'all,* someone else pipes in. *I saw AP coming out of math, she looked awful. She shouldn't be in school.*

Illa steals up to the Mrs. Ancelet's office so she can use the phone; she wants to warn Mercy about Coach's visit. When she knocks on the door to the nurse's office, she can hear someone inside coughing violently. When no one answers, Illa pushes the door open; she sees Brittny Wood reclining on a cot, arm drawn over her eyes. Keisha Freeman holds a blood-speckled tissue in her hand, eyes watering from the force of her hacking.

Mrs. Ancelet sees Illa and says, "Don't tell me you're sick, too?"

Illa shakes her head.

"Oh, thank God." Harried, Mrs. Ancelet turns away, jabbering to herself. "I told them they should have canceled school with this godawful smell, I remember what it was like after the spill in '84, kids lined up down the hall thinking the water was poisoned . . ."

"Can I use the phone?"

She looks back as if surprised that Illa's still there. "Oh. No, come back another time. I've got my hands full. And Illa, shut the door on your way out, please. Don't need anyone else getting any ideas."

Illa nods and does as she's asked, backing out of the room and pulling the door closed behind her. She's glued to the spot, unable to decide which way to go. Maybe she should go home, too. For the first time, she's scared for herself. She can't afford to get sick. How will Mama manage? Illa turns toward the senior hallway and collides with Nancy Cobb, smashing her face against Nancy's shoulder.

"Jesus," Illa says, touching her lip. She can taste blood trickling into her mouth.

"Sorry," says Nancy, already looking past Illa, hand on the door-knob.

"I wouldn't go in there if I were you," Illa says.

"But I don't feel well," Nancy whines. "I think I've got the virus that's going around. Feel my forehead, do I feel hot to you?"

Obligingly, Illa puts her hand to Nancy's forehead, which is cool as a marble slab.

"You feel fine," Illa says before hurrying away.

––––––––––

AT THE END of the day, Illa leaves last period a few minutes early, saying she has to use the bathroom. Instead, she heads to the stilt house. She wants to beat Coach there so she can at least give Mercy a heads-up. Just in case the unthinkable happens and Coach fails to convince Evelia to let Mercy play, Illa has Mercy's uniforms, both home and away, so she'll have something to hold on to during this hard time, something to remind her of who she is.

When Illa arrives, she's glad to see the big Lincoln in the drive-way. She climbs the wooden staircase, knocks on the front door, and waits. After a minute, Mercy answers, eyes puffy and bloodshot. She looks relieved to see Illa.

"Don't go," she hisses. "You have to stay, please, I'm scared . . ."

"What's the matter?" Illa asks.

"She found Charmaine's letters in the trash." Mercy glances over her shoulder, then back at Illa. "She says the letters are proof I've got demons in me, they're planning something, and he said it'll take a few days to get ready, but it's dangerous, I don't want to . . ."

"Who's planning it, Mercy?"

"Pastor Parris."

"Who's there?" Evelia calls.

"No one, Maw Maw," she calls out. She yanks the uniforms from Illa's hand. "Just someone dropping off my old jersey."

Evelia hobbles to the door holding her hip. When she places a hand on her granddaughter's shoulder, a fit of tics overtakes Mercy and she grunts.

"I'm afraid you'll have to be going now," Maw Maw says, and Illa can see why Mercy has spent her life in obeisance to this woman. With her kingmaker's voice, she demands it.

"I . . . I'll . . ." Illa stutters, wanting to stay but not knowing what to say. She recalls Charmaine's warning to Mercy: *If you ever feel unsafe at home, go find someone you trust. Just please, get out of there.* What are they planning to do to Mercy?

"I'm not asking, I'm telling, girl, get," Maw Maw says, corralling Illa and pushing her toward the steps.

Just then, Coach Martin's Explorer appears down the street. She screeches into the driveway and vaults up the steps.

"Coach!" Mercy shouts with hysterical elation, pushing out of the house and running into her arms.

Coach's stern expression softens. "Evelia, I'd like a word with you, if you don't mind," she says, clearing her throat and stepping back from Mercy. "In private."

"I know what you got to say, and you best say it right here," Evelia says. "You ain't coming in the house, you ain't gonna win me with none of your talk. I'm taking her out of school. Times are too serious."

Illa senses the coming confrontation and steps back into the sheltering fronds of the banana plants that lean over the stairway.

"I understand you're afraid, Evelia," Coach says, her voice measured. "We all are. But I don't want us to do anything hasty here. There's a lot at stake . . ."

Evelia snorts. "What do you know about stakes? I'm battling for my girl's *soul*. My life has been spent keeping her safe. You only care for her so long as y'all win at that nonsense game." She waves her hand dismissively. "She's done with all that. There's a reckoning coming."

"Please, Maw Maw," Mercy says. "I want to play again."

"Now wait just a minute, Evelia," Coach says. "You and I had an agreement." She shifts her gaze uneasily to Mercy. "The girl *will* play through her senior year."

"This ain't my decision, Jodi, there are forces at work here you can't imagine. The devil's set his demons roaming, and they've seized my girl. That woman's been in touch, which is proof enough for me that evil walks with us."

Coach shakes her head in bafflement. "I should've been more careful about who I struck deals with. Always knew you were crazier than a loon, Evelia."

At the word *crazy*, Mercy stiffens and steps away from Coach. "Don't call her that! She's not crazy, she's a seer. She foresaw all this, me and the rest of the girls . . ."

But Coach Martin is shaking her head. "I'm sorry, Mercy. I shouldn't have got involved." She reaches out and takes Mercy's hand, but Mercy shakes herself free.

"Don't," Evelia says. "Don't do this, Jodi, it'll only cause her confusion."

"It's wrong, what we did," Coach says. "That woman wants to see her daughter, and who are we to keep her from it?"

"What's she talking about, Maw Maw?" Mercy says, her voice childlike.

"Nothing. Go inside, girl," Evelia says. "Go!"

She starts to close the door on them, but Coach jams her shoe in the doorway to prevent it from closing. "Mercy, listen to me," Coach shouts through the cracked door. "Your mother came for you. Three years ago, she came back for you. I know, because I'm the one who met with her. I'm the one who told her to go away!"

With that, Evelia manages to shove the door shut, leaving Illa and Coach alone on the front stoop, Mercy sealed away inside the house. Coach folds her arms over her chest, hands tucked tightly in her armpits. "I'm sorry, Mercy!" she calls. "I'm so sorry!"

As Coach stares at the closed door, a pained look on her face, Illa asks if she can do anything for her, but she just stares at Illa dazedly like she's never seen her. Taking a few steps back until she hits the balcony railing, she sits down, crosses her legs in front of her, and starts to cry. It's so disturbing a sight that Illa wonders fleetingly if perhaps Evelia is right about the world ending; the world as Illa knew it has already blown apart.

When Illa arrives at the house on Galvez, she's surprised to find her mother waiting for her just inside the front door. Mama swipes at a thin line of drool that shines on her chin. She must have been dozing in her wheelchair.

"Mama, I'm so glad you're here, you'll never believe—"

"Where have you been, Illa?" she interrupts. "I've been so worried. You've hardly been home a minute, and with everything happening with the girls at school . . ."

"But that's just it, Mama," Illa says breathlessly. "That's what I've been doing, trying to help—"

"I've missed you so much," Mama says. She reaches out for Illa's hand, holds the knuckles to her cheek. "I thought you forgot about me."

Illa throws her backpack on the chair by the entryway. "No, Mama. But you have to tell me, do you think Evelia could hurt

Mercy? I mean, physically?" She takes Mama's hand, which is damp and cold. "What did she do to Charmaine that was so awful?"

Mama looks at her, and Illa sees tears welling behind her eyes. "Did you remember my insulin? I'm almost out. Only got another day's worth."

"Mama, please!"

Her mother withdraws her hand. "Evelia Boudreaux probably wouldn't raise a hand to your precious Mercy," she says bitterly. "What she does is far worse than a beating, you ask me. Charmaine needed help, and instead that woman wrecked her."

"Why, Mama? Why did Charmaine need help?"

Her face puckers with tears. "Because Witness Louis took her out on her first date and raped her, that's why."

---

TUESDAY NIGHT, GAME night. The opposing team almost canceled because of the stench—the coach didn't want his girls exposed to any bad chemicals—but in the end, Coach Martin convinced him to come.

The Lady Rays squad hardly resembles the usual team; half the girls have been brought up from junior varsity. They look fearful and green, soldiers sent to the front lines as cannon fodder. Illa is still reeling from what Mama told her about Charmaine, and as the game unfolds, she can't focus on anything. She keeps seeing the crazed look in Evelia's eyes as Coach shouted through the door the day before, and imagining Charmaine, begging her mother for help and not getting it.

Outside, the air is heavy from the pressure of a coming storm, and the gym's AC broke that morning. With hundreds of people crammed inside, the space has become unbearably hot. Illa scans the crowd and sees a few familiar faces, Chole's tia and tio and her cousin Veronica, looking flushed and unhappy; Keisha Freeman's dad sitting next to Zion's stoic parents. What if Charmaine is up there somewhere? Could she have gotten the letter that fast and made the drive? *Please come,* Illa thinks. *Things are bad.* But no. It's too soon. A letter would take at least two days to get to Austin from here. She gulps cold water to fight off a creeping dizziness. *I'm not sick,* she tells herself. *I can't get sick.*

At halftime, Illa watches the dancing girls march onto the floor to the frenetic drums of the blaring techno music (*It's a beautiful life, oh oh oh oh, it's a beautiful life*). She has always envied their easy brightness and the way that, when they dance, their movements are so perfectly coordinated that they appear to be a single forty-legged creature moving across the gym, kicking its white-booted feet, flaunting its rows of glistening teeth. Illa notices that Mackenzie Wolcott's spot in the kick line has been closed up, Abby Williams and Marilee Warren forced to hold on to each other's shoulders and smile about it. The girls' red lipstick and blue eye shadow look garish under the gym's lights, or maybe it's just the extreme discomfort radiating out from behind their wide smiles. Illa heard that the coach makes them wear Vaseline on their teeth so they'll keep smiling no matter what.

A minute into the routine, Abby collapses, followed quickly by Marilee. Illa gasps. When the girls hit the floor, they judder like junkies, and a few of the others trip over them, toppling to join the tangle of shiny limbs. A police officer rushes onto the court and kneels beside Abby, her blond hair spilled onto the floor behind her. Someone cuts the music, and the crowd can hear the animal sounds coming from Marilee's lipsticked mouth: *uuuunnnh-EYE, uuuunnh-EYE.* In the stands, people get on their feet, straining to see what's going on. Students with grease-painted faces hold their spirit posters in front of them like shields. Marilee and Abby's parents rush to the gym floor. Onlookers have clapped hands over their mouths in shock. Illa does the thing she always does when she's ill at ease and in need of distance: she finds her camera from beneath the bench and starts taking pictures of the girls in their strange rapture.

From outside, Illa can hear the scream of ambulances approaching. A minute later, EMTs sprint into the gym. While they strap Abby and Marilee onto stretchers, the Lady Ray players hunker on the sidelines holding hands, surveying the scene. They lose the game by two points, unable to recover from the unsettling halftime show.

That night Illa doesn't sleep. In her head, as on the television news, she replays again and again the image of the two dancers falling, sequins flashing, mouths agape, looking like beautiful, broken dolls.

# MERCY

EARLY WEDNESDAY MORNING, dawn light trickles into my bedroom. I roll to my side and pull the sheet to my chin, careful to press my bad arm deep into the mattress to ward off a fit. As the dawn light steeps around me, I imagine how I would live this day if I had no past and no future, just a weightless present: maybe at the beach with Annie, or on the court with the neighborhood boys at Park Terrace. Maybe with Travis by the river, letting the juice of a watermelon drip down our chins. Not maybe. Definitely. I would spend this day with Travis, anywhere.

But I have a past. *Three years ago, she came back for you.* The past is a trickster—the stories we tell ourselves and the stories we are told.

After Maw Maw closed the door on Coach, I asked her if I'd heard right, if Charmaine came for me. She said yes, Charmaine came back, but she was a mess, still drug-ridden, wanting to see me for her own selfish reasons, so Maw Maw thought it best if I never found out. *Let's pray on it,* Maw Maw said, and so we did. Standing there in the living room, we prayed for protection for me from Charmaine, and we prayed for her, too, that she might find Jesus again and mend her ways.

Since Sunday I've been fasting in preparation for Pastor Parris, living on chicken broth and water. I'm starved, my stomach knotting like a den of blacksnakes. Now I hear a car pull into the driveway and get up quick to see who's come. Pastor Parris's white Cadillac rolls to a stop behind the Lincoln. I hurry to the door and lock it, then move back to the bed and sit, heart thumping. I wait, feeling silly for my fear, listening to their muffled voices as they talk, knowing that when he arrives at the door, I will be told to unlock it and will have to do so. But after several minutes, when no one comes to the door, I unlock it cautiously and stick my head into the hall.

"I won't take her back there," Maw Maw says.

"We're as good as damning the girls of this town if we let this continue. You're the one to convince the people what's really happening, Evelia. After Alicia, they know you're anointed. You're scared, Evelia, I understand that, but people need to look on your girl and see this isn't a common illness. Everyone in that gym today will feel Lucifer's presence in Mercy. We've got to help these girls, *all* the girls, before it's too late."

After a long pause, Maw Maw says, "I put my faith in the Lord that you know what you're doing." I hear the door close behind him.

She calls me to her, says we're going up to the school. Something bad happened last night, more girls were struck down, and Pastor Parris says we're needed at a meeting. She sounds scared.

"I don't want to go up there," I say, shaking my head, realizing this is true only as I say the words. I don't want people to see me this way, especially not Travis. And I don't want to be blamed for what's happening.

"I know, child, but we have an obligation. Those who see the truth must share it. Think of Jesus on the cross and be brave."

I nod, though her words don't make me feel better. After all, Jesus *died* on the cross, in agony.

As we leave the stilt house, we're greeted by the headline from the newspaper on the front stoop: Two Girls Collapse during Half-Time Performance at Game, Mystery Illness Spreads.

In the car, my arm is so bad that I can't buckle my seat belt; Maw Maw reaches across me and straps me in.

By the gym's double doors, camera crews crowd. Mr. Long stands like a human barricade. I hear him say that this is a meeting for Port Sabine High School parents only, and that they're not allowed in. When he sees us coming, he lets us inside, where people spill out of the bleachers and into rows of folding chairs that the janitor has placed in front of a long folding table with several microphones. The rain has picked up, crashing against the metal roof so it sounds like a jet engine overhead. As we pass the bleachers, someone calls out, "*Mercy!*" I look to see Travis waving furiously at me from his spot halfway up. At the sound of my name, people go quiet; Maw Maw puts her hand firm at my back and guides me forward. "Don't speak to him," she says. "Don't speak to anyone."

Superintendent Mack shows us to a spot up front, and when I see who else is there, Annie, Corinne, Mackenzie, Brittny, Keisha, I know this must be the place for the sick girls and their families. There are new cases, Nancy Cobb, Marilee Warren, Abby Williams, Laynie Hibbard, Veronica Gomez, and a handful of underclassmen whose names I don't know. Annie tries to catch my attention as I pass, but I focus my gaze on the ground in front of me. Once seated, I count fourteen of us in all. I look around at the other girls. Some appear scared but normal, their eyes roving and wide as if they're spooked horses. Some move their limbs spastically, and others make odd animal-like sounds. I realize that this is how I must look to everyone.

Suddenly, I feel a welling up, and I'm taken by a fit, my arm flapping. A few of the people in the nearby seats pause to stare, then go back to their nervous chatter: *I blame it on the heat,* one mother says. *Oh, the heat was outrageous,* another agrees. *I could barely breathe myself, those poor girls in their heavy costumes went down so fast, it was terrifying . . .* I realize they're talking about last night, but between the noise of the rain and my struggle to suppress the twitching, I can't follow the conversation. As angry as I am with Annie, I wish she were sitting by me so I could squeeze her hand; we always did that before games as we waited in the locker room tunnel before warm-ups, for luck, for strength.

A hush falls over the packed room as people move to take their places on the panel—Chief McKinney, Principal Long, Superintendent Mack, Coach Martin, a stranger wearing a raspberry suit, and Dr. Joel. Outside, the crack of thunder and angry rain. Staring at the floor, I dig my nails into the flesh of my upper arm and try to focus on breathing; sometimes that helps me fight the urge to twitch. The overhead lights shine on the waxed floor, creating a powerful glare so that when I blink, I see black dots.

"I'd like to thank y'all for joining us here today," Mr. Mack says, tapping his microphone to silence the few talkers. We've got a serious situation on our hands here, and I'm sure you're scared . . . We want to use this chance to address any questions you might have, so we can avoid gossip and rumor."

Someone shouts, "When's Mercy gone be able to play ball again?" People in the crowd hoot and cheer. *Don't look at me, please.* I clutch my arms to my stomach.

Then I hear Coach's voice; she's saying something about how she wants to have the whole team back ASAP. Someone asks if the tics are permanent, and Dr. Joel tries to answer but gets interrupted: *I heard they're part of a cult. I heard they're devil-worshipping out in the swamp, conjuring Beelzebub. That's how that baby got killed, it was a sacrifice.* The crowd murmurs in alarm. As I stare at the lines on the floor, free-throw and three-point and half-court, they wobble and fuzz and blend under the glare of the fluorescents.

Chief McKinney is saying there's no connection between Baby Doe and the . . . sickness, if it can even be called a sickness.

"Of course it's a sickness, it's obviously contagious," says Shelby Williams, Abby's mom. "Our girls are in pain, we need to help them!"

Dr. Joel again, but his words are gobbledygook, *conversion disorder, mass psychogenic illness.*

"It sounds a lot like you're calling our girls crazy."

Mr. Freeman stands, pulling Keisha to her feet. "We need real answers. My girl can barely breathe. Last night me and Mayor Sanchez talked on the phone with Ms. Marlene Upton of Sacramento, California. A company up there, InCom Manufacturers, was poisoning the groundwater and gave a lot of people cancer. Ms. Upton is here today, and she thinks this is due to the chemical spill at the refinery . . ."

"Just a minute," Beau starts.

People are sitting at attention, straining to hear what's being said. Ms. Upton talks into her microphone: "The air has been particularly bad lately, possibly due to a chemical leak at the plant. If the town council approves my request to conduct extensive testing of the water, soil, and air around the school, I think we'll find our answers."

I will myself to rise like a balloon, to nest unseen in the steel beams of the domed ceiling, and I swear I feel myself lift off the chair. Perhaps I do, because Maw Maw grabs my hand and holds it tight, saying, "Sit down, girl."

"Look, Bob, may I have the mic for just a minute?" Beau again, his face contorted with anger, making him look goblinlike.

Mr. Mack, waving him away from the microphone: "Beau, we can't go ruling anything out at this point, we have to at least consider that the refinery might be the culprit."

Cradling his Stetson in his left hand, Beau takes the mic: "As you all know, my Annie is one of the girls afflicted. So I want you to hear my thoughts before we go rushing to conclusions, paying thousands of taxpayer dollars for environmental testing that probably won't get the results you think. This here's my theory: I think Baby Doe belongs to one of the high school girls, and I think all this itching and twitching is a lot of smoke and mirrors to keep us from figuring out who. So I think we need to refocus this investigation, starting with Mercy Louis. I'm not saying she did it, that's not what I'm saying, but she might be trying to protect who did . . ."

The crowd roars, and I'm seized by tics. The blood in my veins drains down, down, out my feet, into the ground. I'm bloodless, freezing. I start to shiver, my teeth chattering so hard that I worry I might break a tooth. Mr. Long tries to get the mic, but Beau stiff-arms him. Some people are standing now, their bodies crowding in on me. *I need air.* I shoot out of my chair, both arms jerking straight up, so fast that people around me startle. Then my knees buckle, and just like that, I'm spilled out on the floor.

"Lord have mercy," Maw Maw cries.

I feel heavy but alert, as if I'm at the bottom of a well looking up at a single slice of sky. My arms and legs and torso sink deeper into the floor. I feel a great weight pushing down on me, and I think of Travis, his body above me, the dip of his shoulder into his collarbone, the veins in his forearms, his broad palms on my back, my breasts. My head thrashes from side to side, my body moves like a snapping whip. I close my eyes.

I see Lucille Cloud's yellow-eyed dog that night in the forest, smell his wet stink. He speaks to me, tells me I'm a rutting bitch. *Live by the senses, as I do,* he says. He has a great grille of yellow teeth and a thick pink tongue dripping saliva. I call out for Maw Maw: *The Loup Garou, the Loup Garou is here to devour me!* I remember that night in the forest, how Lucille watched us through the truck window with devilish, glittering eyes. And I know: in summertime Lucille Cloud lured me to the forest, lured Travis, summoned our lust, took what was rightfully mine. She stole my purity and damned me. *Lucille Cloud, Lucille Cloud, Lucille Cloud!* I scream. *She deals with the devil, this is her doing!*

# ILLA

WHEN MERCY SHOOTS out of her chair and bellows, "Lucille Cloud," it makes the hair on Illa's neck stand up. The gym goes silent. "Lucille Cloud, Lucille Cloud," Mercy repeats, quieter this time, chantlike.

Principal Long attempts crowd control, barking orders into the microphone. "Everyone just stay calm, please! Make your way to the doors in an orderly fashion!" But even if people want to leave, they can't, the room is so jam-packed that progress in any direction is impossible. The families of the sick girls try to shield their daughters from the encroaching crowd.

Illa squeezes her way through the pushing bodies until she can see Mercy lying motionless on the floor, staring up to the ceiling, Evelia and a short man in a seersucker suit bent over her. Chief McKinney appears, herding people toward the door, barking into a walkie-talkie. "She's going to be fine, just fine," he says. "Move along." But how can he be sure? To Illa, Mercy looks half-dead.

With the help of her grandmother, Mercy sits up. Someone hands her a Dixie cup of water from the drinking fountain.

"You want me to call an ambulance, ma'am?" Chief McKinney shouts to Evelia, who shakes her head. "You sure? I've already got backup on the way."

"Yessir," she responds curtly.

"At least let me escort y'all to the door," he says.

"Let's go, *now,*" Pastor Parris says. He positions himself behind Mercy as if he's going to help her up, then hesitates, distaste written on his face. Finally, he puts his hands under her arms and hoists her to her feet. She sways, then falls back against him, deadweight.

"Let me help," Chief McKinney offers, stepping toward Mercy.

Pastor Parris holds up a hand to stop him. "That's not a good idea," he says, lips a grim line. He rights Mercy, then gives her a push in the direction of the back door. "But if you'll clear a path . . . ?"

A confused look flashes across the chief's face, but he turns and begins using his large body to cut through the teeming people. Flanked by Evelia and Pastor Parris, Mercy takes halting steps forward. As soon as they see who's coming, people scuttle out of the way, and Illa notices some of them turn away quick or cover their faces. One woman pulls the neck of her sweater to just below her eyes.

Illa slips unnoticed behind the trio. Once they're out the back door on the sidewalk, she hides behind a concrete pillar. Chief McKinney touches Evelia's elbow, leans slightly forward in a posture of confidence. "I want you to know, Ms. Boudreaux, that I plan to bring Lucille Cloud back in for questioning, but first I'd like to have Mercy come in and make a formal statement. We need to know exactly what she thinks happened with that baby. We'll wait till she's better first, of course." He clears his throat. "And I want to reassure you that Detective LaCroix isn't going to pay heed to loose talk and gossip, even if it comes from Beauregard Putnam."

"Kind of you, sir, but it's not the law we're afraid of," she says.

"Now, if you'll excuse us." They take leave of the chief, hurrying Mercy to the passenger side of the Lincoln.

"We'll begin the exorcism tonight," Pastor Parris says, pushing Mercy down into the backseat like a cop with a cuffed suspect. "We can't wait another day or we'll lose her completely."

"It's too soon," Evelia says. "You said if we didn't prepare everything proper, she might get hurt. I haven't got the house right yet . . ."

"I've never seen someone gripped so tight by the devil," he says. "We can't wait."

Evelia reluctantly assents, and Pastor Parris says he'll come to the house at eight o'clock. He tells her to make sure she takes all the precautions they discussed, removing sharp objects from the room, getting rid of matches and lighters, candles and fire starter logs. Then Pastor Parris shuts the back door and gives a nod. Evelia puts the car in reverse and heads for the highway.

As Illa watches Pastor Parris disappear into the throng, she decides to go in search of Travis Salter. Of the people closest to Mercy, he seems to be the only one who loves her without agenda.

Once inside the building, she learns that Principal Long has canceled school for the day. They're supposed to gather their things and leave campus immediately. Illa hustles to the senior hall, hoping she hasn't missed Travis. As she speed-walks in that direction, students stream past her and out the door to the idling school buses that have been called in for early dismissal.

Along the way, she picks up snippets of talk . . . *she looked possessed, I swear I saw her eyes roll back in her head . . . does this mean the DNA testing is canceled?*

The anxiety in the air reminds her of the day of the explosion four years ago, when students were herded into the cafeteria to the plea of the refinery's emergency sirens. Sitting in the cafeteria listening to the principal explain what had happened at the plant that day, Illa had felt it in her body: life, changing. She has that same dreadful inkling now, that something is badly wrong.

She spots Travis at his locker, packing up his books. He wears a faded Astros cap, his long fair hair curling out from under it, a Farm Aid shirt with a caricature of Willie Nelson's face on it.

"Travis," she says.

He peers around his locker door. "Hey . . ." he says, stretching out the word as he searches for her name.

"Illa Stark," she says, throwing him a bone.

He snaps his fingers as if the name had been on the tip of his tongue. "You're the team manager."

"That's right," she says. "Listen . . ." She hesitates, shifting her weight from foot to foot. "This is probably going to sound kind of cracked out to you, but it's Mercy . . ."

Travis straightens out of his slouch, his eyes thirsty for whatever information she has. "I tried to get down there to help her, but that idiot McKinney shoved me out the doors before I could get to her. I mean, I know she probably doesn't want to see me, but God, I've been a mess wondering about her."

"I need your help."

"What's going on?"

She plunges ahead, the word *exorcism* fantastical and melodramatic there in the senior hallway, with its rows of colorful lockers, girls calling out *Heyyyyy bitch* to passersby. He takes off his ball cap and wrings it between his hands. "Unreal," he says.

"Last time I saw Mercy at Evelia's, she was so scared. And my mom told me something awful about Mercy's mom. She was . . ." She pauses, then whispers, " . . . raped by Mercy's dad."

"But I thought her parents were married. Mercy never talked about it, but my mom remembered something about a wedding."

"I don't know," Illa says. "But we can't trust Evelia to take care of Mercy."

He shakes the hair out of his eyes. "What does Lucille have to do with anything?"

"Judging by what happened to her dog, someone thinks she's guilty of something. I know Mercy visited Lucille this weekend." She takes the amethyst necklace out of her pocket; she scooped it up after Mercy threw it into the brush. "Lucille gave this to her, and Mercy tried to get rid of it. Maybe she thinks it's cursed."

"Lucille found us once," he says. "In the woods. Caught us fooling around."

Just then Annie descends on them, sneers at Illa, then says to Travis: "My God, you're the hardest fucking person to find. Look, Mercy is really messed up right now, I think she needs us . . ." When she realizes Illa is still standing there, she pauses and stares at her. "Get lost, stalker, this has nothing to do with you."

"You get lost, Putnam," Travis says. "Quit pretending you give a shit about Mercy. Illa and I have it under control."

Annie's mouth hangs open in shock, but she quickly collects herself and looks witheringly at Illa. "God, you're a sicko, preying on Mercy when she's helpless like this." She flicks her hair over her shoulder. "Enjoy it while it lasts, because when this is all over, she's going to go right back to not giving a shit about you."

"Fuck off, Annie," Travis says.

"I was just leaving."

They watch her storm away, and Illa's hatred of Annie threatens to consume her until she sees Annie pause at the end of the hallway, head jerking *one-two, one-two.*

"We'll figure something out," Travis says. He doesn't sound very certain.

"Why don't I pick you up tonight?" she says.

"I'm on the east side of town. On Bird of Paradise."

"I'll be there at seven-thirty."

As Illa makes her way to the student lot, she thinks about Annie's accusation that she is somehow enjoying all of this. Everything about the last week has been a nightmare, not a dream. Though Mercy knows who Illa is now, this isn't the kind of closeness she prayed for all these years. She wanted a friendship predicated on love and respect, not need. But from Mercy, she is starting to grasp what she was never able to learn from Mama: that there is grace in serving someone who can give you nothing; and that sometimes love is purest in such needs-meeting.

———————

THAT EVENING ILLA steals out to her car and slides behind the wheel. She's about to turn the engine when a voice comes from the backseat: "Hello."

Illa wheels around to see who it is, heart drumming. "Jesus, Annie."

"I see myself as more of a Judas, really," Annie says. "I would tell you to lock your car, but no one would ever steal this POS."

"How long have you been out here?"

Annie twitches *one-two one-two,* then smiles the kind of spacey grin Illa sees on the faces of the alcoholics who drink from paper bags under the Sabine River Bridge. From her shoulder bag, Annie procures a fat manila envelope and holds it out between the shoulders of the two front seats. "Here," she says.

"What is that?"

"An internal report created by the refinery's safety chief in the fall of 1995." She withdraws the envelope, pulls out a stack of half-shredded papers, and flips to a dog-eared page. "And I quote from the concluding paragraph: 'In my career at this plant, I have never seen a situation where the notion "I could die today" was so real as it is now.'"

She holds Illa's gaze through the mirror before Illa looks away.

She stares at the shaggy shadows of the bougainvillea bushes, trying to absorb what she's just heard. Tears have sprung to her eyes, and she doesn't want Annie to see.

Annie continues: "This report predicts an accident on the level of the explosion that took your mama's legs four months before it happened; it recommends immediate action to fix a number of problems they term 'not potentially, but inevitably, lethal.' You know what Daddy did when they gave him this report?" She paused. "He brought it home to shred, but he was so shit-faced that he didn't notice it was too thick for the machine, only made it halfway through. My mama found it like that."

"Why would she hang on to something like this?"

"Same reason Monica Lewinsky didn't wash that dress, I guess."

"Seriously, Annie."

Annie looks out the back window, nodding. "When the leak happened last week, Mom decided she'd had enough of nothing changing, so she gave the report to me. I've been sitting on it a few days. Didn't know what to do with it until now."

Stuffing the papers back in the envelope, Annie again holds it out over the console, where Illa can feel it pulsing with the truth her mother sensed all along.

"Why hasn't anyone blown the whistle on this?" Illa asks, trying to keep her voice steady. "It's been years."

"The men who wrote this knew how easy it would be for them to wind up on the wrong end of a blown pipe. Especially after the explosion, they knew how little their lives were worth, let alone their jobs."

"Why are you doing this?" Illa asks. "Won't your dad go to jail?"

"I doubt it. But if the story breaks big enough, it'll keep him from becoming mayor next week." *One-two one-two,* she twitches.

"So why me? What's the point in me having it?"

"The point is, it's the truth. Isn't that what your mama wants? I know my mom and I are sick to death of his lies, of the company's lies." She shakes her head hard, like she's trying to dislodge bad memories. "And Illa?"

"Yeah?"

"I'm sorry. Really, this time. For . . . everything. It's just, every time I saw you, it made me think of my dad, and . . . it just pissed me off." Illa nods wordlessly, then dabs her eyes with her sleeve. After a pause, Annie says: "So are you going to take me to Mercy or what?" When Illa doesn't answer, Annie continues. "Look, I'm the first to admit, I've been a shit to Mercy." She places a hand on Illa's shoulder. "But we've got years between us, and I've got love in my heart for her, that's not nothing. I know she's hurting. I want to be there for her."

Turning the engine of the car, Illa nods. She knows that Mercy needs all the help she can get.

"Let's go, then," Annie says, climbing into the front seat. They bump out of the driveway, the jalopy groaning from the sudden movement. When Illa guns it, the engine lets out a slow but triumphal roar. As they drive, Illa fills Annie in on what she knows.

Across town, Travis eyes Annie warily, then slides into the backseat. "What the hell's she doing here?" he asks.

"Don't worry about me," Annie says. "I'm going to be a goddamn Girl Scout."

"I'll explain later." *Oh God,* Illa thinks. What are they doing?

When they're a quarter mile from the house, Illa pulls up under the branches of a sprawling live oak that leans out over the road. The windows of the stilt house glow with lamplight. She notices Pastor Parris's ragtop Cadillac parked in front of the mailbox.

"You think they already started?" Travis asks nervously.

"We're fixing to find out," Annie says.

Even with the aid of Travis's pocket flashlight, the ground is a dark swell empty as outer space, with only the squishing of muddy turf beneath Illa's sneakers to let her know it's earth. There's a damp maritime chill in the air; Illa zips her hoodie farther up her neck. She shows them the back way into Mercy's room, where she helped Mercy climb up the afternoon she collapsed in the woods by Lucille Cloud's lean-to. They arrive under Mercy's window and stare up at it.

"Okay," Travis says, turning to Illa. "Let's get her out of the house. Illa, you're the smallest of us, I'll hoist you so you can tell us what's going on."

"Okay, then," Illa says. "Hurry."

They lift her up, and from there, she grabs the rungs of the balcony railing and, monkeylike, shimmies her hands higher until she's standing upright at the edge of the balcony and can slide over the railing.

Through the window, Illa sees Mercy curled on the bed, eyes closed. She's dressed like a baby for a baptism in the froufy, ill-fitting white dress she wore to Annie's Purity Ball. Illa taps softly on the glass, then harder when Mercy doesn't respond. Nothing. Depressing the door handle, she eases into the room and tiptoes to Mercy's bedside. "Mercy," she whispers. "Mercy, wake up."

She nudges her shoulder gently, then again, this time harder, but Mercy doesn't stir. Not even an eyelid flutters. Alarmed, Illa checks her neck for a pulse and is relieved to feel one strong against her fingertips. Up close, she notices a pinkish tinge around Mercy's mouth. That's when she spots the empty bottle of Benadryl on the bedside table.

From down the hall, Illa hears the doorbell, then the rumble of voices. Scurrying back to the door, she leans over the railing. "Who's at the door?" she asks.

Below, Travis and Annie stare up at her. "Someone just pulled up and went to the door," Travis whispers. "Too dark to see who."

"She's out cold," Illa says. "I'm going to need help. We'll have to haul her out." She takes a breath to calm her runaway heart. The moon is a yellowed fingernail, shining dirty light on the bayou, which shimmers blackly.

"Okay," Annie says, bouncing once, twice on the balls of her feet. "I'm coming up."

Travis gives Annie a boost, and soon she's standing next to Illa. Downstairs, the voices grow louder, Evelia shouting, "Get out, get out of my house!"

"Mercy," Annie says, going to her and brushing the hair off her forehead. "What did they do to you?" she whispers, voice cracking.

"We need to wake her," Illa says. Looking around, she grabs a half-full water glass off the vanity. "Move," she says to Annie before splashing the water over Mercy's face and giving her a few light slaps on the cheek. "Come *on,* Mercy. Wake up."

Sputtering water out of her nose and mouth, Mercy rolls over, eyes fighting to open. Illa grabs her shoulder and tries to sit her upright, but Mercy slumps to the side. "You'll not get the girl!" Evelia's cry carries down the hallway.

"We've gotta get out *now,*" Illa says to Mercy, feeling frantic.

Footsteps heavy against the creaking floorboards, then the bedroom door bursts open, banging against the wall behind it. Mercy starts at the noise, then turns and vomits pink ribbons over the side of the bed. She gasps as saliva drips out of her mouth. Evelia enters first, then someone vaguely familiar. The woman from the yearbook photo. Charmaine Boudreaux. *She came,* Illa thinks. She glances at

Mercy, who still looks zonked out of her head, then at Annie, whose shocked expression confirms Illa's suspicions

"Keep that devil dog away from the girl!" Evelia says, as if instructing Illa. "She's come to steal her, body and soul!"

"We are engaged in spiritual warfare every minute of every day," Pastor Parris says as he enters. "The apostle Paul was frequently called upon to cast out the devil from his congregants."

"Mercy, are you okay?" Charmaine says, stepping toward her. Mercy recoils into the bed pillows, a series of vehement grunts spilling from her mouth, *huh huh huh.*

"Jesus Christ witnessed demonic possession," Pastor Parris continues, his voice shifting into a strange, high whine. Seemingly oblivious to what's happening, he keeps a white-hot focus on Mercy. "But He had only to speak the Gospel and the demons fled before Him."

"Are you going to tell me again how much *better off* Mercy is without me, Evelia?" Charmaine spits. "Look at her, shaking like a kicked dog! What did you people do to her?"

Evelia wheels around to face Charmaine. "Have faith in the Lord, and He shall protect you, Mercy child. Say Jesus' name and you shall be saved from these demons!"

"The devil is a master of disguise," Pastor Parris says, rocking back and forth on the balls of his feet, eyes closed. "His demons have many faces. Speak Jesus' name and be saved."

Adrenaline rampages through Illa's body. Just as she starts to contemplate what to do, Mercy stands up, her white party dress streaked in pink vomit, and the shouting stops.

"I must've died a thousand times, thinking about you," Mercy says to Charmaine, her voice cracking with the last word. She sniffs, clutching her elbows against her body, staring at the floor as she talks. Standing in her little girl's dress, she looks wrenchingly vulnerable. Evelia's jaw is set, but her hands shake badly.

"Why don't you tell her the truth, Mother," Charmaine says. "Tell her!" She takes Evelia by the shoulders and gives her a shake. "Tell Mercy the truth."

"You destroyed this family . . ." Evelia whispers.

"It was *rape,* and it was me that got destroyed." Charmaine sobs. "You made me *marry* that criminal."

"*Jesus,*" says Illa. Mercy's face is twisted with shock, mouth open, eyes wide and blinking.

Evelia looks around at the others as if expecting someone to come to her aid. "I was only trying—"

"You were only *nothing,*" Charmaine says, wiping furiously at her face to stop the tears. The streaks of wet make her cheeks gleam in the room's low light. "You *sacrificed* me, all because you were worried they'd kick you and your whore daughter out of church, shame you in front of the town."

"If you'd been a good girl, if you'd obeyed me and not gone out . . ."

"I was a *girl,*" Charmaine says. "I was a girl who wanted to go on a *date.* That man took a girl who'd never been kissed and raped her three times. And after I got pregnant, you told me it was God's plan, that even if life started in a terrible place, we had to respect His will." She takes a step toward Evelia. "Witness Louis stole my joy, and all you could think about was your reputation." Charmaine turns to Mercy. "I wanted you out of my belly because I couldn't carry that man's child for nine months, I just didn't think I could do that and live."

Mercy says, "I want to . . ." She pauses as a fit takes hold of her arm. "I want to know one thing from you." Pause. *Huh huh huh.* "What happened three years ago? When you came back?"

Charmaine tugs at her shirt. "After I'd been clean for a while, I decided to try to come down and see you. Evelia wouldn't meet me, though. She sent Jodi Martin to run me out of town. She told me you were better off here and I ought to leave you be if I wanted what was best for you."

"You were sober when you came?" Mercy asks.

"I was a year and a half clean."

Mercy nods deliberatively.

"She was . . ." Evelia starts, but Mercy simply says no, then picks her way across the wrecked room and walks out the door.

# MERCY

---

LLA, TRAVIS, AND Annie drive me to the Starlite Motel, where Charmaine is staying, and Charmaine follows in her truck. I feel as if I'm suffocating in this too-small dress, the satin tight against my ribs. Inside the car, the smell of vomit is stifling.

At the motel, I rush into Charmaine's room, knowing only that I need to get unzipped and *out* of this reeking dress so I can breathe again. From behind me, Travis says they'll be right there waiting if I need them.

In the privacy of the room, I fumble with the zipper but can't quite reach. "*Fuck!*" I say, pounding my fist on the glass of the window.

"Here, let me help you," Charmaine says, hurrying over. In one motion, she unzips the dress and pulls it down over my hips. I step out of it. Folding my arms over my chest; I can't stop shivering. Our eyes meet; she looks confused about what to do next, but then she rummages in a suitcase and takes out some clothes. "Put these on."

After pulling on the T-shirt and shorts, I feel a little calmer. At least I can breathe again. I walk to the window and stare at Illa's beater, sitting in the empty parking lot under a halo of light from the streetlamp. I can see their heads in silhouette, and I consider going back out to them, taking refuge with my friends, leaving behind this messy part of my life once and for all.

From behind me, the muffled sussings of Charmaine's feet on cheap carpet. She comes up behind me and takes my hair in her hands, starts a braid. The gentle tug of the hair at my scalp feels good. When she's finished, she leans her face into the back of my head. "Mercy, will you turn around? Will you let me hug you?"

Something about the way she asks me to do this, in a voice that shimmers with care, makes me want to, so I turn and let myself be held, her face warm on my neck, hands at my back. Soon I'm holding on, too, arms looped around her waist. "You're going to be okay," she says. "We'll get you better."

We stay that way awhile, till she starts us rocking side to side like a dance. From time to time, my bad arm flies out. When it does, she catches my hand and holds it loosely, her arm moving with mine. She hums the same three notes over and over. I feel a yawning hole in me, the wind whistling through. All the lullabies, the dances, the nonsense talk, the time spent skin to skin, rocking, rocking, rocking. The countless moments that fill years shared by mother and child—we missed that. This is only a single moment; we share no common book of memory. How can we start from here?

"Tell me about three years ago," I say, turning back toward the window. It is easier to stare at the empty parking lot than her face. The fact is, I don't know this person.

She takes a breath, releases it audibly. "I had a job, I'd saved enough to rent a place of my own, so I came down here to see what Evelia thought about letting me have my baby back. See, Witness left a few weeks after you were born, took the first chunk of money Ma promised him and ran. I couldn't afford the place we were living in, so I moved back in with Mama. Pretty soon I went to see Father Dubois up at All Hallows, to see if I could get an annulment. I didn't want Witness's name or anything to do with him anymore. I hadn't planned on telling the priest everything, but I was all hormones, I just broke down and told him the whole story, the rape, how Mama paid Witness to marry me, even though *he* was the one that did wrong. Father Dubois called Mama up to church to confirm everything I said, and she didn't dare lie to a priest, but I could tell she was steamed at me. He helped me through the annulment paperwork, and that was it, Ma was so angry she wouldn't let me in the house, said I wasn't fit to touch you now that I'd gone and made you a bastard after all she'd done to prevent it. She left the church after that, too.

"I was so young, didn't realize I had any rights, I thought I was the lowest, worst scum of the earth. That's when I got in a bad way with the booze and other poison. Got myself two DUIs, courts packed me off to rehab, and Mama had me declared an unfit mother. She became your guardian and I spent my time trying to erase my brain, just wipe everything clean, forget about Witness and you and Evelia and Port Sabine. I did a pretty good job of it, nearly killed myself. Whatever other lies she might have told you about me, Evelia couldn't have exaggerated how bad things got between me and the stuff. We were doing a death dance, that's the God's honest.

"When I'd been straight awhile, I just got this feeling every time I thought about you, like when you get a bad flu and your whole body hurts and you can barely move. And I knew how hard it could be, living by Evelia's rules. I started wondering about you, how you were doing, what you were like. I knew adopted kids looked for their real parents thirty, forty years down the line, so maybe I had a chance.

Maybe I could go down to Port Sabine, take bank statements and letters of reference from my boss and caseworker, and work something out." She pauses. "I was so stupid."

"She never told me," I say. "She said you never looked back."

"I didn't get very far once I got here. Evelia holds a deep grudge. Wouldn't let me in the door. Jodi met me at the Waffle House," she continues. "And I got out my folder, showed her my pay stubs and all the other paperwork. I told her I wanted to see if you might like to live with me in Austin over the summer, just a trial run to see how we both took to it. But she told me it'd be too disruptive if I showed up after so many years, said you were really happy, a great ball player who showed real potential within the program . . ."

"Potential within the program?" I say. "I *was* her program."

"I could tell she thought I was a first-class loser who shouldn't be allowed within a hundred yards of you. I played for Jodi her first two years at Port Sabine. Even back then, fresh out of college, the woman couldn't stand losing and couldn't abide losers. When I sat down across from her at the Waffle House, she had me pegged. She said it was okay, that some women just weren't mother material, and how could I be sure I wouldn't relapse, and what kind of life would that be for a girl, always living with the threat of her mama's addiction, and what kind of example would I set for you? What would I tell you when I had to go to my NA meetings, or when you asked why I didn't have a beer now and again. And boy, if I hadn't been a loser long enough to believe everything she said." Charmaine shakes her head. "So I put all my papers back in my folder, went out to my car, and drove away, telling myself you were better off where you were."

Fury burns through me. I grab the closest thing to me, the TV remote, and hurl it sidearm across the room, where it cracks against the opposite wall, bits of black plastic spraying out.

I grip my bad arm, trying to stop its movement. "What she *knew* was that her program would collapse without me. *Player like you comes along once in a lifetime,* she said. Some might say that about a mother."

My body is tingly with tired. Charmaine steps back, doesn't try to soothe me, and I'm glad, because I am a downed telephone wire sparking in the street, waiting for someone to grab hold.

The digital clock on the end table reads 8:43 in blinking red numerals. I want to get in Illa's car and go and keep going, away from everyone, because I'm eighteen years old and there's not a person on this green earth who can do a thing about it. But as much as I want to go, where would I end up? I'm not so foolish as to think I don't need somewhere to land.

And Travis, my heart. Even though we haven't talked in so long, I've taken comfort from the fact that he falls asleep in the same town I do, looking at the same piece of sky night after night. If I leave, then we'll lose even that fragile connection.

Charmaine walks to the sink adjacent to the bathroom to splash water on her face. She leans up against the sink, pats at the water with a paper-thin white washcloth. I see again the woman-me, a fine-boned face aged too fast, filled with loss, clearly the root from which I grew. She sits on the edge of the bed facing me.

"I came for you the once," she says. "And when I came, I was weak. I might not be proper mother material or anything like the mother you want, but me and others been making that decision for you for years, and it's time you got it figured for yourself." We sit in silence, Charmaine staring at the floor like a criminal awaiting sentencing, me a quarter turn away from her, watching the headlights come and go on the frontage road. Finally, she says: "'Course, I'd be lying if I didn't admit I'm back for selfish reasons, too. A solid job, a monthly rental, and a collection of sober days are what I got to show for my thirty-five years. And then there's you. Look at you. So beautiful and talented, I can't hardly believe you're anything to do with me, but I see it written all over your face that you're my girl."

My brain fizzes with new truth. "This is kind of a lot for me to process," I say, and to my surprise, she lets out a laugh, first just one bark but then a whole bunch, so she has to tilt her chin up as if to keep all the laughter from spilling out at once.

"Yeah," she says, barely squeezing in the syllable before another cascade of laughs. "Oh, girl . . ." She reaches across the narrow lane of carpet that separates us and puts her hand on my cheek; her thumb moves softly back and forth against my cheekbone. I lean in to it to extract more pressure. She laughs until it gets inside me and I'm laughing, too, not a joyful laugh but one that makes room for the absurdity of this night. "Keep in mind," she says, "I'm asking, not telling, when I say that I got a spare bedroom up in Austin and you're welcome to it. We could get to know each other a little. I've written the address on the notepad by the phone."

Too tired to do much more, I nod to acknowledge I've heard the offer. "I should find my friends," I say.

"Why don't you stay here with me," she says. "I could run you a bath . . ."

"No," I say. "I don't think I better do that."

"Got someplace else, then? Besides Evelia's?"

"I'll figure it out," I say. "I won't go back there tonight."

"I'm heading home to Austin tomorrow morning," she says. "Around eight o'clock, so I can make my shift. I hope you'll consider coming with me."

"I don't know," I say. Still, she presses the notepad into my hand.

We step through the door and into the night. Travis and Annie sit on the walkway, surrounded by Coke bottles and candy wrappers. Illa must have gone home. It's late, after all, Annie asleep, her head resting on Travis's shoulder. From somewhere, they've procured a brown blanket against the wind. When Travis hears the door creak, his head swivels in our direction. Annie stirs, opens her eyes, looks at us foggily. I smile, shake my head. Though I'm unsure how to classify what's happened over the last couple hours, *done* seems a poor word for it. But it's not a beginning, either. I wonder if it's possible to be in the middle with someone you've just met, because that's how it feels with Charmaine this early-November night—like we are travelers on a train, and now we're moving—perhaps by chance, perhaps by fate—in the same direction.

"Where's Illa?" I ask.

"She freaked out and bolted a few minutes ago," Annie says. "Something about her mom's medicine?"

"Meg Stark . . ." Charmaine says, wistfulness softening the name. "How's she doing?"

"Not great," I say. "She's in a wheelchair, and Illa takes care of her."

"How awful," Charmaine says. "I'll drive y'all where you're going. I might stop at the Stark house on my way back. I feel like I ought to have been told about Meg. It's crazy, but I used to be the first person she told anything to . . ." Her voice trails off, a distracted look on her face. But she snaps back quick, ushers us to her truck. "Come on, now, before we freeze."

Travis jumps in the truck bed, and Annie and I cram into the front seat, where I sit straddling the gearshift, pressed against Charmaine. It feels good. I remember her letter about wanting to touch my hand and let all the love flow into me from her fingertips. Maybe that's what this warmth between us is. When she stops the truck at Travis's house, I consider driving with her to Austin just like this.

But when Travis holds out his hand to help me down from the truck, I take it. Because it was through his hands, not hers, that I first felt love. And because I'm not yet sure I want to leave this town.

# ILLA

LLA SCURRIES INTO the all-night L&S drugstore, pays for Mama's Lantus prescription, and flies home, the paper bag scrunched tight in her fist. As she enters the house, she can hear the television going. When she sees the kitchen, she thinks they've been burglarized. Cupboards hang open, the fridge stands ajar. Peanut butter and mayonnaise jars sit lidless on the counter, knife handles sticking out of them. Half a loaf of white bread has tumbled out of its plastic bag, fanning across the counter. As she walks into the room, something crunches underfoot—a mix of Cap'n Crunch and potato chips. Behind the kitchen island, Mama is slumped against the wall, urine spreading in a clear pool on the tile around her. She's shaking as if palsied.

Illa drops her bag and crouches beside her mother, whose eyes are sleepy slits. Groping for the phone that hangs on the wall, she dials 911. As they wait for the ambulance, she cradles her mother's head to her chest, listening for each breath, imploring: *Please be okay, please be okay.*

THE EMTS HEAVE Mama's bulk into the ambulance bay. For a moment, her eyes flutter open, and she looks around, her gaze uncomprehending. Illa says, "I'm here, Mama," but when her mother looks at her, her eyes are swimming.

"Did you pack your swimsuit?" Mama asks, her speech slurred.

"No," Illa answers, as if this is an appropriate question.

"Well, hurry up, can't go to the shore without a suit."

"She's disoriented," one of the EMTs says. "That happens with hypoglycemia." Gently, he brushes Mama's hair from her forehead, and Illa wonders how a person could summon such tenderness for a stranger. When did Illa stop letting Mama stroke her hair before bed, rub her back as they watched TV? Their touches are purely functional now—pinching flesh between fingers in preparation for a needle, arms crooked under armpits at bathtime.

The EMT pulls the door shut. As the ambulance moves away, the siren slashes through the nighttime quiet of Galvez Street. Illa follows in the car, trying to remember the last time they went to the beach, but it's been too long, the memories of their many trips sliding into a single golden day spent paddling in the bathwater-warm Gulf, watching Mama stretched elegantly on the sand in her black two-piece, slender legs bent into triangles, rib cage moving up and down with her breath, a paperback propped on her chest. When she gets too hot, she joins Illa in the water, diving under, keeping her legs pressed tightly together as she dolphin-kicks her way forward. For a moment, her mother is a mermaid moving through the sea.

When Illa arrives at the hospital, they've already wheeled Mama into the critical care unit and won't let her follow. "She had a seizure of some kind on the way over," a nurse says. "She's in danger of a coma. I'm sorry, hon."

Illa panics. "But she was awake when they left, she was talking to me . . ."

"I'll let you know as soon as I hear anything," the nurse says.

Illa promises whatever overworked angel of mercy tasked with watching over Meg Stark that if her mother comes out of this alive, Illa will perform any caretaking tasks required of her, with no grousing. *Just please, give me a chance to be a better daughter,* she prays. *Give her a chance to be happy again.*

While waiting for news, Illa sees a man pull up in a truck and stumble in, blood saturating a towel balled around his right hand. "Lost me a finger to the outboard," he says with preternatural calm. He trails ruby dots on the hallway's white linoleum. It doesn't seem fair that some things are irrevocable, and that you never know which decision will lead to those things.

An hour later, the same nurse finds Illa and ushers her into her mother's room. On the room's muted television set, they're replaying footage of yesterday's basketball game. Mama, eyes closed, has half a dozen tubular tentacles springing from her arms.

As Illa sits down next to the bed, a doctor blows into the room, white coat floating behind him like a cape. He tells her accusingly that Mama's sugars were sky-high and that she nearly fell into a diabetic coma because of it.

"So she's not in a coma?" Illa asks.

"No, but she's going to be groggy for a while. Let her rest."

He has secured his wavy hair into place with reeking pomade, as if he works in a nightclub and not a place where he might witness a person's last hours on earth. His name tag reads *Dr. Chet Bilikins.* Illa watches his eyes, full of reprobation, rove over Mama's body, and she wants to confess her part in the problem. *It was my fault, I left her in the house without any Lantus. I left her alone with her depression. For weeks. Years, even.* Instead, she says only, "She has a binging problem. She just . . ." She pauses. "It got out of hand."

She can tell by the way the doctor looks at her mother that he's judging her, and Illa wants to say something cutting to him. But what right does she have to get defensive when she has registered the same callous thoughts countless times?

"Could she have died?" she asks quietly.

"She's badly dehydrated, but we've got her on fluids. Potassium and insulin, too. She might not have made it much longer if you hadn't found her when you did." He looks at Illa for the first time. "She's lucky."

"I don't know about that," Illa says.

"We'll keep her closely monitored," he says. "Has your mother been depressed lately, do you think?"

"No," she lies, still feeling defensive. "She just has an issue with food sometimes."

"Okay," he says. "So she hasn't exhibited any troubling behavior? Difficulty getting out of bed, hopelessness, detachment . . ."

*Oh, God,* thinks Illa. Is he implying that Mama tried to kill herself? In the years since the accident, her sadness has been static, a melancholy that could be managed. But perhaps their fight changed that, and Illa didn't notice because, in its affect, despair so closely resembled the status quo. She thinks about the report tucked in its manila envelope. Maybe, just maybe, the information it contains will be enough to bring her mother back from the edge.

While Mama dozes, Illa slips outside to the car to get the report. She will give it to Mama as soon as she seems ready. On the way back into the hospital, Illa stops before the plumeria tree planted by the entrance. Ducking under the low branches of the tree, she stands near the slender trunk, hidden within a chamber of fragrant white blossoms. Pressing a cheek to the smooth bark, she inhales the honeyed scent. When she's had her fill, she gently plucks a dozen of the snowy blossoms from the branches. She wants to take something beautiful to Mama to counterbalance the ugliness of the report.

When she enters the room, her mother is sitting upright, sipping water through a straw.

"Mama!" she exclaims, rushing to her bedside.

"What's the occasion?" Mama asks, pointing to the flowers. Her voice is weak and scratchy, but it's the loveliest sound Illa's heard in years.

"Can't a girl do something for her mama without raising suspicion?" she says, voice thick with tears.

"Doctor said there was no damage because you found me so quick."

"Oh, Mama." Illa drops the flowers on a chair, kisses her mother's cheeks, her forehead, her chin, burying her face in Mama's neck. Today she is glad for every part of her mother's body.

"We used to be great friends, you and me," Mama says. She tries to wipe at her eyes, but her arms are so densely intubated that she can't raise them. To respond that they are still friends would be false, Illa knows that. They are mother and daughter, nurse and patient, housemates, none of which amounts to what they were before.

"We can get back there," Illa says, and she believes it. Giving Mama the report won't guarantee change. But with the manila envelope burning beneath her fingertips, she feels rankled by something close to hope. Mama will be vindicated, and there's tremendous power and relief in that. "Mama, I know I forgot your Lantus, but I got so caught up in what was happening to Mercy . . . By the time I got home with it, it was too late. It was my fault . . ."

"You stop right there," Mama says. "I was headed down a bad road. I've been binging a lot, not just that time you caught me a few weeks ago. When you didn't show with the Lantus, I got to feeling so sorry for myself, I decided not to take the NovoLog, either. And to eat all the food I'd been stockpiling. *I'm* the fool."

"I should have been there for you," Illa says. "Not just tonight but all the other nights."

"I read those letters out of jealousy," Mama says quietly. "I was jealous of how much attention you paid that girl. I thought maybe by reading them, I could feel Mercy's pain in getting left, that it might make me feel better or dislike her less."

"I love you, Mama, more than anyone."

"I know you do," she says. "I leaned on you too hard."

"All I want's my mama back."

"I love you, my Lilla," she says, calling Illa by a nickname she hasn't heard in a long time. "And I'm sorry. Especially for this." She raises her chin to indicate the hospital room.

"We'll do better."

"We will."

With that, Illa opens the manila envelope and pulls out the report.

"What you got?"

Illa says: "You were right, Mama."

Then she reads the report aloud, glancing up from time to time to gauge her mother's reaction, which is oddly tranquil. When Illa finishes reading, Mama says, "What a waste. What a terrible waste." Pause. And then: "I've wanted blood for so long, but now that I have proof, I don't know what to do. What should we do?"

"See if we can shame the shameless," Illa says. "I know a guy who's been waiting years to break a story like this."

A nurse appears in the doorway. "Your sister is here to see you," she says.

Mama raises an eyebrow. "But I . . ." Charmaine's entrance silences her midsentence. The nurse leaves. "I'll be damned."

"Meg," Charmaine says, tugging at the hem of her denim jacket. If she's shocked by the way Mama looks, she doesn't show it, and Illa is grateful to her. "Your neighbor told me I'd find you here." Charmaine hovers by the door as if uncertain of her welcome. "How you feeling?"

"Better now you're here."

"You mean that?"

"I was mad over your going away, why would I be mad at you for coming back? Like getting run over by a car twice, no thank you."

Charmaine smiles, and Illa sees Mercy in every detail of the expression, down to the dusky rose of her lips. "Fair enough," she says.

"How's your girl doing?"

"Always trying to change the subject away from yourself," Charmaine says. "But I came here to say something to you, and I'm going to say it. I figure while I'm on my knees begging forgiveness from just about everyone, why not you, too." She smiles, though it's the kind of chagrined smile a cheating husband gives a wife before confessing. "I ought not to have blamed you, Meg."

Neither woman speaks. Mama just stares out the window. When the women's silence becomes too much, Illa blurts, "For what? Blame her for what?"

Mama looks sharply at Charmaine, as if to say, *Let me tell it.* And she does: "I'm the one that set her up with Witness Louis." Chin drops to chest. "I used to rib her something awful for being a prude and not having any fun. I pushed her to go on that date, said it'd be good for her. He was handsome and keen on Char, so I set them up." Pause. "Gave her a puff of her first joint when she came to me crying afterward, told her it'd help take the edge off. I . . ."

The silence of tears being choked down, and Illa is reminded how tough her mother can be when she sets her mind to it. In the years since the accident, she's never seen Mama cry, only heard her from time to time, late at night from behind a closed bedroom door. And yet for so long she has believed in her mother's whole and total weakness. How easy it is to ignore contrary evidence when you've already made up your mind about a person.

Charmaine goes to the other side of the bed, across from Illa. She takes Mama's hand, kneels down and kisses the knuckles, holds the hand to her cheek. "Wasn't your fault," she says. "You were just doing what friends do. I know that now. I shouldn't have cut you off like I did, but I just grouped you in with everyone else in this town and didn't want nothing to do with any of y'all."

From outside, the wail of an ambulance. In the hall, nurses appear out of nowhere, bustling here and there in preparation for what's coming in the double doors Mama was wheeled through only a few hours ago. How much can change in a handful of hours, after years of running in place.

"You're here, I'm alive," Mama says. "That's a good enough place to start."

# MERCY

AT TRAVIS'S HOUSE, his parents and sisters are already asleep. In the kitchen, he cuts two slices of bread pudding out of a pan balancing on the stove's burners, heats them in the microwave. I devour mine, then eat his.

Travis asks if I remember anything from today, the town hall meeting or what happened at Evelia's before everyone stormed the place. *Did they hurt you?* he wants to know. But the day unfolded like a dream faintly recollected, and I tell him so.

When Charmaine asked where I wanted to go, I said this address. I wanted to be in this house where I learned happiness. In the bathroom, Travis runs a hot bath for me, dumps in half a box of bubble bath so the suds go up to my chin. It smells of lavender, like Sylvie did that first day she embraced me. I close my eyes, feel my fingertips grow rubbery and start to prune. Travis sits cross-legged on the counter, reading a book. The silence between us is full and satisfying, and I remember the first night he talked to me at Park Terrace, how several minutes of silence visited us as we walked to the big oak, and how it felt like a benediction then, too.

He slides off the sink and walks to the tub. Fingertips kneading my scalp, he washes my hair, tilting my chin up and pouring water over the crown of my head. I think of Jean de l'Ours watching the king's daughter bathe, of David watching from his palace window as Bathsheba washed herself and the ill that came of it, Uriah's death that David arranged so he could marry Bathsheba. It's a sin to let Travis see my nakedness, I know, but somehow it feels baptismal.

When I stand from the tub, I wring out my hair slowly as he watches me. His gaze is serious, not lascivious, not admiring. In his room, he undresses and we burrow beneath the comforter. It's the first time we've had the legitimacy of a bed, which feels both glorious and sad, for it marks us as beyond the kids we were last summer, stealing time and fumbling in his truck.

I ask him to hold me. Tonight, between Charmaine and Travis, I've been held more than ever in my life. We don't make love, but under the sheets we entangle ourselves, arms and legs twining, unable to get close enough, nearly two hundred degrees of heat. Later, hovering above me, he holds my bad hand and good over my head against the pillow; I let my arms go soft, and he lowers himself so we're chest to chest. For a few blessed minutes, with the pressure of his weight on me, I'm not fighting the sneezy urge beneath my skin. He kisses my ear. Before we fall asleep, my body curled into his, I fight to keep my eyes open, trying to memorize his face because I'm not sure who I owe for this happiness, God or the devil. Perhaps I am a fool to stake my life on this boy, but I'd do it again. Without this touch, I'm only half alive, anyway.

The next morning, the sound of a dog barking wakes me. The bluish light coming in at the window tells me it's early. The smell of coffee drifts in from the kitchen. Friday, a workday. Travis's scratchy chin on my shoulder as he sleeps on his belly beside me. I touch my neck with both hands, my face, feel my breath against my palm. I'm alive, I've lived through the night. As I blink my way further into the day, I realize it's not a dog barking after all, but someone crying in short rhythmic bursts. Sylvie, maybe, or one of the girls. I slip out of bed and back into my clothes.

I open the door and steal toward the sound, find Sylvie hunched over the kitchen island, a half-empty mug of coffee abandoned, the cream filmy on top.

"What is it, Sylvie?" I say. "What's happened?"

She covers her mouth with a tissue, slides the newspaper toward me. BABY DOE SUSPECT CLOUD BADLY BEATEN, POLICE SAY NO SUSPECTS.

"It's brutal what they did to that girl . . ." She hiccups a sob, then folds me into a tight hug. "They beat her half to death . . ."

Before she can finish, I'm wriggling out of her arms, running back down the hall to Travis, her words trailing after me. I push into the room, the door slamming against the wall. Travis sits up, startled.

"Travis, what did I say yesterday about Lucille? *What did I say?*"

He rubs his eyes, blinks. "I don't remember exactly . . . something about Lucille Cloud dealing with the devil." He stares at me. "Why?"

*Clever, cruel you, letting me have him, letting me live but giving me the black mark of her torment in my soul.*

"I have to go," I say. "Take me to the Starlite."

———————

THROUGH THE STREETS of downtown Charmaine drives fast, past the ruined storefronts, broken glass sprayed across the wide deserted sidewalks that were built for men and women to promenade down arm in arm, now split by crabgrass and anthills. Past the hulking high school, the Dome where I scored thousands of points, and where I finally fell. The buildings are quiet, they don't try to make me stay.

Soon we arrive at the city limit, where the Hotel Sabine stands sentry, forlorn against the bright autumn sky. I think of the party that August night, me sitting on the windowsill breaking up with Travis, knowing it was useless, that he had my heart no matter what I did, that I had paid a high price and would keep paying for that boy with his sweet words.

There is Park Terrace, and I remember summer nights, the wild freedom of the game. *Our bodies spun / On swivels of bone & faith, / Through a lyric slipknot / Of joy, & we knew we were / Beautiful & dangerous.* Behind the hotel's redbrick shell are the Praying Hands, blinding white in the sunlight, the refinery rising like a city of steel and smoke. As we pass by, I smell its choking stink, feel a shiver for the souls who departed this life from its labyrinth of pipes. I hold my breath and count *one two three four five six.* By the time I count *ten,* we have reached the interstate, and soon we are barreling west, which is the only direction for people like us, trying to erase the past.

# ILLA

*May 2000*


GRADUATION DAY. The students have been placed in the
middle of the soggy football field, balancing precariously on
plastic folding chairs so as to keep the metal legs from puncturing
the grass and sending them ass over tassel into the mud. In front of
the students, Principal Long stands atop a sheet-draped platform
on the track, calling graduates up to receive their diplomas: "Kyle
Henkie, Laynie Hibbard, Clint Hoakum . . ."

From here, Illa can see Mama sitting in the home stands with the
other parents, wearing a wide-brimmed straw hat they picked out
together at the Houston Dillard's. Illa told her it reminded her of a
hat a woman might wear in the French countryside, sitting next to
a picnic basket. Not that she'd ever seen such a thing, but she could
imagine it, she said, touching the hat's fat black ribbon. Mama said
maybe they should find out. *Find out what?* Illa said. *What kind of
hats women wear while sitting next to picnic baskets in the French countryside,* Mama responded. *Maybe we'll go before your internship starts.*
And then Mama walked to the Lancôme counter and bought a bottle of perfume called Trésor that smelled of apricots and roses, as if

holding a small glass bottle made in France were a down payment on the trip.

Illa could hardly believe it. Her mother was a woman who bought French perfume and talked about travel abroad, a woman who was ready to let Illa leave, first to New York City for the photography internship, then to Austin for college at the University of Texas.

After six months of physical therapy and regular meetings with a dietician, Illa's mother is also a woman who walks. Illa has used up dozens of roles of film documenting Mama's progress, like the proud parent of a newly walking toddler—an irony that is not lost on her. Some days, though, Mama stays in bed with the lights off, and Illa can hear her whimpering.

Illa waves to Mama, who waves back. They didn't go to Houston to shop; they went to meet with the people at the bank where Mama's settlement money was held. Illa pictured it sitting in the vault, stacks of hundred-dollar bills piled into towers. They found out that in four years the towers had grown a few stories, enough that Illa would be able to go to college on the interest alone. At Dillard's, they bought the hat, perfume, and some black slacks for Illa to wear on graduation day. Size four. *I've made it into positive integers,* she thought.

Illa and Annie aren't friends, but sometimes they get together to talk about Mercy. For an hour every couple weeks, they drive around trying to talk Mercy back into their lives. *Remember remember remember,* Annie says, and Illa nods even if she doesn't. Where Annie had years with Mercy, Illa had less than one week. For a few days in late autumn of 1999, she was the most important person in Mercy Louis's life. As quickly as it happened, it was over, Mercy separated from her not by her magnificence but by hundreds of miles of highway.

If Illa had been told last summer that it would play out like this, such a swift giving and taking away, she might have cried from frustration, but here, standing on the other side, she feels glad about the small role she was able to play in Mercy's life. Perhaps they didn't become friends, but their lives would be forever entwined. From that violence years ago, Mercy Louis was born. And wasn't her singular presence a gift to them all?

Mr. Long continues down the list of names. When he reads out "Lennox McBaine," Illa can hear some hissing mixed in with the scattered applause, the hooting of his dad and siblings. His father had surprised everyone by recovering. As he receives his diploma, Lennox grins like a Cheshire cat. There was talk about not letting him walk with the class—some parents who worked at the refinery said it would be a slap in the face—but in the end, Mr. Long dismissed their complaints. The Sunday before the mayoral election, the *Houston Chronicle* published an article detailing the cover-up that Beau Putnam orchestrated at the refinery, quoting sections of the report Annie gave Illa. Lennox cowrote the piece with a *Chronicle* reporter. Two days later, Beau lost the election, and Annie took Illa out for milk shakes to celebrate. But even while toasting *Hizzdishonor Beau Putnam,* Annie's smile was tight. Illa imagines it isn't as satisfying to skewer an asshole when he's your father.

When Annie's name is called, she glides across the stage, flashing a pageant-worthy smile. Illa can tell Annie is pleased with herself for the speech she gave earlier in the ceremony, which she dedicated to Mercy. In the fall, she's off to Pomona on a full academic scholarship, which is lucky, since Beau disowned her and kicked her out of the big house on the hill after the story broke. Annie tried to talk her mother into leaving with her, but Mrs. Putnam decided to stay with Beau, which infuriated and then saddened Annie. Illa offered her a room in the house on Galvez, but she declined, choosing instead to move into the McBaine apartment in the GB, where she shares a bedroom with his sister. Sometimes, remembering the kiss she and Lennox had on that long-ago night, Illa feels the old simmering jealousy of Annie returning, but then she remembers how much has been returned to her in the past year, and how much Annie has lost, and her jealousy is replaced with a sense of generosity.

Up on stage, Annie's neck jerks *one-two one-two*. When she wears her long hair down, as she does that day, it's not as noticeable, but Illa sees it. Of all the girls who developed tics last fall, Annie and Marilee are the only girls still twitching. Or at least Marilee was, before she dropped out of school to go live with her aunt in Baton Rouge. Rumor was she got pregnant.

"Abby Williams, Corinne Wolcott," Mr. Long says. Abby, Corinne, and the others, they all got better with time, their symptoms petering out along with the national news stories and the refinery stench. Keisha, on the other hand, was found to have a benign growth on her lung that aggravated the asthma. In December, she underwent surgery to have it removed. That same month, Marlene Upton's environmental tests revealed what everyone in town already knew—that the air and water quality in Port Sabine were terrible. For a while, she and Mr. Freeman tried to link the findings to the girls' symptoms, but again and again, doctors found that none of the victims had nerve or brain damage attributable to organic causes. Dr. Joel became so frustrated with Ms. Upton that at one point, he went on TV and said that while he understood the desire to find an environmental culprit, particularly in a place with Port Sabine's history, he wished that Ms. Upton would hurry up and leave town because all the distractions, the *media circus* and the *witch hunts,* were keeping the girls from getting down to the hard business of healing themselves after what, he hoped everyone could agree, had been a *very difficult year.*

"Travis Salter," Mr. Long calls out. Travis unfolds himself from his plastic chair and ambles to the stage. Mercy's sudden departure has hit him the hardest. He never carries his guitar around anymore.

In late January, Mercy and Charmaine came back for an afternoon to bury Evelia, whom Pastor Parris discovered at the stilt house after she missed church several days in a row. Illa wonders if it was guilt that killed her or the shock of Mercy's departure. Or maybe she was just in poor health. The last few times Illa saw her, she seemed frail, her face drawn and skeletal. Now that Lucille's gone, kids have a new bogeyman: *Sleep under the angel over Evelia's grave, I dare you.*

Every once in a while, Illa gets a letter from that familiar address, PO Box 1984, Austin, Texas, only this time they're from Mercy, not Charmaine. She's better now, no longer twitching. Best of all, she's playing basketball again.

Illa watches a plane divide the sky overhead, twin plumes of exhaust like the tail of a bird. The roaring of its engine reaches her on a delay. That's how she felt when she heard the news about Lucille. Like it was being shouted at her from across a canyon, echoing and reverberating. *Maybe,* she thought, *that's what happens with news we can't quite believe: that a thirty-ton metal bird can fly; that a girl's life is worth so little, she can be badly beaten and a town barely blinks.*

Illa recalls what the Sonic carhop said that night, about being a girl in a town where that felt like a crime. Even the news stories dismissed Lucille, describing her as mentally ill and homeless. The thing Lucille did have in common with the LeBlanc Avenue baby was that people in town were eager to forget about both of them and move on. Lucille never pressed charges; no one knew where she went.

At last, Mr. Long calls her name. "Illa Stark." He says it gentler than Coach Martin used to. After the disastrous start to the season, somehow Jodi Martin was able to rally her ragtag group of girls to a 21–9 season and third place in the district. In the spring, she resigned from Port Sabine High School, still the winningest coach in the history of Texas high school basketball. No one knows if she'll coach again. Rumor has it she's headed for Port Aransas, to a beach cottage she bought there.

Illa trips up the stairs to shake the principal's hand and collect the slip of paper that proves she survived high school. Never would she have imagined that she would make it to this stage and Mercy Louis would not. But she has arrived at the realization that not much separates her from someone as exceptional as Mercy, and what distinguishes them from each other isn't beauty or talent or control, as Illa so often imagined. The first two proved unreliable currency, and the last, an illusion. In the end, all that really mattered was whether or not you had a person who loved you well when you were young.

# MERCY

*June 2000*

**T**HERE'S A PLACE in Austin that makes me believe in the full-throated freedom of summer, a natural spring in the middle of the city that bubbles up from a hidden place beneath the drought-parched earth, cold and clear and miraculous.

This June Saturday, we pack a picnic lunch and go early to beat the crowds. On our way, Charmaine asks if I'm nervous, and I say yeah, a little. But it's the good kind of nervous, the kind that makes you tingle in anticipation. Today Travis is driving up. He's got orientation at UT this week. He asked to see me, and I said okay.

We spread our towels over the Bermuda grass on the hillside that flanks the pool, slip out of our shoes and shorts, grab our goggles, and scramble to the concrete ledge, where we count three and leap in. My body absorbs the frigid shock of water, the pleasant sensation of dropping down, down, before naturally reversing direction to bob to the surface.

Treading water to secure my goggles, I then pull myself the length of the spring, using the ugly but functional freestyle I developed last winter at the Y, where me and Charmaine swam laps together every morning before she went to her NA meeting and then to work. She thought swimming might help with my arm the way it helped with her cravings, the repetitive strokes a replacement for bringing a long-neck or a pipe to her lips. *It's amazing how little you can think about when you're trying to keep yourself from drowning,* she said.

Amazingly, she was right. Where Xanax and therapy had failed, swimming saved me. When I threw myself into the deep end of the pool, I guess my survival instinct kicked in, my arms doing what I told them to simply because I would sink if they didn't. I swam and swam, losing myself in the numbing routine, focusing only on taking a breath every two strokes, kicking my legs, drawing my arms close to my ears and back through the water. Afterward, I showered and caught the city bus to the big high school where Charmaine enrolled me, letting my hair air dry in first period like I used to after morning practice.

After two months of swimming, the twitching stopped. I started playing basketball again, over on the courts by the community college. First just games of horse against myself, then knockout with the middle school kids who showed up after the last bell, then street ball with the men who strapped braces over aging knees but still played fierce.

Through my goggles, I watch fish dart between the fronds of vegetation that grow thick along the rocky bottom of the spring. Each time I turn my head to take a breath, I hear the squeals of children splashing nearby, mothers calling to them, the lifeguard whistle, the groan of the diving board as it releases someone into the air.

I was on the blacktop when the assistant coach from St. Ed's walked by. *What's your name?* he asked after the game. *Mercy Louis,* I said. *I'll be damned,* he said before asking me how I'd feel about being a Hilltopper. I called Charmaine at work, and she met me at his office. We signed the papers that afternoon. There was a time when I would've been disappointed to play D-II ball, but I was so happy dragging the pen across those papers that day, I about kissed the man. When I asked him if there was a team meal plan, he laughed and said, *Girl, this is college, not the army.*

When I'm too tired to draw another stroke, I climb the ladder out of the spring and scramble up the hill, where Charmaine is shaking water from her curly hair. She gives me a wet kiss, then pats the towel next to her; I sit and devour a PB and J. Later, dreamy from the sun, I scoot to her and lay my head in her lap like a puppy dog. She brushes my hair away from my forehead and tucks it behind my ear, then strokes my cheek absently with her thumb.

This is how we sat on the chilled pavement of her driveway the night of December 31. Only I shook uncontrollably then, scared the earth would split open and tumble me into hellfire. When the clock struck midnight, though, all we heard were the pop and fizz of bottle rockets, the distant cannon boom of fireworks. Holding tight to Charmaine, I wept with relief.

By that point, two months had passed since I'd left Port Sabine, and I was still a mess, twitching, wrecked over Lucille, missing so much about my old life even though I hated who I had become down there. But one thing emerged with clarity on that cloudless New Year's morning: Maw Maw was wrong. It made me wonder if, when she woke to discover herself in bed in the stilt house, she was sad or glad. And it made me wonder what else she had been wrong about all those years. When we got news of her death, my first thought was that she had done it to spite everyone because she couldn't bear to be wrong. But even Maw Maw didn't have the power to will herself to death, and I realized what I'd failed to see for so many months: that she had been sick and hadn't told me, or anyone, maybe because she was afraid she would pass before the Rapture, or maybe because she saw illness and weakness as the same thing. Sometimes I wonder if she was in pain, and I wish she would have told me so I could have tried to comfort her. But then, she never believed in the power of love or touch unless it was divine. What she didn't understand is that when we hold each other, when we love each other, God feels closer than ever.

Sometimes I miss my grandmother, and when I confess it to Charmaine, she tells me stories about Evelia in the early days, before fear and pride and disappointment ruled her. Like when she found toddler Charmaine hiding behind the Christmas tree, eating all the candy canes, and, instead of scolding, crawled in beside her to eat one, too.

If forgiveness can be found in us, it will be through these small reparations to our memory of Evelia Boudreaux. I know goodness existed in her, and I love her because I've always loved her, and love is not something that you can will away because you no longer want to feel it.

With my eyes closed, I relish Charmaine's fingertips on my brow, the lacy, delicate feel of them. I picture Travis in his truck on the highway. He is coming to me. After so long, me refusing his calls for months out of guilt over Lucille, he is coming. I think of Evangeline and Gabriel and wonder if, when we embrace, the boys playing street ball at Park Terrace will pause at the sound of the wind like lovers' voices through the leaves of the big oak. See, I am ready for my corny story now. A happy heart can stand sentiment better than an unhappy one.

Lazy with contentment, I launch us into another round of our game. "Favorite time of day?" I ask Charmaine.

"Sunrise," she says. "You?"

"Just after sunset on the blacktop," I say. "Before the lights kick on. You guide the ball on faith, the bucket just a suggestion."

"Nice," she says. "Burger or hot dog?"

"Burger, for sure," I reply. "Extra ketchup and pickled jalapeños."

"Mmmm," she says. "What about hot sausage? I love me some Elgin hot sausage. Does that count?"

"Why not?"

"Favorite word?"

"Hmmm. *Euphoric*?"

"A real college girl already."

"Learned it from a friend. *Et toi, maman*?"

"That's the first time you've called me *mother*."

"It won't be the last. Answer the question."

"Easy one—*mercy*."

# ACKNOWLEDGMENTS

F OR WHAT SUCCEEDS in this novel, I am indebted to a number of generous souls. I thank Rebecca Gradinger for her keen editorial eye, tireless advocacy, and steadfast encouragement. Thanks, too, to Sylvie Greenberg, Grainne Fox, Melissa Chinchillo, Jennifer Herrera, and everyone else at Fletcher and Company. Thank you to Maya Ziv for believing in this book when it was just a will-o'-the-wisp idea I was chasing, and for shepherding the eventual manuscript through every step of the publication process so graciously and thoughtfully. I'm grateful to my team at Harper: Gregory Henry, Katie O'Callaghan, Amanda Pelletier, and so many others. Huge thanks to my insightful readers: Signe Cohen, Jennifer duBois, Jill Hicks, Aisha Ginwalla, Adam Krause, Marlene Lee, Susan Maxey, Laura McHugh, Rose Metro, Carolyn Nash, Jill Orr, Leah Sanchez, Allison Smythe, Lauren Williams, Michael Robertson, and Mark Viator, who hails from Southeast Texas and told me many colorful stories about the area, traces of which found their way into the book. For providing a beautiful writing refuge when I needed one, I thank Alan and Lori Kehr, Emily Edgington Andrews, Janice Gaston, Steve Weinberg, and Katie Tesoro. In this area, I would like to especially thank my dear neighbors Sarah Wolcott and Andrew Twaddle, for opening their home to me for several months, offering not only a cozy writing office but also interesting conversation and an endless stream of delicious smells wafting from their productive kitchen. Dr. Joel Shenker and Dr. Barbara Bauer helped me understand more about conversion disorder and mass psychogenic illness. Dr. Chris Greenman elucidated the ins and outs of emergency room procedure. Detectives Richard Faithful and Angel Polansky of the Austin Police Department were kind enough to speak with me about Baby Doe cases. Krystle Wattenbarger, MS, RD, CDE, walked me through the basics of type 2 diabetes. Shannon Brown helped me understand more about the legal ramifications of industrial disasters in Texas, and Shane Epping guided me into the mindset of a photographer. Thanks to my students at the Quarry Heights Writers' Workshop and Louisiana State University, who inspire me. Finally, thank you to my family: Michael, my true love; Malcolm Fionn, my sweet, scrumptious boy; Mom, Dad, Malcolm Lee, Janice, John, Laura, and the Settles and Sloan families. Your love and support give me strength, joy, and purpose.

KEIJA PARSSINEN is the author of *The Ruins of Us*, which won a Michener-Copernicus award, was chosen by Don George as *National Geographic Traveler*'s Book of the Month, and was a 2012 Ingram Book Club pick. A graduate of Princeton University and the Iowa Writers' Workshop, where she was a Truman Capote fellow, Parssinen was a visiting professor of creative writing at Louisiana State University in 2014. She grew up in Saudi Arabia and Texas, and now directs the Quarry Heights Writers' Workshop in Columbia, Missouri, where she lives with her husband and son.